Top Cow Productions Presents...

punderworld

Created by Linda Sejic

Published by Top Cow Productions, Inc.
Los Angeles

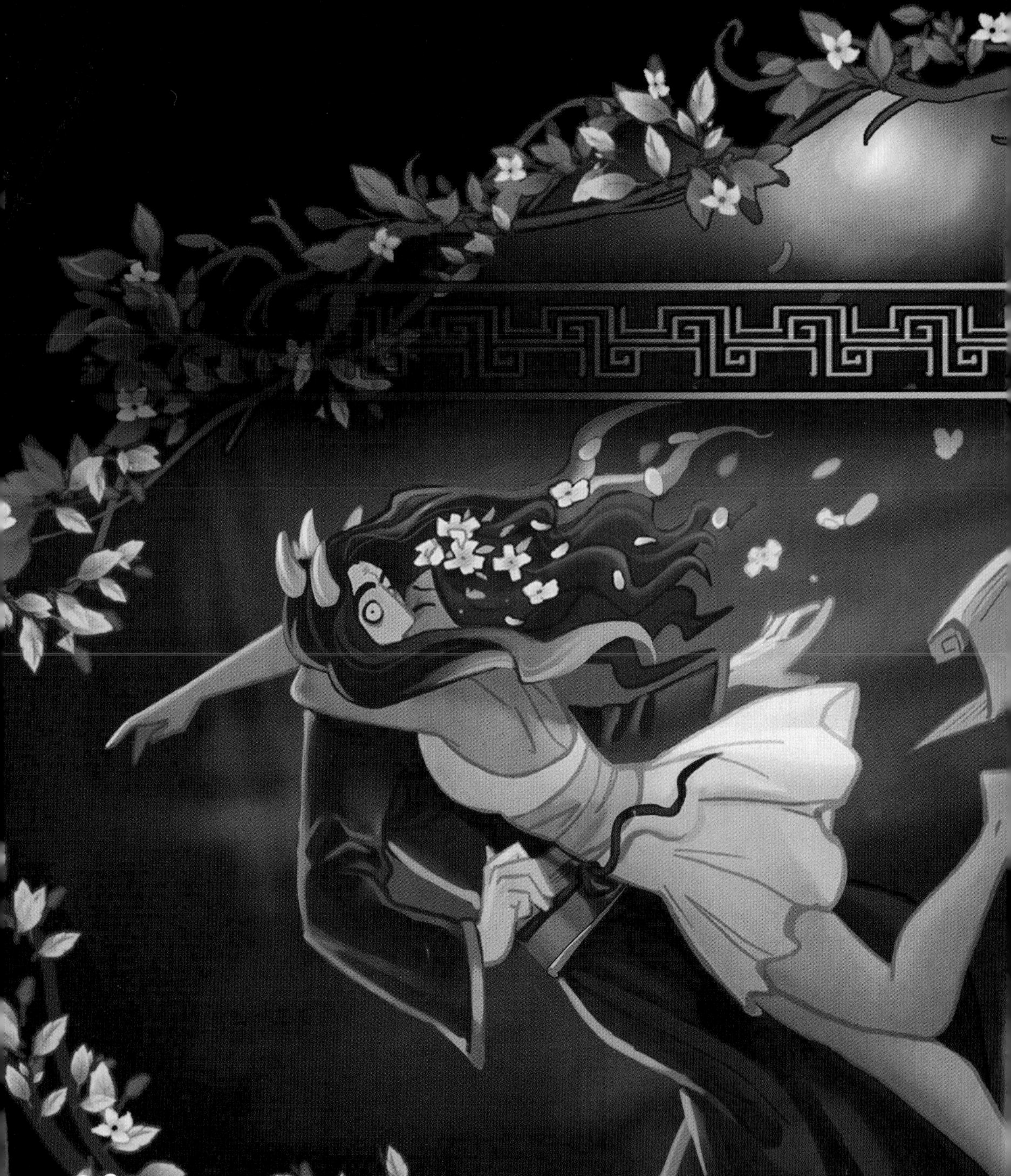

For Top Cow Productions, Inc.
Marc Silvestri - CEO
Matt Hawkins - President & COO
Elena Salcedo - Vice President of Operations
Vincent Valentine - Lead Production Artist
Henry Barajas - Director of Operations

IMAGE COMICS, INC. • **Todd McFarlane**: President • **Jim Valentino**: Vice President • **Marc Silvestri**: Chief Executive Officer • **Erik Larsen**: Chief Financial Officer • **Robert Kirkman**: Chief Operating Officer • **Eric Stephenson**: Publisher / Chief Creative Officer • **Nicole Lapalme**: Controller • **Leanna Caunter**: Accounting Analyst • **Sue Korpela**: Accounting & HR Manager • **Marla Eizik**: Talent Liaison • **Jeff Boison**: Director of Sales & Publishing Planning • **Dirk Wood**: Director of International Sales & Licensing • **Alex Cox**: Director of Direct Market Sales • **Chloe Ramos**: Book Market & Library Sales Manager • **Emilio Bautista**: Digital Sales Coordinator • **Jon Schlaffman**: Specialty Sales Coordinator • **Kat Salazar**: Director of PR & Marketing • **Drew Fitzgerald**: Marketing Content Associate • **Heather Doornink**: Production Director • **Drew Gill**: Art Director • **Hilary DiLoreto**: Print Manager • **Tricia Ramos**: Traffic Manager • **Melissa Gifford**: Content Manager • **Erika Schnatz**: Senior Production Artist • **Ryan Brewer**: Production Artist • **Deanna Phelps**: Production Artist • **IMAGECOMICS.COM**

PUNDERWORLD VOL 1. FIRST PRINTING. August 2021. Published by Image Comics, Inc. Office of publication: PO BOX 14457, Portland, OR 97293.

ISBN: 978-1-5343-2072-7

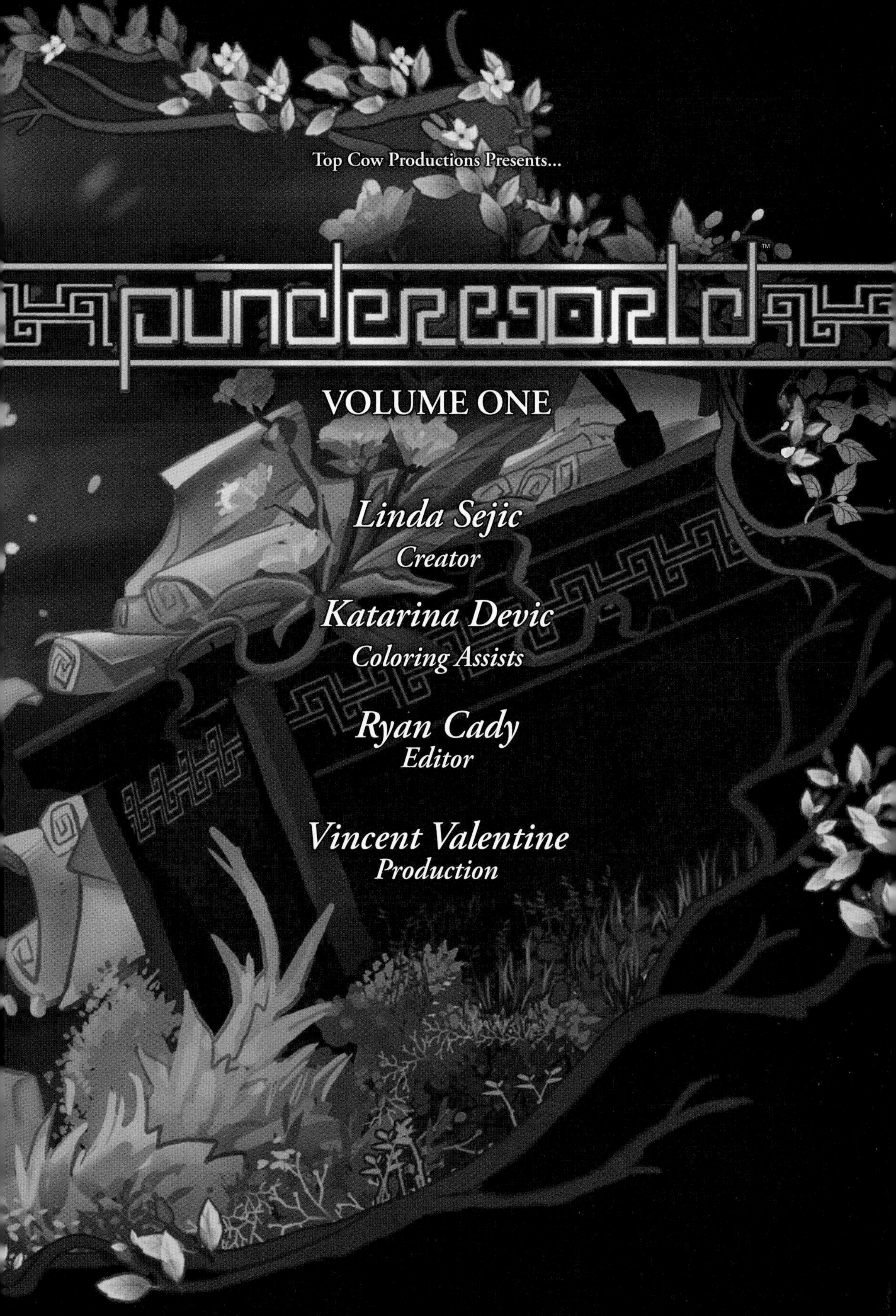

Top Cow Productions Presents...

Punderworld™

VOLUME ONE

Linda Sejic
Creator

Katarina Devic
Coloring Assists

Ryan Cady
Editor

Vincent Valentine
Production

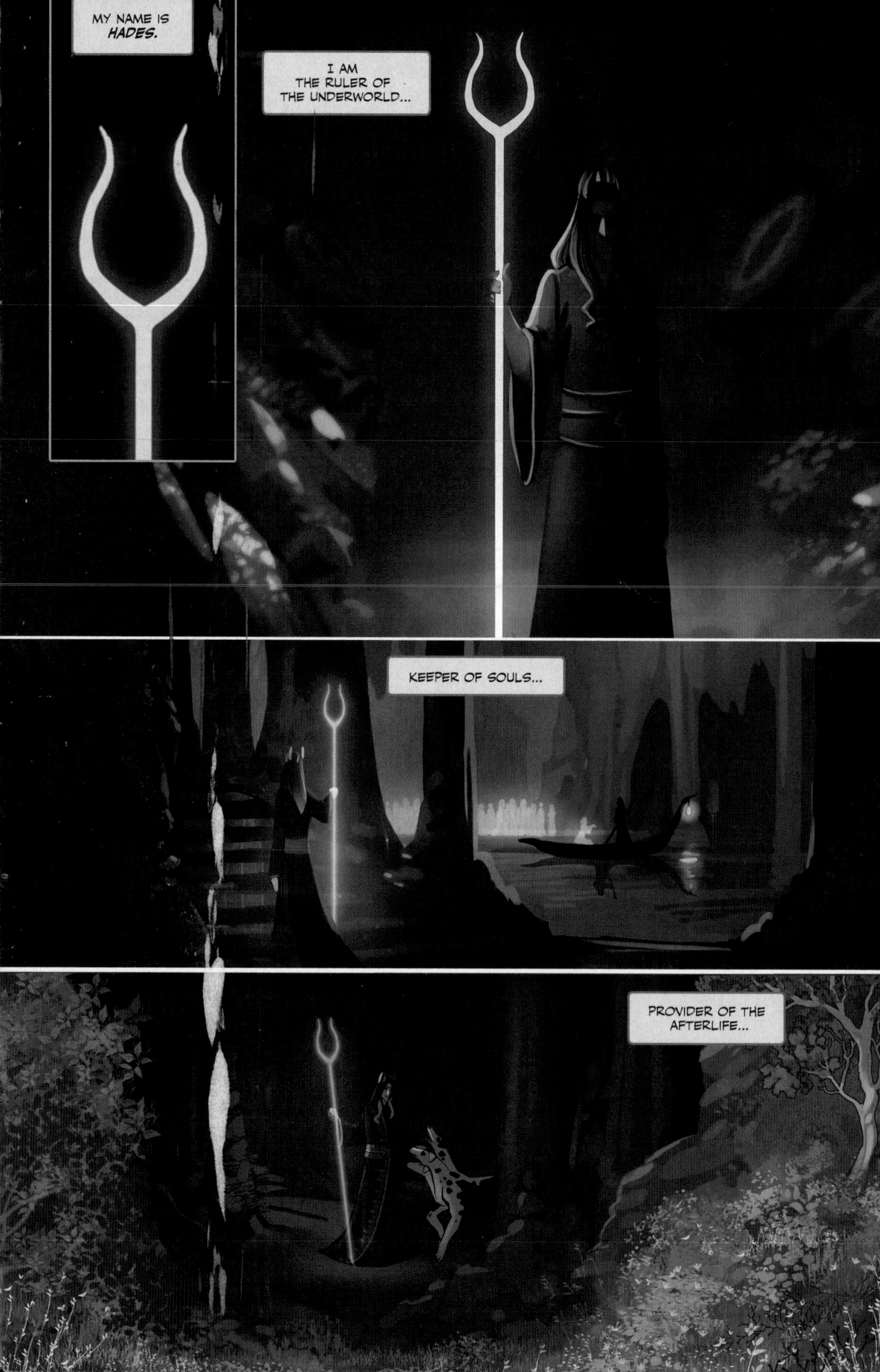
MY NAME IS *HADES.*
I AM THE RULER OF THE UNDERWORLD...
KEEPER OF SOULS...
PROVIDER OF THE AFTERLIFE...

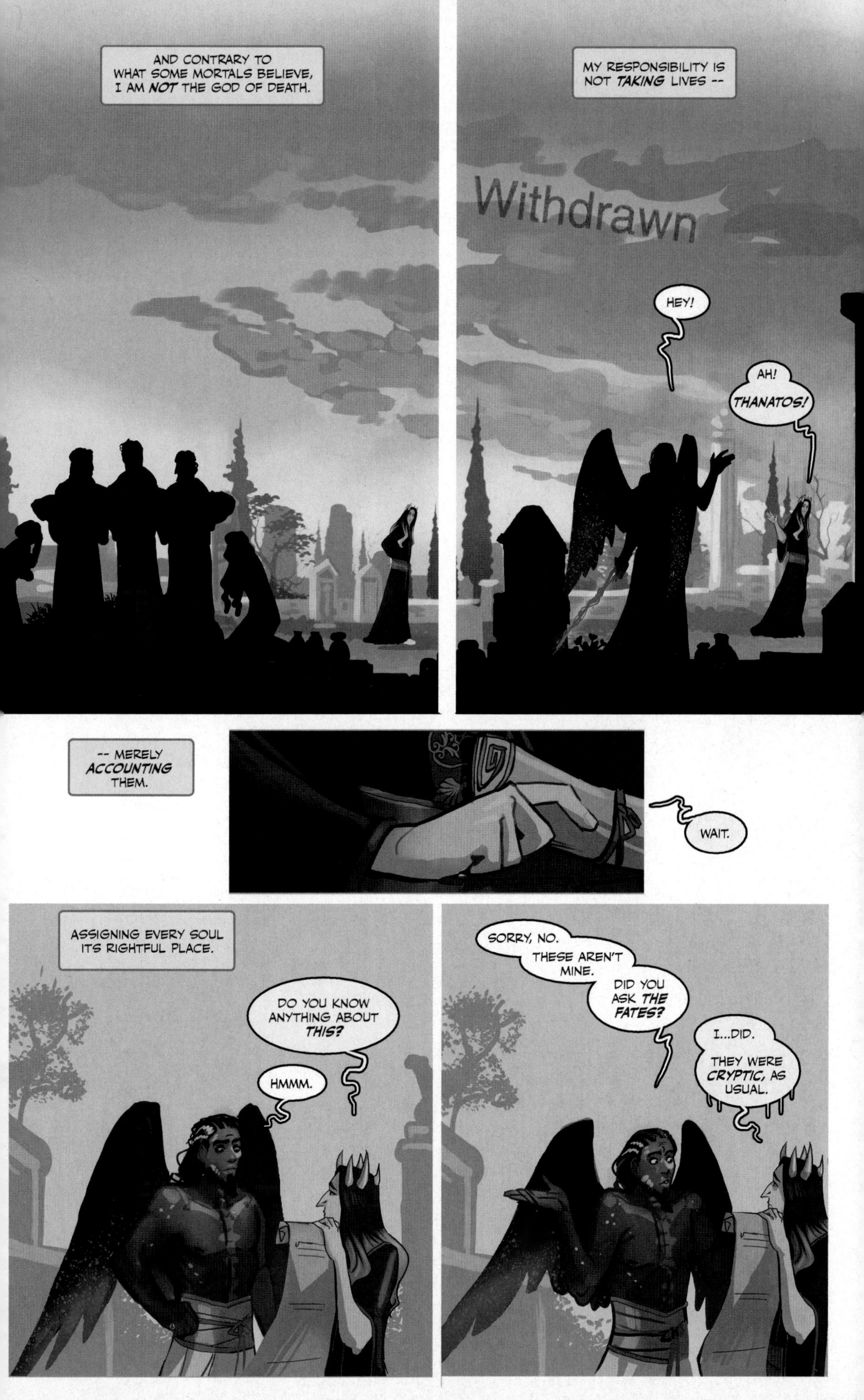
AND CONTRARY TO WHAT SOME MORTALS BELIEVE, I AM NOT THE GOD OF DEATH.
MY RESPONSIBILITY IS NOT TAKING LIVES --
HEY!
AH! THANATOS!
-- MERELY ACCOUNTING THEM.
WAIT.
ASSIGNING EVERY SOUL ITS RIGHTFUL PLACE.
DO YOU KNOW ANYTHING ABOUT THIS?
HMMM.
SORRY, NO.
THESE AREN'T MINE.
DID YOU ASK THE FATES?
I...DID.
THEY WERE CRYPTIC, AS USUAL.

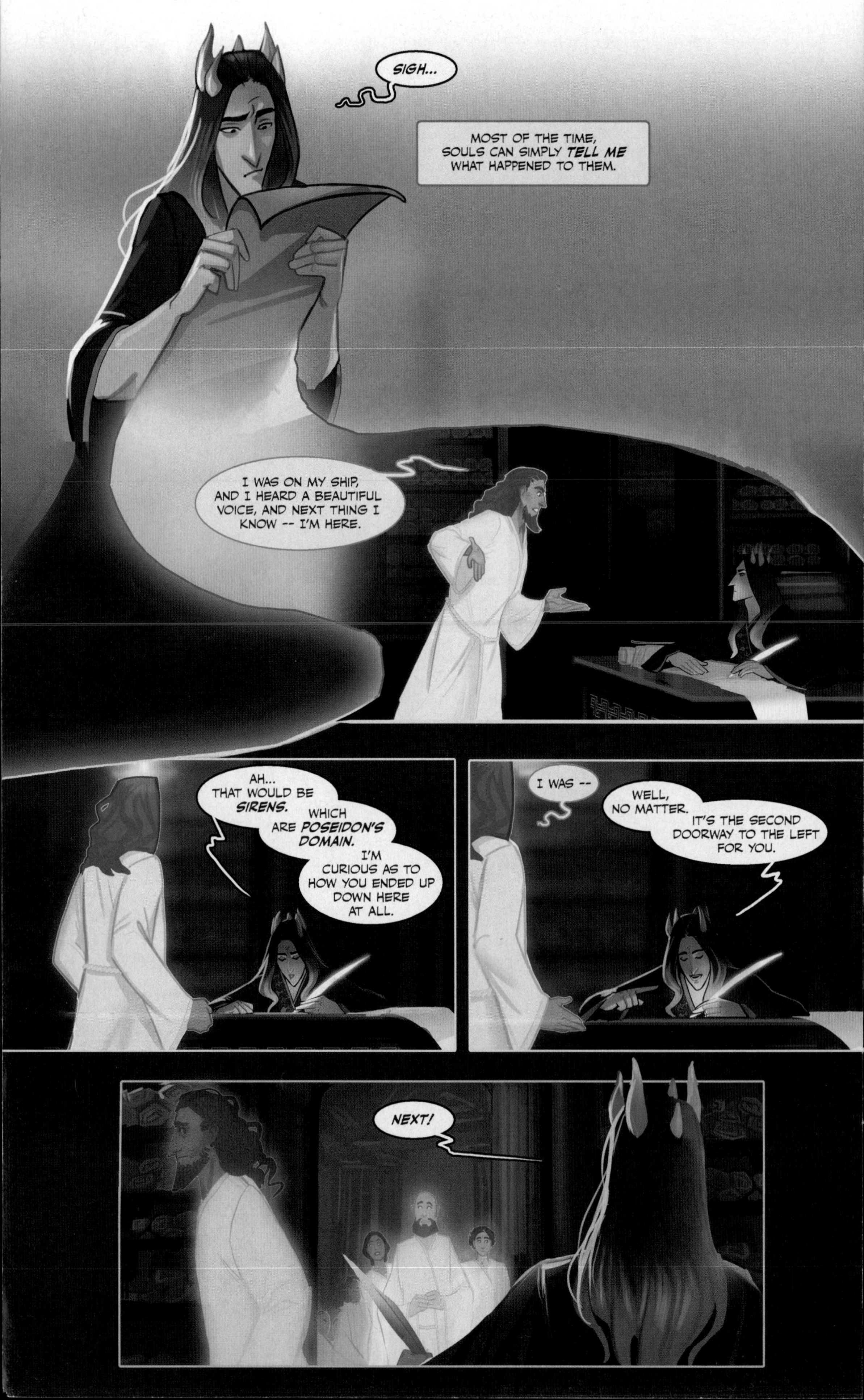
SIGH...
MOST OF THE TIME, SOULS CAN SIMPLY TELL ME WHAT HAPPENED TO THEM.
I WAS ON MY SHIP, AND I HEARD A BEAUTIFUL VOICE, AND NEXT THING I KNOW -- I'M HERE.
AH... THAT WOULD BE SIRENS.
WHICH ARE POSEIDON'S DOMAIN.
I'M CURIOUS AS TO HOW YOU ENDED UP DOWN HERE AT ALL.
I WAS --
WELL, NO MATTER.
IT'S THE SECOND DOORWAY TO THE LEFT FOR YOU.
NEXT!

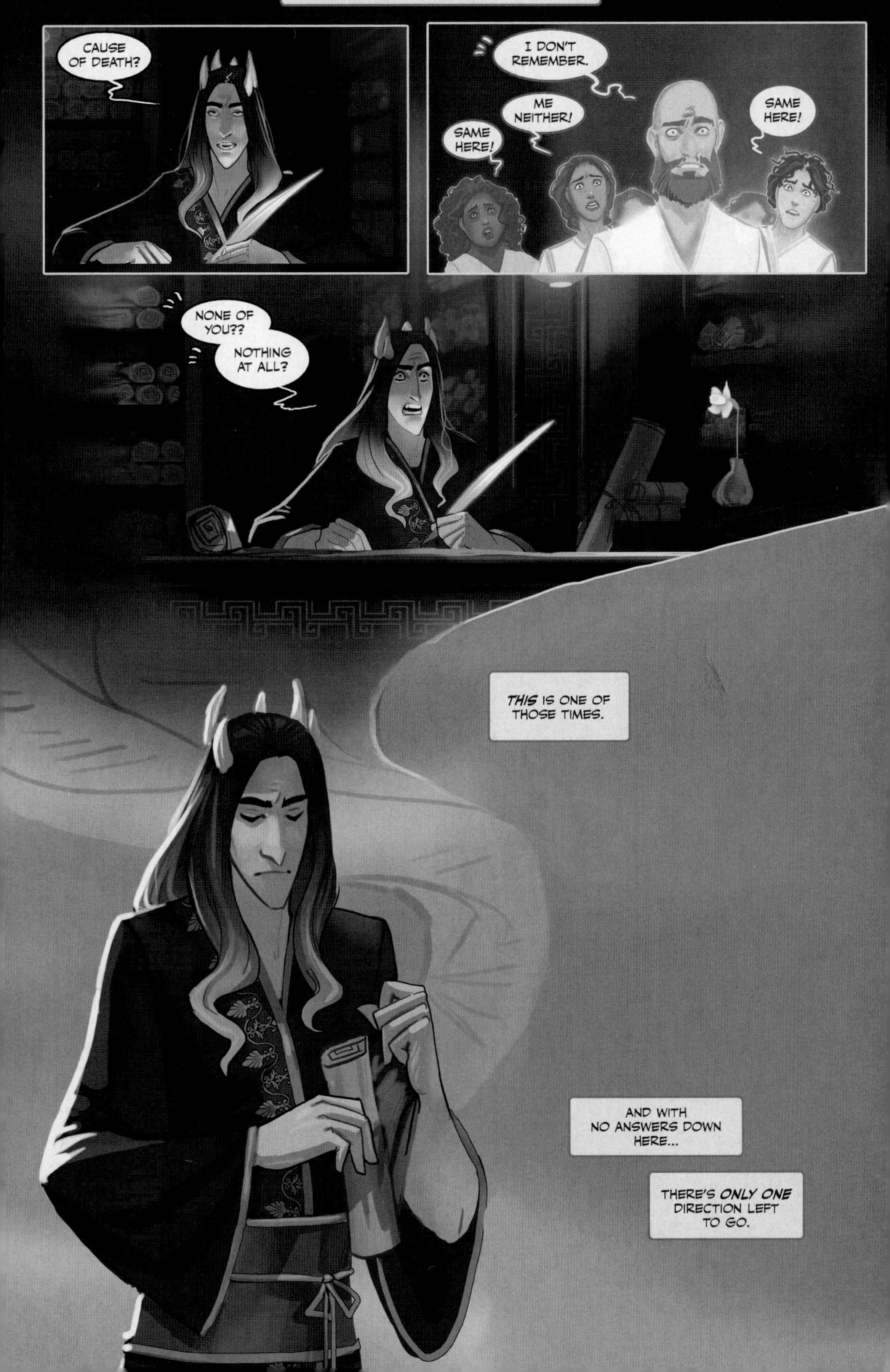
CAUSE OF DEATH?
I DON'T REMEMBER.
SAME HERE!
ME NEITHER!
SAME HERE!
NONE OF YOU??
NOTHING AT ALL?
THIS IS ONE OF THOSE TIMES.
AND WITH NO ANSWERS DOWN HERE...
THERE'S ONLY ONE DIRECTION LEFT TO GO.

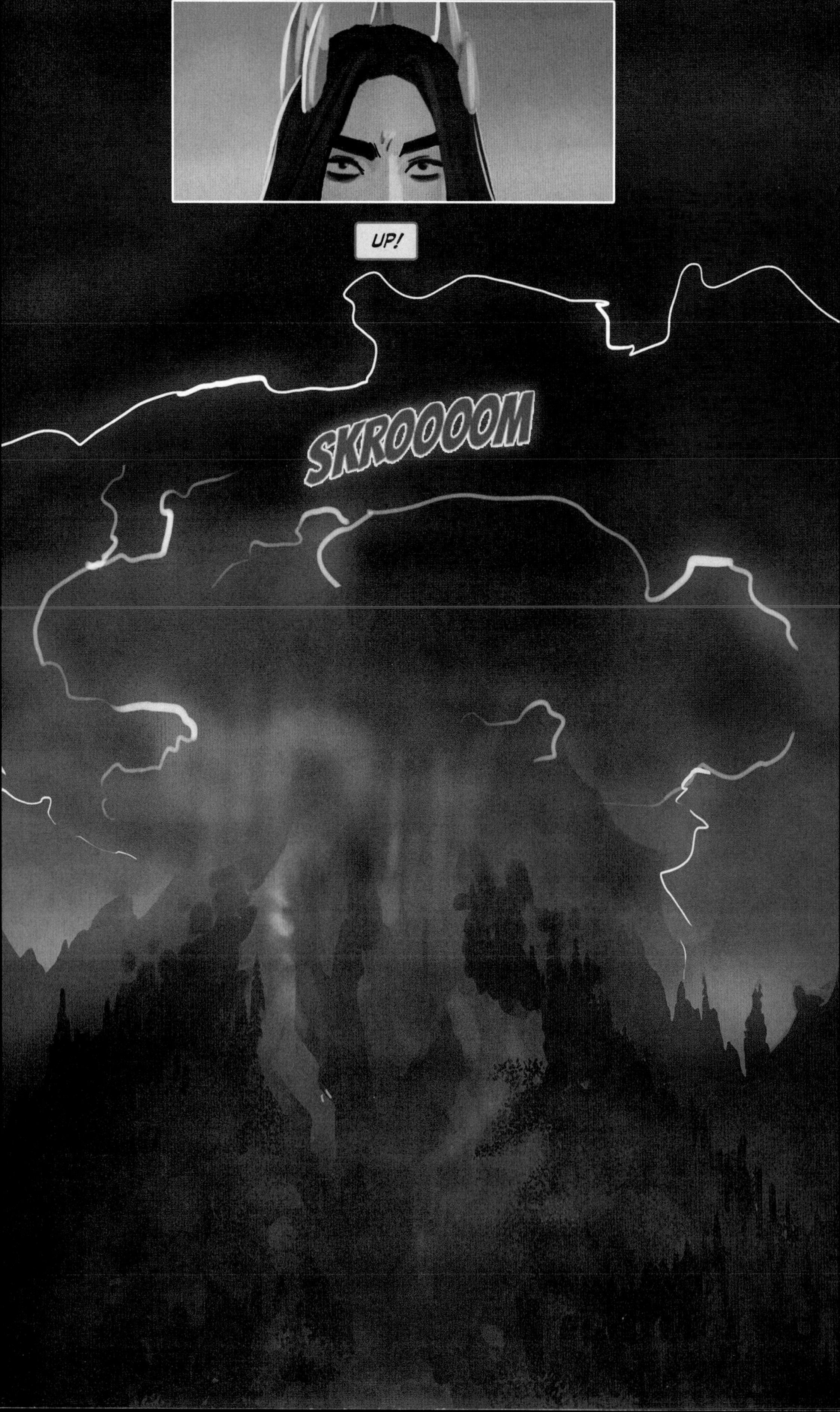
UP!
SKROOOOM

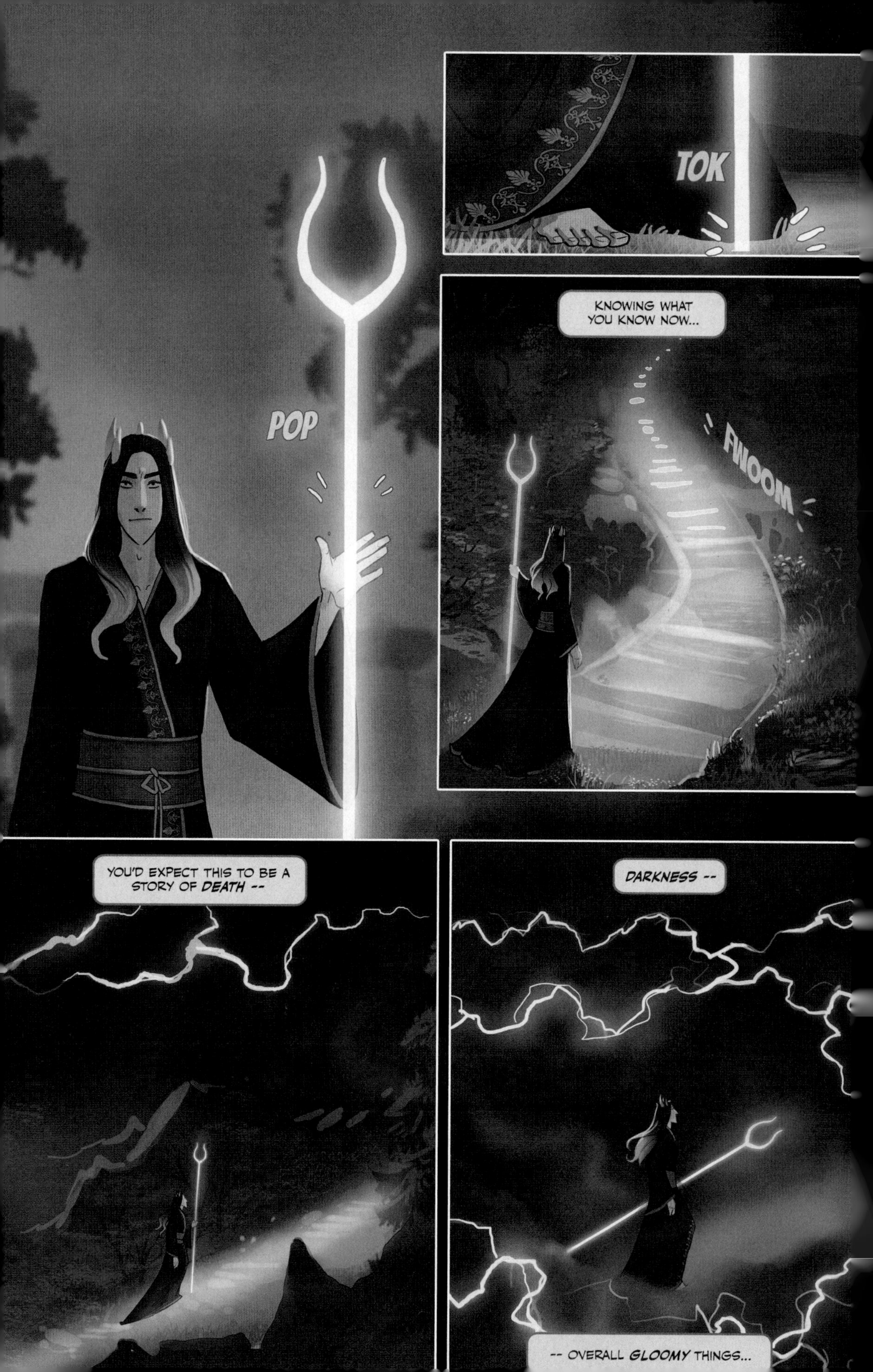
TOK
POP
KNOWING WHAT YOU KNOW NOW...
FWOOM
YOU'D EXPECT THIS TO BE A STORY OF DEATH --
DARKNESS --
-- OVERALL GLOOMY THINGS...

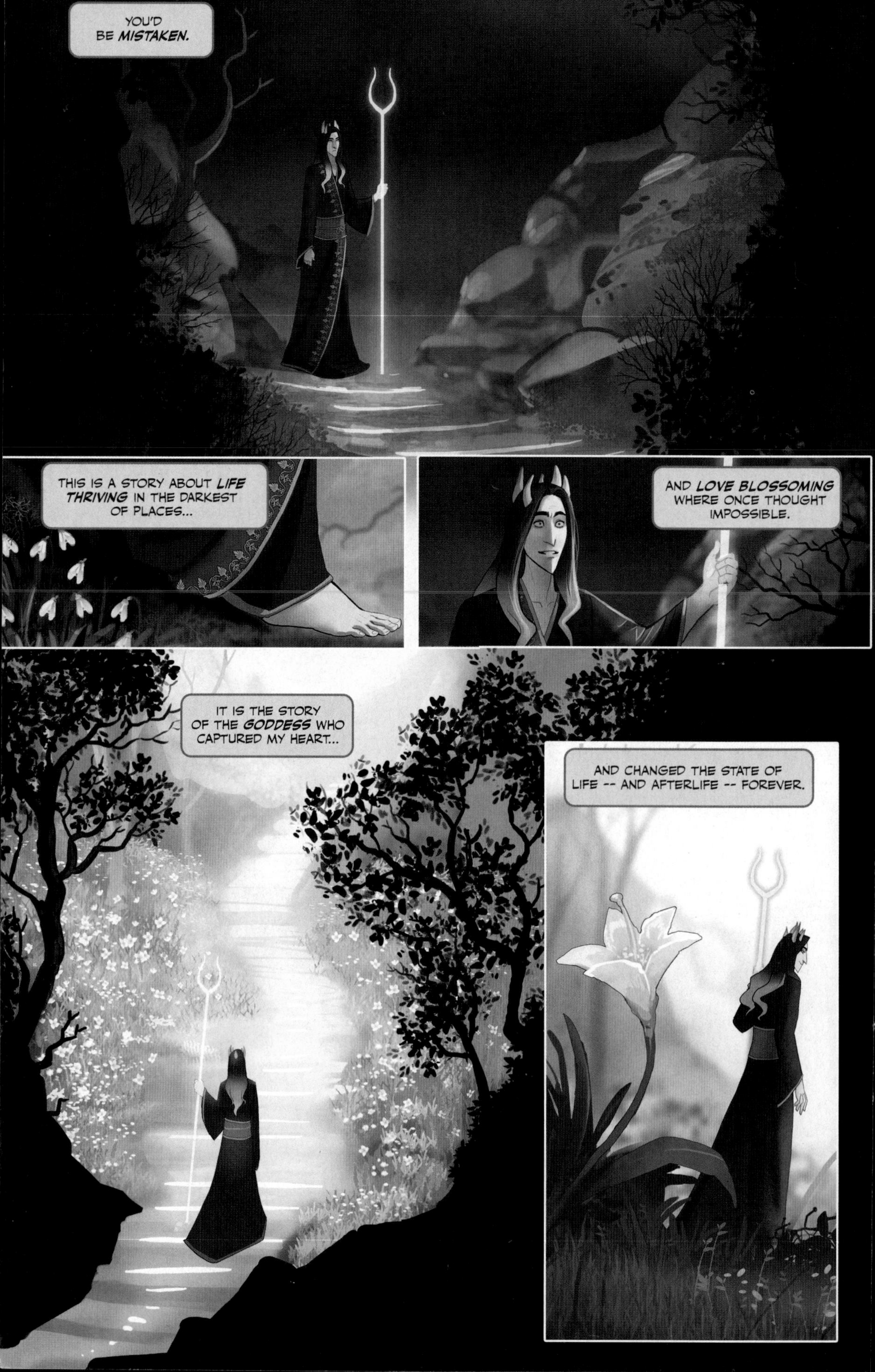
YOU'D BE MISTAKEN.
THIS IS A STORY ABOUT LIFE THRIVING IN THE DARKEST OF PLACES...
AND LOVE BLOSSOMING WHERE ONCE THOUGHT IMPOSSIBLE.
IT IS THE STORY OF THE GODDESS WHO CAPTURED MY HEART...
AND CHANGED THE STATE OF LIFE -- AND AFTERLIFE -- FOREVER.

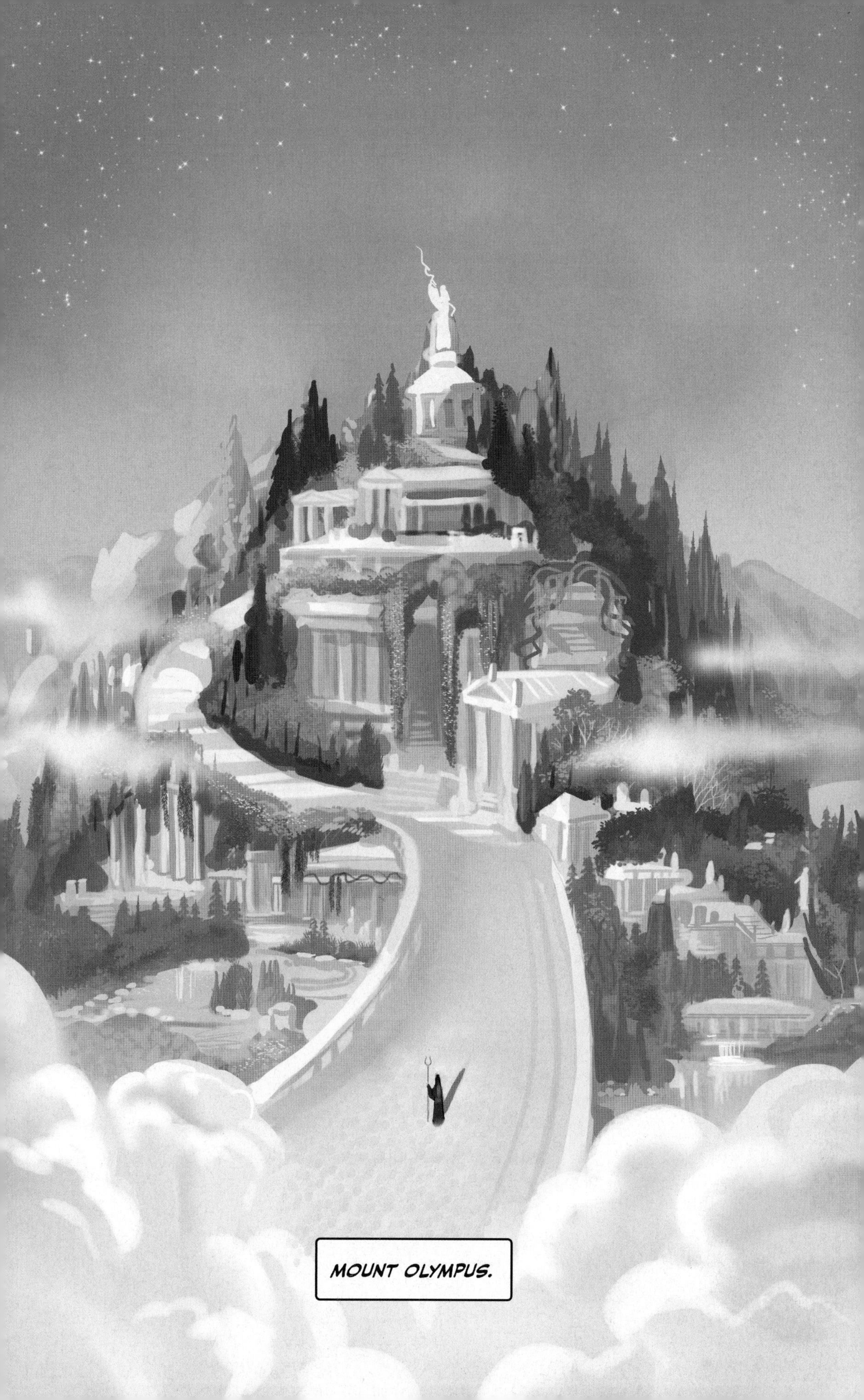
MOUNT OLYMPUS.

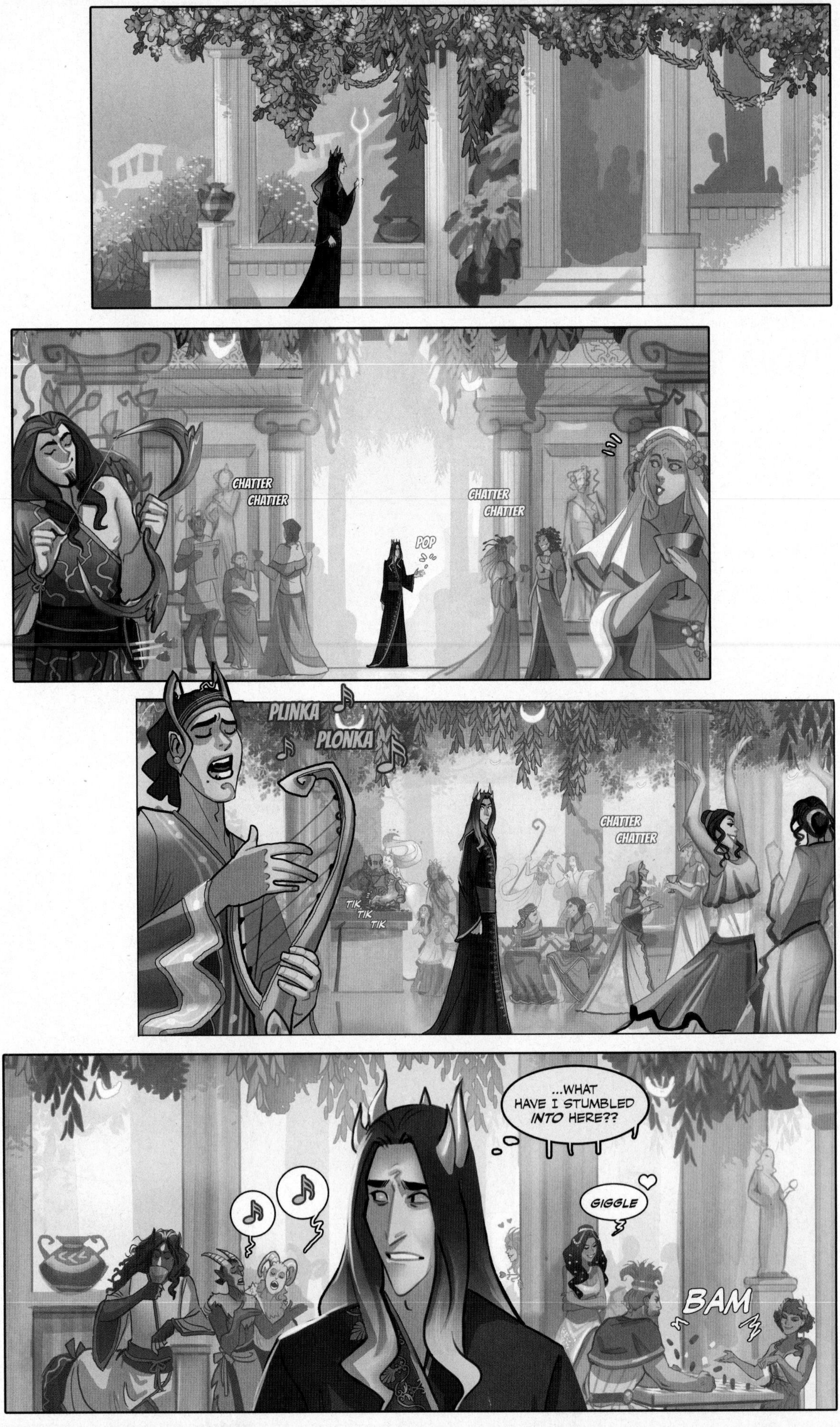
CHATTER
CHATTER
POP
CHATTER
CHATTER
PLINKA
PLONKA
TIK
TIK
TIK
CHATTER
CHATTER
...WHAT HAVE I STUMBLED *INTO* HERE??
GIGGLE
BAM

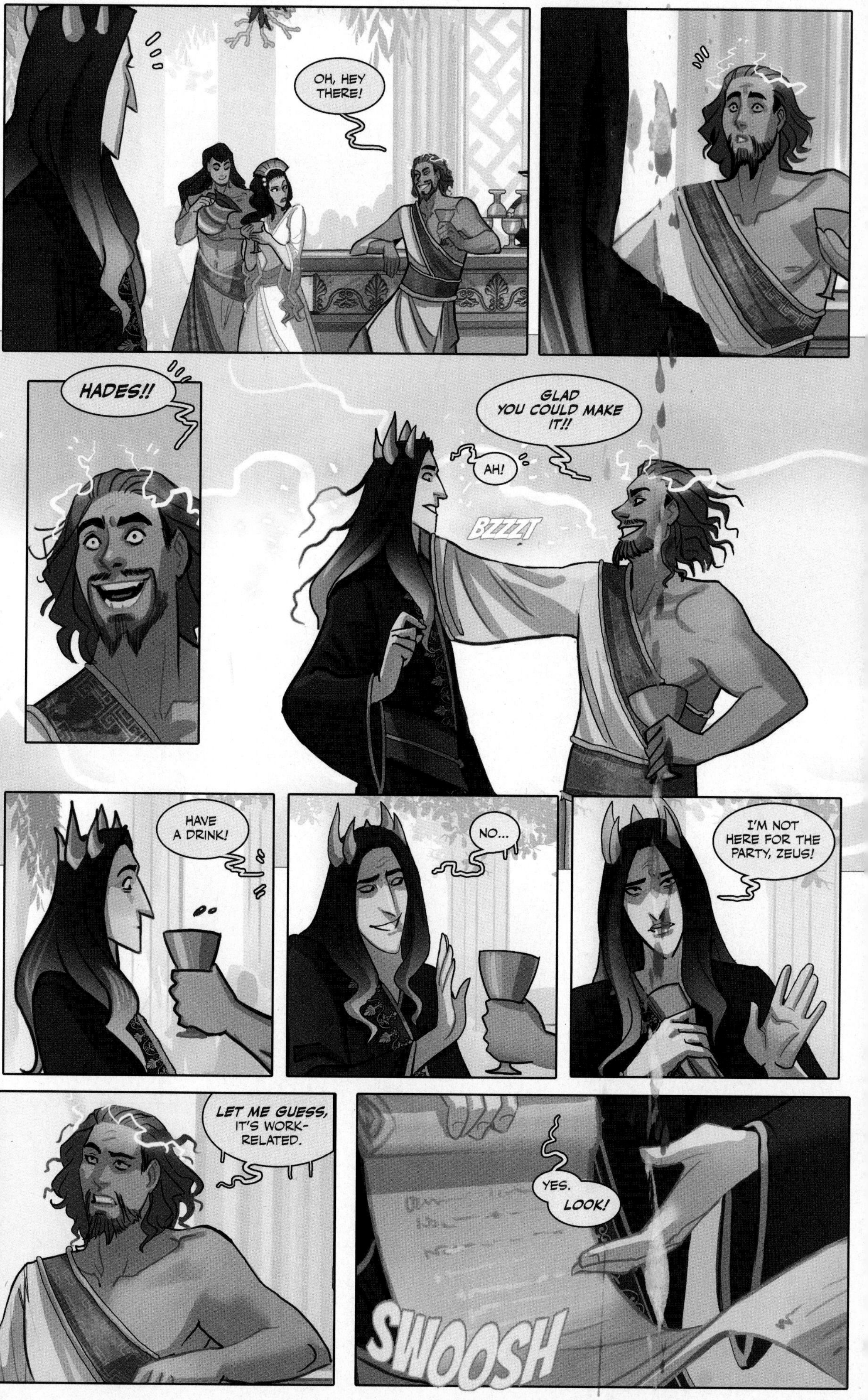
OH, HEY THERE!
HADES!!
GLAD YOU COULD MAKE IT!!
AH!
BZZZZT
HAVE A DRINK!
NO...
I'M NOT HERE FOR THE PARTY, ZEUS!
LET ME GUESS, IT'S WORK-RELATED.
YES.
LOOK!
SWOOSH

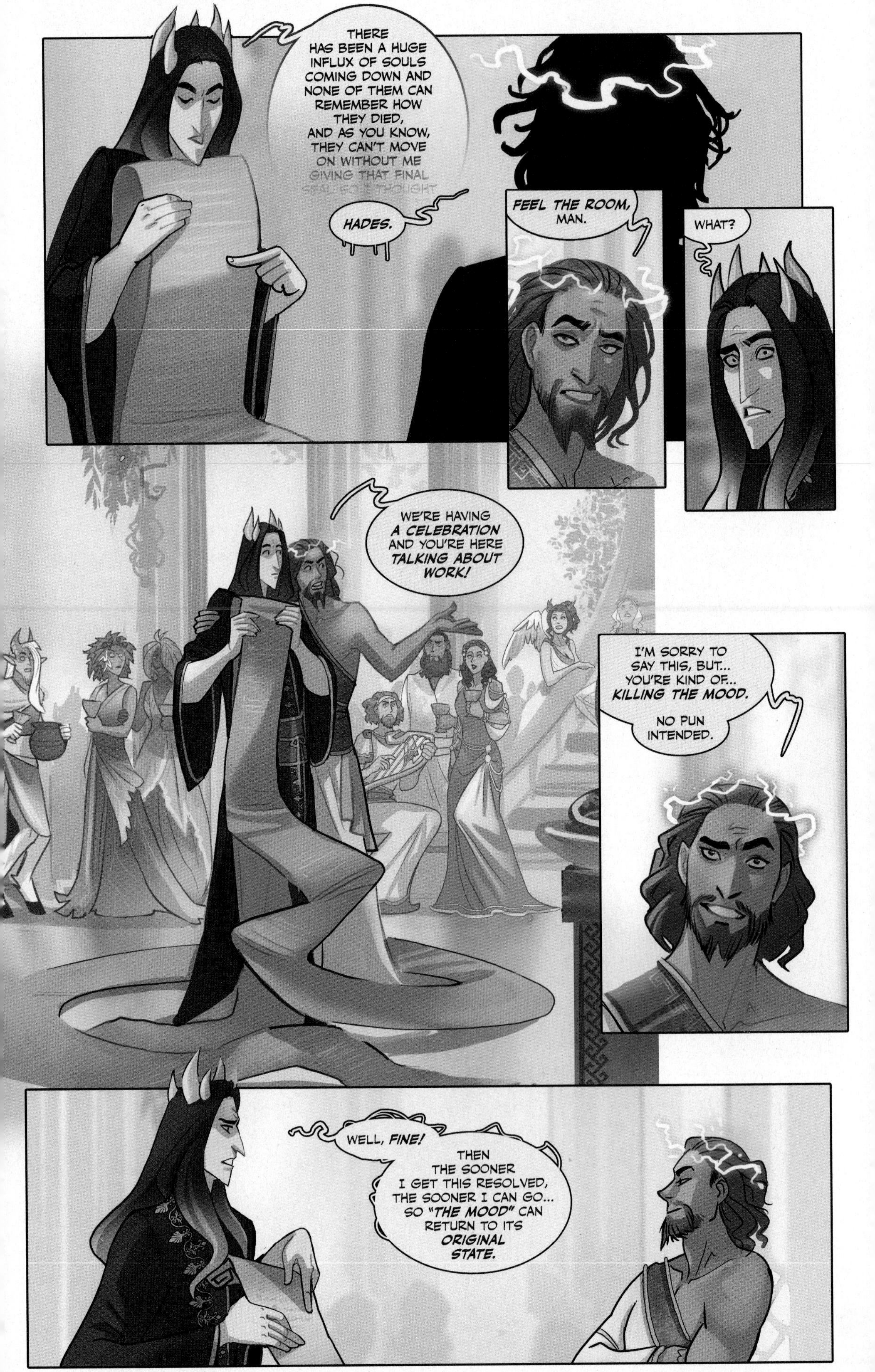
THERE HAS BEEN A HUGE INFLUX OF SOULS COMING DOWN AND NONE OF THEM CAN REMEMBER HOW THEY DIED, AND AS YOU KNOW, THEY CAN'T MOVE ON WITHOUT ME GIVING THAT FINAL SEAL SO I THOUGHT
HADES.
FEEL THE ROOM, MAN.
WHAT?
WE'RE HAVING A CELEBRATION AND YOU'RE HERE TALKING ABOUT WORK!
I'M SORRY TO SAY THIS, BUT... YOU'RE KIND OF... KILLING THE MOOD.
NO PUN INTENDED.
WELL, FINE!
THEN THE SOONER I GET THIS RESOLVED, THE SOONER I CAN GO... SO "THE MOOD" CAN RETURN TO ITS ORIGINAL STATE.

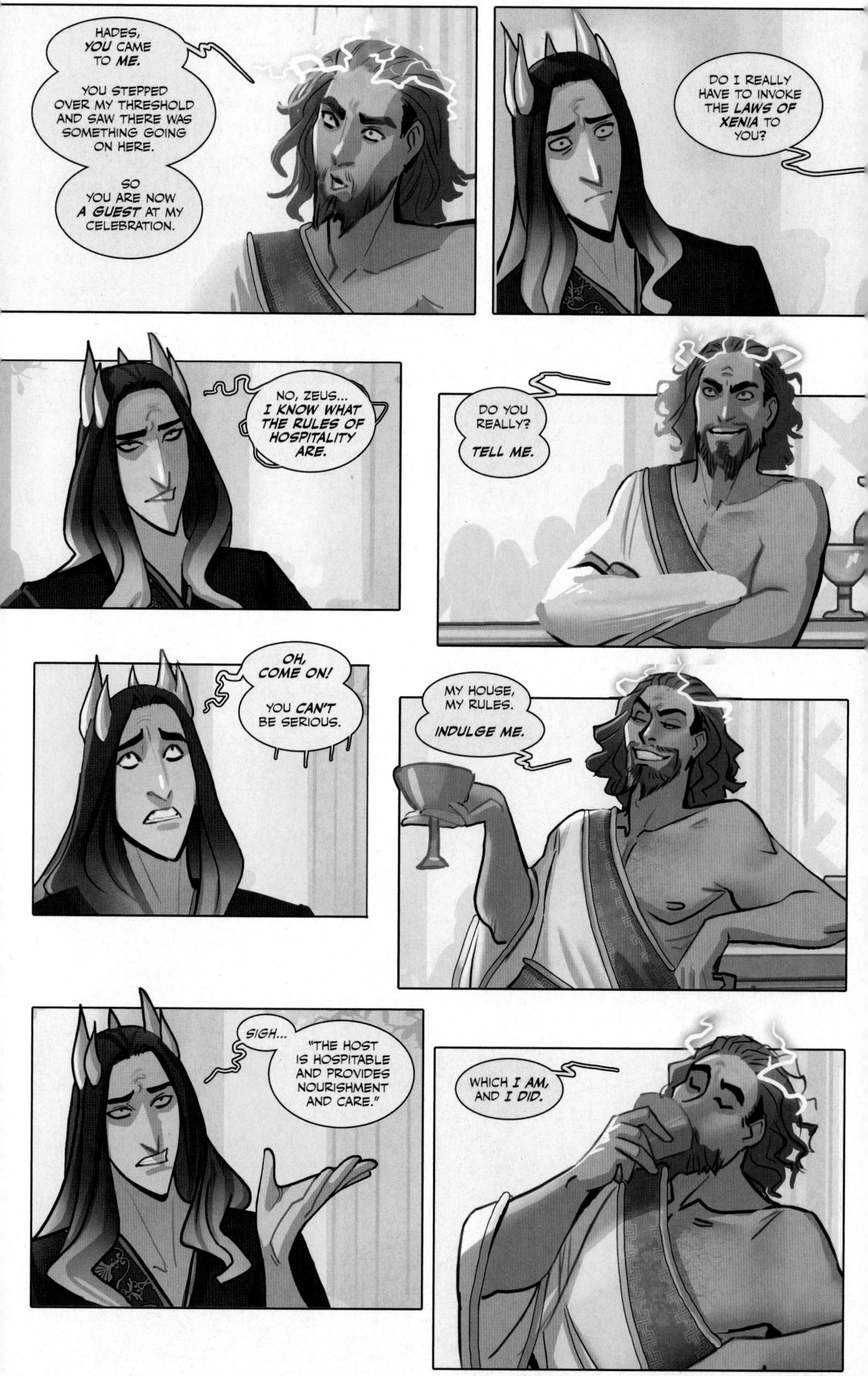

HADES, YOU CAME TO ME.
YOU STEPPED OVER MY THRESHOLD AND SAW THERE WAS SOMETHING GOING ON HERE.
SO YOU ARE NOW A GUEST AT MY CELEBRATION.
DO I REALLY HAVE TO INVOKE THE LAWS OF XENIA TO YOU?
NO, ZEUS... I KNOW WHAT THE RULES OF HOSPITALITY ARE.
DO YOU REALLY?
TELL ME.
OH, COME ON!
YOU CAN'T BE SERIOUS.
MY HOUSE, MY RULES.
INDULGE ME.
SIGH...
"THE HOST IS HOSPITABLE AND PROVIDES NOURISHMENT AND CARE."
WHICH I AM, AND I DID.

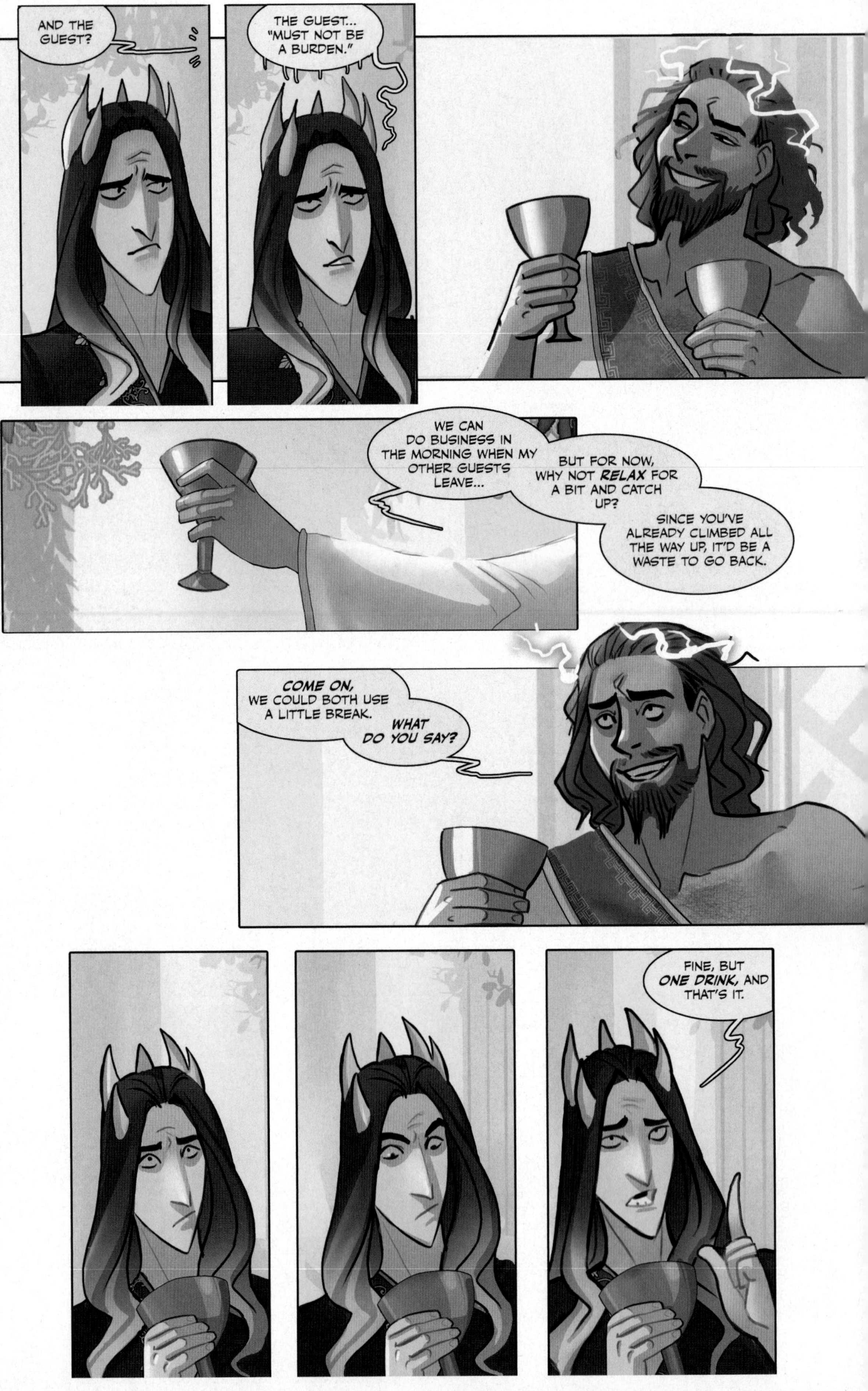
AND THE GUEST?
THE GUEST... "MUST NOT BE A BURDEN."
WE CAN DO BUSINESS IN THE MORNING WHEN MY OTHER GUESTS LEAVE...
BUT FOR NOW, WHY NOT RELAX FOR A BIT AND CATCH UP?
SINCE YOU'VE ALREADY CLIMBED ALL THE WAY UP, IT'D BE A WASTE TO GO BACK.
COME ON, WE COULD BOTH USE A LITTLE BREAK.
WHAT DO YOU SAY?
FINE, BUT ONE DRINK, AND THAT'S IT.

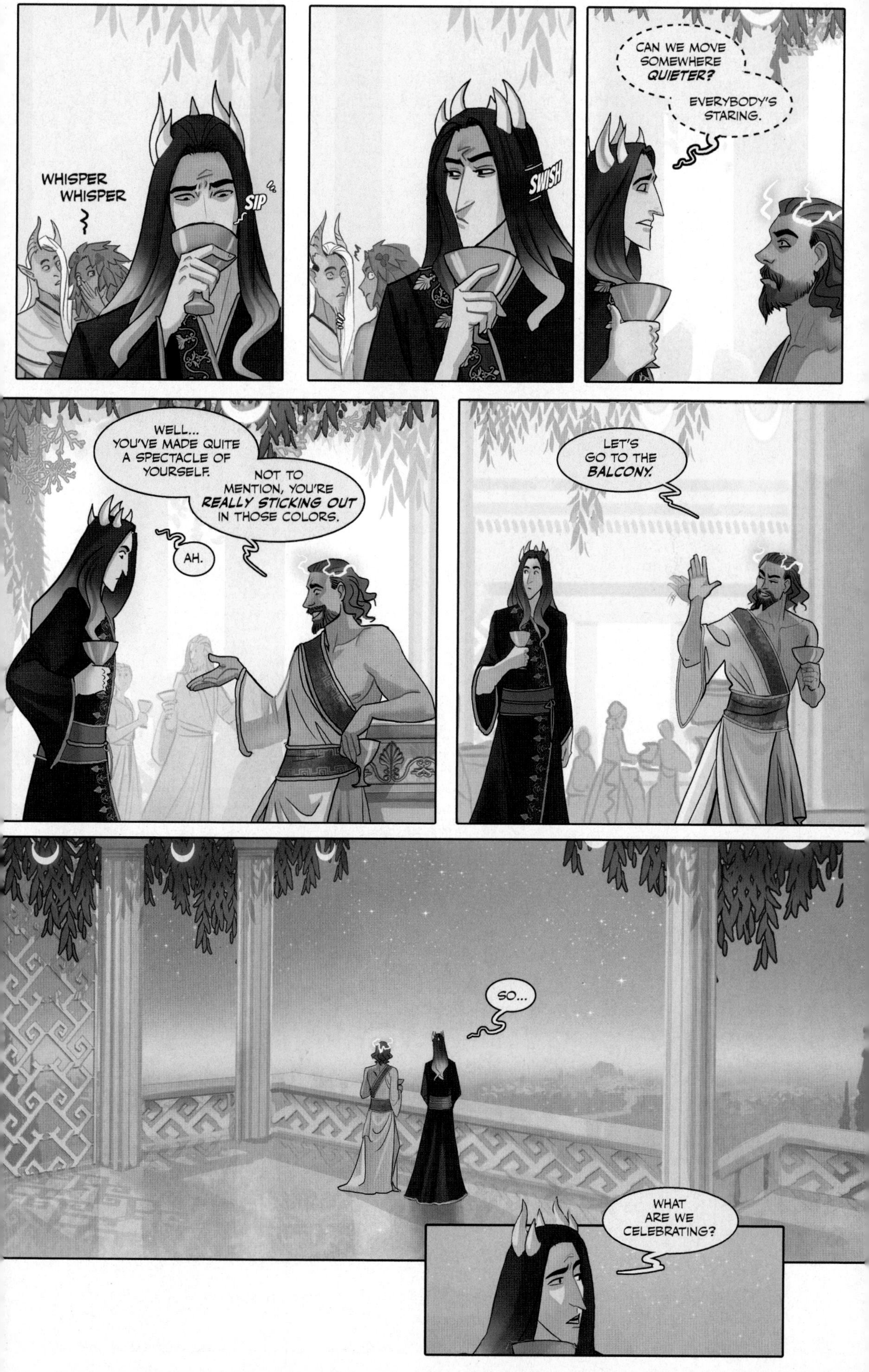
WHISPER
WHISPER
SIP
SWISH
CAN WE MOVE SOMEWHERE QUIETER?
EVERYBODY'S STARING.
WELL... YOU'VE MADE QUITE A SPECTACLE OF YOURSELF.
NOT TO MENTION, YOU'RE REALLY STICKING OUT IN THOSE COLORS.
AH.
LET'S GO TO THE BALCONY.
SO...
WHAT ARE WE CELEBRATING?

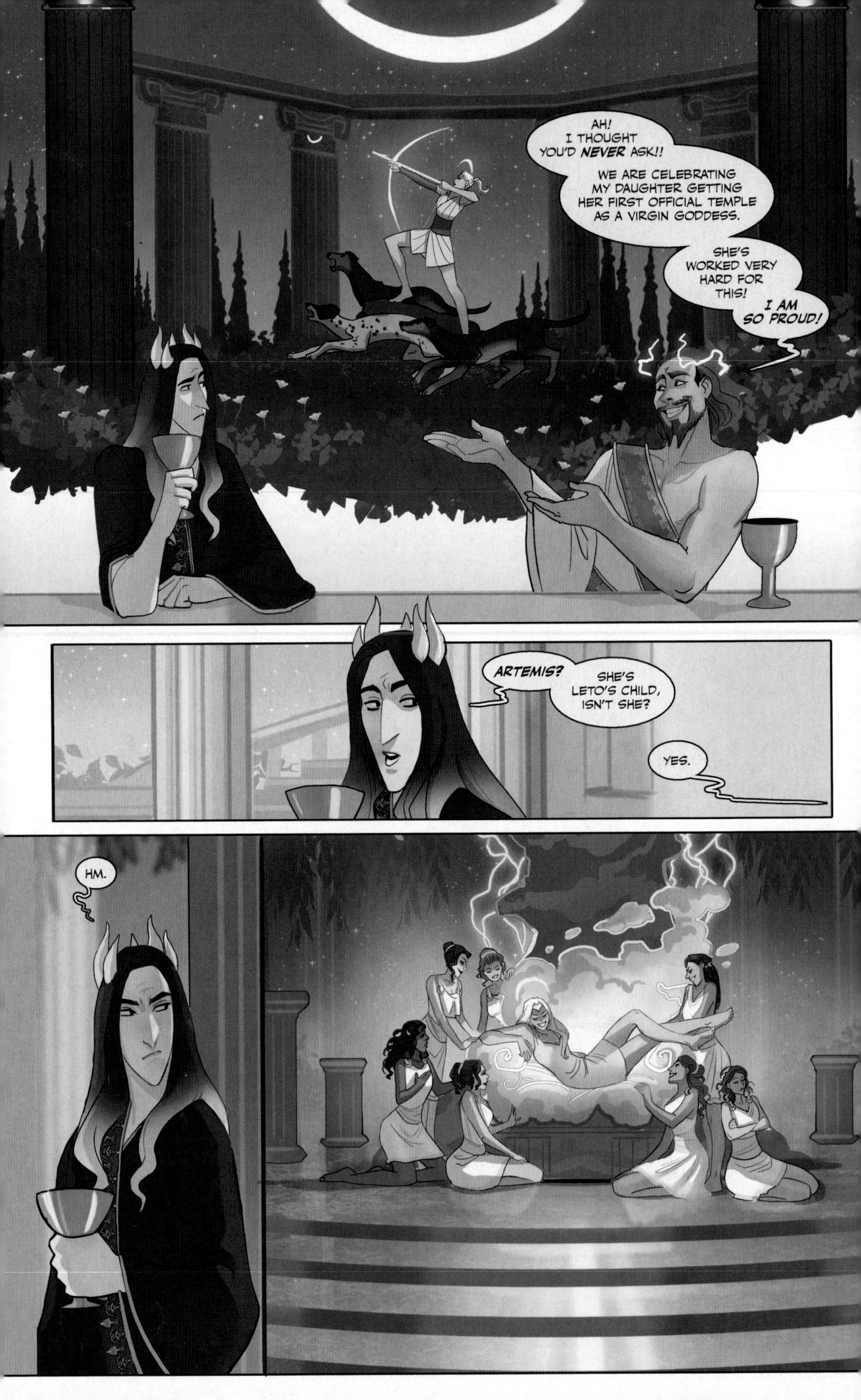
AH! I THOUGHT YOU'D NEVER ASK!!
WE ARE CELEBRATING MY DAUGHTER GETTING HER FIRST OFFICIAL TEMPLE AS A VIRGIN GODDESS.
SHE'S WORKED VERY HARD FOR THIS!
I AM SO PROUD!
ARTEMIS?
SHE'S LETO'S CHILD, ISN'T SHE?
YES.
HM.

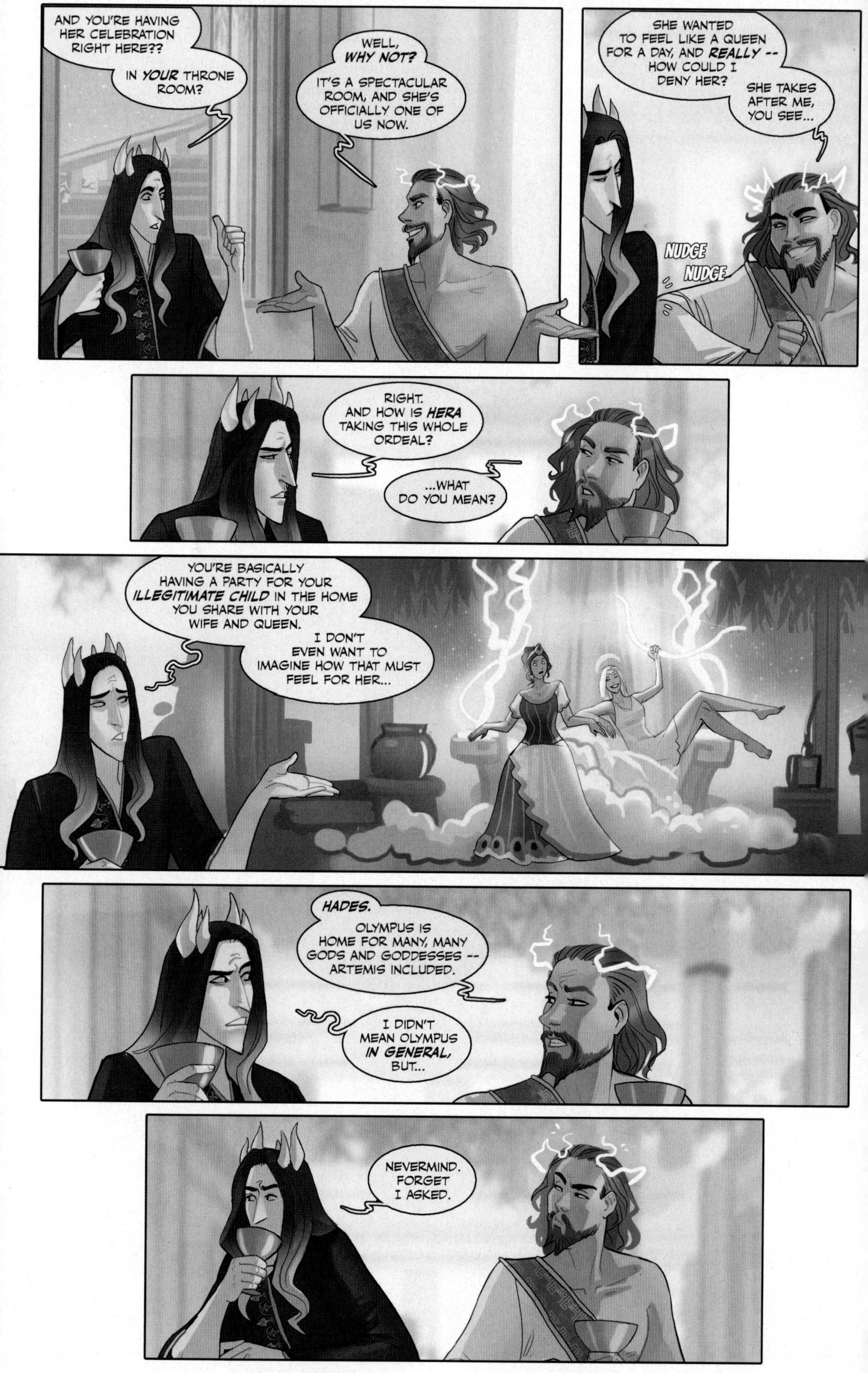
AND YOU'RE HAVING HER CELEBRATION RIGHT HERE??
IN YOUR THRONE ROOM?
WELL, WHY NOT?
IT'S A SPECTACULAR ROOM, AND SHE'S OFFICIALLY ONE OF US NOW.
SHE WANTED TO FEEL LIKE A QUEEN FOR A DAY, AND REALLY -- HOW COULD I DENY HER?
SHE TAKES AFTER ME, YOU SEE...
NUDGE
NUDGE
RIGHT. AND HOW IS HERA TAKING THIS WHOLE ORDEAL?
...WHAT DO YOU MEAN?
YOU'RE BASICALLY HAVING A PARTY FOR YOUR ILLEGITIMATE CHILD IN THE HOME YOU SHARE WITH YOUR WIFE AND QUEEN.
I DON'T EVEN WANT TO IMAGINE HOW THAT MUST FEEL FOR HER...
HADES.
OLYMPUS IS HOME FOR MANY, MANY GODS AND GODDESSES -- ARTEMIS INCLUDED.
I DIDN'T MEAN OLYMPUS IN GENERAL, BUT...
NEVERMIND. FORGET I ASKED.

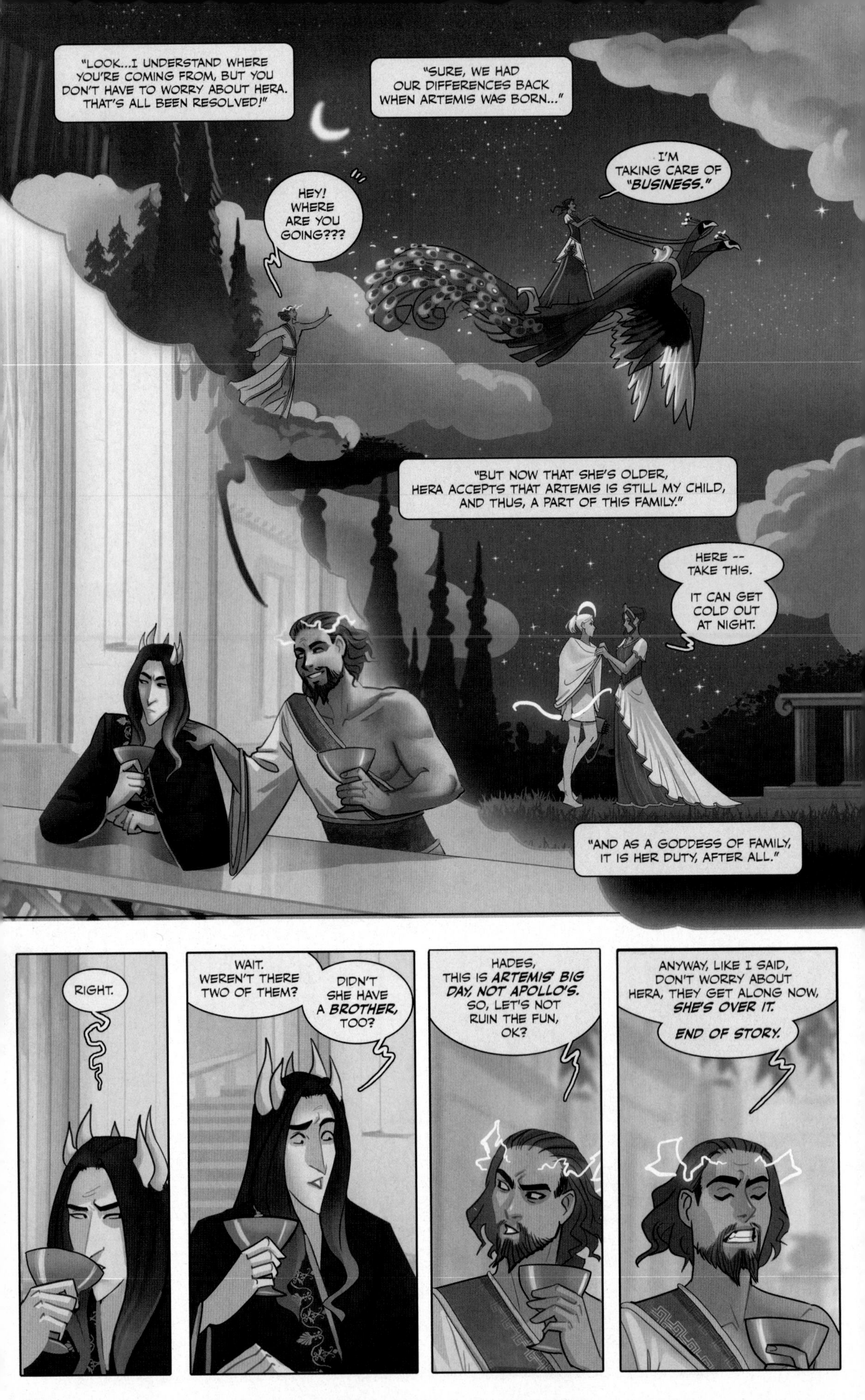
"LOOK...I UNDERSTAND WHERE YOU'RE COMING FROM, BUT YOU DON'T HAVE TO WORRY ABOUT HERA. THAT'S ALL BEEN RESOLVED!"
"SURE, WE HAD OUR DIFFERENCES BACK WHEN ARTEMIS WAS BORN..."
HEY! WHERE ARE YOU GOING???
I'M TAKING CARE OF "BUSINESS."
"BUT NOW THAT SHE'S OLDER, HERA ACCEPTS THAT ARTEMIS IS STILL MY CHILD, AND THUS, A PART OF THIS FAMILY."
HERE -- TAKE THIS.
IT CAN GET COLD OUT AT NIGHT.
"AND AS A GODDESS OF FAMILY, IT IS HER DUTY, AFTER ALL."
RIGHT.
WAIT. WEREN'T THERE TWO OF THEM?
DIDN'T SHE HAVE A BROTHER, TOO?
HADES, THIS IS ARTEMIS' BIG DAY, NOT APOLLO'S. SO, LET'S NOT RUIN THE FUN, OK?
ANYWAY, LIKE I SAID, DON'T WORRY ABOUT HERA, THEY GET ALONG NOW, SHE'S OVER IT.
END OF STORY.

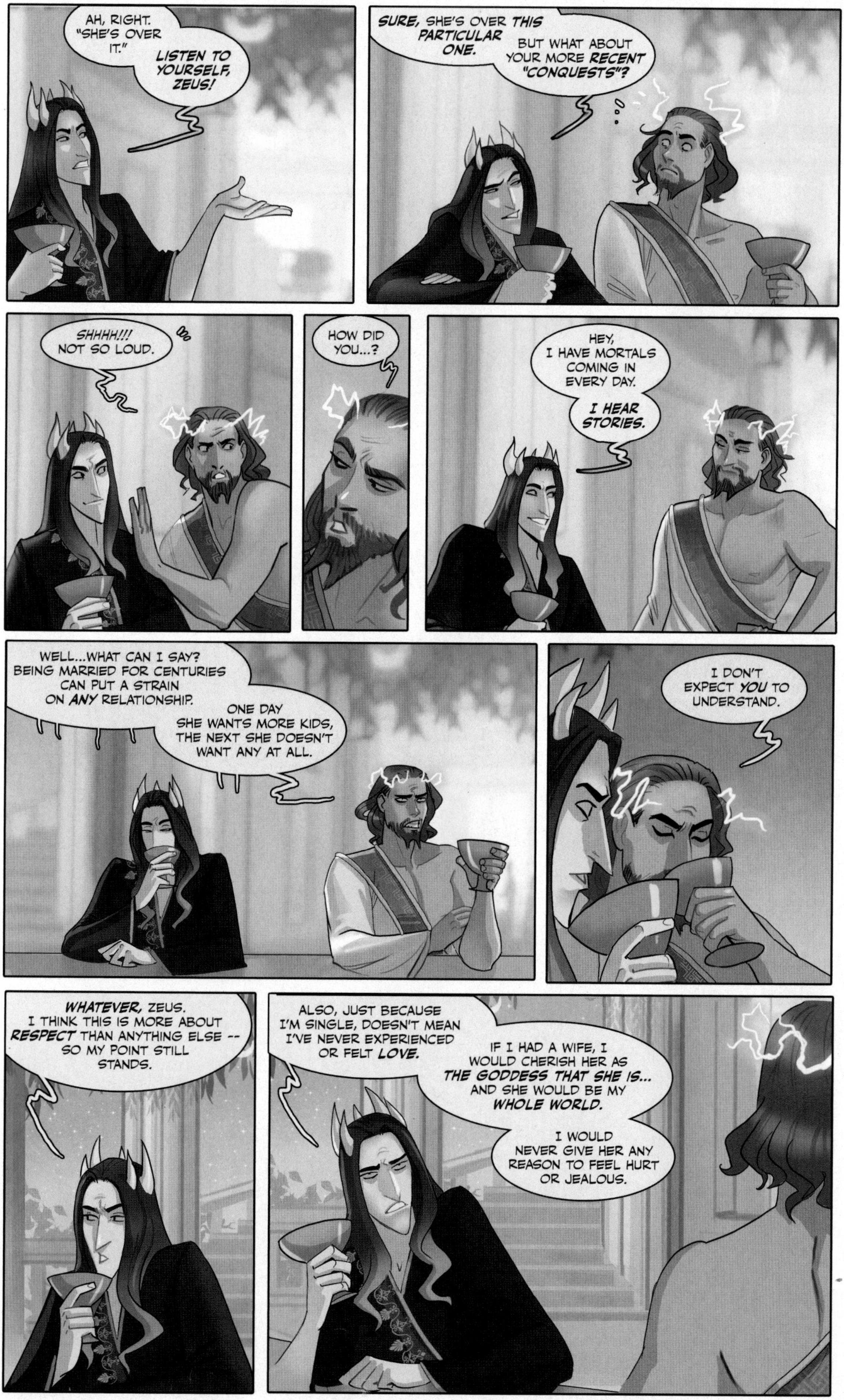
AH, RIGHT. "SHE'S OVER IT."
LISTEN TO YOURSELF, ZEUS!
SURE, SHE'S OVER THIS PARTICULAR ONE.
BUT WHAT ABOUT YOUR MORE RECENT "CONQUESTS"?
SHHHH!!! NOT SO LOUD.
HOW DID YOU...?
HEY, I HAVE MORTALS COMING IN EVERY DAY.
I HEAR STORIES.
WELL...WHAT CAN I SAY? BEING MARRIED FOR CENTURIES CAN PUT A STRAIN ON ANY RELATIONSHIP.
ONE DAY SHE WANTS MORE KIDS, THE NEXT SHE DOESN'T WANT ANY AT ALL.
I DON'T EXPECT YOU TO UNDERSTAND.
WHATEVER, ZEUS. I THINK THIS IS MORE ABOUT RESPECT THAN ANYTHING ELSE -- SO MY POINT STILL STANDS.
ALSO, JUST BECAUSE I'M SINGLE, DOESN'T MEAN I'VE NEVER EXPERIENCED OR FELT LOVE.
IF I HAD A WIFE, I WOULD CHERISH HER AS THE GODDESS THAT SHE IS... AND SHE WOULD BE MY WHOLE WORLD.
I WOULD NEVER GIVE HER ANY REASON TO FEEL HURT OR JEALOUS.

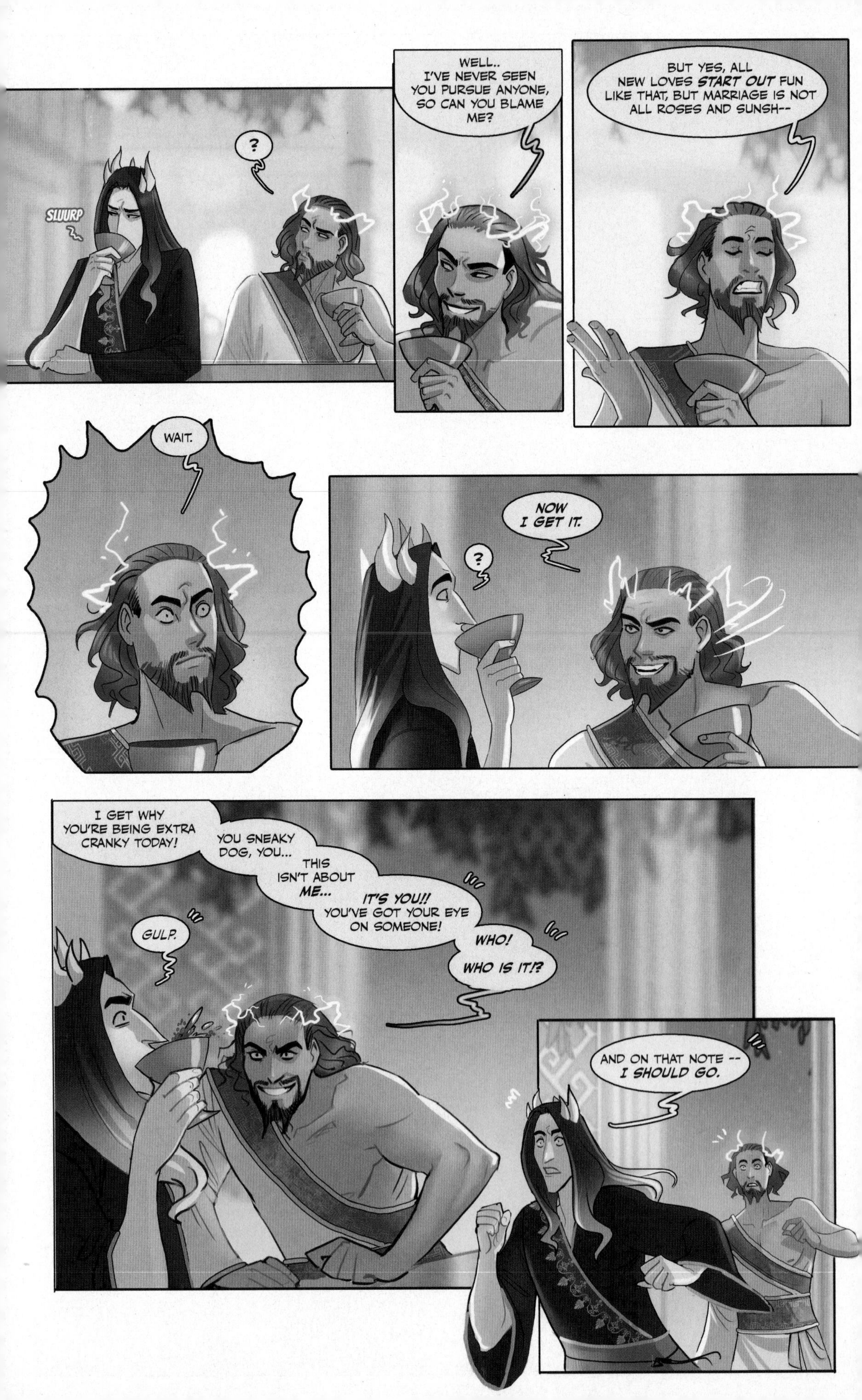

SLUURP
?
WELL..
I'VE NEVER SEEN YOU PURSUE ANYONE, SO CAN YOU BLAME ME?
BUT YES, ALL NEW LOVES START OUT FUN LIKE THAT, BUT MARRIAGE IS NOT ALL ROSES AND SUNSH--
WAIT.
NOW I GET IT.
?
I GET WHY YOU'RE BEING EXTRA CRANKY TODAY!
YOU SNEAKY DOG, YOU...
THIS ISN'T ABOUT ME...
IT'S YOU!! YOU'VE GOT YOUR EYE ON SOMEONE!
WHO!
WHO IS IT!?
GULP.
AND ON THAT NOTE -- I SHOULD GO.

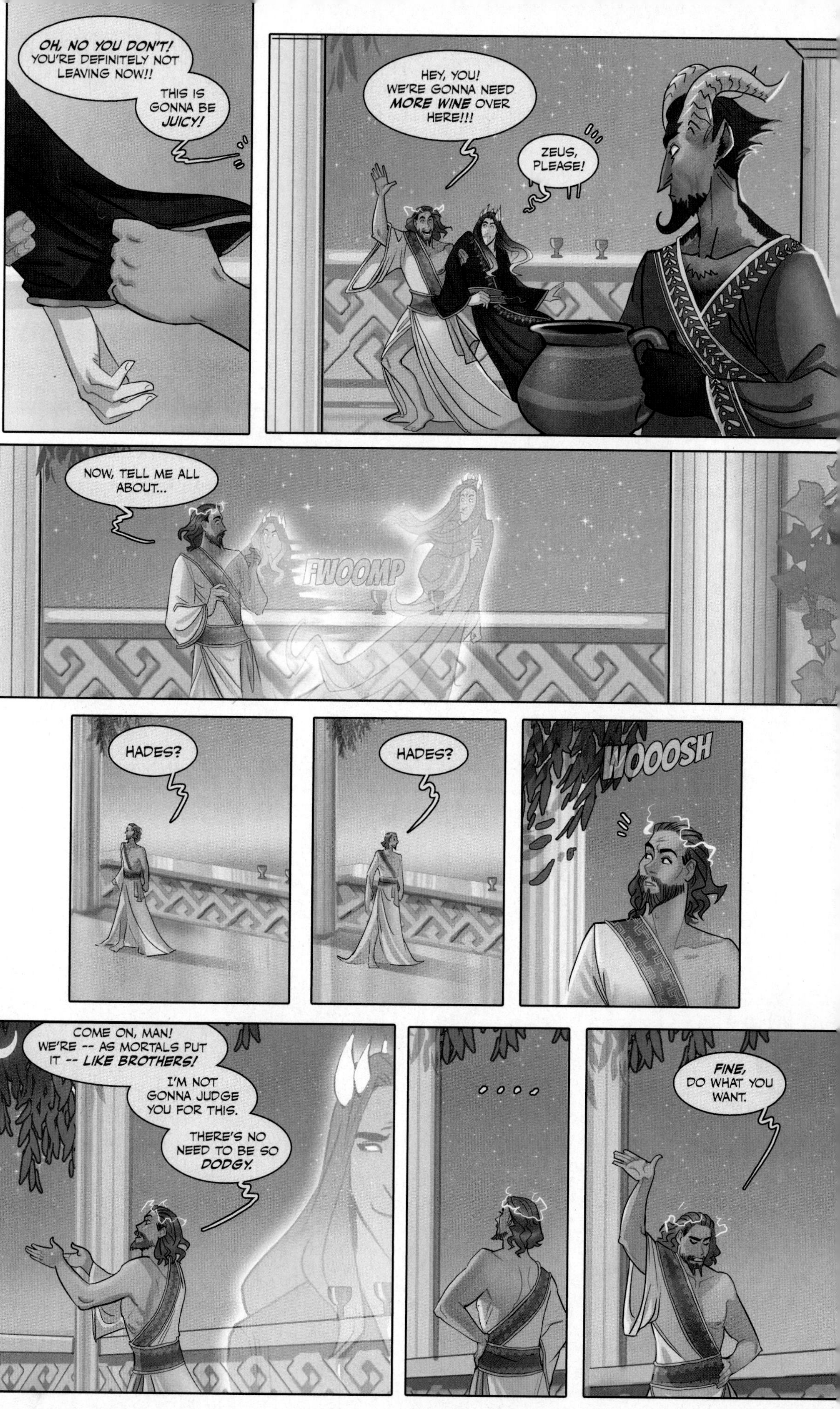
OH, NO YOU DON'T! YOU'RE DEFINITELY NOT LEAVING NOW!!
THIS IS GONNA BE JUICY!
HEY, YOU! WE'RE GONNA NEED MORE WINE OVER HERE!!!
ZEUS, PLEASE!
NOW, TELL ME ALL ABOUT...
FWOOMP
HADES?
HADES?
WOOOSH
COME ON, MAN! WE'RE -- AS MORTALS PUT IT -- LIKE BROTHERS!
I'M NOT GONNA JUDGE YOU FOR THIS.
THERE'S NO NEED TO BE SO DODGY.
....
FINE, DO WHAT YOU WANT.

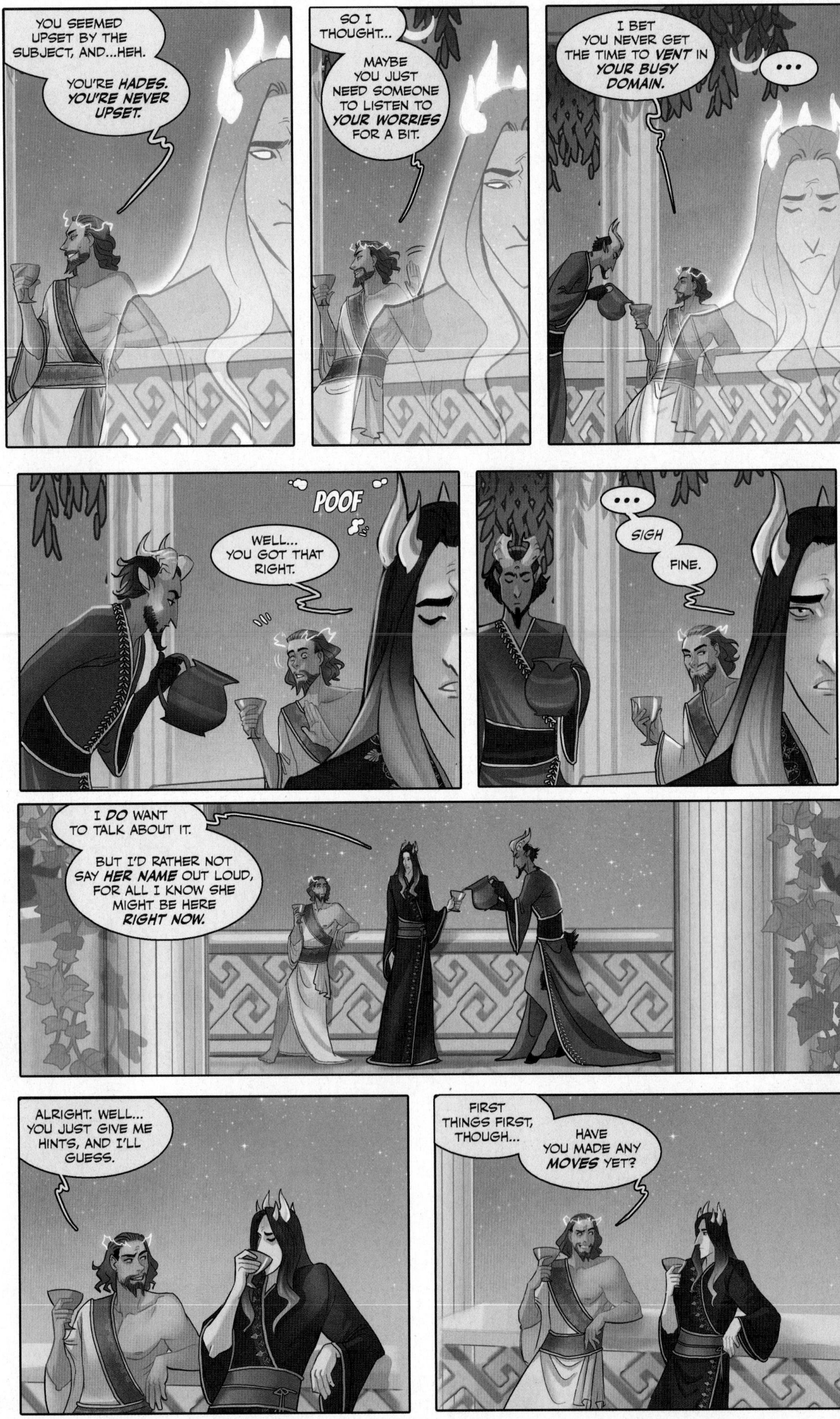

YOU SEEMED UPSET BY THE SUBJECT, AND...HEH.
YOU'RE HADES. YOU'RE NEVER UPSET.
SO I THOUGHT...
MAYBE YOU JUST NEED SOMEONE TO LISTEN TO YOUR WORRIES FOR A BIT.
I BET YOU NEVER GET THE TIME TO VENT IN YOUR BUSY DOMAIN.
...
POOF
WELL... YOU GOT THAT RIGHT.
...
SIGH
FINE.
I DO WANT TO TALK ABOUT IT.
BUT I'D RATHER NOT SAY HER NAME OUT LOUD, FOR ALL I KNOW SHE MIGHT BE HERE RIGHT NOW.
ALRIGHT. WELL... YOU JUST GIVE ME HINTS, AND I'LL GUESS.
FIRST THINGS FIRST, THOUGH...
HAVE YOU MADE ANY MOVES YET?

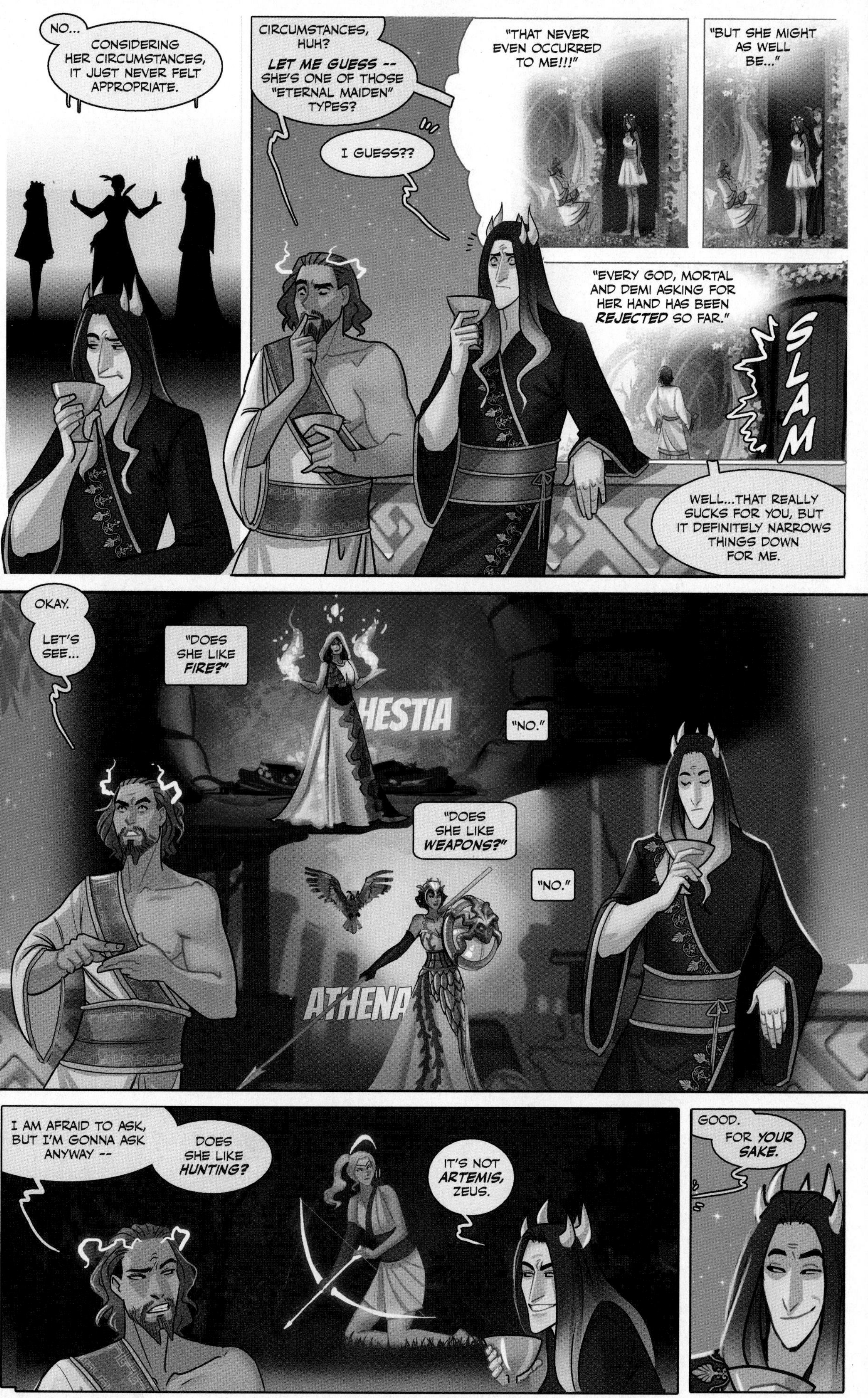
NO... CONSIDERING HER CIRCUMSTANCES, IT JUST NEVER FELT APPROPRIATE.
CIRCUMSTANCES, HUH? *LET ME GUESS --* SHE'S ONE OF THOSE "ETERNAL MAIDEN" TYPES?
I GUESS??
"THAT NEVER EVEN OCCURRED TO ME!!!"
"BUT SHE MIGHT AS WELL BE..."
"EVERY GOD, MORTAL AND DEMI ASKING FOR HER HAND HAS BEEN *REJECTED* SO FAR."
SLAM
WELL...THAT REALLY SUCKS FOR YOU, BUT IT DEFINITELY NARROWS THINGS DOWN FOR ME.
OKAY.
LET'S SEE...
"DOES SHE LIKE *FIRE?*"
HESTIA
"NO."
"DOES SHE LIKE *WEAPONS?*"
"NO."
ATHENA
I AM AFRAID TO ASK, BUT I'M GONNA ASK ANYWAY --
DOES SHE LIKE *HUNTING?*
IT'S NOT *ARTEMIS,* ZEUS.
GOOD.
FOR *YOUR SAKE.*

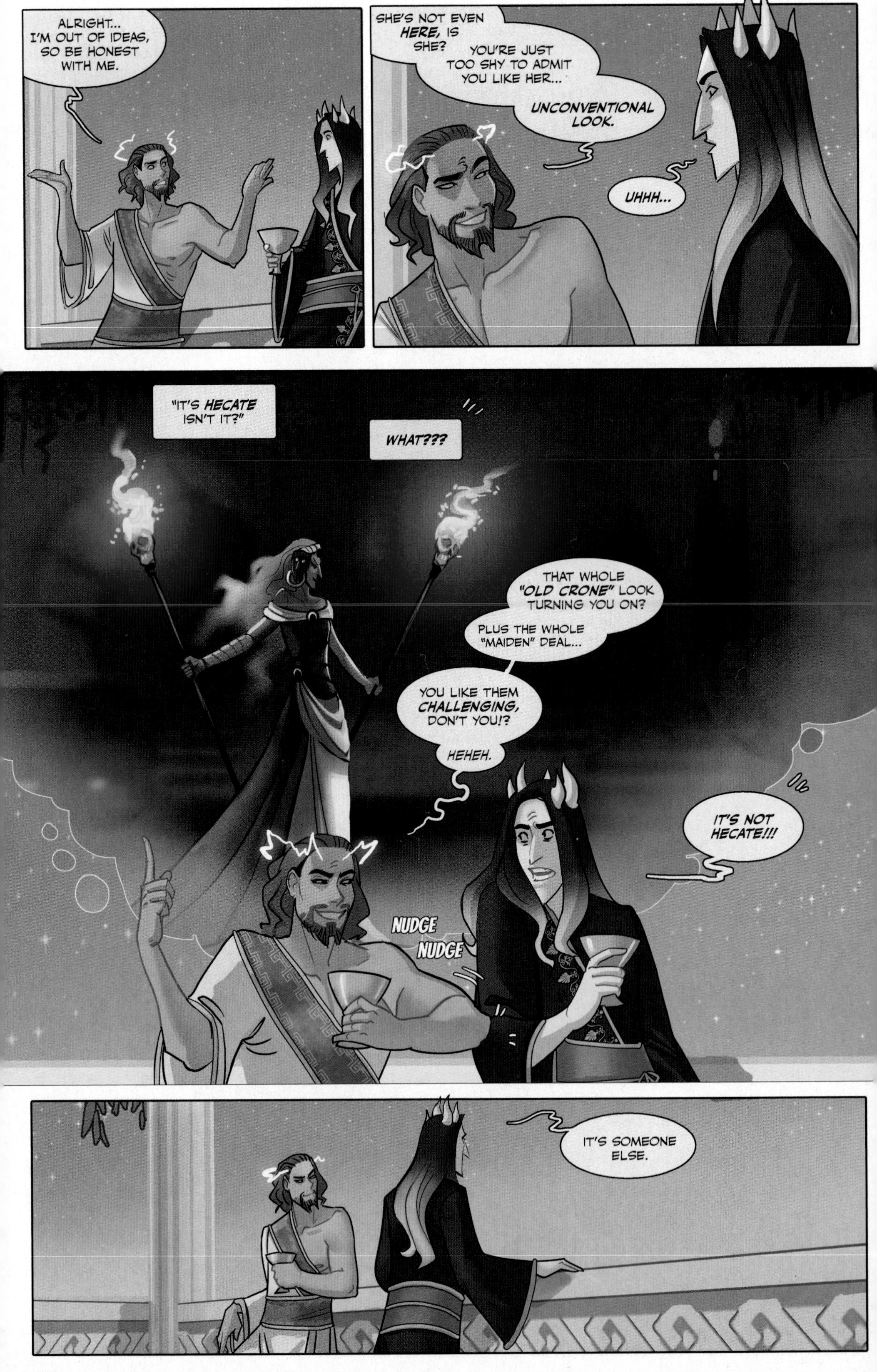
ALRIGHT... I'M OUT OF IDEAS, SO BE HONEST WITH ME.
SHE'S NOT EVEN *HERE,* IS SHE?
YOU'RE JUST TOO SHY TO ADMIT YOU LIKE HER...
UNCONVENTIONAL LOOK.
UHHH...
"IT'S *HECATE* ISN'T IT?"
WHAT???
THAT WHOLE *"OLD CRONE"* LOOK TURNING YOU ON?
PLUS THE WHOLE "MAIDEN" DEAL...
YOU LIKE THEM *CHALLENGING,* DON'T YOU!?
HEHEH.
IT'S NOT HECATE!!!
NUDGE
NUDGE
IT'S SOMEONE ELSE.

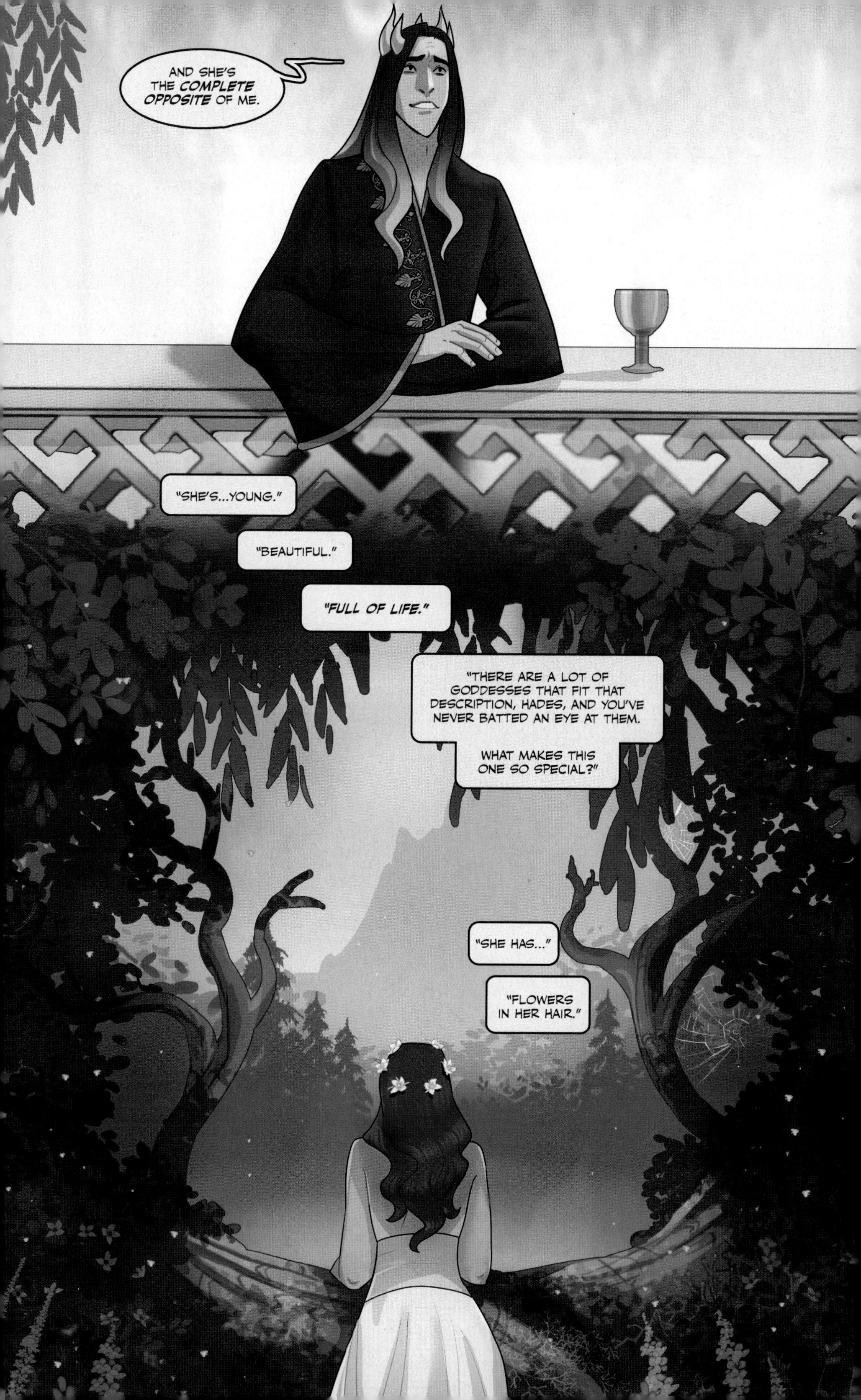
AND SHE'S THE COMPLETE OPPOSITE OF ME.
"SHE'S...YOUNG."
"BEAUTIFUL."
"FULL OF LIFE."
"THERE ARE A LOT OF GODDESSES THAT FIT THAT DESCRIPTION, HADES, AND YOU'VE NEVER BATTED AN EYE AT THEM.
WHAT MAKES THIS ONE SO SPECIAL?"
"SHE HAS..."
"FLOWERS IN HER HAIR."

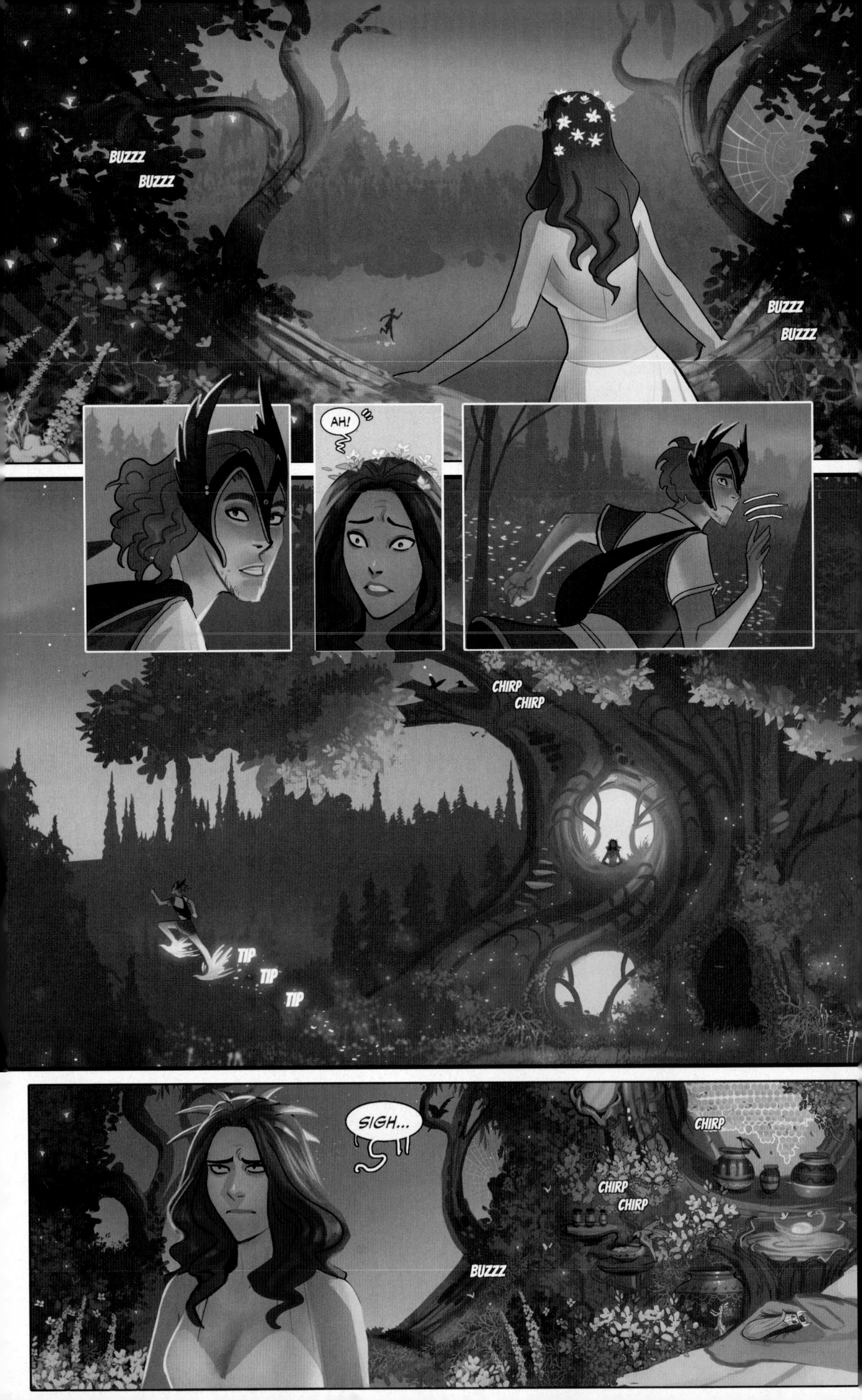
BUZZZ
BUZZZ
BUZZZ
BUZZZ
AH!
CHIRP
CHIRP
TIP
TIP
TIP
SIGH...
CHIRP
CHIRP
CHIRP
BUZZZ

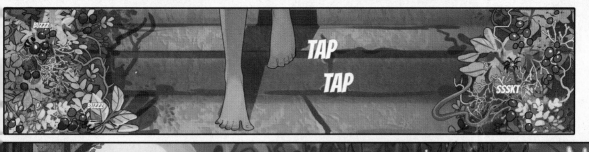

TAP

TAP

BUZZZ

SSSKT

MOM, YOU SAID WE COULD GO!

HERMES WAS HERE TO PICK US UP!!!

BUZZZ

BUZZZ

BUZZZ

I SAID "MAYBE."

BUT...I DECIDED IT WOULD MAKE A MUCH BIGGER IMPACT IF WE DIDN'T ATTEND.

UGH... WHAT IMPACT? WE NEVER GO ANYWHERE, UNLESS IT'S THESMOPHORIA...*

AND THAT'S A WOMEN-ONLY FESTIVAL, STRICTLY AND SPECIFICALLY CONNECTED TO OUR WORK.

CHIRP CHIRP

THE TRULY IMPORTANT FESTIVAL, YES.

BUZZZ BUZZZ

BUZZZ

*HARVEST FESTIVAL HONORING DEMETER AND PERSEPHONE.

WELL...YES! THAT'S WHAT I'M GETTING AT.

WE ONLY EVER GO TO EVENTS THAT ARE WORK-RELATED.

IT'S NEVER JUST FOR...FUN.

FUN?

SQUISH

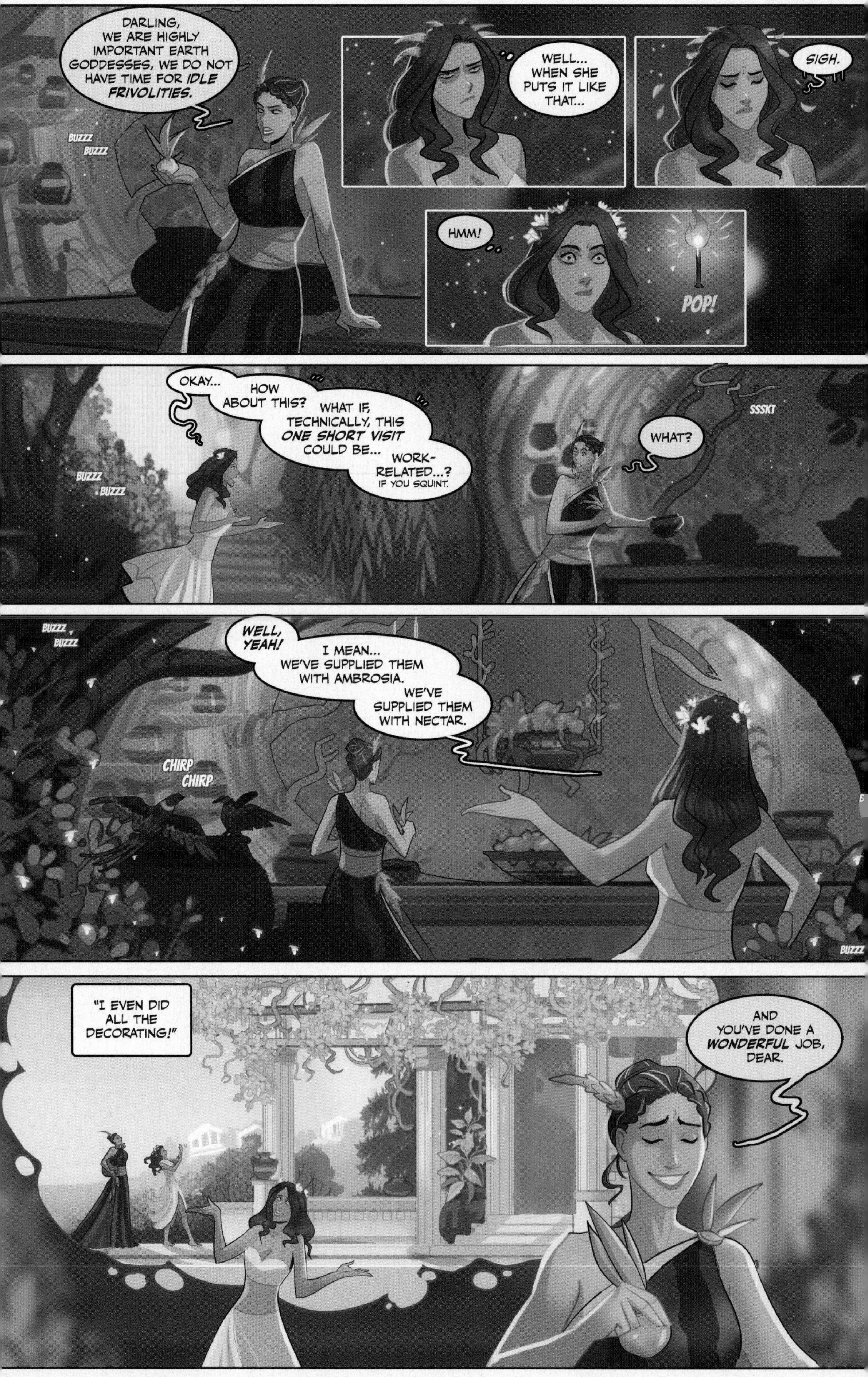
DARLING, WE ARE HIGHLY IMPORTANT EARTH GODDESSES, WE DO NOT HAVE TIME FOR IDLE FRIVOLITIES.
BUZZZ BUZZZ
WELL... WHEN SHE PUTS IT LIKE THAT...
SIGH.
HMM!
POP!
OKAY... HOW ABOUT THIS? WHAT IF, TECHNICALLY, THIS ONE SHORT VISIT COULD BE... WORK-RELATED...? IF YOU SQUINT.
BUZZZ BUZZZ
SSSKT
WHAT?
BUZZZ BUZZZ
WELL, YEAH! I MEAN... WE'VE SUPPLIED THEM WITH AMBROSIA. WE'VE SUPPLIED THEM WITH NECTAR.
CHIRP CHIRP
BUZZZ
"I EVEN DID ALL THE DECORATING!"
AND YOU'VE DONE A WONDERFUL JOB, DEAR.

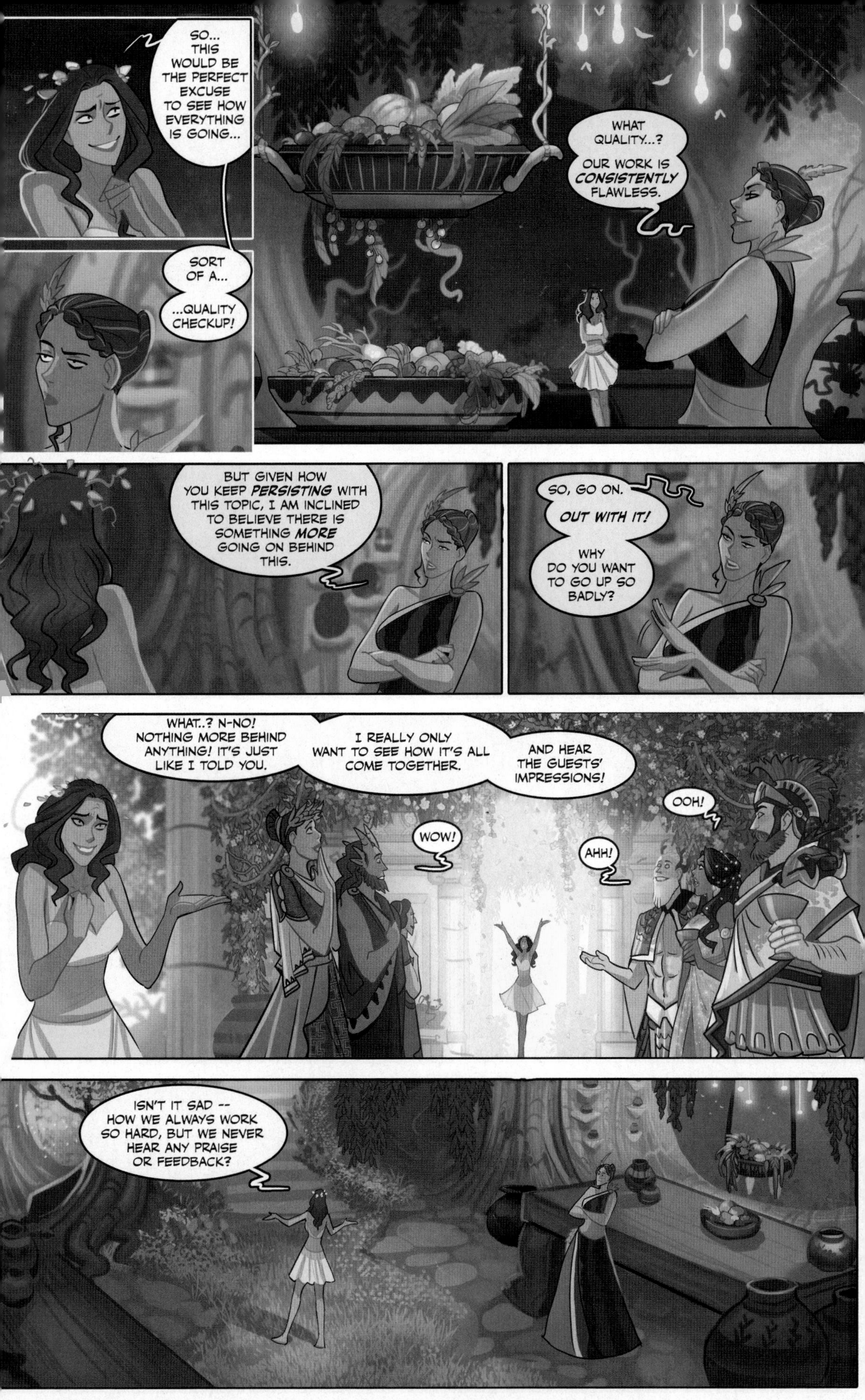
SO... THIS WOULD BE THE PERFECT EXCUSE TO SEE HOW EVERYTHING IS GOING...
SORT OF A...
...QUALITY CHECKUP!
WHAT QUALITY...?
OUR WORK IS CONSISTENTLY FLAWLESS.
BUT GIVEN HOW YOU KEEP PERSISTING WITH THIS TOPIC, I AM INCLINED TO BELIEVE THERE IS SOMETHING MORE GOING ON BEHIND THIS.
SO, GO ON.
OUT WITH IT!
WHY DO YOU WANT TO GO UP SO BADLY?
WHAT..? N-NO! NOTHING MORE BEHIND ANYTHING! IT'S JUST LIKE I TOLD YOU.
I REALLY ONLY WANT TO SEE HOW IT'S ALL COME TOGETHER.
AND HEAR THE GUESTS' IMPRESSIONS!
WOW!
AHH!
OOH!
ISN'T IT SAD -- HOW WE ALWAYS WORK SO HARD, BUT WE NEVER HEAR ANY PRAISE OR FEEDBACK?

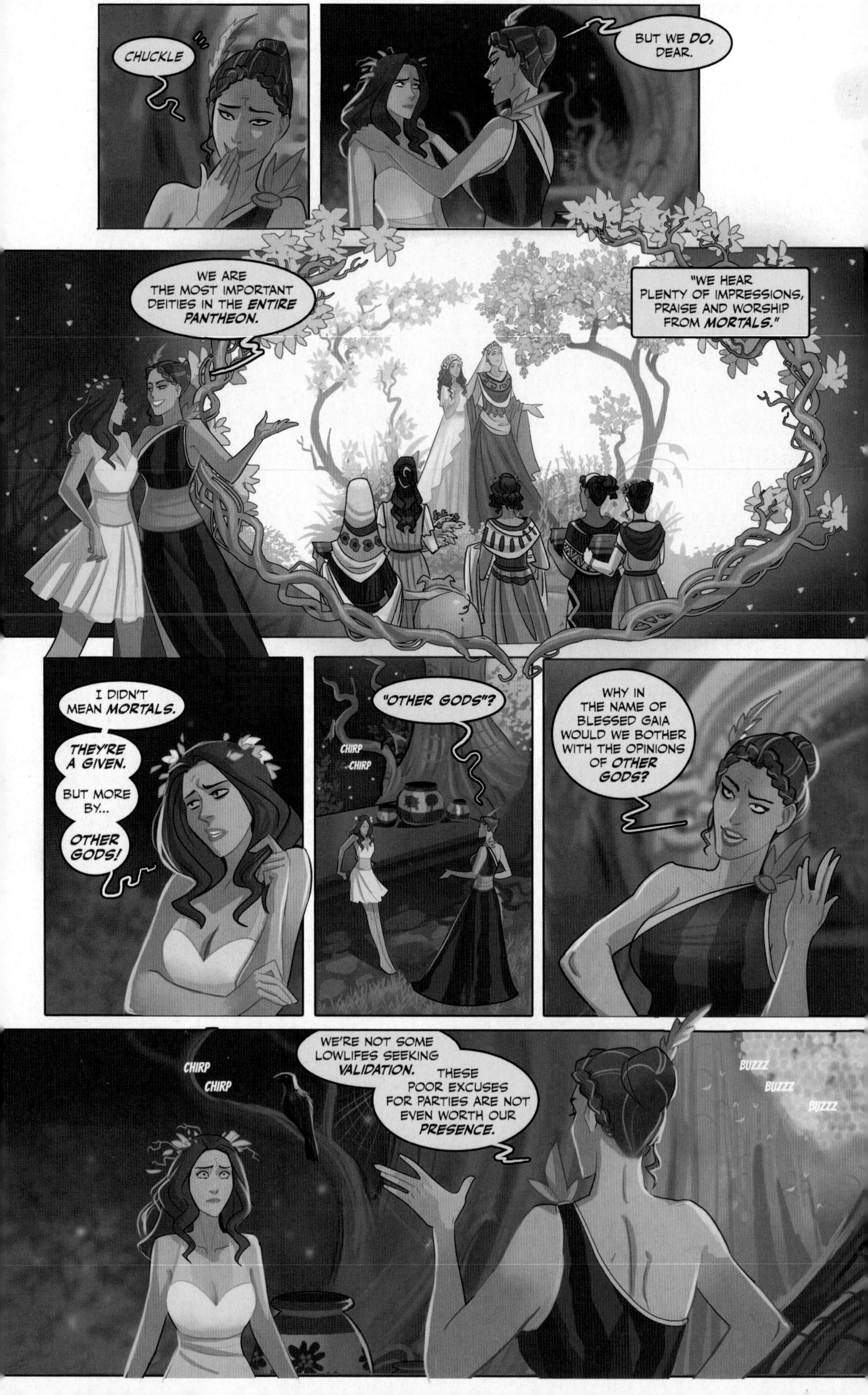
CHUCKLE
BUT WE DO, DEAR.
WE ARE THE MOST IMPORTANT DEITIES IN THE ENTIRE PANTHEON.
"WE HEAR PLENTY OF IMPRESSIONS, PRAISE AND WORSHIP FROM MORTALS."
I DIDN'T MEAN MORTALS.
THEY'RE A GIVEN.
BUT MORE BY...
OTHER GODS!
"OTHER GODS"?
CHIRP
CHIRP
WHY IN THE NAME OF BLESSED GAIA WOULD WE BOTHER WITH THE OPINIONS OF OTHER GODS?
CHIRP
CHIRP
WE'RE NOT SOME LOWLIFES SEEKING VALIDATION.
THESE POOR EXCUSES FOR PARTIES ARE NOT EVEN WORTH OUR PRESENCE.
BUZZZ
BUZZZ
BUZZZ

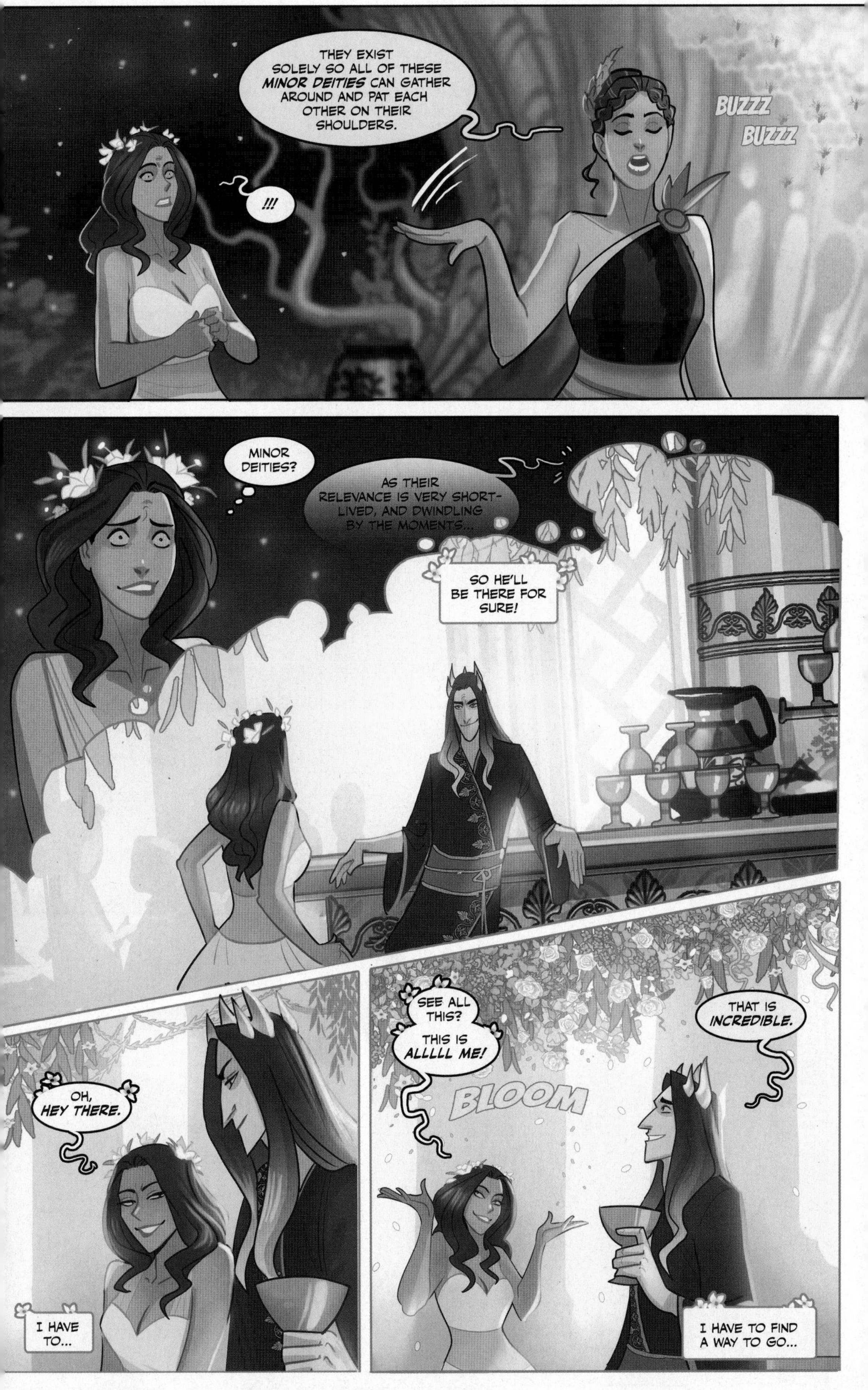
THEY EXIST SOLELY SO ALL OF THESE MINOR DEITIES CAN GATHER AROUND AND PAT EACH OTHER ON THEIR SHOULDERS.
!!!
BUZZZ
BUZZZ
MINOR DEITIES?
AS THEIR RELEVANCE IS VERY SHORT-LIVED, AND DWINDLING BY THE MOMENTS...
SO HE'LL BE THERE FOR SURE!
OH, HEY THERE.
I HAVE TO...
SEE ALL THIS?
THIS IS ALLLLL ME!
BLOOM
THAT IS INCREDIBLE.
I HAVE TO FIND A WAY TO GO...

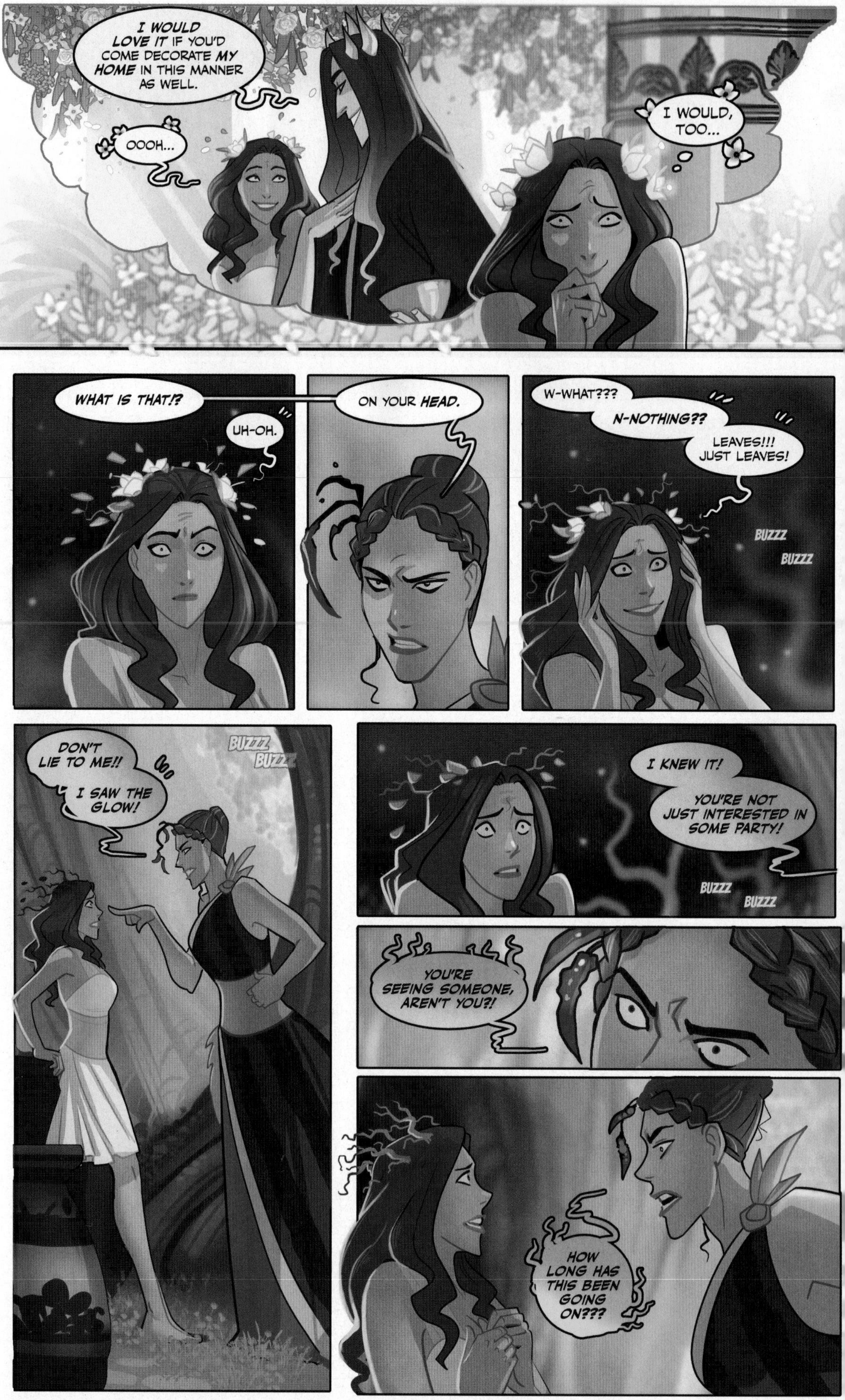
I WOULD LOVE IT IF YOU'D COME DECORATE MY HOME IN THIS MANNER AS WELL.
OOOH...
I WOULD, TOO...
WHAT IS THAT!?
UH-OH.
ON YOUR HEAD.
W-WHAT???
N-NOTHING??
LEAVES!!! JUST LEAVES!
BUZZZ
BUZZZ
DON'T LIE TO ME!!
I SAW THE GLOW!
BUZZZ
BUZZZ
I KNEW IT!
YOU'RE NOT JUST INTERESTED IN SOME PARTY!
BUZZZ
BUZZZ
YOU'RE SEEING SOMEONE, AREN'T YOU?!
HOW LONG HAS THIS BEEN GOING ON???

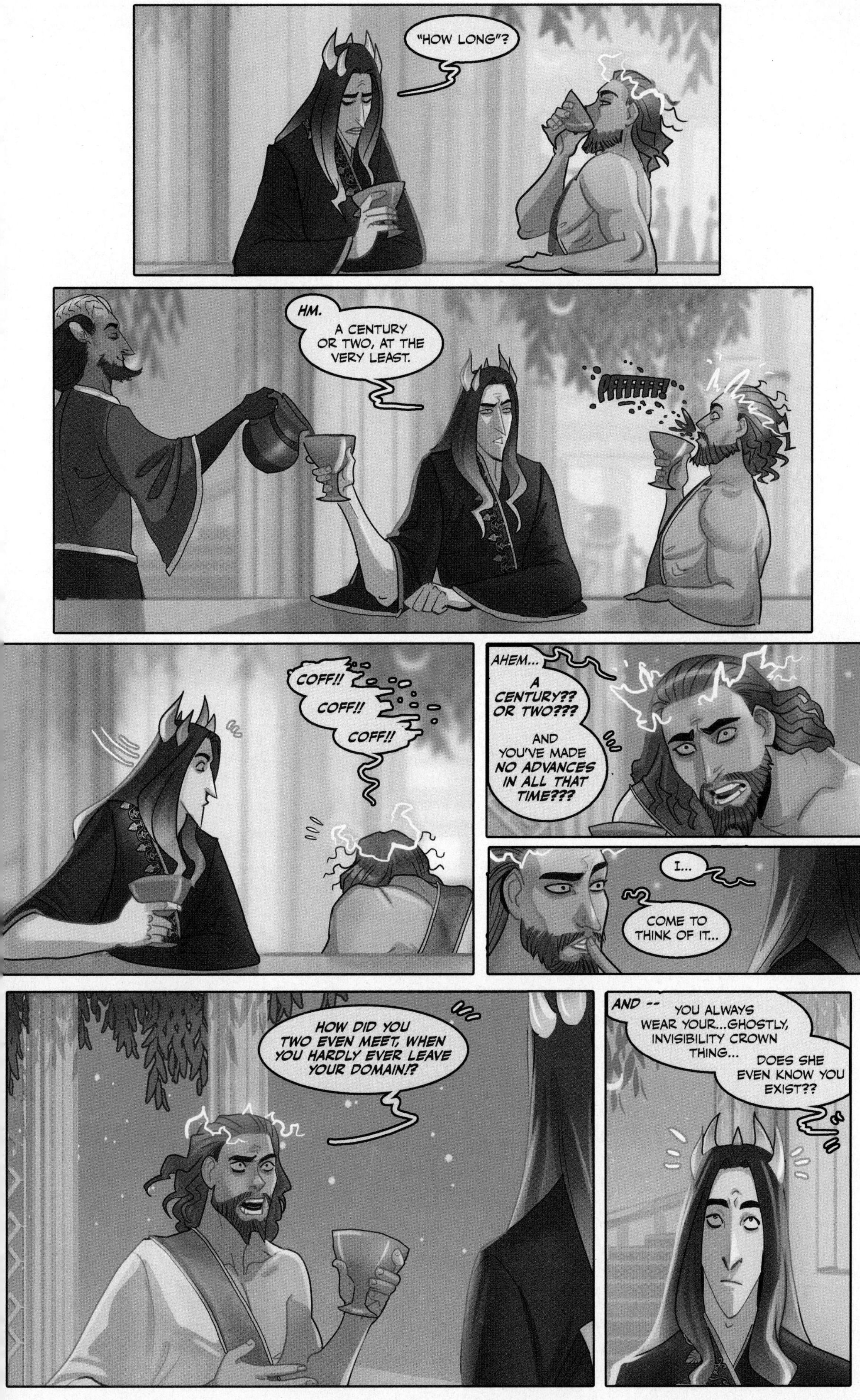
"HOW LONG"?
HM.
A CENTURY OR TWO, AT THE VERY LEAST.
PFFFFFFT!
COFF!!
COFF!!
COFF!!
AHEM...
A CENTURY?? OR TWO???
AND YOU'VE MADE NO ADVANCES IN ALL THAT TIME???
I...
COME TO THINK OF IT...
HOW DID YOU TWO EVEN MEET, WHEN YOU HARDLY EVER LEAVE YOUR DOMAIN!?
AND --
YOU ALWAYS WEAR YOUR...GHOSTLY, INVISIBILITY CROWN THING...
DOES SHE EVEN KNOW YOU EXIST??

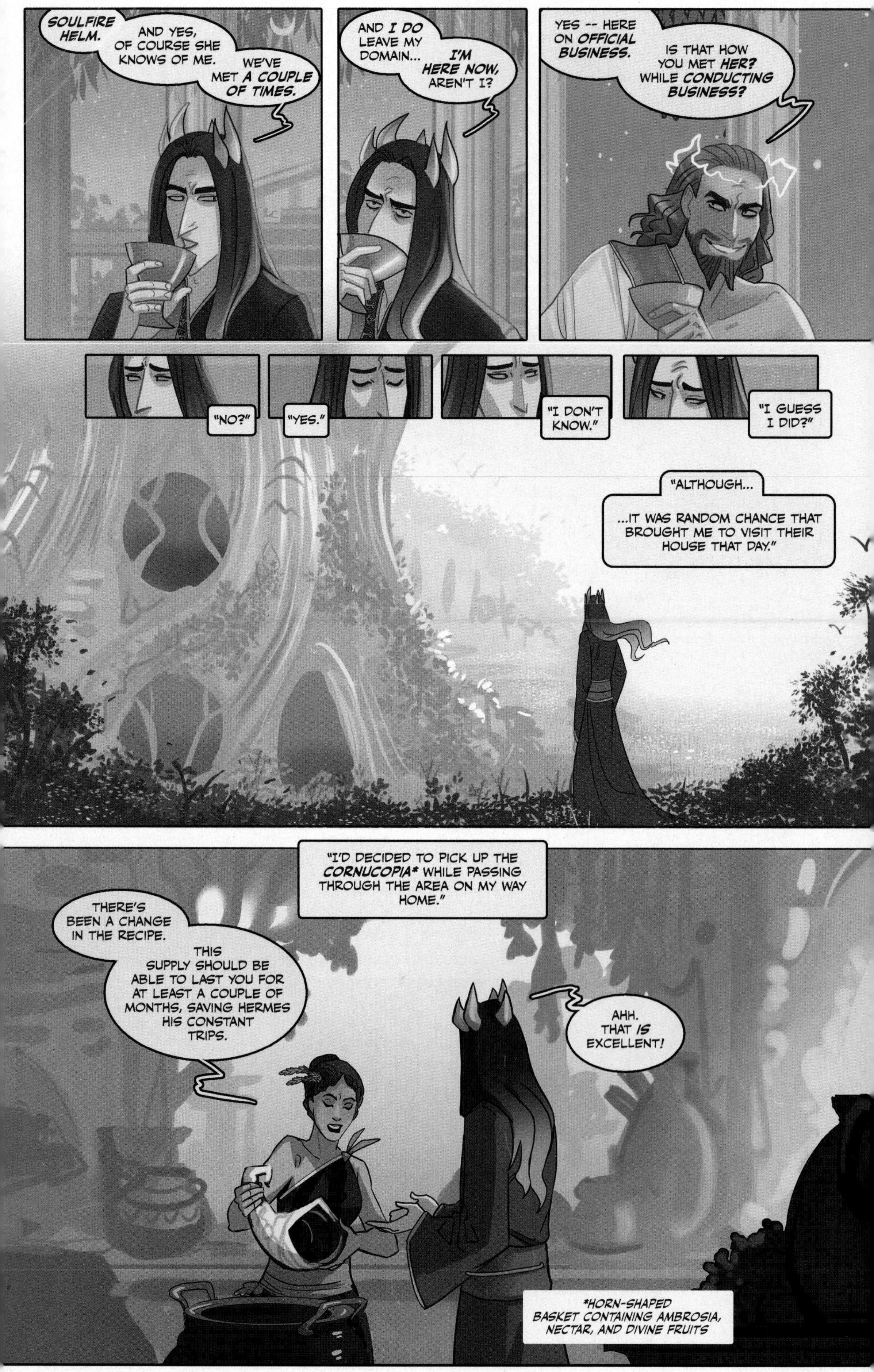
SOULFIRE HELM.
AND YES, OF COURSE SHE KNOWS OF ME.
WE'VE MET A COUPLE OF TIMES.
AND I DO LEAVE MY DOMAIN...
I'M HERE NOW, AREN'T I?
YES -- HERE ON OFFICIAL BUSINESS.
IS THAT HOW YOU MET HER? WHILE CONDUCTING BUSINESS?
"NO?"
"YES."
"I DON'T KNOW."
"I GUESS I DID?"
"ALTHOUGH...
...IT WAS RANDOM CHANCE THAT BROUGHT ME TO VISIT THEIR HOUSE THAT DAY."
"I'D DECIDED TO PICK UP THE CORNUCOPIA* WHILE PASSING THROUGH THE AREA ON MY WAY HOME."
THERE'S BEEN A CHANGE IN THE RECIPE.
THIS SUPPLY SHOULD BE ABLE TO LAST YOU FOR AT LEAST A COUPLE OF MONTHS, SAVING HERMES HIS CONSTANT TRIPS.
AHH. THAT IS EXCELLENT!
*HORN-SHAPED BASKET CONTAINING AMBROSIA, NECTAR, AND DIVINE FRUITS

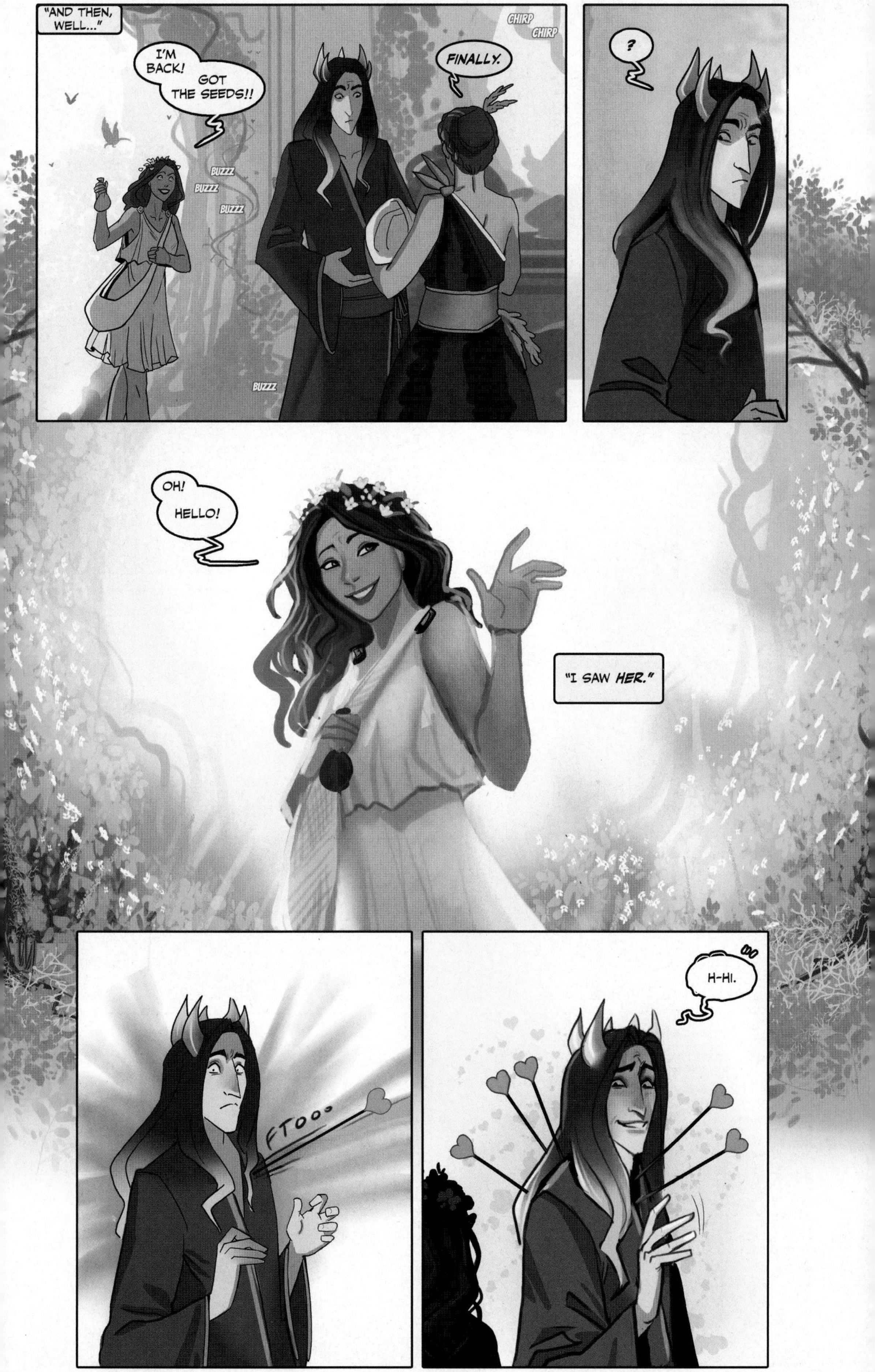
"AND THEN, WELL..."
CHIRP
CHIRP
I'M BACK!
GOT THE SEEDS!!
FINALLY.
BUZZZ
BUZZZ
BUZZZ
BUZZZ
?
OH!
HELLO!
"I SAW HER."
FTOOO
H-HI.

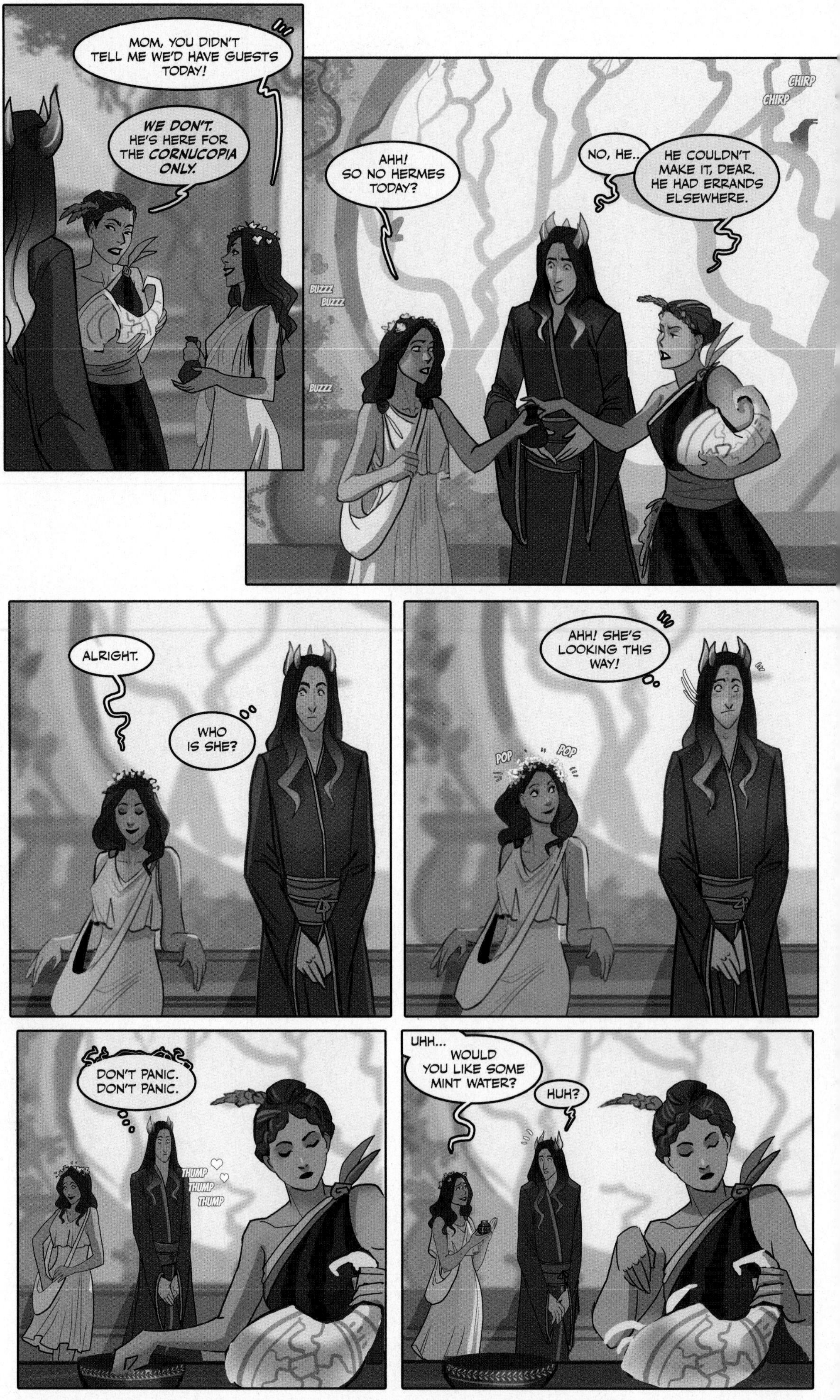

MOM, YOU DIDN'T TELL ME WE'D HAVE GUESTS TODAY!
WE DON'T. HE'S HERE FOR THE CORNUCOPIA ONLY.
BUZZZ
BUZZZ
BUZZZ
CHIRP
CHIRP
AHH! SO NO HERMES TODAY?
NO, HE...
HE COULDN'T MAKE IT, DEAR. HE HAD ERRANDS ELSEWHERE.
ALRIGHT.
WHO IS SHE?
AHH! SHE'S LOOKING THIS WAY!
POP
POP
DON'T PANIC. DON'T PANIC.
THUMP
THUMP
THUMP
UHH... WOULD YOU LIKE SOME MINT WATER?
HUH?

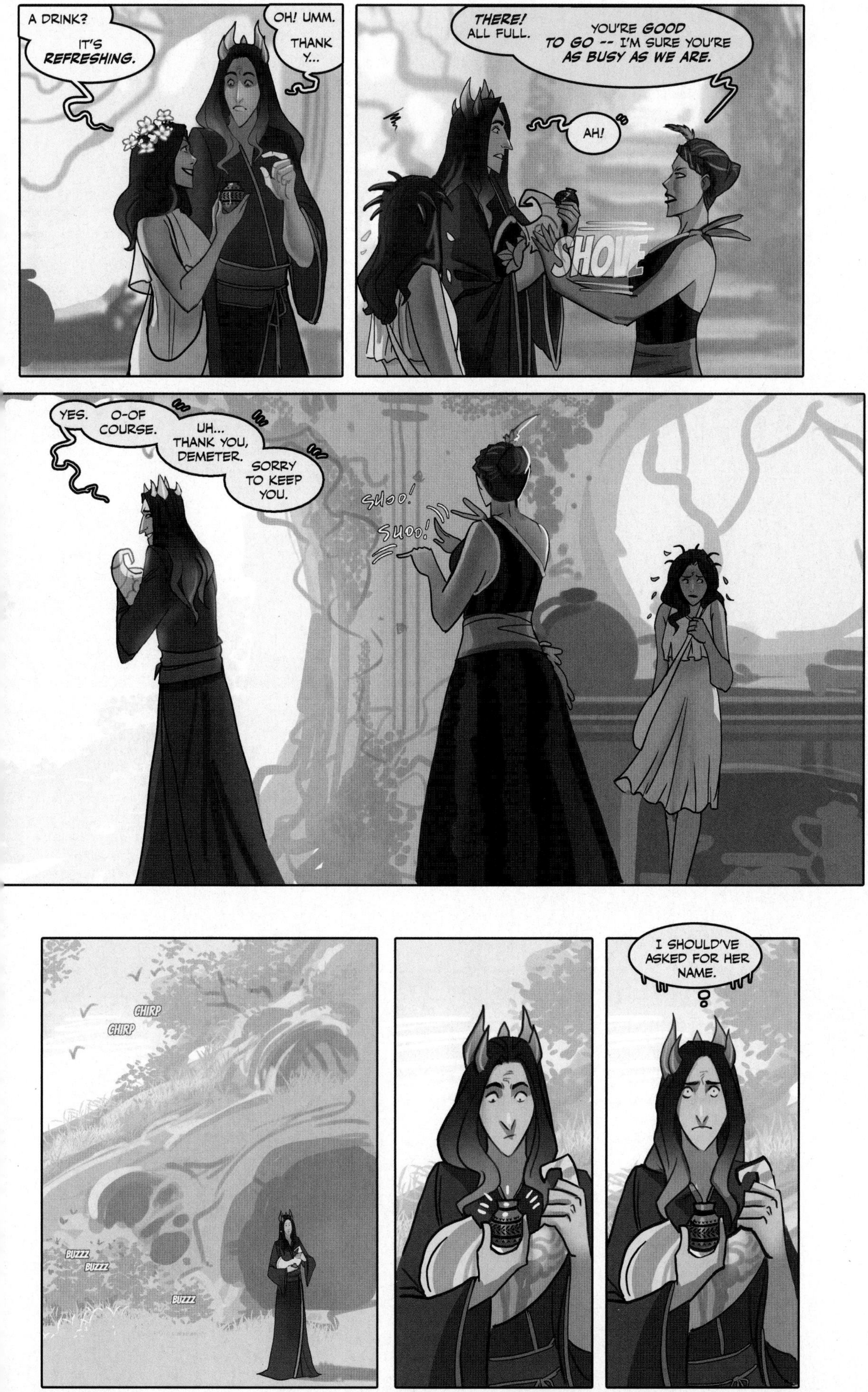
A DRINK?
IT'S REFRESHING.
OH! UMM.
THANK Y...
THERE! ALL FULL.
YOU'RE GOOD TO GO -- I'M SURE YOU'RE AS BUSY AS WE ARE.
AH!
SHOVE
YES.
O-OF COURSE.
UH... THANK YOU, DEMETER.
SORRY TO KEEP YOU.
SHOO!
SHOO!
CHIRP
CHIRP
BUZZZ
BUZZZ
BUZZZ
I SHOULD'VE ASKED FOR HER NAME.

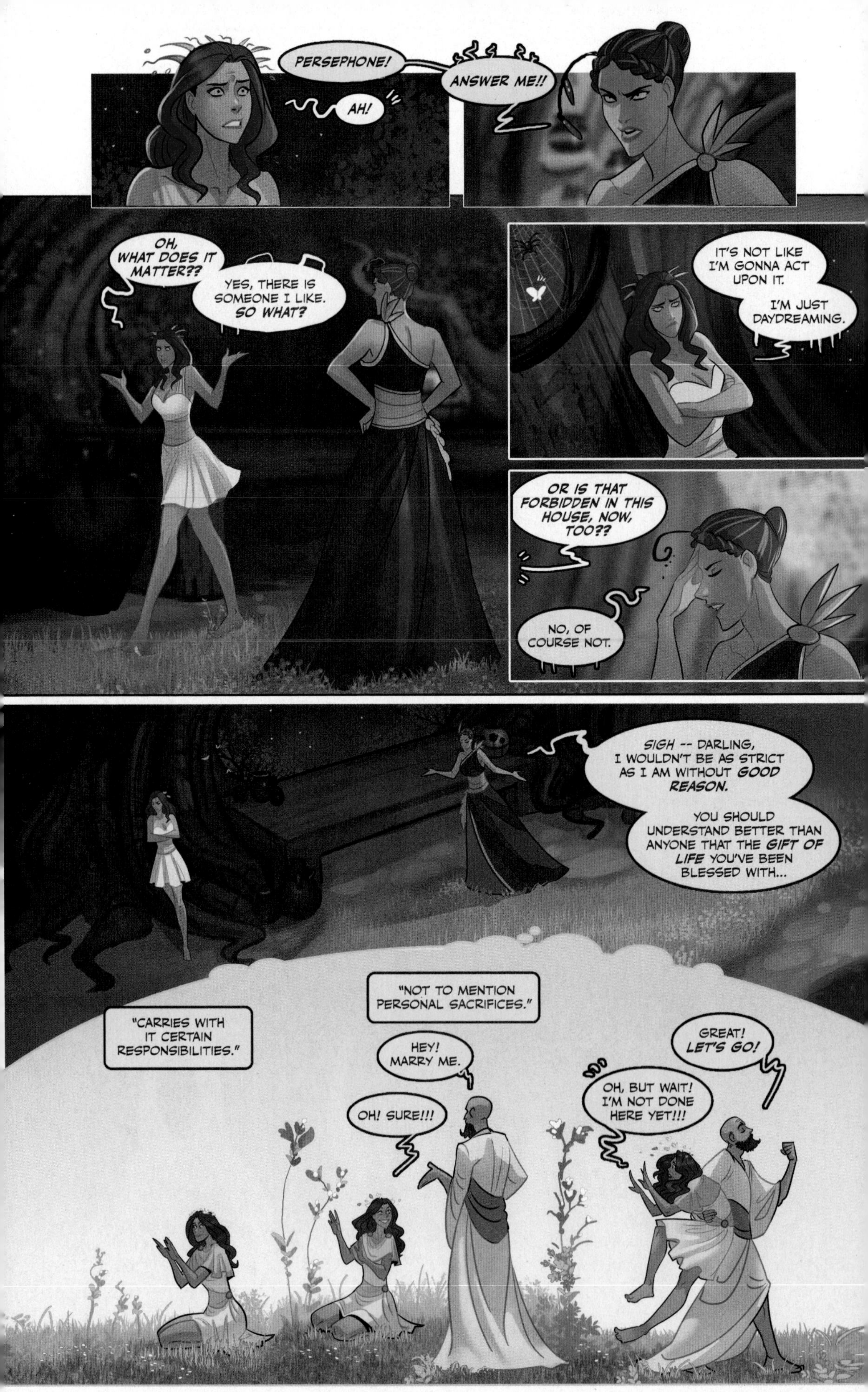
PERSEPHONE!
AH!
ANSWER ME!!
OH, WHAT DOES IT MATTER??
YES, THERE IS SOMEONE I LIKE. SO WHAT?
IT'S NOT LIKE I'M GONNA ACT UPON IT.
I'M JUST DAYDREAMING.
OR IS THAT FORBIDDEN IN THIS HOUSE, NOW, TOO??
NO, OF COURSE NOT.
SIGH -- DARLING, I WOULDN'T BE AS STRICT AS I AM WITHOUT GOOD REASON.
YOU SHOULD UNDERSTAND BETTER THAN ANYONE THAT THE GIFT OF LIFE YOU'VE BEEN BLESSED WITH...
"CARRIES WITH IT CERTAIN RESPONSIBILITIES."
"NOT TO MENTION PERSONAL SACRIFICES."
HEY! MARRY ME.
OH! SURE!!!
GREAT! LET'S GO!
OH, BUT WAIT! I'M NOT DONE HERE YET!!!

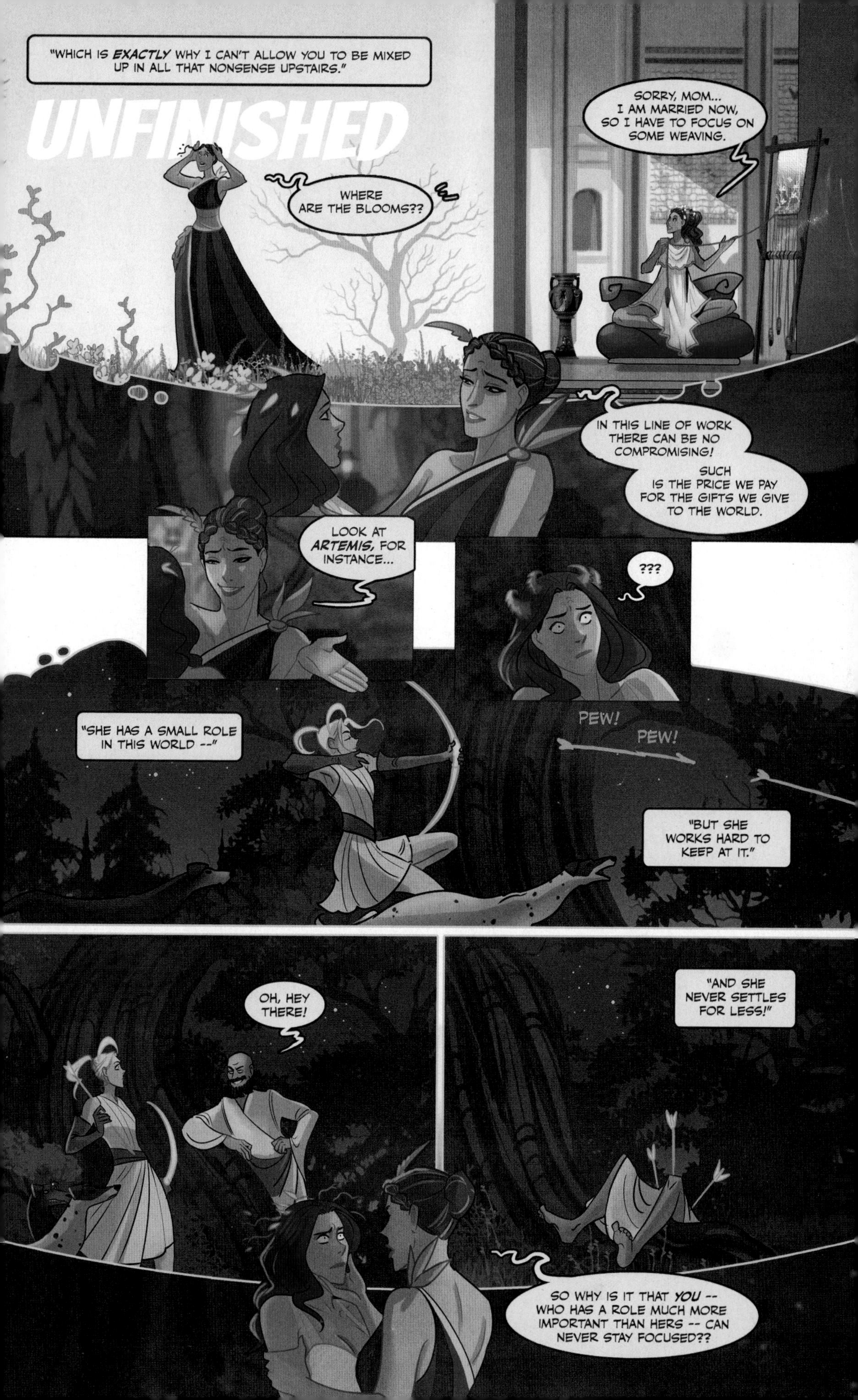
"WHICH IS EXACTLY WHY I CAN'T ALLOW YOU TO BE MIXED UP IN ALL THAT NONSENSE UPSTAIRS."
UNFINISHED
WHERE ARE THE BLOOMS??
SORRY, MOM... I AM MARRIED NOW, SO I HAVE TO FOCUS ON SOME WEAVING.
IN THIS LINE OF WORK THERE CAN BE NO COMPROMISING!
SUCH IS THE PRICE WE PAY FOR THE GIFTS WE GIVE TO THE WORLD.
LOOK AT ARTEMIS, FOR INSTANCE...
???
"SHE HAS A SMALL ROLE IN THIS WORLD --"
PEW!
PEW!
"BUT SHE WORKS HARD TO KEEP AT IT."
OH, HEY THERE!
"AND SHE NEVER SETTLES FOR LESS!"
SO WHY IS IT THAT YOU -- WHO HAS A ROLE MUCH MORE IMPORTANT THAN HERS -- CAN NEVER STAY FOCUSED??

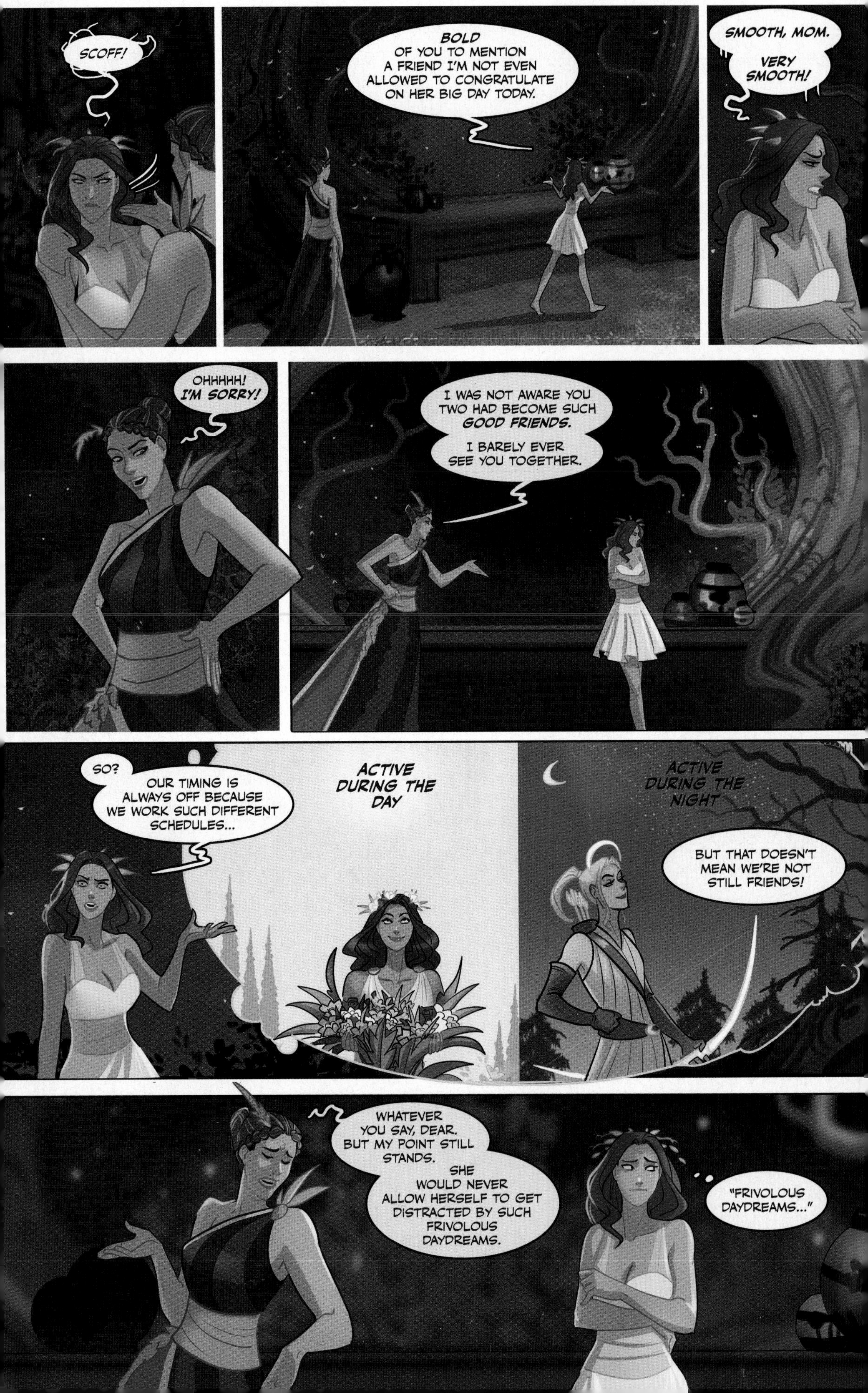
SCOFF!
BOLD OF YOU TO MENTION A FRIEND I'M NOT EVEN ALLOWED TO CONGRATULATE ON HER BIG DAY TODAY.
SMOOTH, MOM.
VERY SMOOTH!
OHHHHH! I'M SORRY!
I WAS NOT AWARE YOU TWO HAD BECOME SUCH GOOD FRIENDS.
I BARELY EVER SEE YOU TOGETHER.
SO?
OUR TIMING IS ALWAYS OFF BECAUSE WE WORK SUCH DIFFERENT SCHEDULES...
ACTIVE DURING THE DAY
ACTIVE DURING THE NIGHT
BUT THAT DOESN'T MEAN WE'RE NOT STILL FRIENDS!
WHATEVER YOU SAY, DEAR. BUT MY POINT STILL STANDS.
SHE WOULD NEVER ALLOW HERSELF TO GET DISTRACTED BY SUCH FRIVOLOUS DAYDREAMS.
"FRIVOLOUS DAYDREAMS..."

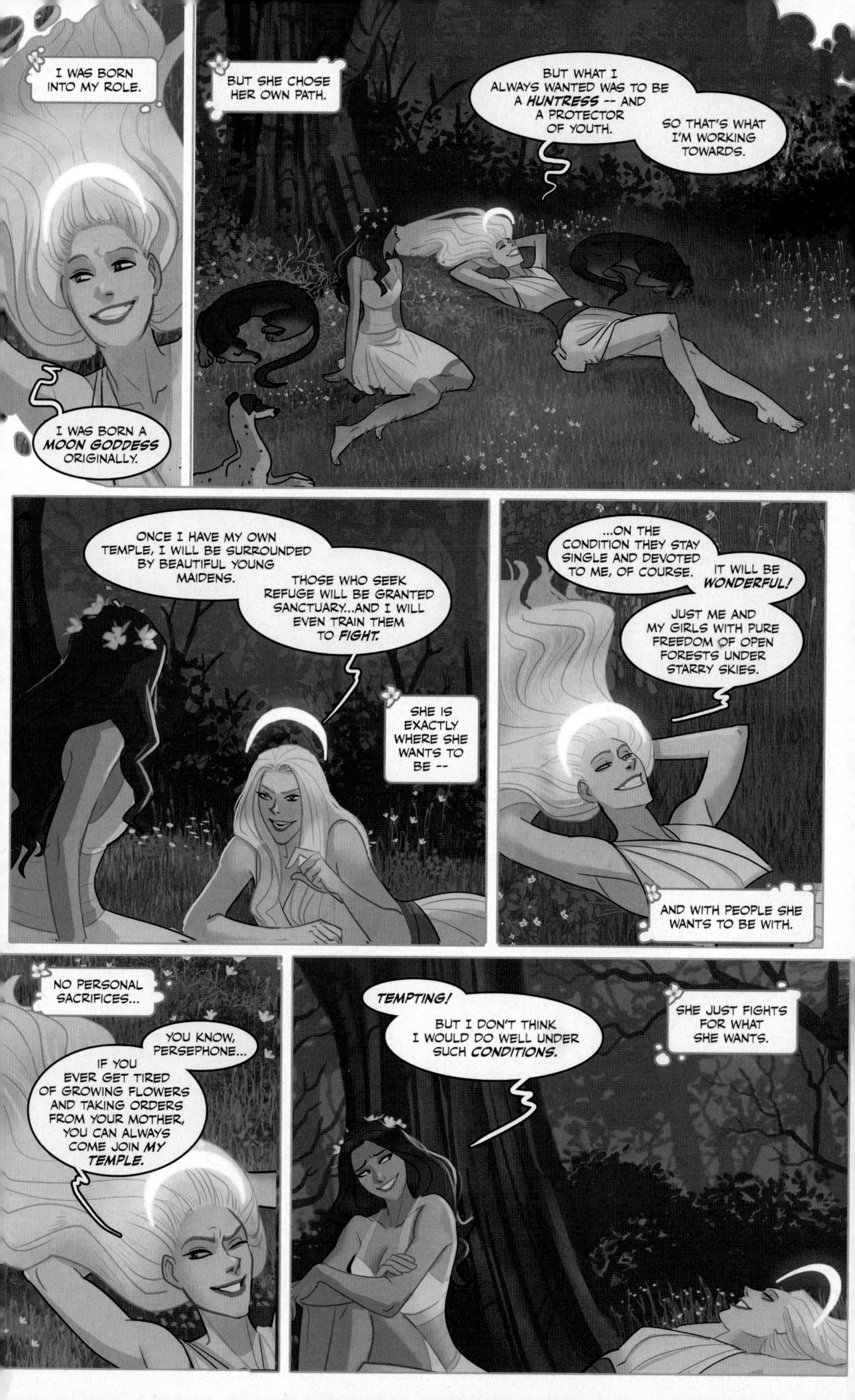
I WAS BORN INTO MY ROLE.
I WAS BORN A MOON GODDESS ORIGINALLY.
BUT SHE CHOSE HER OWN PATH.
BUT WHAT I ALWAYS WANTED WAS TO BE A HUNTRESS -- AND A PROTECTOR OF YOUTH.
SO THAT'S WHAT I'M WORKING TOWARDS.
ONCE I HAVE MY OWN TEMPLE, I WILL BE SURROUNDED BY BEAUTIFUL YOUNG MAIDENS.
THOSE WHO SEEK REFUGE WILL BE GRANTED SANCTUARY...AND I WILL EVEN TRAIN THEM TO FIGHT.
SHE IS EXACTLY WHERE SHE WANTS TO BE --
...ON THE CONDITION THEY STAY SINGLE AND DEVOTED TO ME, OF COURSE.
IT WILL BE WONDERFUL!
JUST ME AND MY GIRLS WITH PURE FREEDOM OF OPEN FORESTS UNDER STARRY SKIES.
AND WITH PEOPLE SHE WANTS TO BE WITH.
NO PERSONAL SACRIFICES...
YOU KNOW, PERSEPHONE...
IF YOU EVER GET TIRED OF GROWING FLOWERS AND TAKING ORDERS FROM YOUR MOTHER, YOU CAN ALWAYS COME JOIN MY TEMPLE.
TEMPTING!
BUT I DON'T THINK I WOULD DO WELL UNDER SUCH CONDITIONS.
SHE JUST FIGHTS FOR WHAT SHE WANTS.

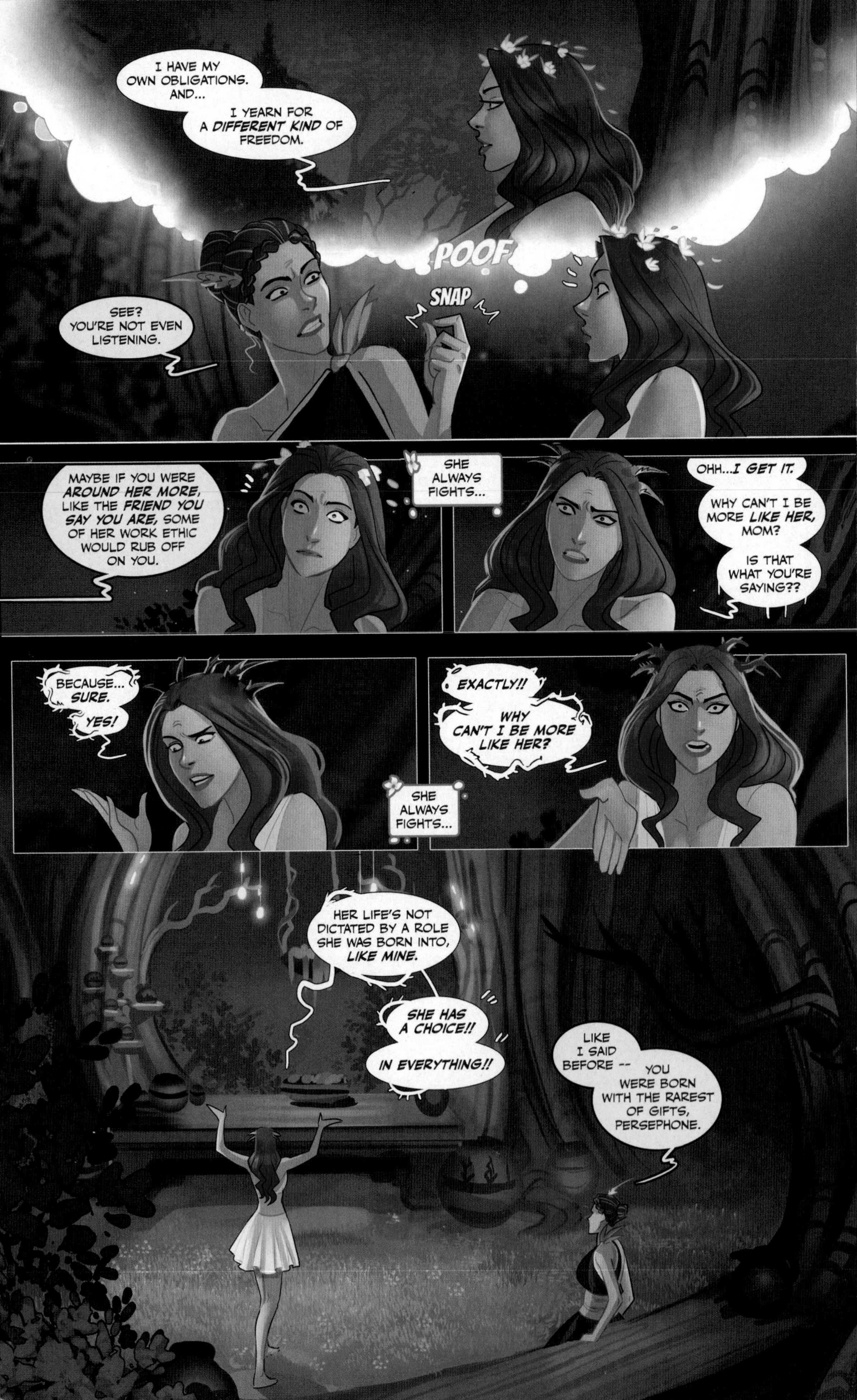
I HAVE MY OWN OBLIGATIONS. AND...
I YEARN FOR A *DIFFERENT KIND* OF FREEDOM.
POOF
SEE? YOU'RE NOT EVEN LISTENING.
SNAP
MAYBE IF YOU WERE *AROUND HER MORE,* LIKE THE *FRIEND YOU SAY YOU ARE,* SOME OF HER WORK ETHIC WOULD RUB OFF ON YOU.
SHE ALWAYS FIGHTS...
OHH...*I GET IT.*
WHY CAN'T I BE MORE *LIKE HER,* MOM?
IS THAT WHAT YOU'RE SAYING??
BECAUSE... *SURE.*
YES!
EXACTLY!!
WHY CAN'T I BE MORE LIKE HER?
SHE ALWAYS FIGHTS...
HER LIFE'S NOT DICTATED BY A ROLE SHE WAS BORN INTO, *LIKE MINE.*
SHE HAS A CHOICE!!
IN EVERYTHING!!
LIKE I SAID BEFORE --
YOU WERE BORN WITH THE RAREST OF GIFTS, PERSEPHONE.

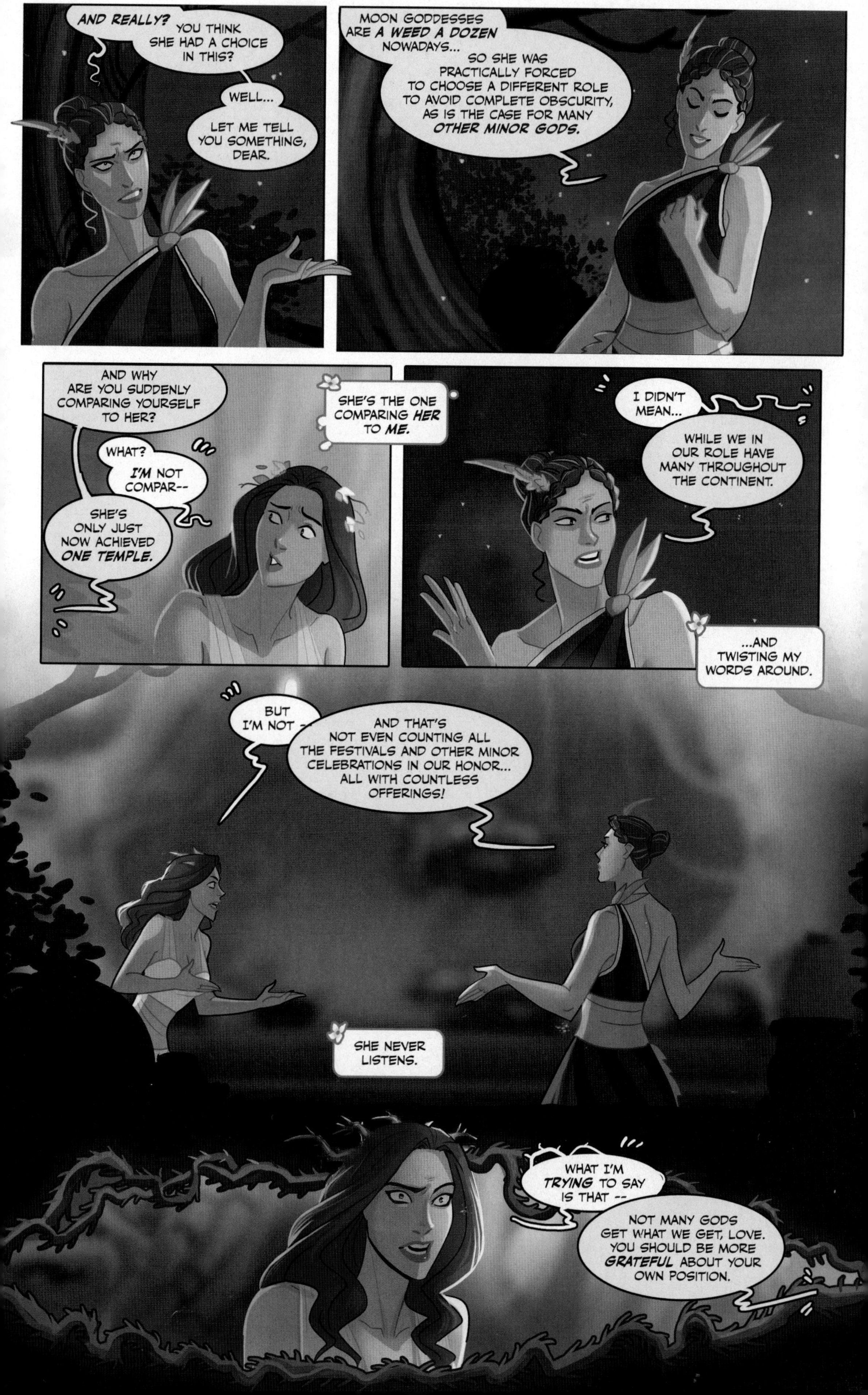
AND REALLY? YOU THINK SHE HAD A CHOICE IN THIS?
WELL...
LET ME TELL YOU SOMETHING, DEAR.
MOON GODDESSES ARE A WEED A DOZEN NOWADAYS...
SO SHE WAS PRACTICALLY FORCED TO CHOOSE A DIFFERENT ROLE TO AVOID COMPLETE OBSCURITY, AS IS THE CASE FOR MANY OTHER MINOR GODS.
AND WHY ARE YOU SUDDENLY COMPARING YOURSELF TO HER?
WHAT? I'M NOT COMPAR--
SHE'S ONLY JUST NOW ACHIEVED ONE TEMPLE.
SHE'S THE ONE COMPARING HER TO ME.
I DIDN'T MEAN...
WHILE WE IN OUR ROLE HAVE MANY THROUGHOUT THE CONTINENT.
...AND TWISTING MY WORDS AROUND.
BUT I'M NOT --
AND THAT'S NOT EVEN COUNTING ALL THE FESTIVALS AND OTHER MINOR CELEBRATIONS IN OUR HONOR... ALL WITH COUNTLESS OFFERINGS!
SHE NEVER LISTENS.
WHAT I'M TRYING TO SAY IS THAT --
NOT MANY GODS GET WHAT WE GET, LOVE. YOU SHOULD BE MORE GRATEFUL ABOUT YOUR OWN POSITION.

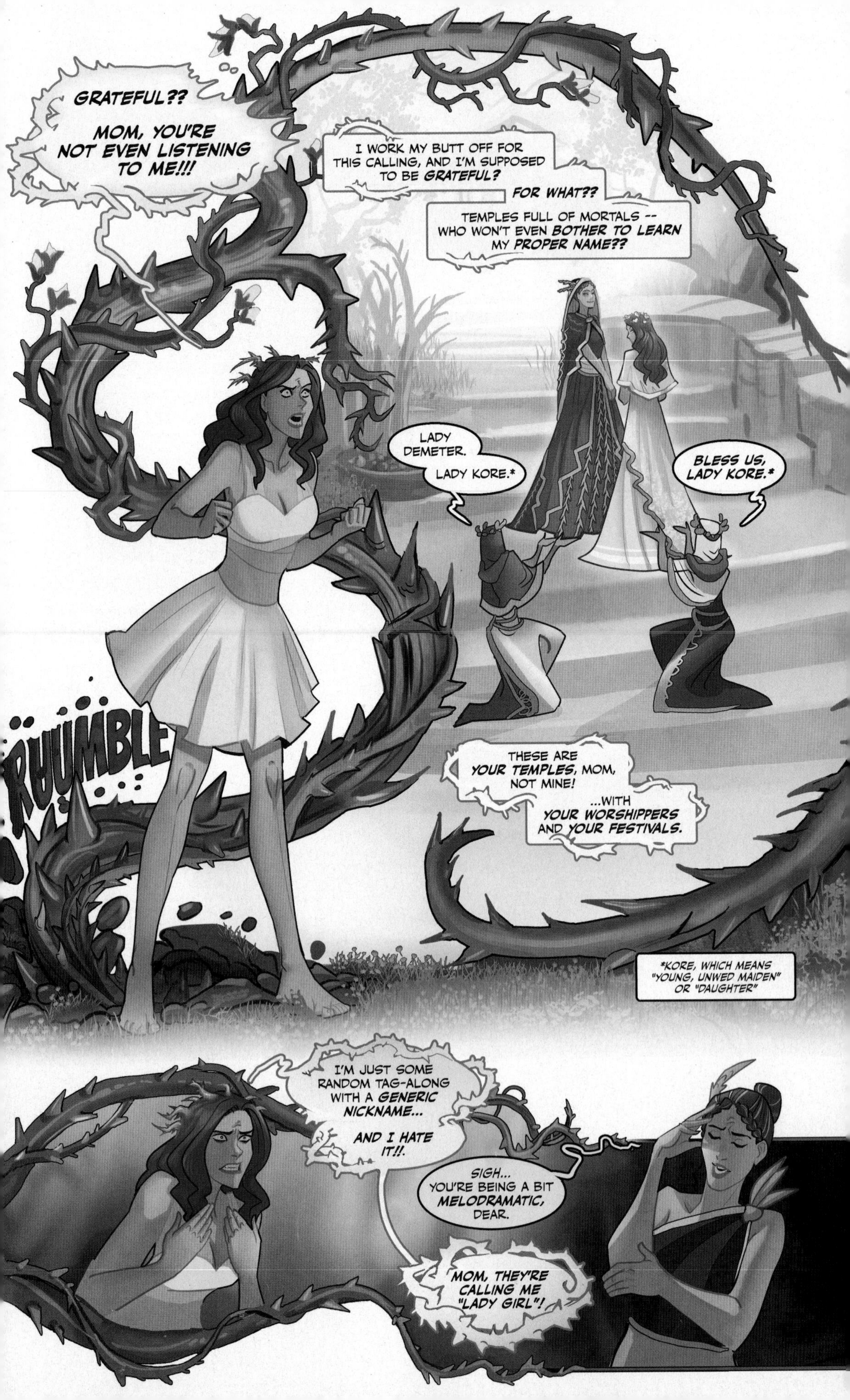
GRATEFUL??
MOM, YOU'RE NOT EVEN LISTENING TO ME!!!
I WORK MY BUTT OFF FOR THIS CALLING, AND I'M SUPPOSED TO BE GRATEFUL?
FOR WHAT??
TEMPLES FULL OF MORTALS -- WHO WON'T EVEN BOTHER TO LEARN MY PROPER NAME??
LADY DEMETER.
LADY KORE.*
BLESS US, LADY KORE.*
RUUMBLE
THESE ARE YOUR TEMPLES, MOM, NOT MINE!
...WITH YOUR WORSHIPPERS AND YOUR FESTIVALS.
*KORE, WHICH MEANS "YOUNG, UNWED MAIDEN" OR "DAUGHTER"
I'M JUST SOME RANDOM TAG-ALONG WITH A GENERIC NICKNAME...
AND I HATE IT!!.
SIGH... YOU'RE BEING A BIT MELODRAMATIC, DEAR.
MOM, THEY'RE CALLING ME "LADY GIRL"!

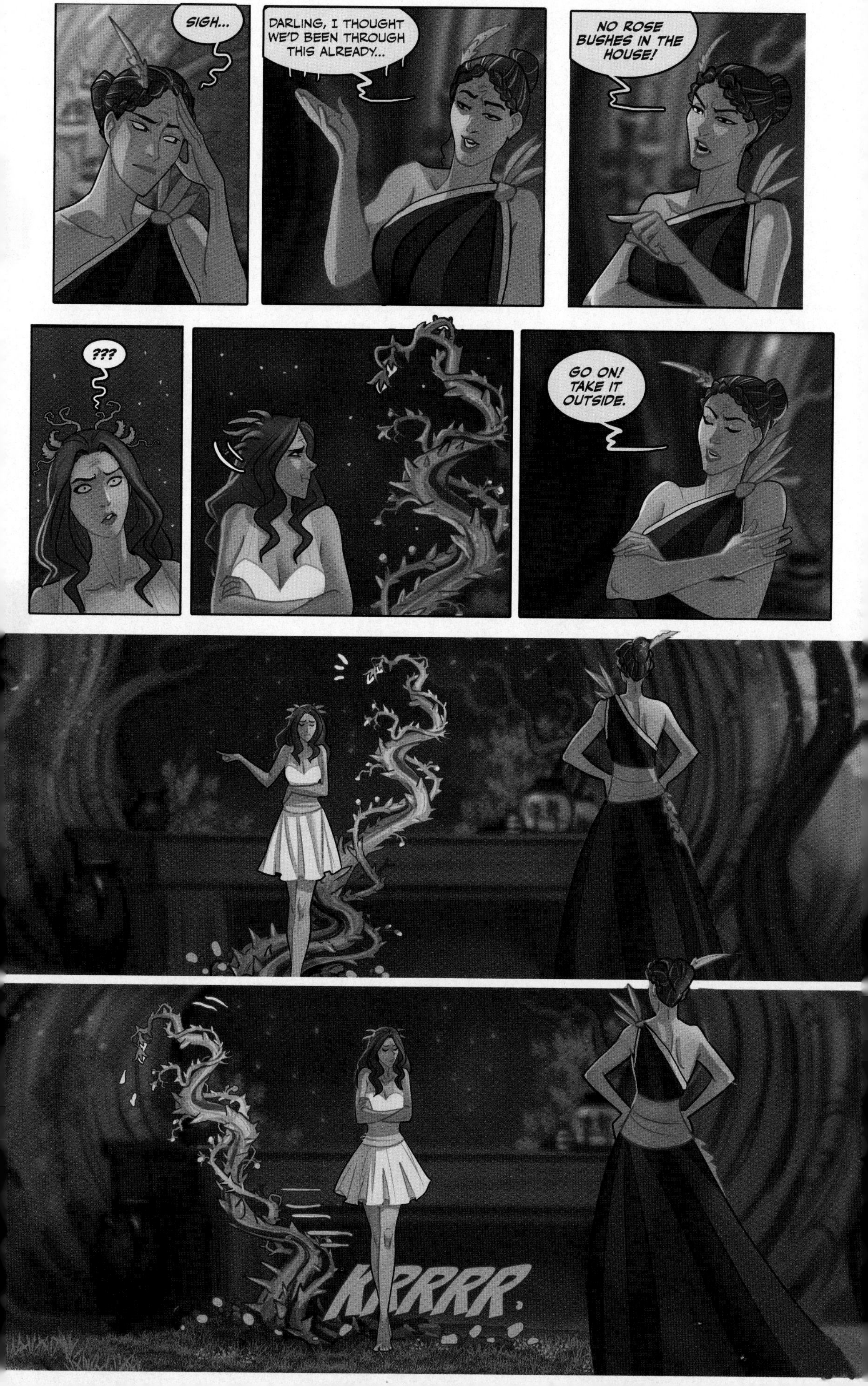
SIGH...
DARLING, I THOUGHT WE'D BEEN THROUGH THIS ALREADY...
NO ROSE BUSHES IN THE HOUSE!
???
GO ON! TAKE IT OUTSIDE.
KRRRR

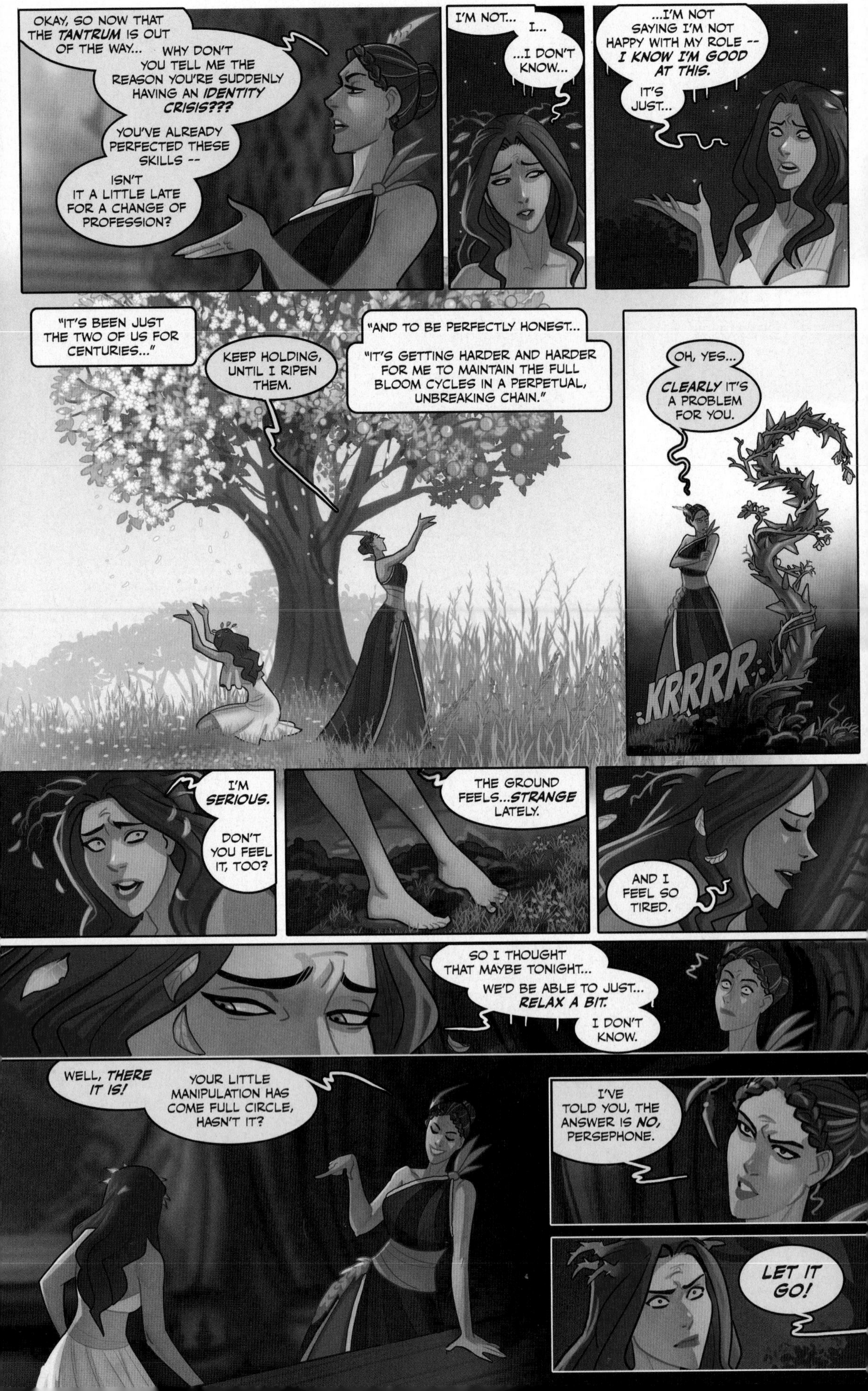

OKAY, SO NOW THAT THE *TANTRUM* IS OUT OF THE WAY...
WHY DON'T YOU TELL ME THE REASON YOU'RE SUDDENLY HAVING AN *IDENTITY CRISIS???*
YOU'VE ALREADY PERFECTED THESE SKILLS --
ISN'T IT A LITTLE LATE FOR A CHANGE OF PROFESSION?
I'M NOT... I...
...I DON'T KNOW...
...I'M NOT SAYING I'M NOT HAPPY WITH MY ROLE -- *I KNOW I'M GOOD AT THIS.*
IT'S JUST...
"IT'S BEEN JUST THE TWO OF US FOR CENTURIES..."
KEEP HOLDING, UNTIL I RIPEN THEM.
"AND TO BE PERFECTLY HONEST...
"IT'S GETTING HARDER AND HARDER FOR ME TO MAINTAIN THE FULL BLOOM CYCLES IN A PERPETUAL, UNBREAKING CHAIN."
OH, YES...
CLEARLY IT'S A PROBLEM FOR YOU.
KRRRR
I'M *SERIOUS.*
DON'T YOU FEEL IT, TOO?
THE GROUND FEELS...*STRANGE* LATELY.
AND I FEEL SO TIRED.
SO I THOUGHT THAT MAYBE TONIGHT...
WE'D BE ABLE TO JUST... *RELAX A BIT.*
I DON'T KNOW.
WELL, *THERE IT IS!*
YOUR LITTLE MANIPULATION HAS COME FULL CIRCLE, HASN'T IT?
I'VE TOLD YOU, THE ANSWER IS *NO,* PERSEPHONE.
LET IT GO!

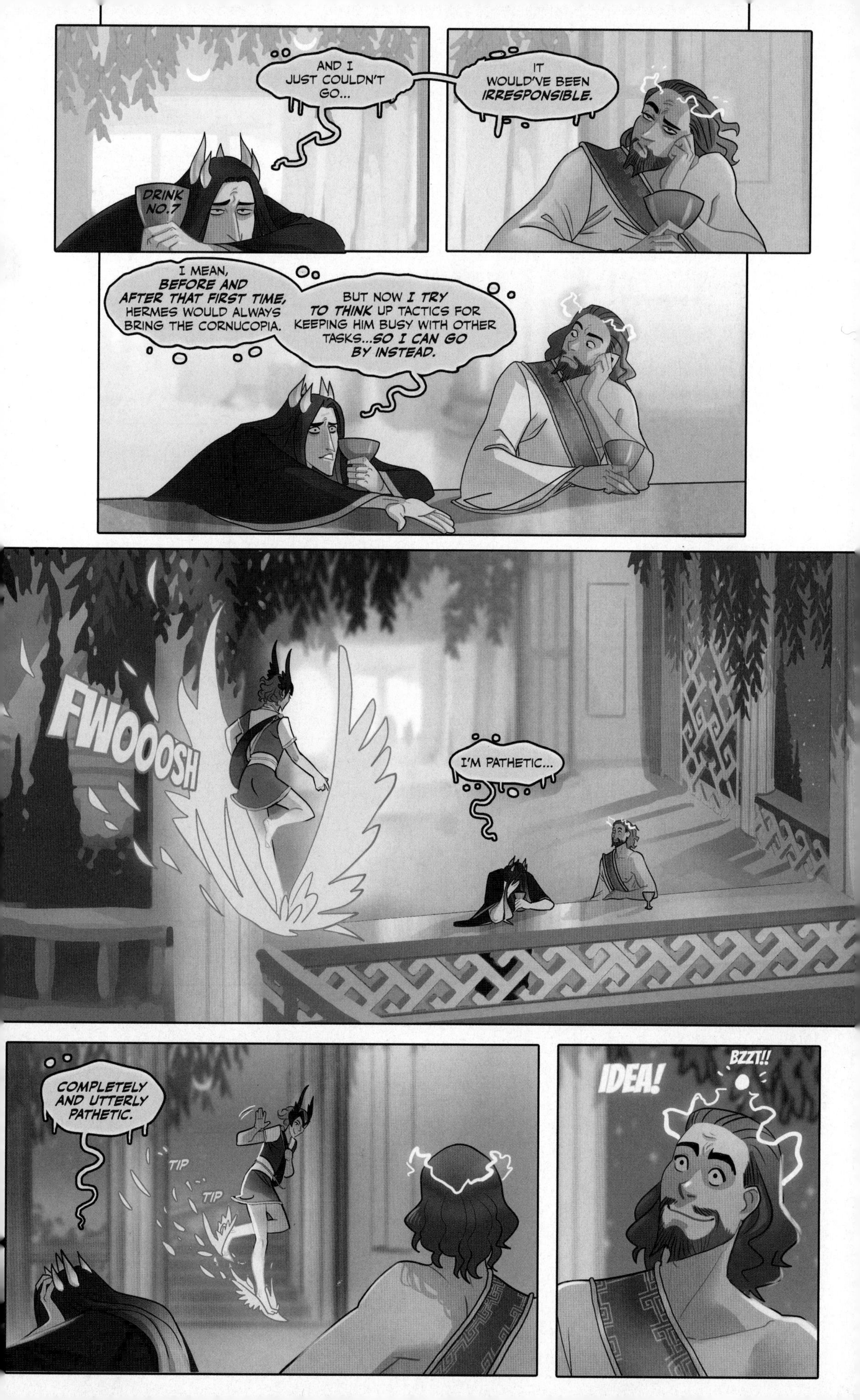
DRINK NO.7
AND I JUST COULDN'T GO...
IT WOULD'VE BEEN IRRESPONSIBLE.
I MEAN, BEFORE AND AFTER THAT FIRST TIME, HERMES WOULD ALWAYS BRING THE CORNUCOPIA.
BUT NOW I TRY TO THINK UP TACTICS FOR KEEPING HIM BUSY WITH OTHER TASKS...SO I CAN GO BY INSTEAD.
FWOOOSH
I'M PATHETIC...
COMPLETELY AND UTTERLY PATHETIC.
TIP
TIP
IDEA!
BZZT!!

AND JUST SO WE'RE CLEAR...

THIS IS NOT DUE A LACK OF MY OWN RESPONSIBILITIES...

?

HERMES, WAIT.

OH, NO!!! I HAVE *PLENTY* TO DO!

SCRIBBLE
SCRIBBLE

CLICK

FSSS

THIS IS JUST ME BEING COMPLETELY ILLOGICAL...

...DREAMING UP ELABORATE WAYS TO COMPLICATE EVERYBODY'S LIVES...

...INCLUDING MY OWN.

SWISH

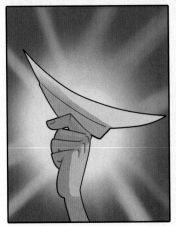

GOT IT!

SIGH...

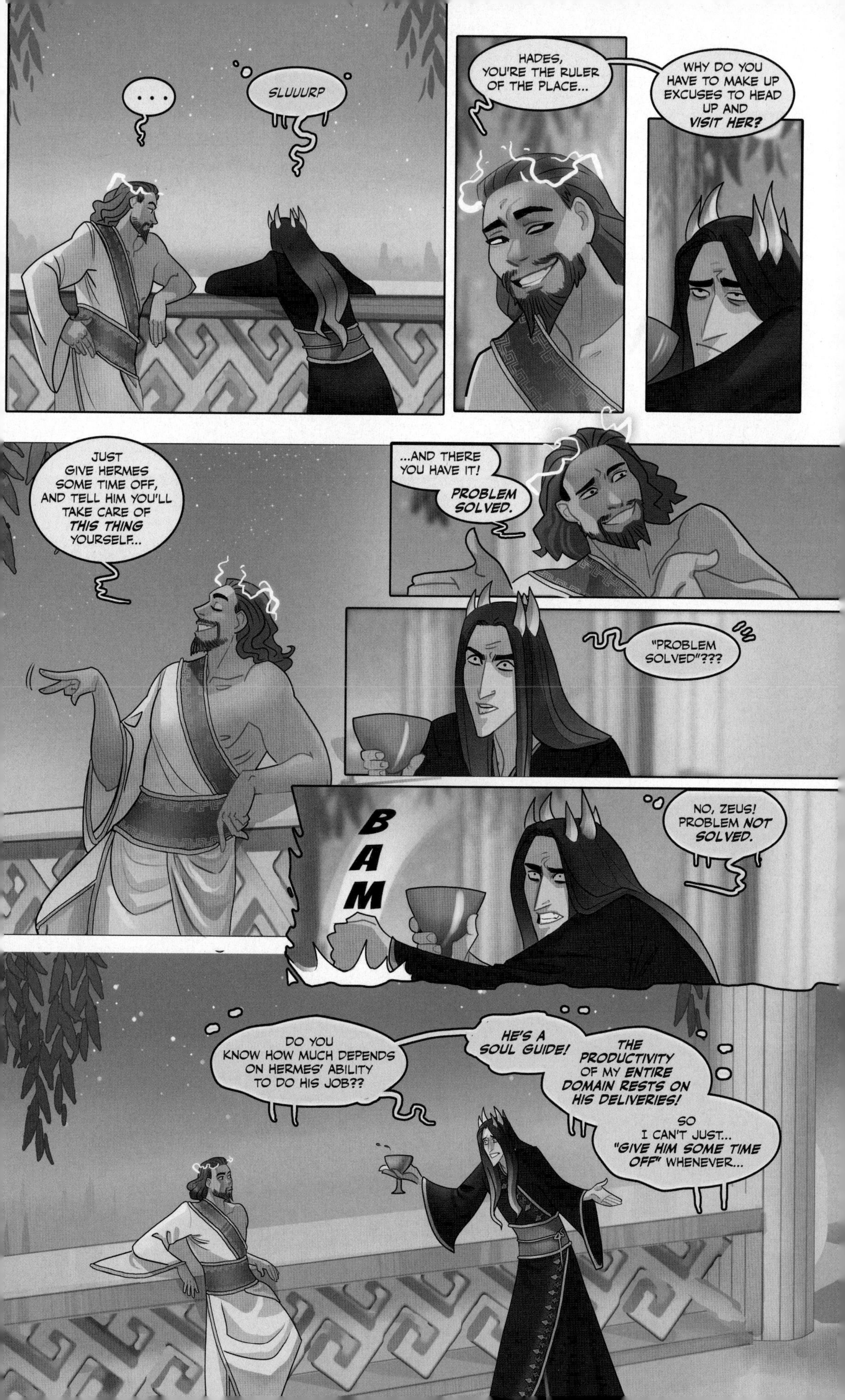

...
SLUUURP
HADES, YOU'RE THE RULER OF THE PLACE...
WHY DO YOU HAVE TO MAKE UP EXCUSES TO HEAD UP AND VISIT HER?
JUST GIVE HERMES SOME TIME OFF, AND TELL HIM YOU'LL TAKE CARE OF THIS THING YOURSELF...
...AND THERE YOU HAVE IT! PROBLEM SOLVED.
"PROBLEM SOLVED"???
BAM
NO, ZEUS! PROBLEM NOT SOLVED.
DO YOU KNOW HOW MUCH DEPENDS ON HERMES' ABILITY TO DO HIS JOB??
HE'S A SOUL GUIDE!
THE PRODUCTIVITY OF MY ENTIRE DOMAIN RESTS ON HIS DELIVERIES!
SO I CAN'T JUST... "GIVE HIM SOME TIME OFF" WHENEVER...

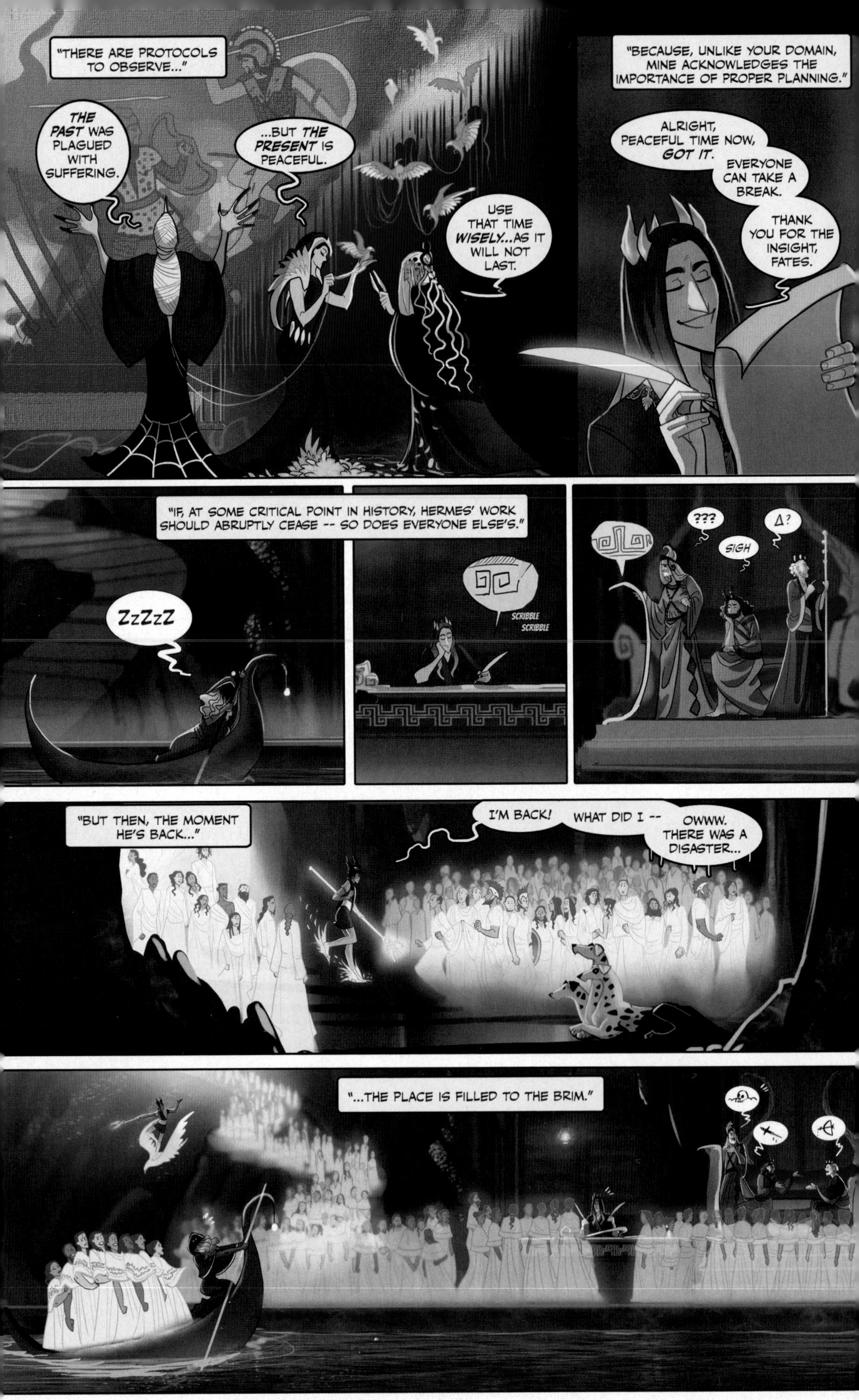
"THERE ARE PROTOCOLS TO OBSERVE..."
THE PAST WAS PLAGUED WITH SUFFERING.
...BUT THE PRESENT IS PEACEFUL.
USE THAT TIME WISELY...AS IT WILL NOT LAST.
"BECAUSE, UNLIKE YOUR DOMAIN, MINE ACKNOWLEDGES THE IMPORTANCE OF PROPER PLANNING."
ALRIGHT, PEACEFUL TIME NOW, GOT IT.
EVERYONE CAN TAKE A BREAK.
THANK YOU FOR THE INSIGHT, FATES.
"IF, AT SOME CRITICAL POINT IN HISTORY, HERMES' WORK SHOULD ABRUPTLY CEASE -- SO DOES EVERYONE ELSE'S."
ZzZzZ
SCRIBBLE
SCRIBBLE
???
SIGH
Δ?
"BUT THEN, THE MOMENT HE'S BACK..."
I'M BACK!
WHAT DID I --
OWWW. THERE WAS A DISASTER...
"...THE PLACE IS FILLED TO THE BRIM."

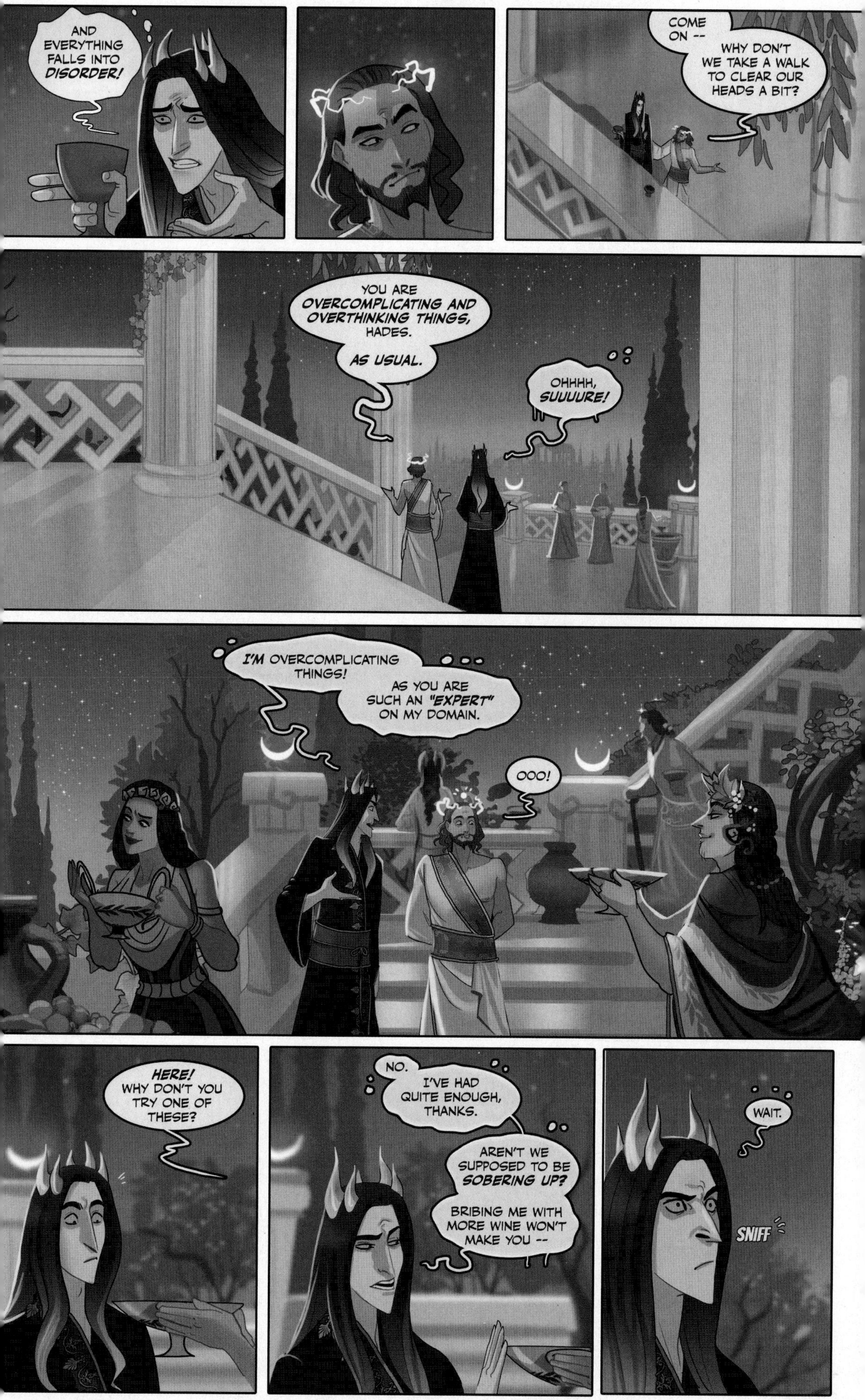
AND EVERYTHING FALLS INTO DISORDER!
COME ON --
WHY DON'T WE TAKE A WALK TO CLEAR OUR HEADS A BIT?
YOU ARE OVERCOMPLICATING AND OVERTHINKING THINGS, HADES.
AS USUAL.
OHHHH, SUUUURE!
I'M OVERCOMPLICATING THINGS!
AS YOU ARE SUCH AN "EXPERT" ON MY DOMAIN.
OOO!
HERE! WHY DON'T YOU TRY ONE OF THESE?
NO.
I'VE HAD QUITE ENOUGH, THANKS.
AREN'T WE SUPPOSED TO BE SOBERING UP?
BRIBING ME WITH MORE WINE WON'T MAKE YOU --
WAIT.
SNIFF

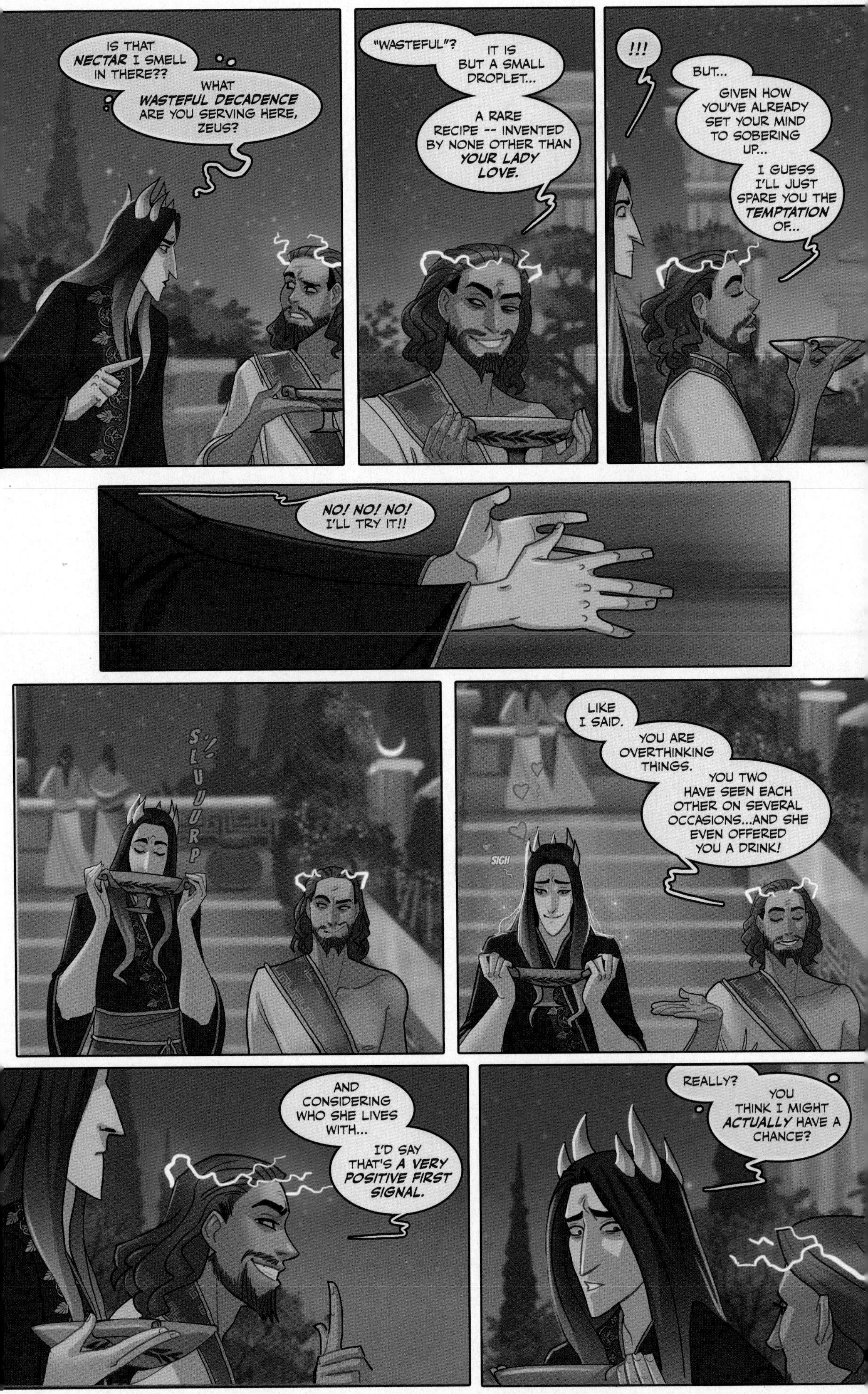
IS THAT NECTAR I SMELL IN THERE??
WHAT WASTEFUL DECADENCE ARE YOU SERVING HERE, ZEUS?
"WASTEFUL"? IT IS BUT A SMALL DROPLET...
A RARE RECIPE -- INVENTED BY NONE OTHER THAN YOUR LADY LOVE.
!!!
BUT...
GIVEN HOW YOU'VE ALREADY SET YOUR MIND TO SOBERING UP...
I GUESS I'LL JUST SPARE YOU THE TEMPTATION OF...
NO! NO! NO! I'LL TRY IT!!
SLUUURP
SIGH
LIKE I SAID.
YOU ARE OVERTHINKING THINGS.
YOU TWO HAVE SEEN EACH OTHER ON SEVERAL OCCASIONS...AND SHE EVEN OFFERED YOU A DRINK!
AND CONSIDERING WHO SHE LIVES WITH...
I'D SAY THAT'S A VERY POSITIVE FIRST SIGNAL.
REALLY?
YOU THINK I MIGHT ACTUALLY HAVE A CHANCE?

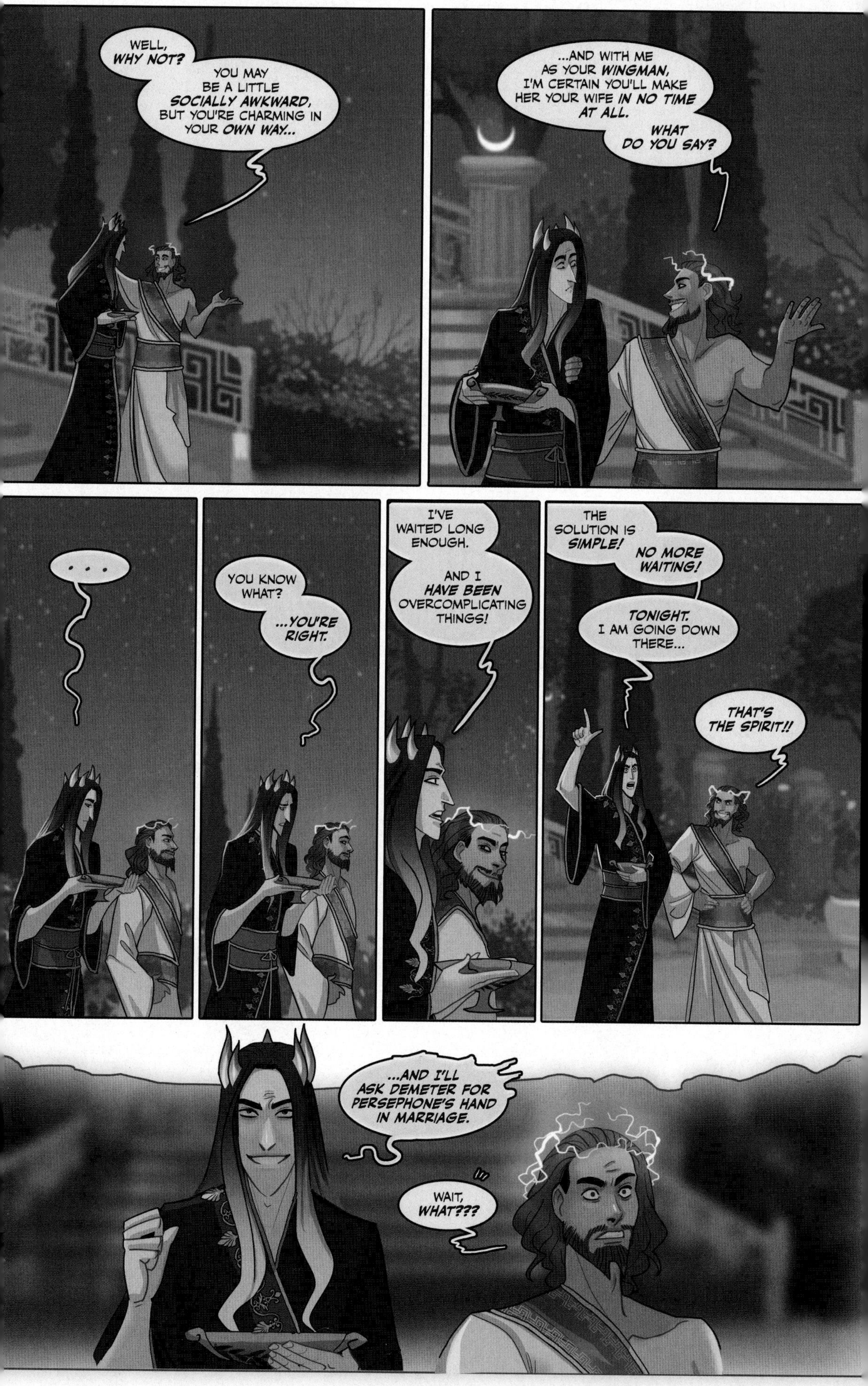
WELL, WHY NOT?
YOU MAY BE A LITTLE SOCIALLY AWKWARD, BUT YOU'RE CHARMING IN YOUR OWN WAY...
...AND WITH ME AS YOUR WINGMAN, I'M CERTAIN YOU'LL MAKE HER YOUR WIFE IN NO TIME AT ALL.
WHAT DO YOU SAY?
. . .
YOU KNOW WHAT?
...YOU'RE RIGHT.
I'VE WAITED LONG ENOUGH.
AND I HAVE BEEN OVERCOMPLICATING THINGS!
THE SOLUTION IS SIMPLE!
NO MORE WAITING!
TONIGHT. I AM GOING DOWN THERE...
THAT'S THE SPIRIT!!
...AND I'LL ASK DEMETER FOR PERSEPHONE'S HAND IN MARRIAGE.
WAIT, WHAT???

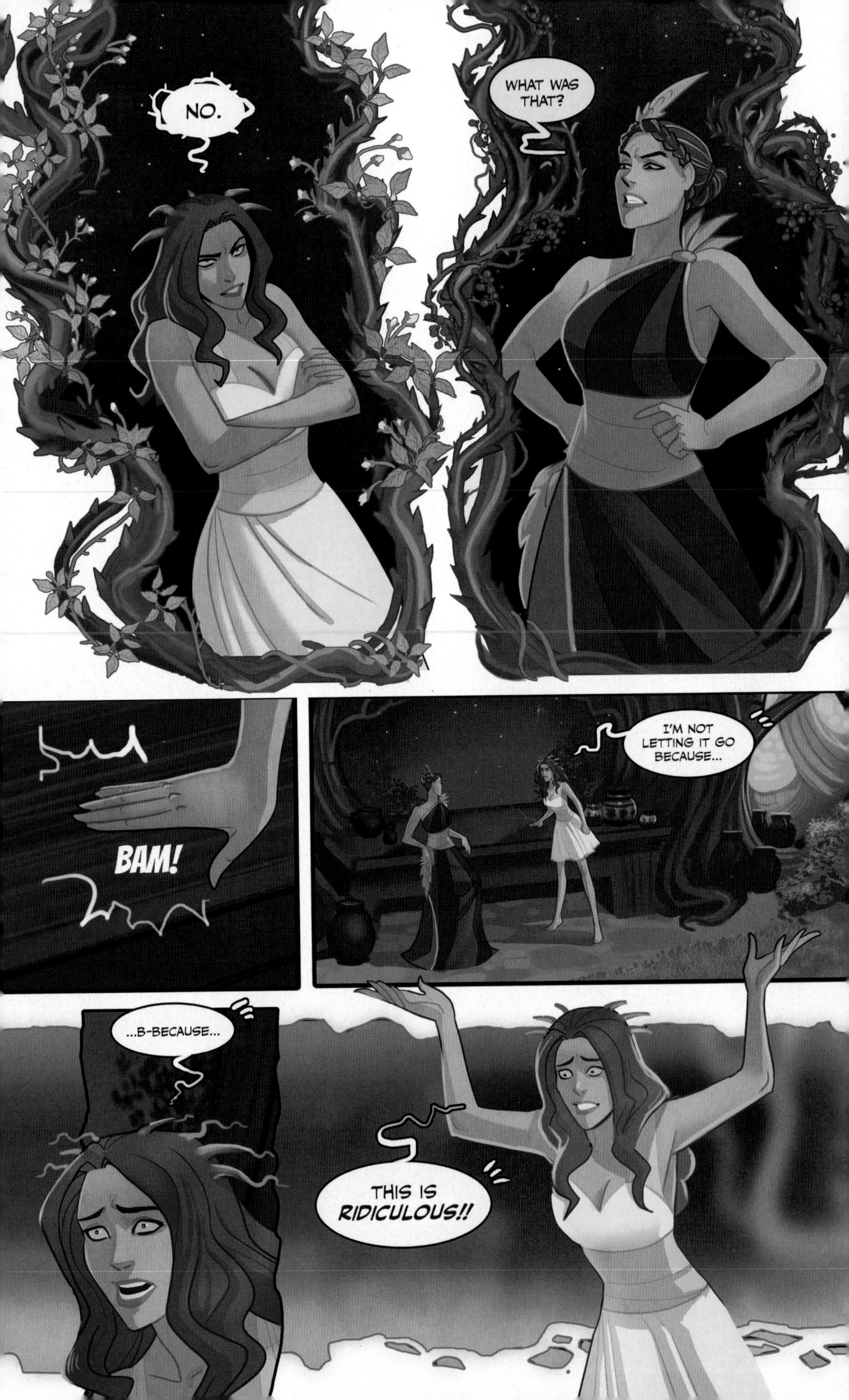
NO.
WHAT WAS THAT?
BAM!
I'M NOT LETTING IT GO BECAUSE...
...B-BECAUSE...
THIS IS RIDICULOUS!!

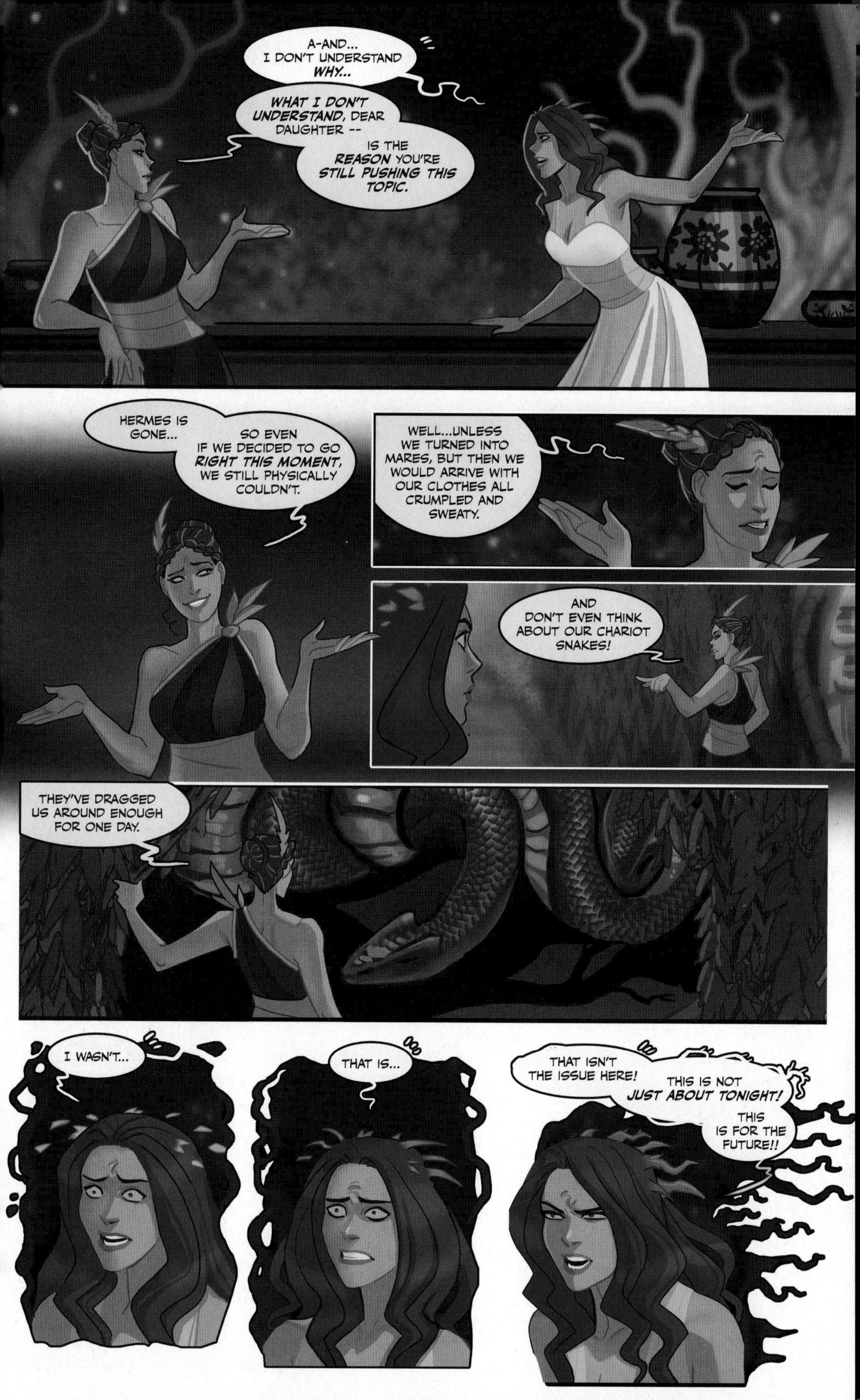
A-AND... I DON'T UNDERSTAND WHY...
WHAT I DON'T UNDERSTAND, DEAR DAUGHTER --
IS THE REASON YOU'RE STILL PUSHING THIS TOPIC.
HERMES IS GONE...
SO EVEN IF WE DECIDED TO GO RIGHT THIS MOMENT, WE STILL PHYSICALLY COULDN'T.
WELL...UNLESS WE TURNED INTO MARES, BUT THEN WE WOULD ARRIVE WITH OUR CLOTHES ALL CRUMPLED AND SWEATY.
AND DON'T EVEN THINK ABOUT OUR CHARIOT SNAKES!
THEY'VE DRAGGED US AROUND ENOUGH FOR ONE DAY.
I WASN'T...
THAT IS...
THAT ISN'T THE ISSUE HERE!
THIS IS NOT JUST ABOUT TONIGHT!
THIS IS FOR THE FUTURE!!

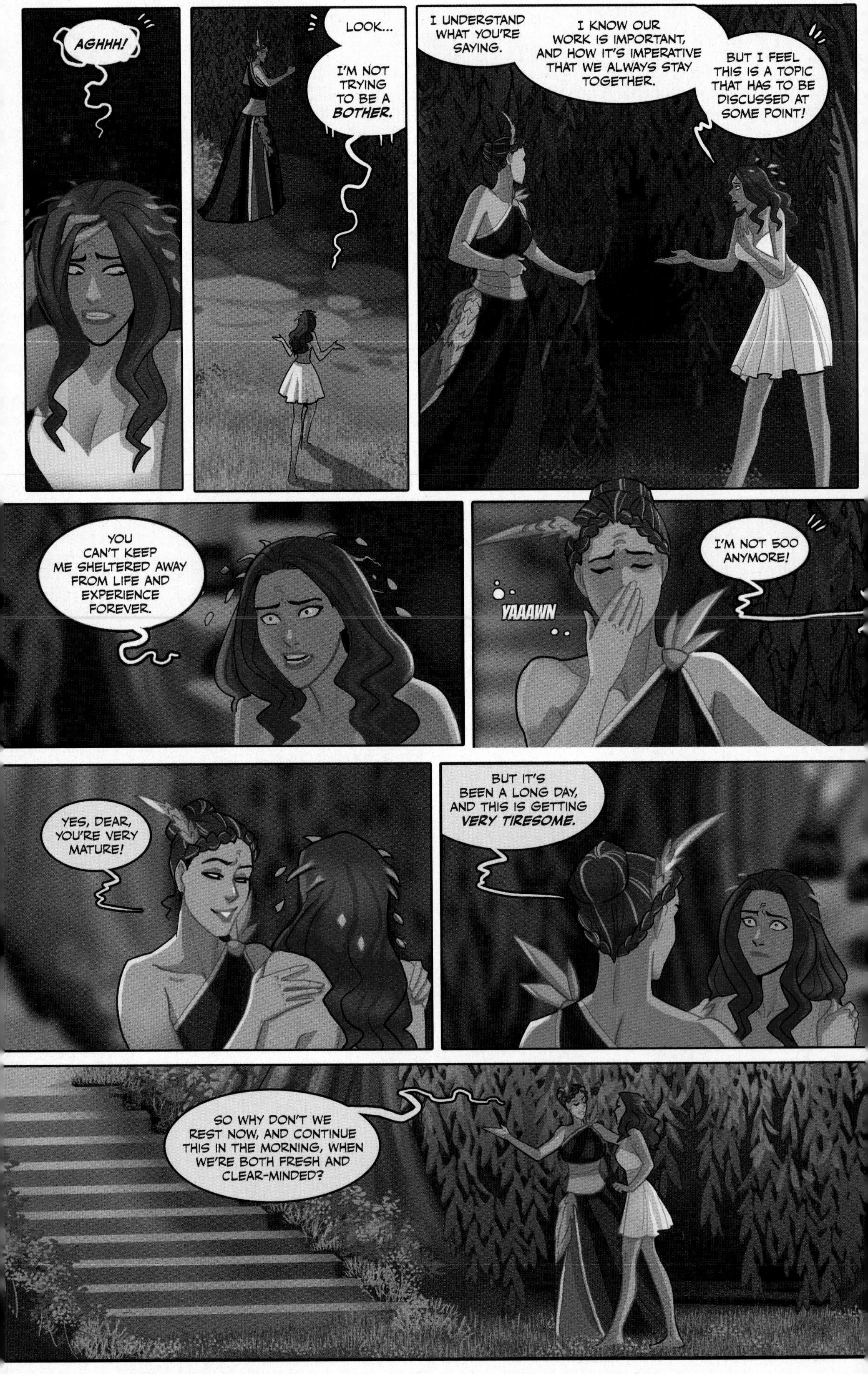
AGHHH!
LOOK...
I'M NOT TRYING TO BE A BOTHER.
I UNDERSTAND WHAT YOU'RE SAYING.
I KNOW OUR WORK IS IMPORTANT, AND HOW IT'S IMPERATIVE THAT WE ALWAYS STAY TOGETHER.
BUT I FEEL THIS IS A TOPIC THAT HAS TO BE DISCUSSED AT SOME POINT!
YOU CAN'T KEEP ME SHELTERED AWAY FROM LIFE AND EXPERIENCE FOREVER.
I'M NOT 500 ANYMORE!
YAAAWN
YES, DEAR, YOU'RE VERY MATURE!
BUT IT'S BEEN A LONG DAY, AND THIS IS GETTING VERY TIRESOME.
SO WHY DON'T WE REST NOW, AND CONTINUE THIS IN THE MORNING, WHEN WE'RE BOTH FRESH AND CLEAR-MINDED?

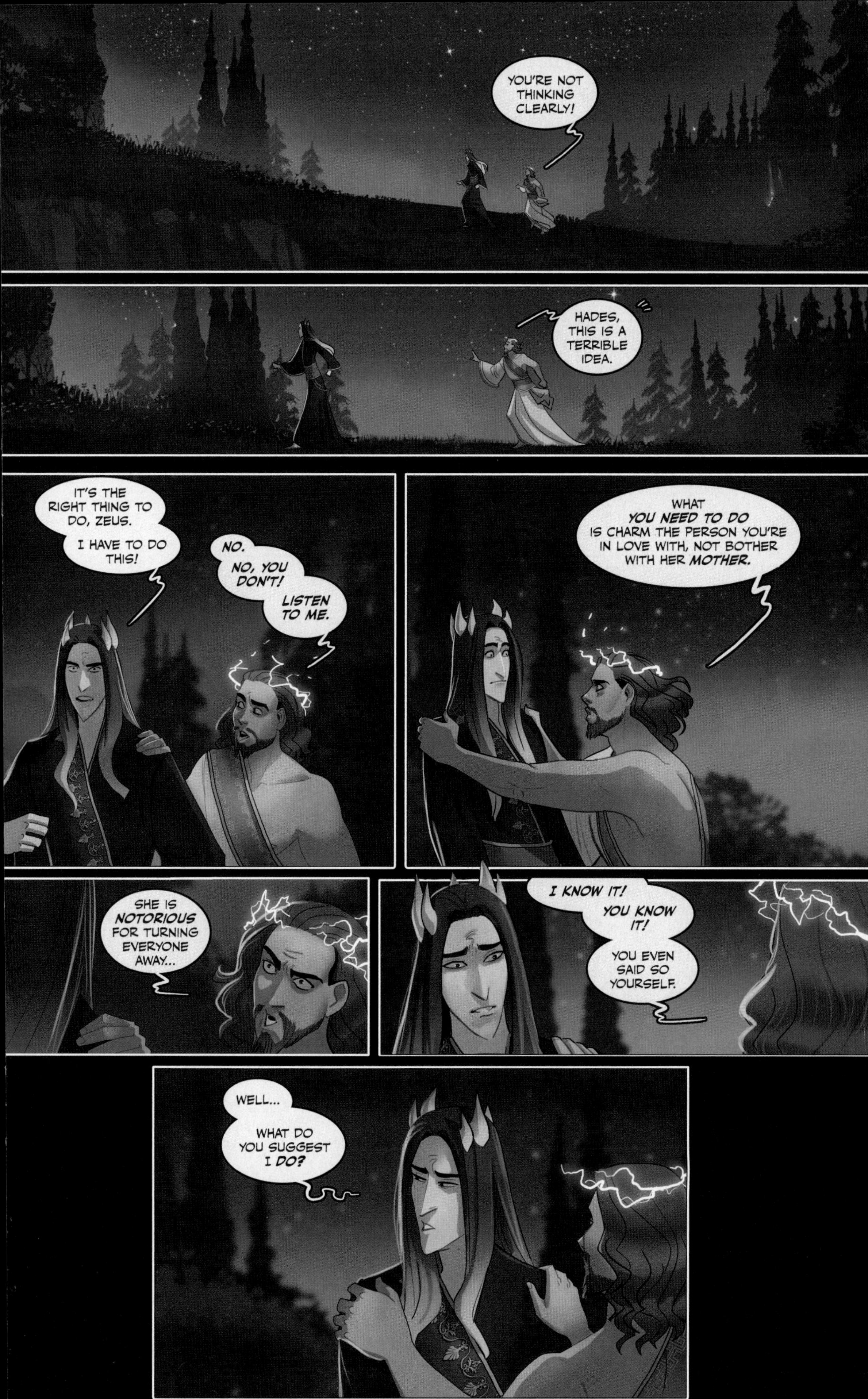
YOU'RE NOT THINKING CLEARLY!
HADES, THIS IS A TERRIBLE IDEA.
IT'S THE RIGHT THING TO DO, ZEUS.
I HAVE TO DO THIS!
NO.
NO, YOU DON'T!
LISTEN TO ME.
WHAT *YOU NEED TO DO* IS CHARM THE PERSON YOU'RE IN LOVE WITH, NOT BOTHER WITH HER *MOTHER.*
SHE IS *NOTORIOUS* FOR TURNING EVERYONE AWAY...
I KNOW IT!
YOU KNOW IT!
YOU EVEN SAID SO YOURSELF.
WELL...
WHAT DO YOU SUGGEST I *DO?*

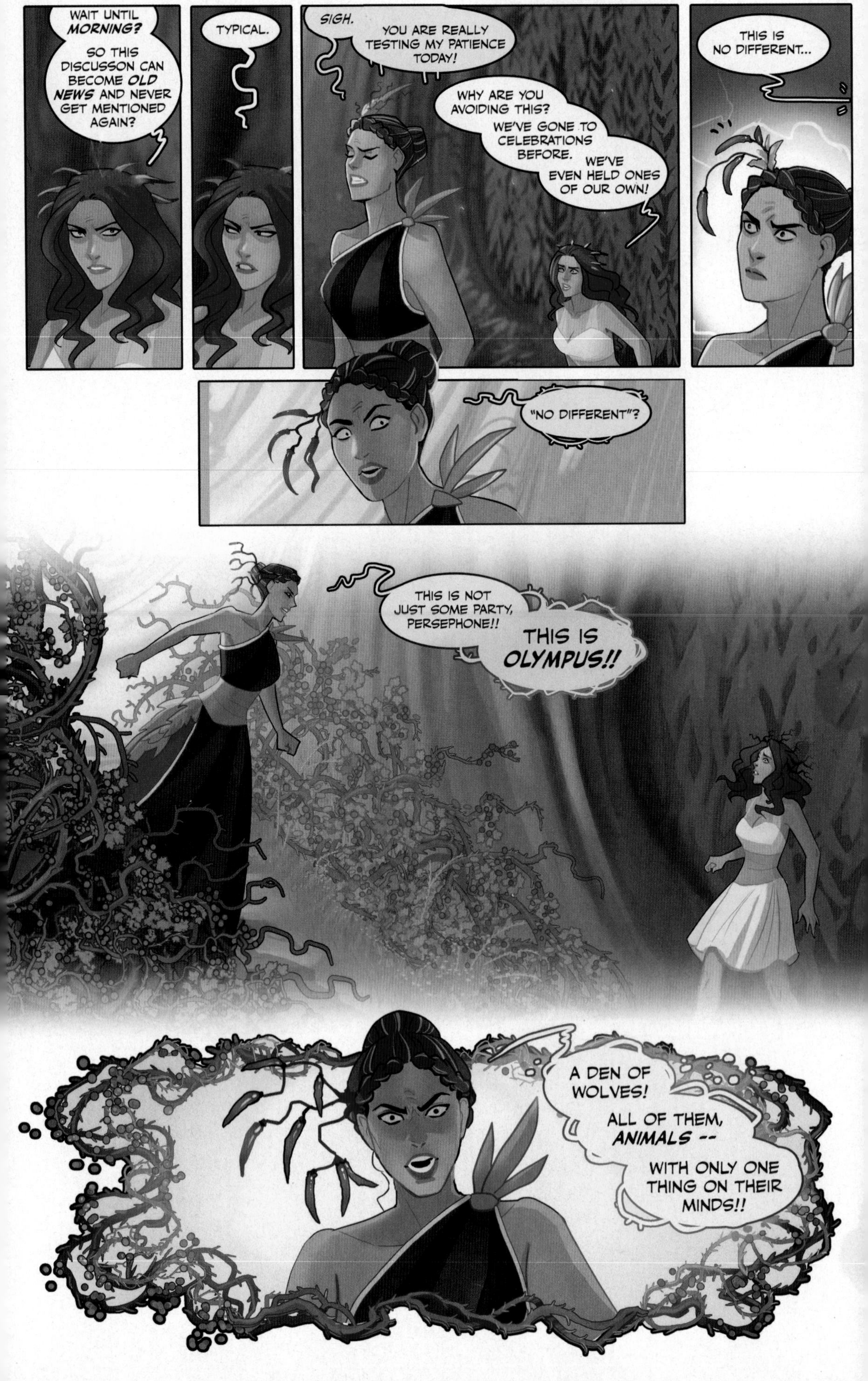

WAIT UNTIL MORNING? SO THIS DISCUSSON CAN BECOME OLD NEWS AND NEVER GET MENTIONED AGAIN?
TYPICAL.
SIGH.
YOU ARE REALLY TESTING MY PATIENCE TODAY!
WHY ARE YOU AVOIDING THIS?
WE'VE GONE TO CELEBRATIONS BEFORE.
WE'VE EVEN HELD ONES OF OUR OWN!
THIS IS NO DIFFERENT...
"NO DIFFERENT"?
THIS IS NOT JUST SOME PARTY, PERSEPHONE!!
THIS IS OLYMPUS!!
A DEN OF WOLVES!
ALL OF THEM, ANIMALS --
WITH ONLY ONE THING ON THEIR MINDS!!

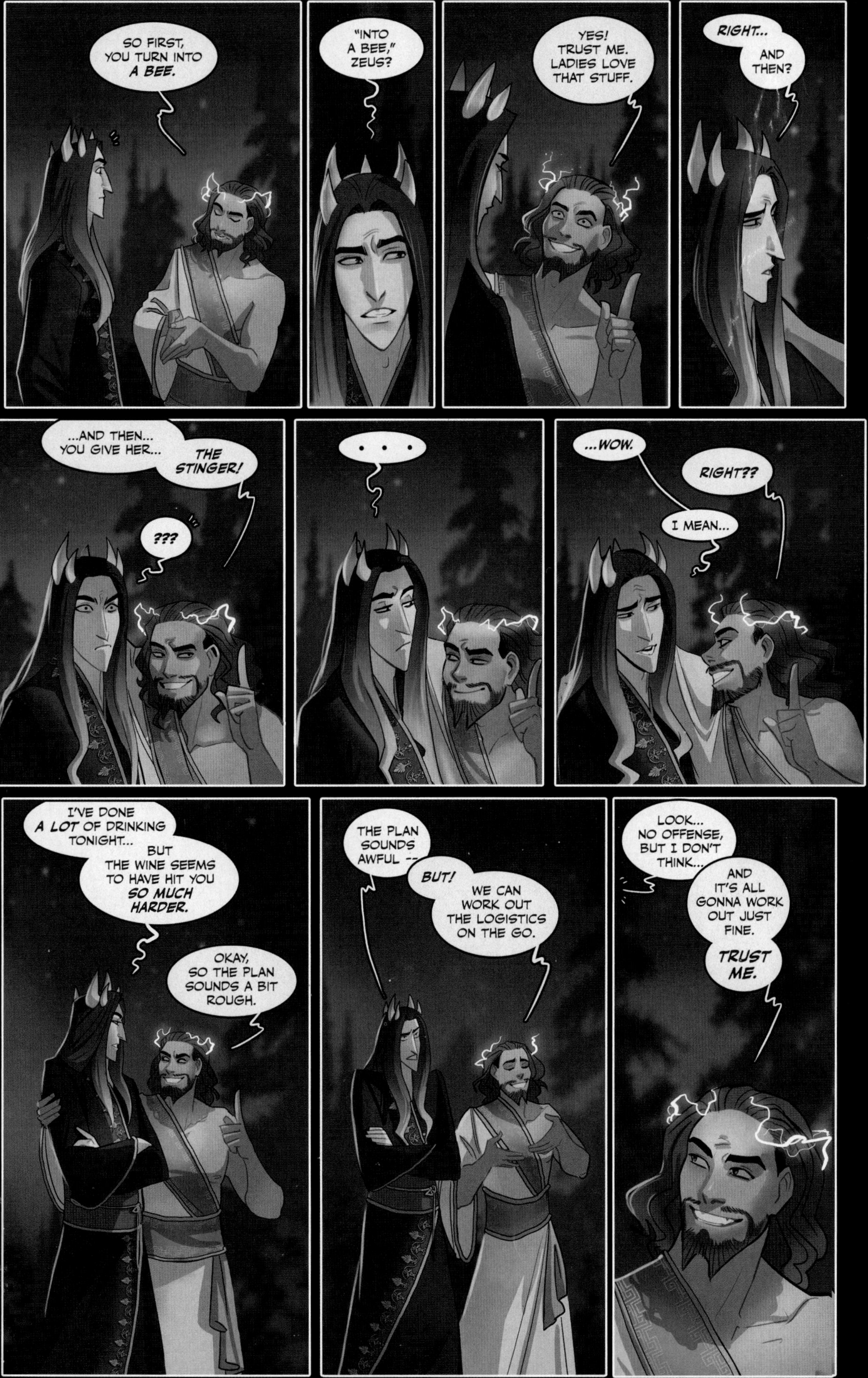
SO FIRST, YOU TURN INTO A BEE.
"INTO A BEE," ZEUS?
YES! TRUST ME. LADIES LOVE THAT STUFF.
RIGHT...
AND THEN?
...AND THEN... YOU GIVE HER...
THE STINGER!
???
. . .
...WOW.
RIGHT??
I MEAN...
I'VE DONE A LOT OF DRINKING TONIGHT...
BUT THE WINE SEEMS TO HAVE HIT YOU SO MUCH HARDER.
OKAY, SO THE PLAN SOUNDS A BIT ROUGH.
THE PLAN SOUNDS AWFUL --
BUT!
WE CAN WORK OUT THE LOGISTICS ON THE GO.
LOOK... NO OFFENSE, BUT I DON'T THINK...
AND IT'S ALL GONNA WORK OUT JUST FINE.
TRUST ME.

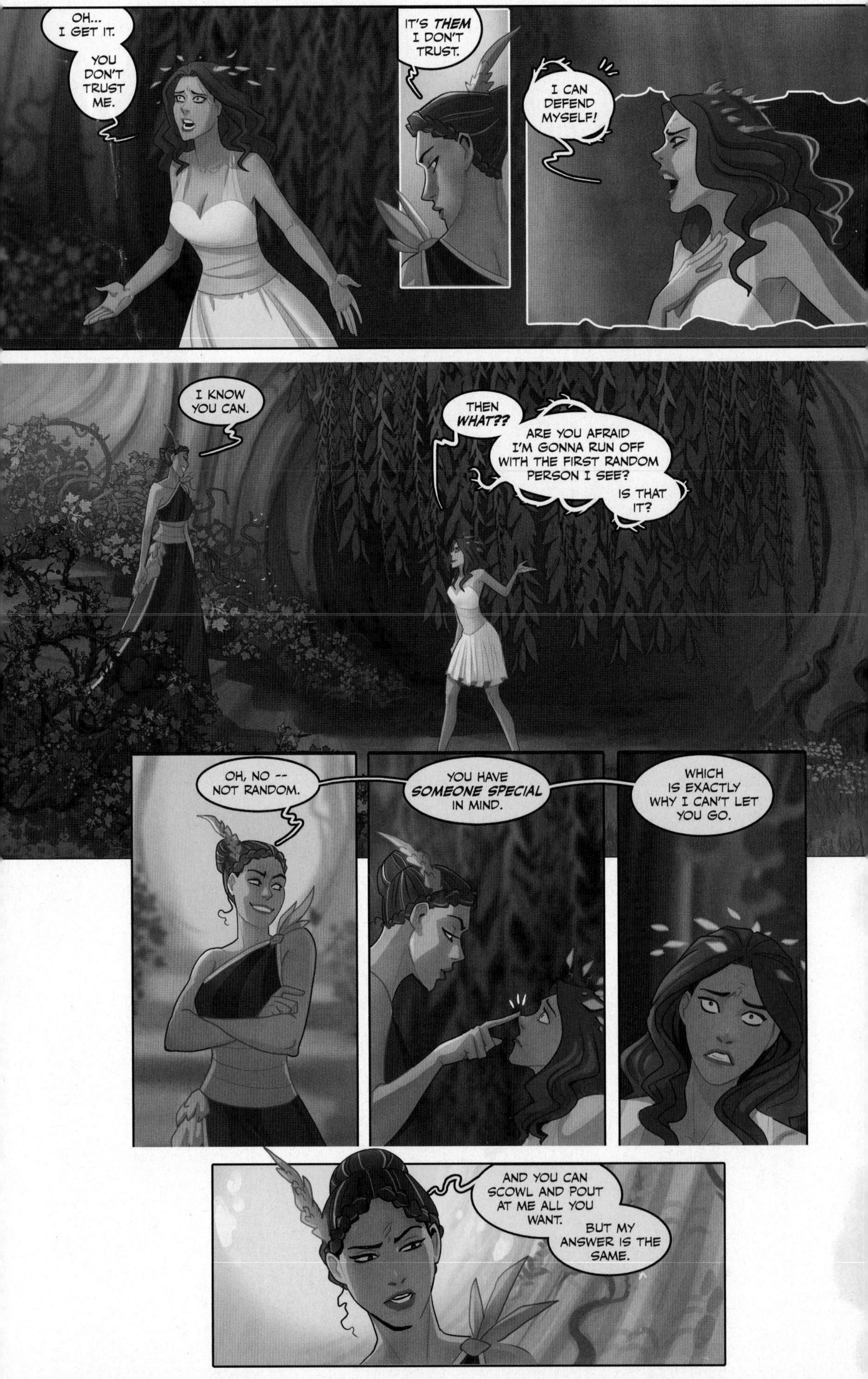
OH... I GET IT.
YOU DON'T TRUST ME.
IT'S THEM I DON'T TRUST.
I CAN DEFEND MYSELF!
I KNOW YOU CAN.
THEN WHAT??
ARE YOU AFRAID I'M GONNA RUN OFF WITH THE FIRST RANDOM PERSON I SEE?
IS THAT IT?
OH, NO -- NOT RANDOM.
YOU HAVE SOMEONE SPECIAL IN MIND.
WHICH IS EXACTLY WHY I CAN'T LET YOU GO.
AND YOU CAN SCOWL AND POUT AT ME ALL YOU WANT.
BUT MY ANSWER IS THE SAME.

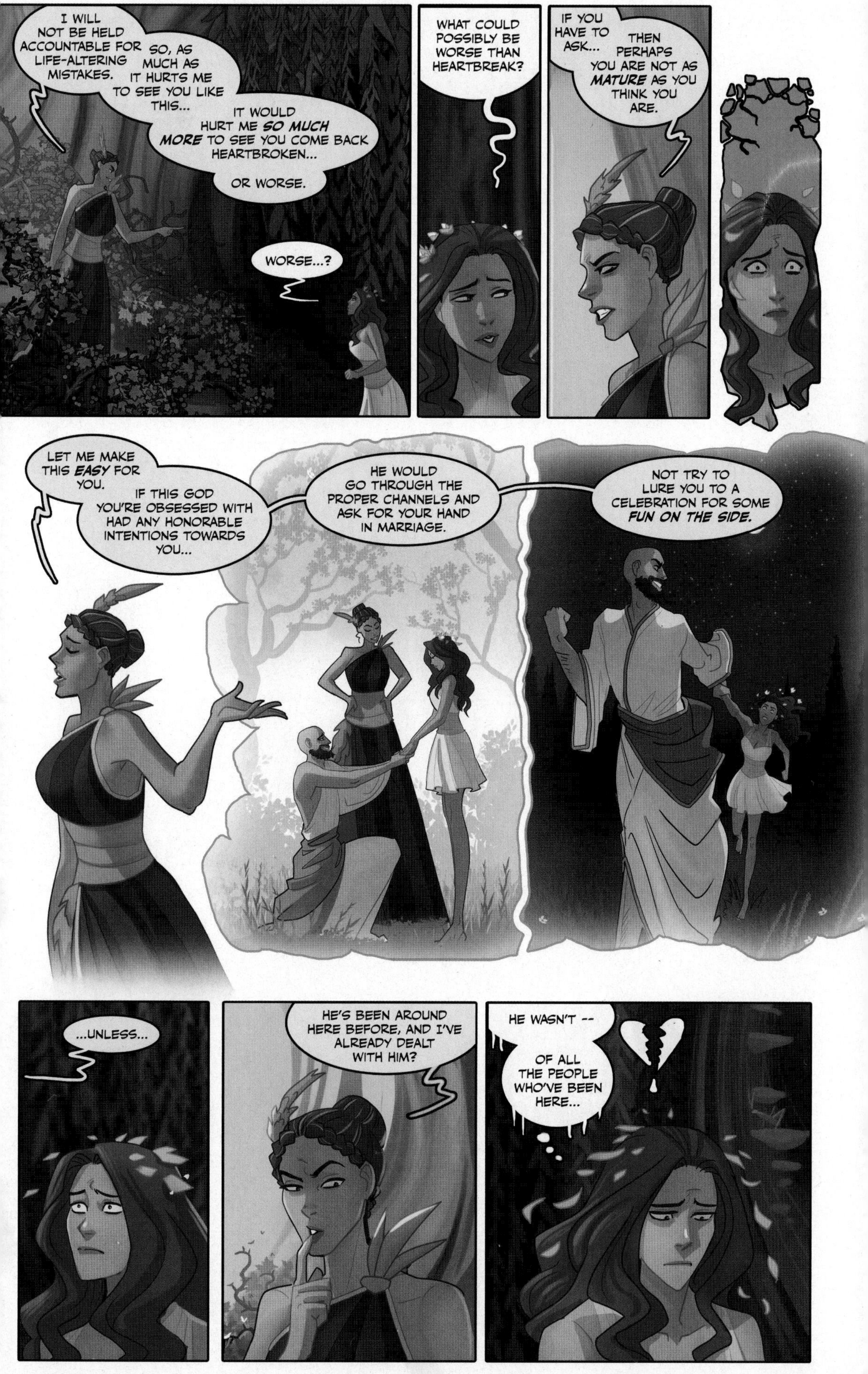
I WILL NOT BE HELD ACCOUNTABLE FOR LIFE-ALTERING MISTAKES.
SO, AS MUCH AS IT HURTS ME TO SEE YOU LIKE THIS...
IT WOULD HURT ME SO MUCH MORE TO SEE YOU COME BACK HEARTBROKEN...
OR WORSE.
WORSE...?
WHAT COULD POSSIBLY BE WORSE THAN HEARTBREAK?
IF YOU HAVE TO ASK...
THEN PERHAPS YOU ARE NOT AS MATURE AS YOU THINK YOU ARE.
LET ME MAKE THIS EASY FOR YOU.
IF THIS GOD YOU'RE OBSESSED WITH HAD ANY HONORABLE INTENTIONS TOWARDS YOU...
HE WOULD GO THROUGH THE PROPER CHANNELS AND ASK FOR YOUR HAND IN MARRIAGE.
NOT TRY TO LURE YOU TO A CELEBRATION FOR SOME FUN ON THE SIDE.
...UNLESS...
HE'S BEEN AROUND HERE BEFORE, AND I'VE ALREADY DEALT WITH HIM?
HE WASN'T --
OF ALL THE PEOPLE WHO'VE BEEN HERE...

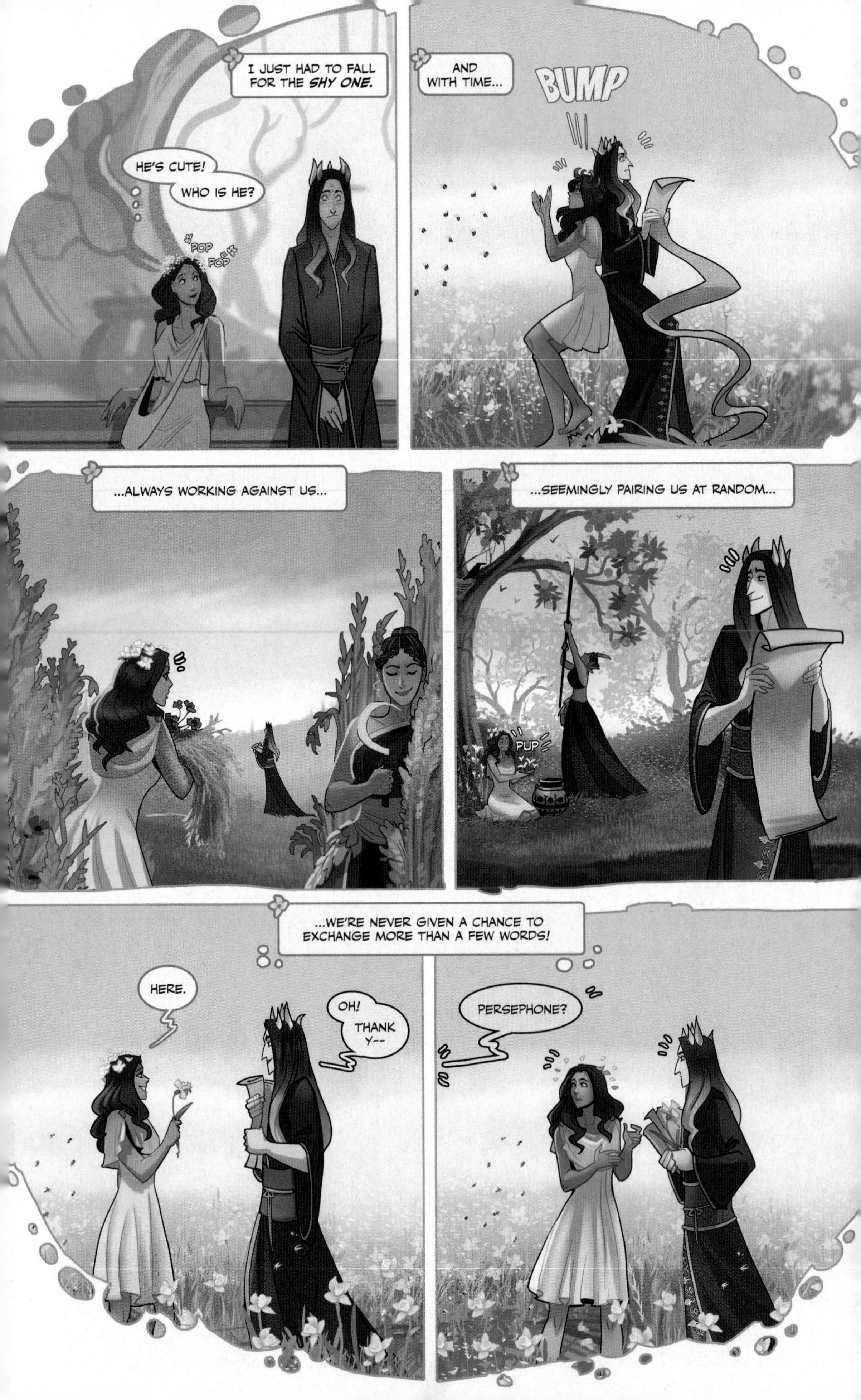
I JUST HAD TO FALL FOR THE SHY ONE.
HE'S CUTE!
WHO IS HE?
POP
POP
AND WITH TIME...
BUMP
...ALWAYS WORKING AGAINST US...
...SEEMINGLY PAIRING US AT RANDOM...
PUP
...WE'RE NEVER GIVEN A CHANCE TO EXCHANGE MORE THAN A FEW WORDS!
HERE.
OH! THANK Y--
PERSEPHONE?

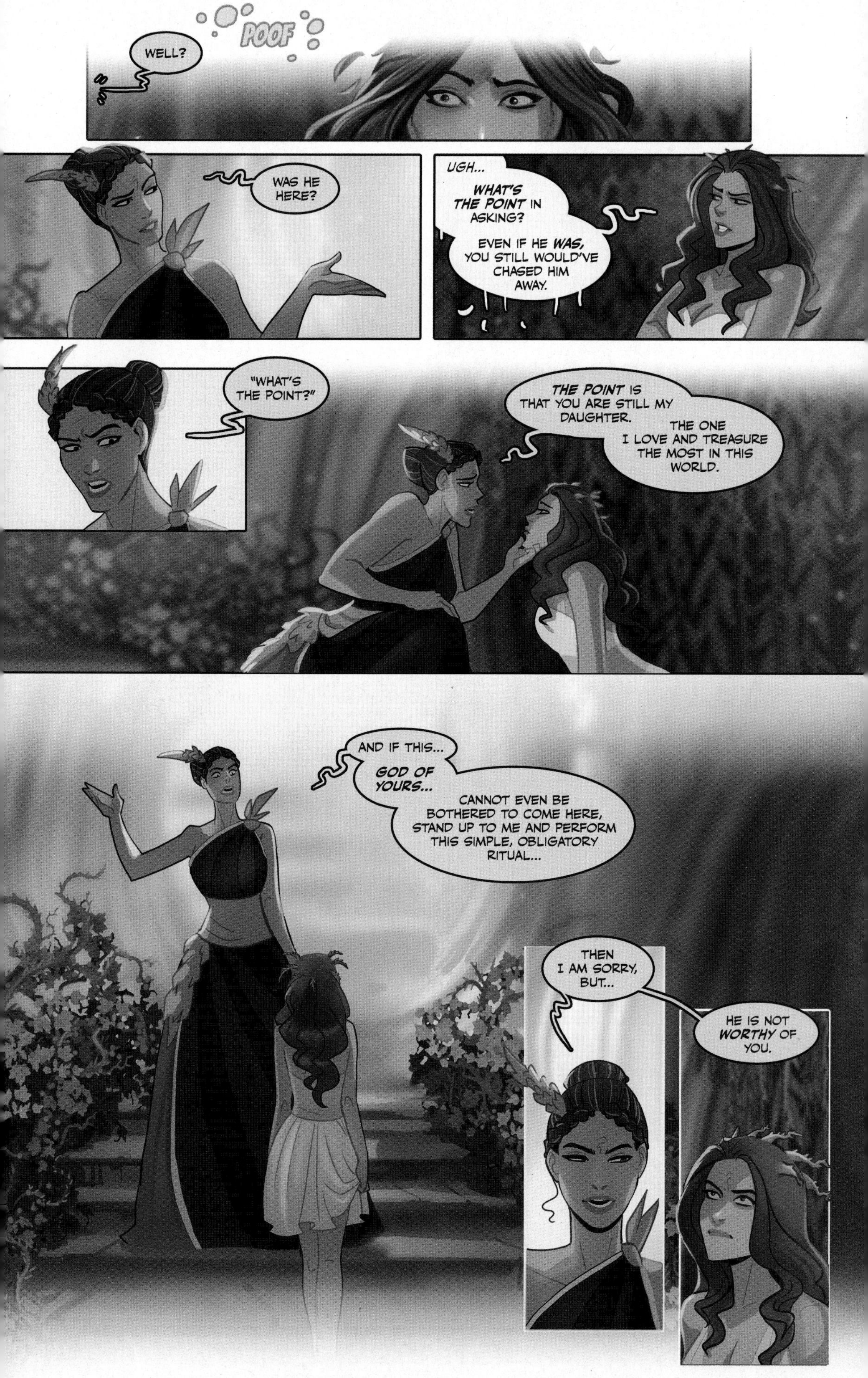
POOF
WELL?
WAS HE HERE?
UGH...
WHAT'S THE POINT IN ASKING?
EVEN IF HE WAS, YOU STILL WOULD'VE CHASED HIM AWAY.
"WHAT'S THE POINT?"
THE POINT IS THAT YOU ARE STILL MY DAUGHTER.
THE ONE I LOVE AND TREASURE THE MOST IN THIS WORLD.
AND IF THIS...
GOD OF YOURS...
CANNOT EVEN BE BOTHERED TO COME HERE, STAND UP TO ME AND PERFORM THIS SIMPLE, OBLIGATORY RITUAL...
THEN I AM SORRY, BUT...
HE IS NOT WORTHY OF YOU.

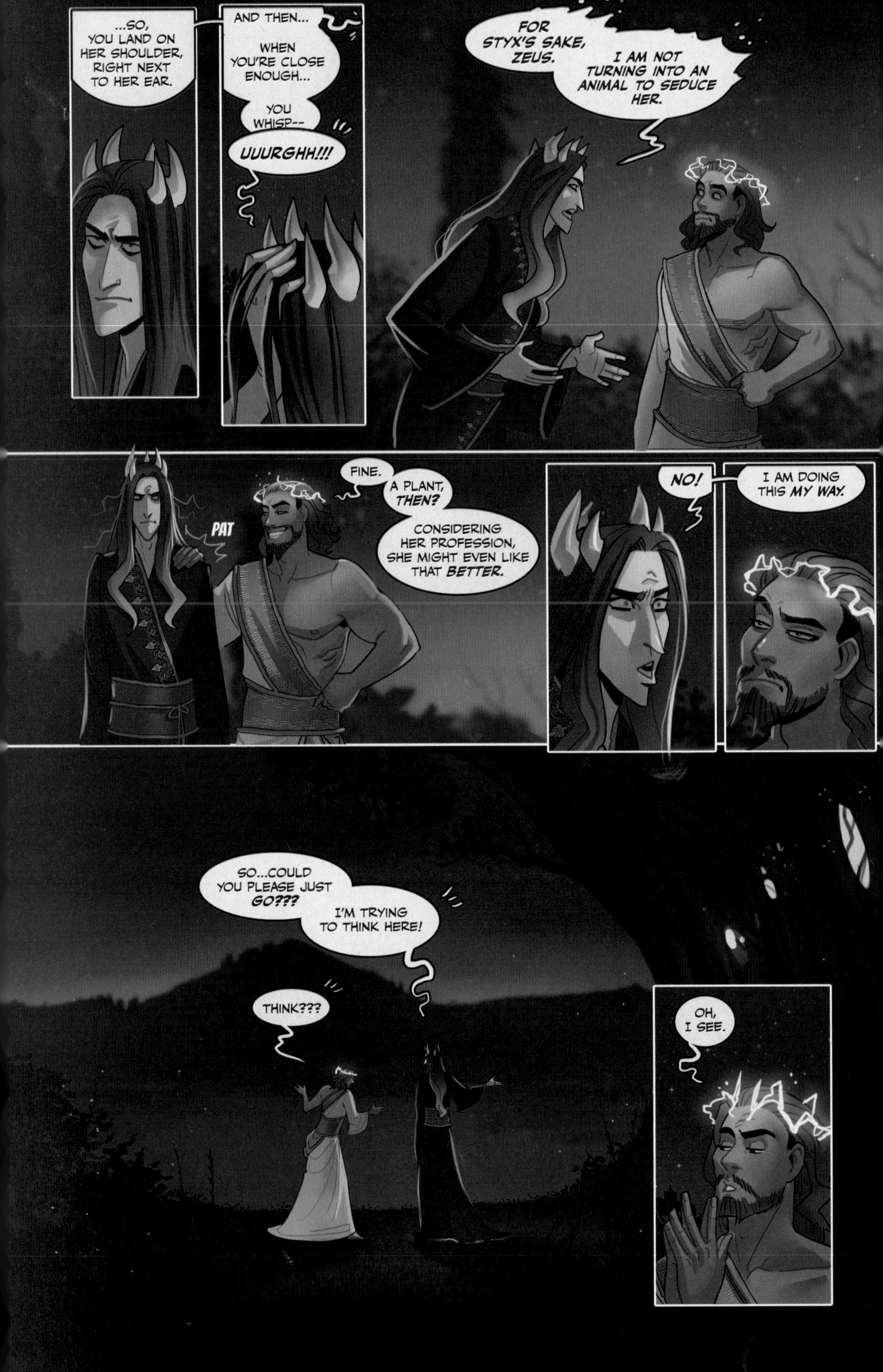

...SO, YOU LAND ON HER SHOULDER, RIGHT NEXT TO HER EAR.
AND THEN...
WHEN YOU'RE CLOSE ENOUGH...
YOU WHISP--
UUURGHH!!!
FOR STYX'S SAKE, ZEUS.
I AM NOT TURNING INTO AN ANIMAL TO SEDUCE HER.
PAT
FINE.
A PLANT, THEN?
CONSIDERING HER PROFESSION, SHE MIGHT EVEN LIKE THAT BETTER.
NO!
I AM DOING THIS MY WAY.
SO...COULD YOU PLEASE JUST GO???
I'M TRYING TO THINK HERE!
THINK???
OH, I SEE.

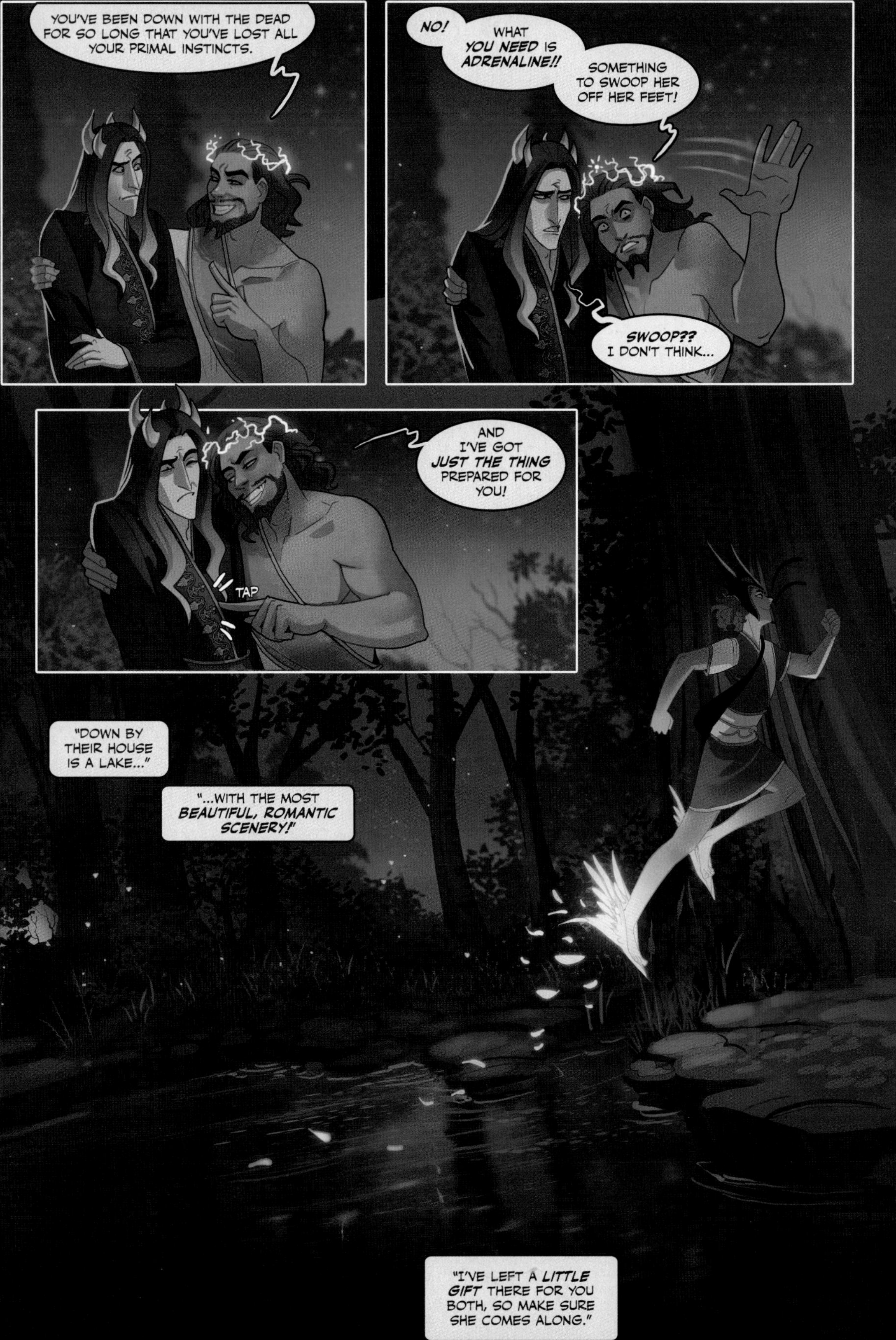
YOU'VE BEEN DOWN WITH THE DEAD FOR SO LONG THAT YOU'VE LOST ALL YOUR PRIMAL INSTINCTS.
NO!
WHAT YOU NEED IS ADRENALINE!!
SOMETHING TO SWOOP HER OFF HER FEET!
SWOOP?? I DON'T THINK...
AND I'VE GOT JUST THE THING PREPARED FOR YOU!
TAP
"DOWN BY THEIR HOUSE IS A LAKE..."
"...WITH THE MOST BEAUTIFUL, ROMANTIC SCENERY!"
"I'VE LEFT A LITTLE GIFT THERE FOR YOU BOTH, SO MAKE SURE SHE COMES ALONG."

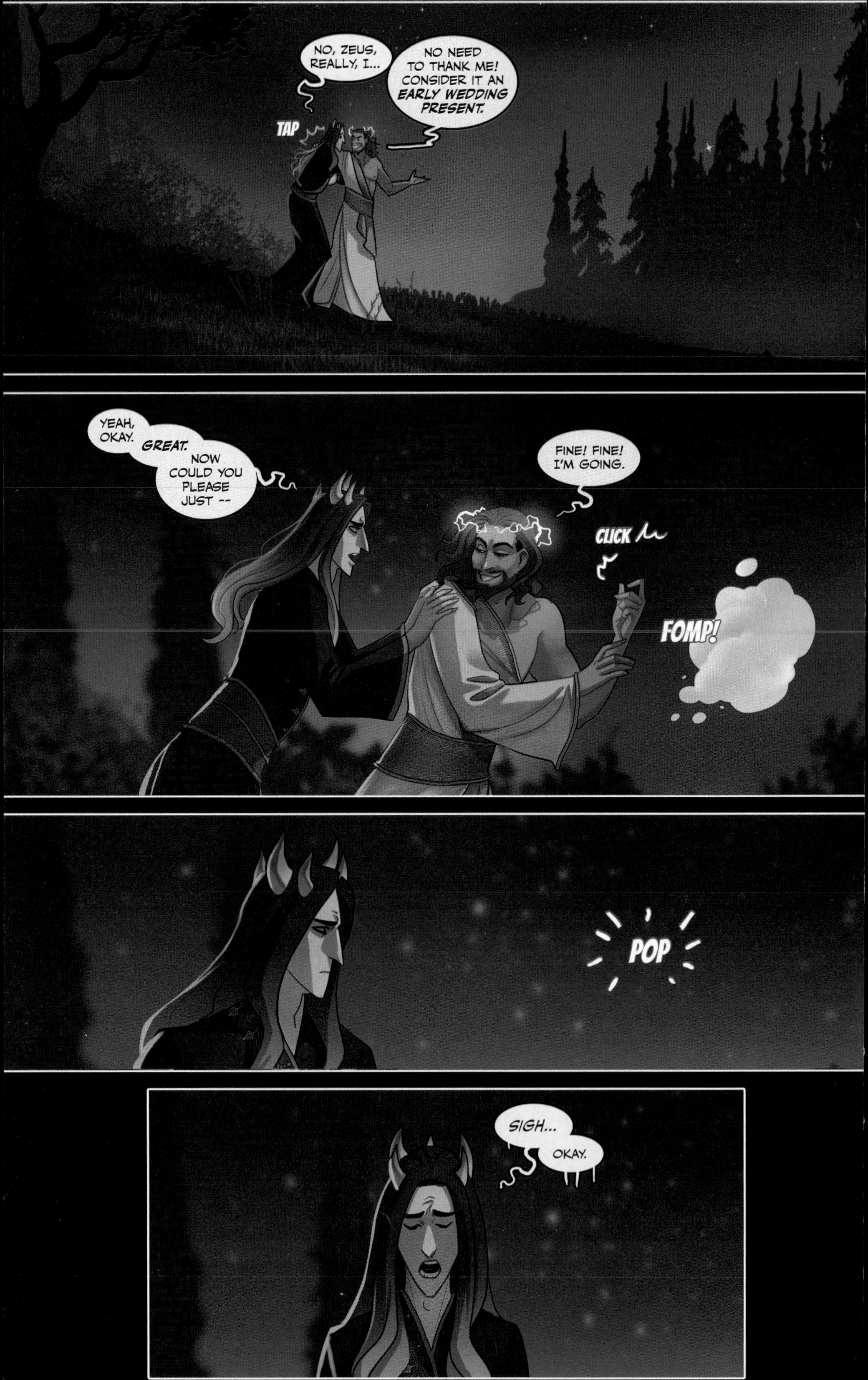
NO, ZEUS, REALLY, I...
NO NEED TO THANK ME! CONSIDER IT AN EARLY WEDDING PRESENT.
TAP
YEAH, OKAY.
GREAT.
NOW COULD YOU PLEASE JUST --
FINE! FINE! I'M GOING.
CLICK
FOMP!
POP
SIGH...
OKAY.

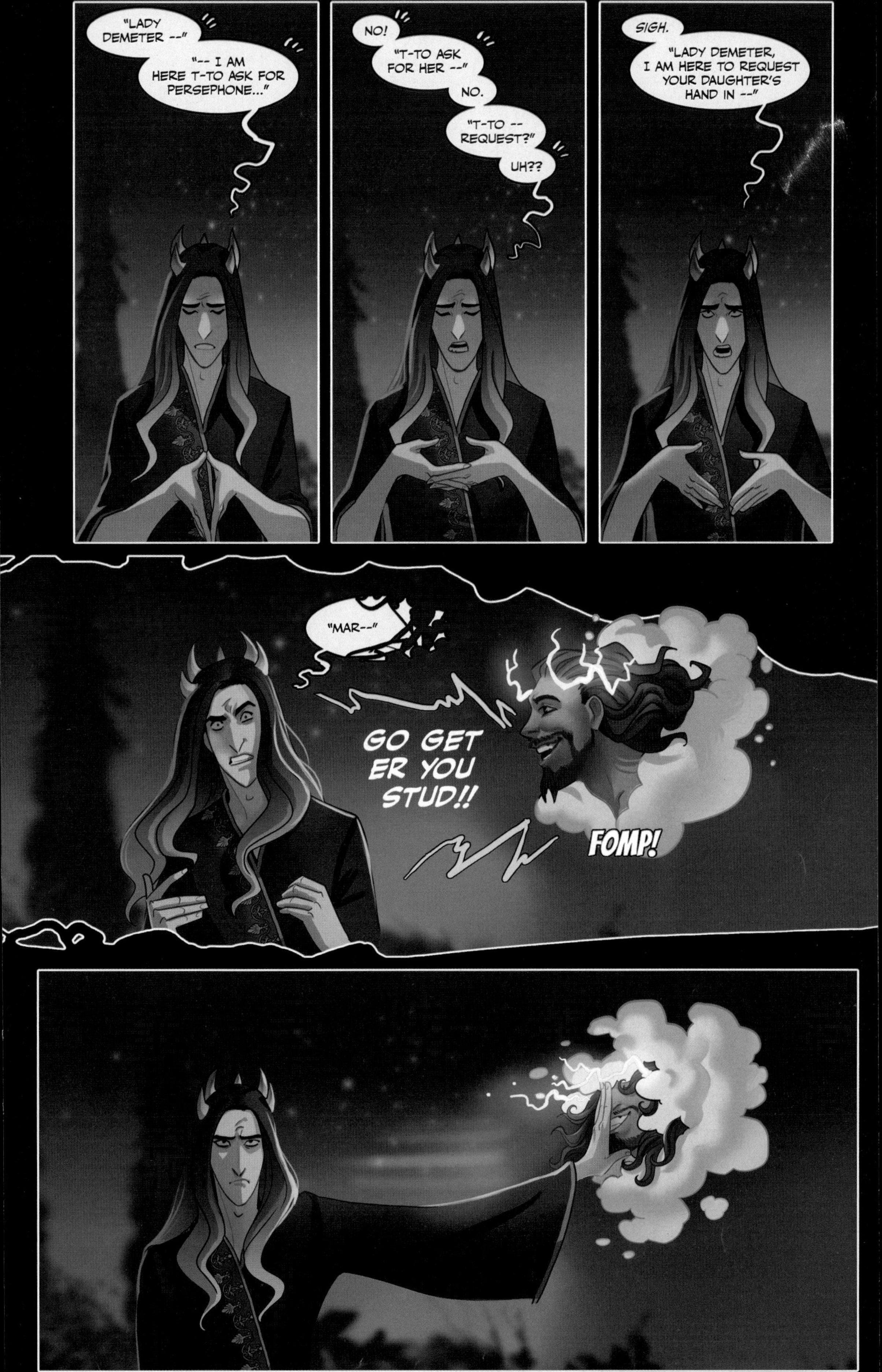
"LADY DEMETER --"
"-- I AM HERE T-TO ASK FOR PERSEPHONE..."
NO!
"T-TO ASK FOR HER --"
NO.
"T-TO -- REQUEST?"
UH??
SIGH.
"LADY DEMETER, I AM HERE TO REQUEST YOUR DAUGHTER'S HAND IN --"
"MAR--"
GO GET ER YOU STUD!!
FOMP!

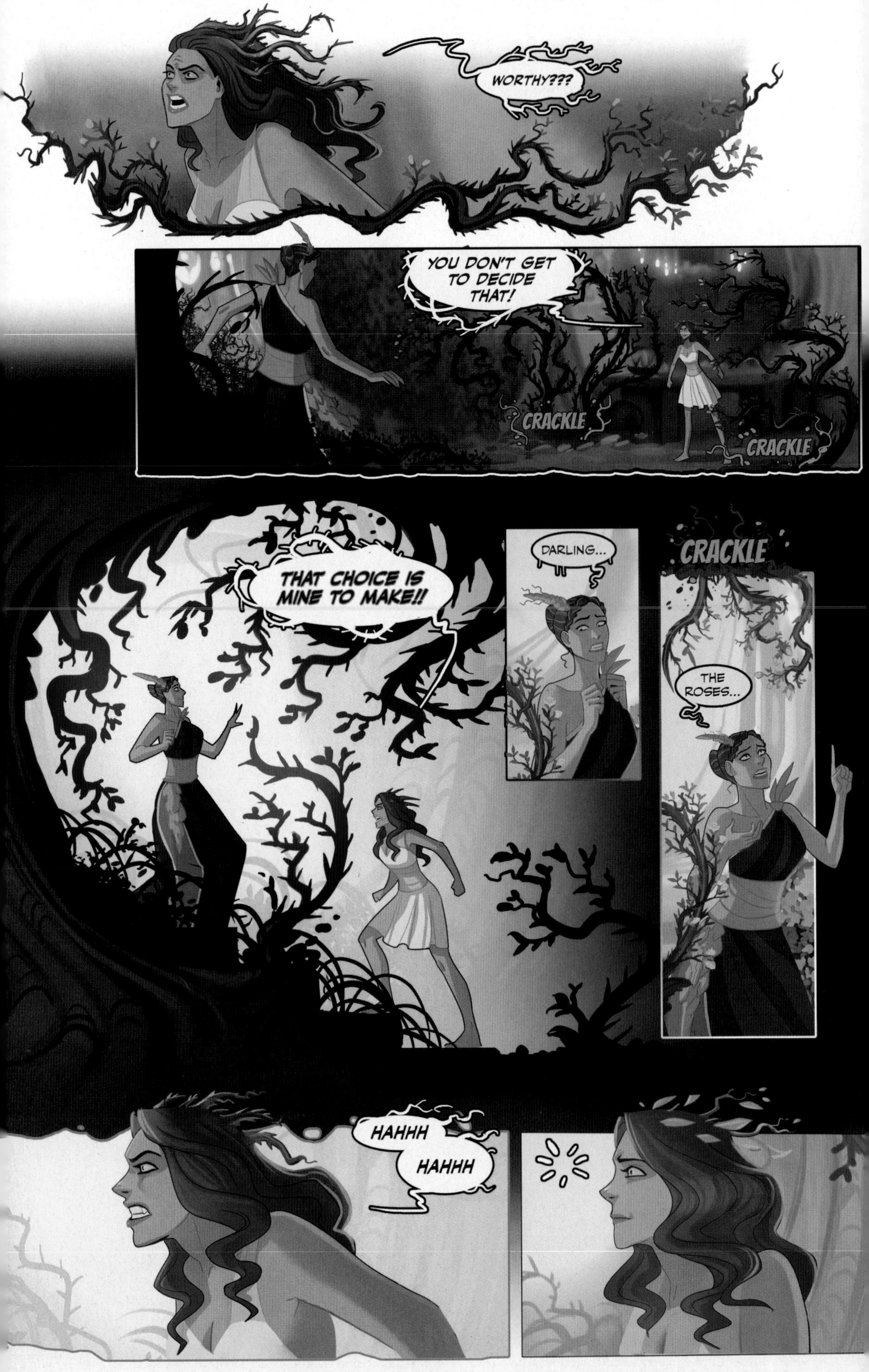
WORTHY???
YOU DON'T GET TO DECIDE THAT!
CRACKLE
CRACKLE
THAT CHOICE IS MINE TO MAKE!!
DARLING...
CRACKLE
THE ROSES...
HAHHH HAHHH

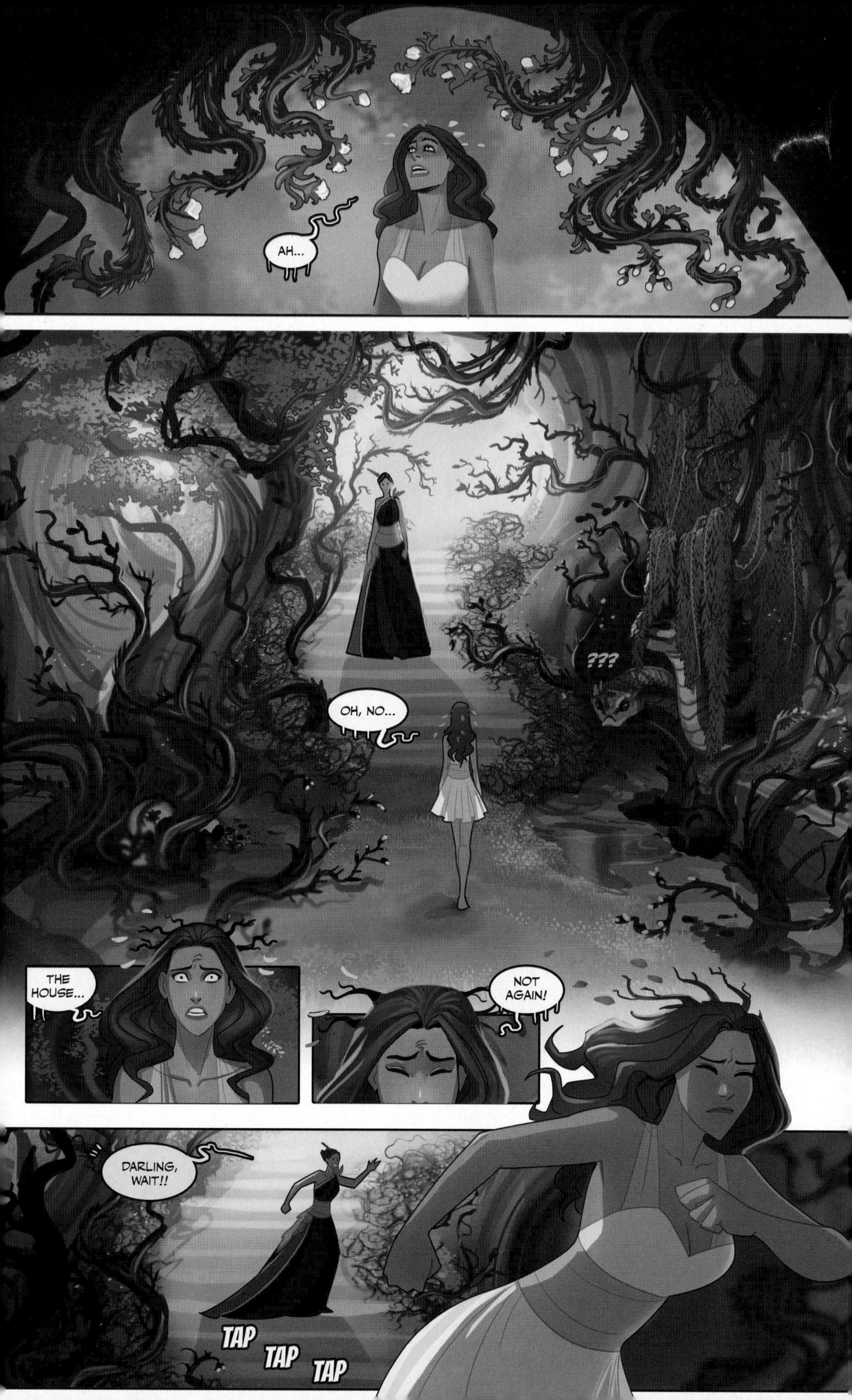
AH...
OH, NO...
???
THE HOUSE...
NOT AGAIN!
DARLING, WAIT!!
TAP
TAP
TAP

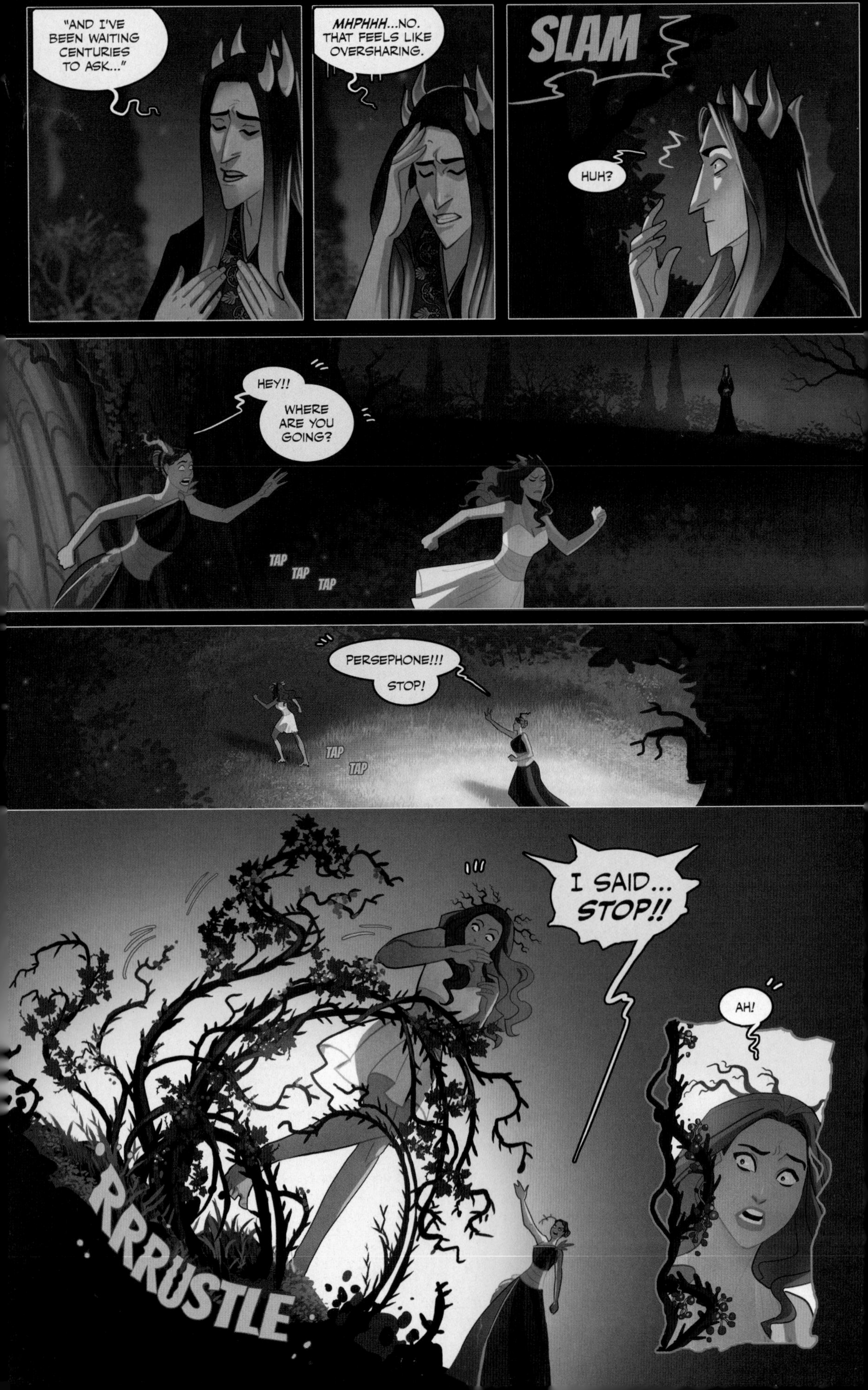
"AND I'VE BEEN WAITING CENTURIES TO ASK..."
MHPHHH...NO. THAT FEELS LIKE OVERSHARING.
SLAM
HUH?
HEY!!
WHERE ARE YOU GOING?
TAP
TAP
TAP
PERSEPHONE!!!
STOP!
TAP
TAP
I SAID... STOP!!
AH!
RRRUSTLE

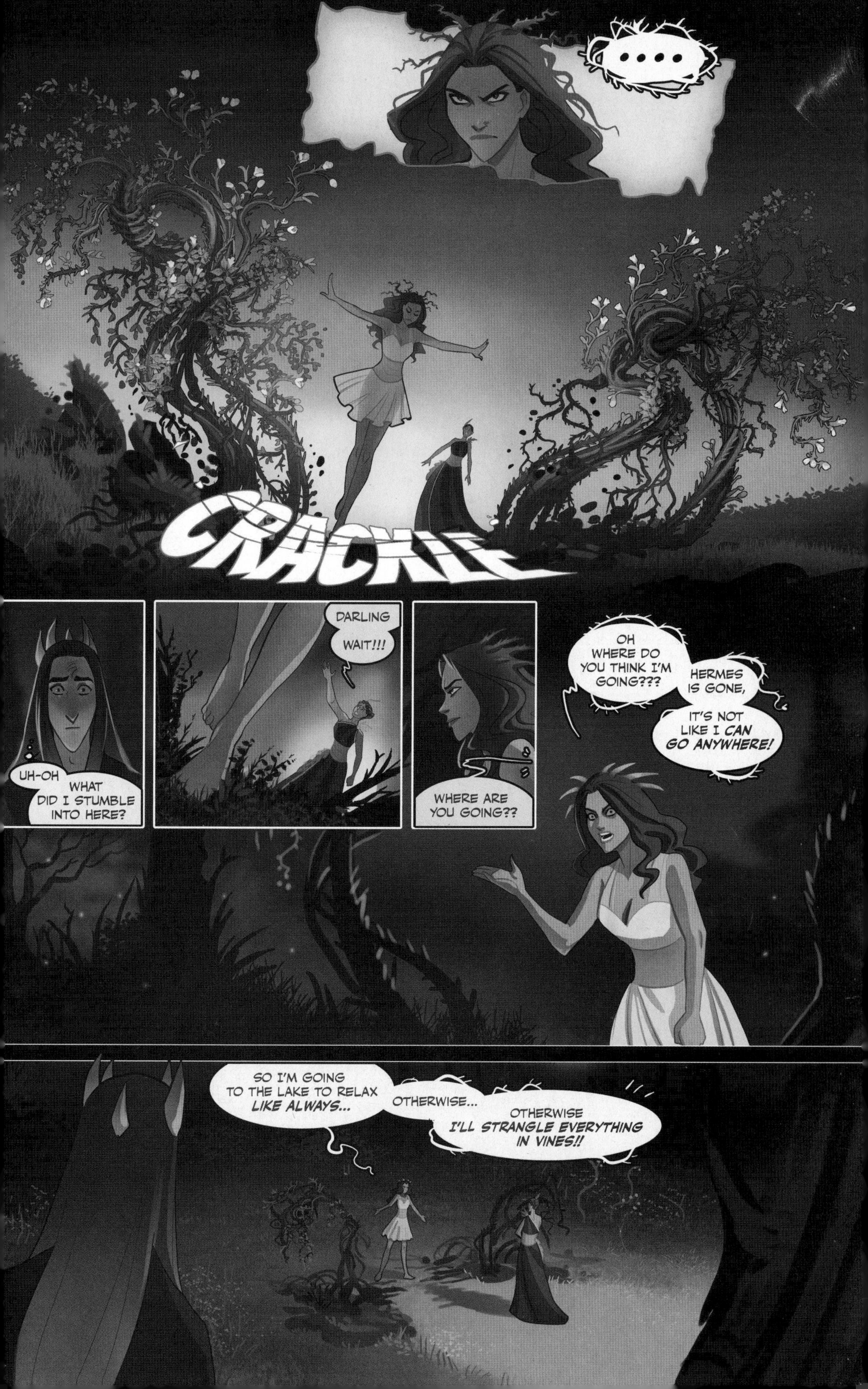
....
CRACKLE
UH-OH
WHAT DID I STUMBLE INTO HERE?
DARLING
WAIT!!!
WHERE ARE YOU GOING??
OH WHERE DO YOU THINK I'M GOING???
HERMES IS GONE,
IT'S NOT LIKE I CAN GO ANYWHERE!
SO I'M GOING TO THE LAKE TO RELAX LIKE ALWAYS...
OTHERWISE...
OTHERWISE I'LL STRANGLE EVERYTHING IN VINES!!

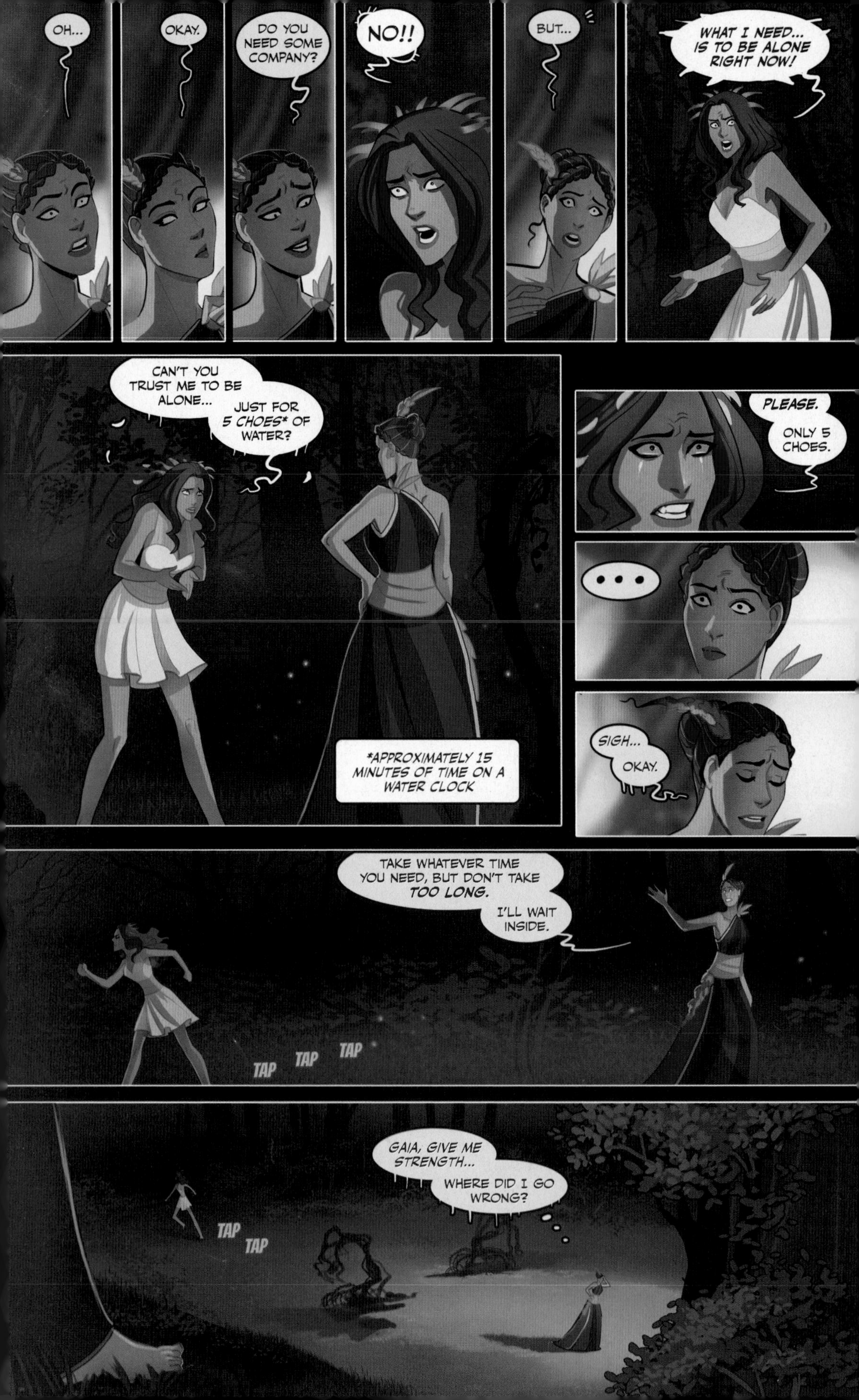
OH...
OKAY.
DO YOU NEED SOME COMPANY?
NO!!
BUT...
WHAT I NEED... IS TO BE ALONE RIGHT NOW!
CAN'T YOU TRUST ME TO BE ALONE...
JUST FOR 5 CHOES* OF WATER?
*APPROXIMATELY 15 MINUTES OF TIME ON A WATER CLOCK
PLEASE.
ONLY 5 CHOES.
...
SIGH...
OKAY.
TAKE WHATEVER TIME YOU NEED, BUT DON'T TAKE TOO LONG.
I'LL WAIT INSIDE.
TAP
TAP
TAP
GAIA, GIVE ME STRENGTH...
WHERE DID I GO WRONG?
TAP
TAP

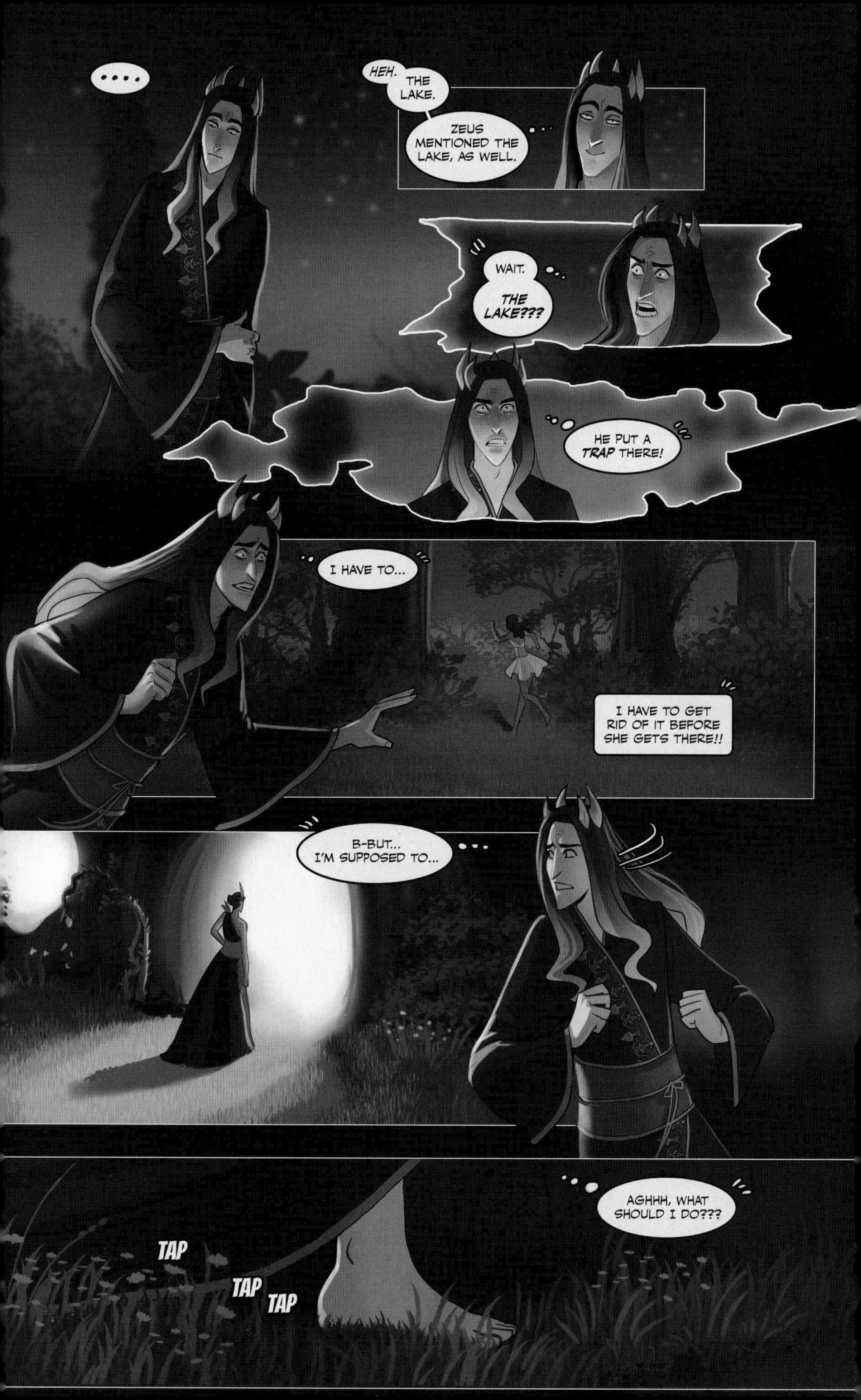
....
HEH. THE LAKE.
ZEUS MENTIONED THE LAKE, AS WELL.
WAIT. THE LAKE???
HE PUT A TRAP THERE!
I HAVE TO...
I HAVE TO GET RID OF IT BEFORE SHE GETS THERE!!
B-BUT... I'M SUPPOSED TO...
AGHHH, WHAT SHOULD I DO???
TAP
TAP
TAP

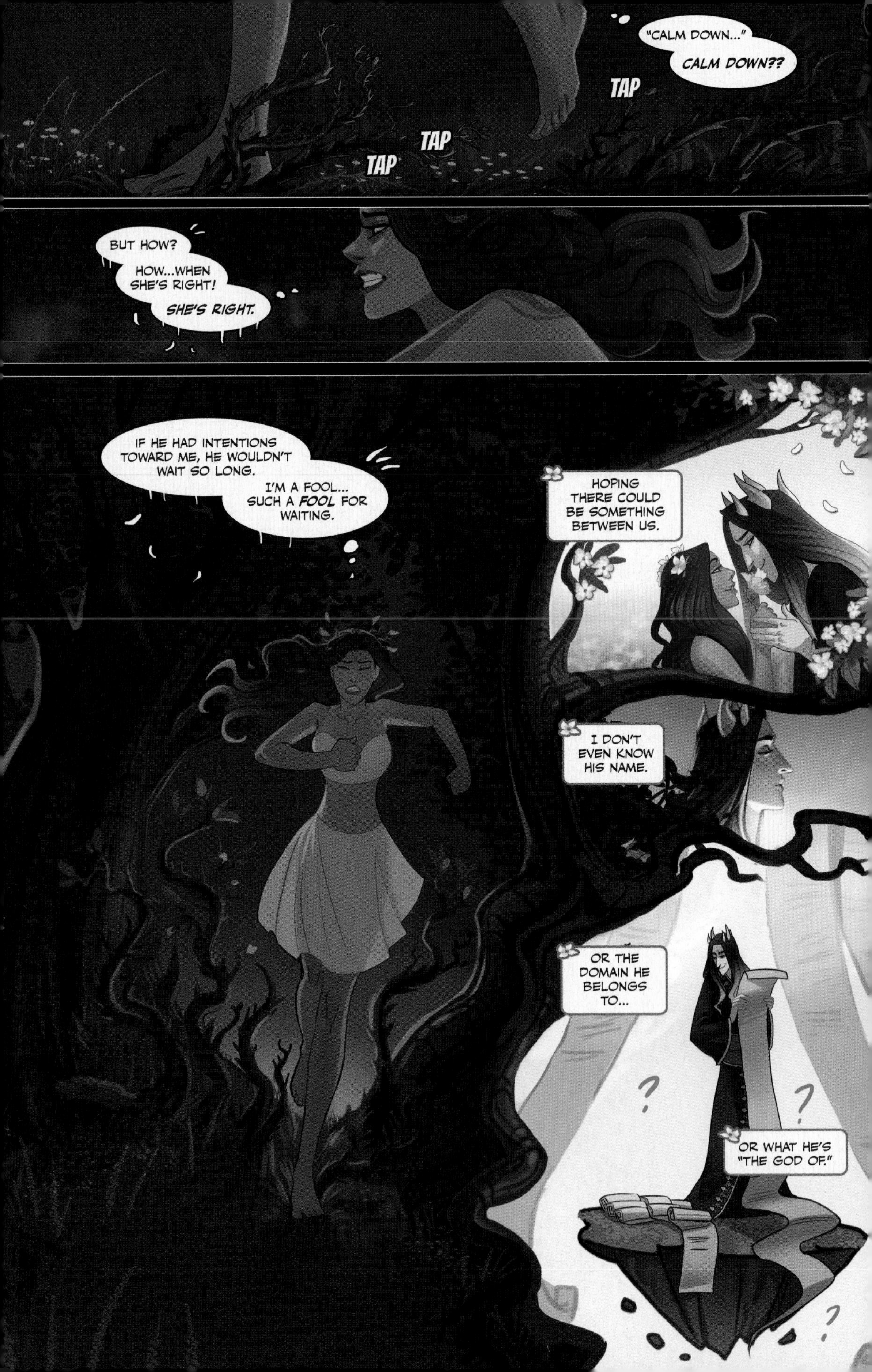
"CALM DOWN..."
CALM DOWN??
TAP
TAP
TAP
BUT HOW?
HOW...WHEN SHE'S RIGHT!
SHE'S RIGHT.
IF HE HAD INTENTIONS TOWARD ME, HE WOULDN'T WAIT SO LONG.
I'M A FOOL... SUCH A FOOL FOR WAITING.
HOPING THERE COULD BE SOMETHING BETWEEN US.
I DON'T EVEN KNOW HIS NAME.
OR THE DOMAIN HE BELONGS TO...
OR WHAT HE'S "THE GOD OF."

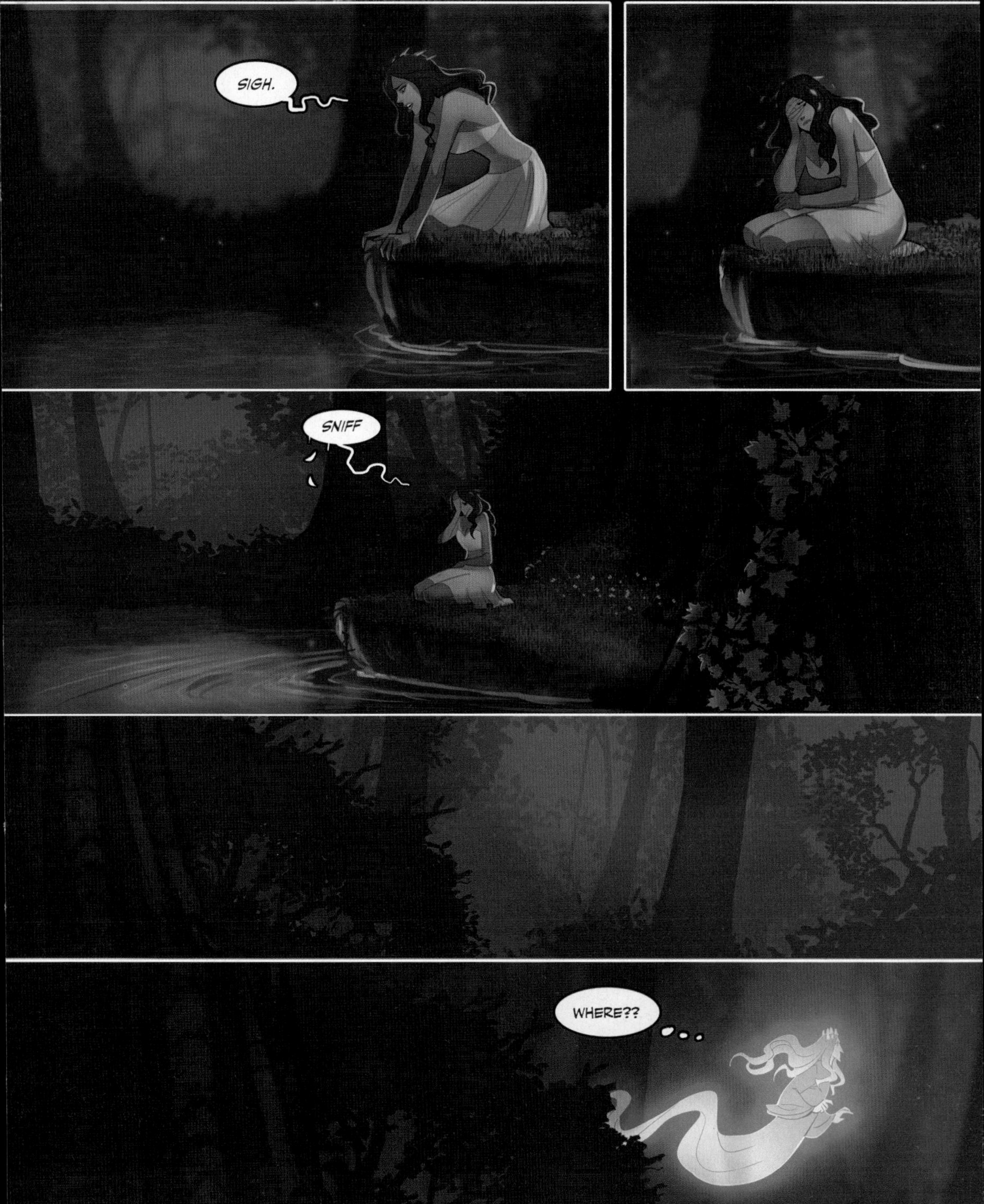
SIGH.
SNIFF
WHERE??

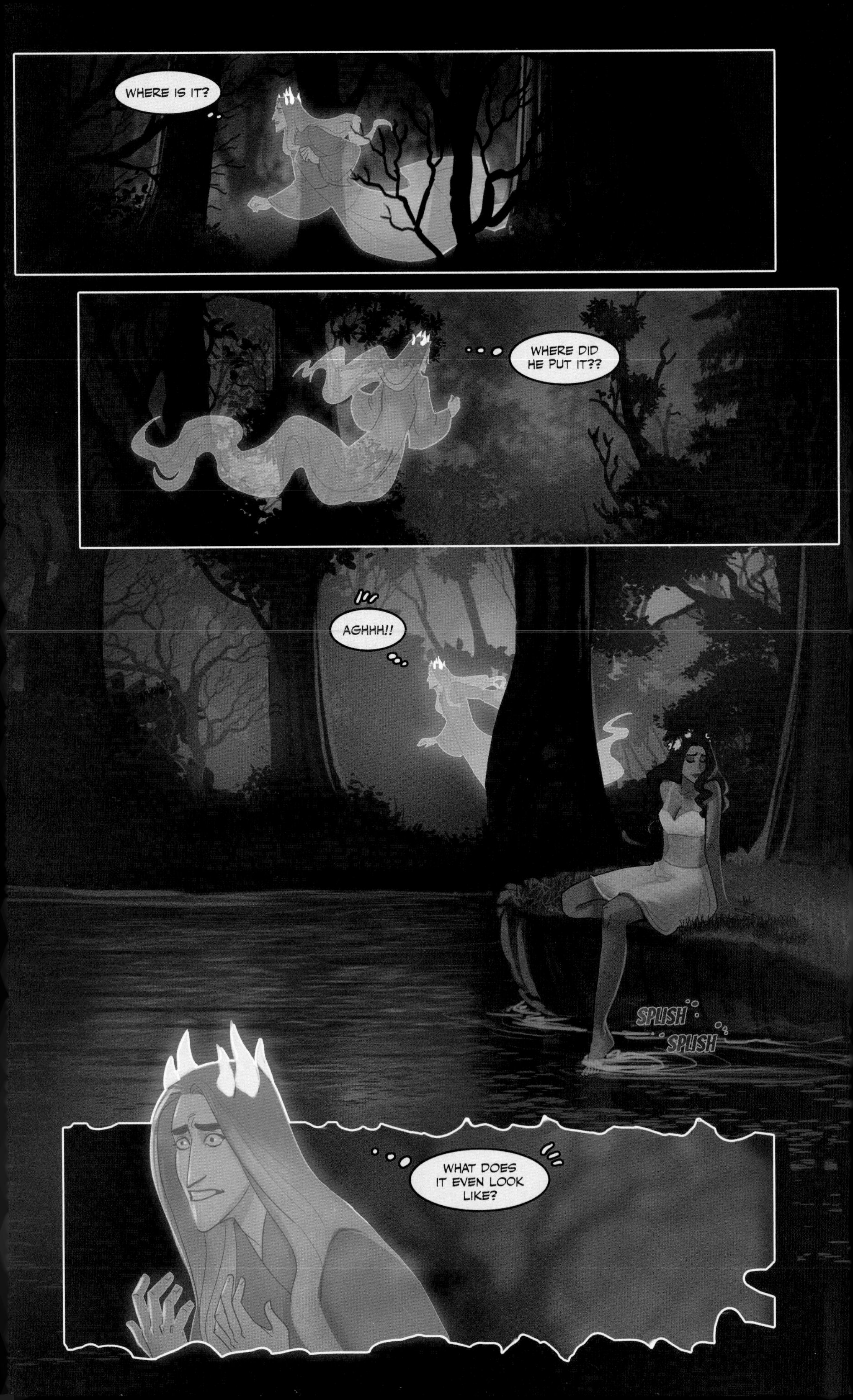
WHERE IS IT?
WHERE DID HE PUT IT??
AGHHH!!
SPLISH
SPLISH
WHAT DOES IT EVEN LOOK LIKE?

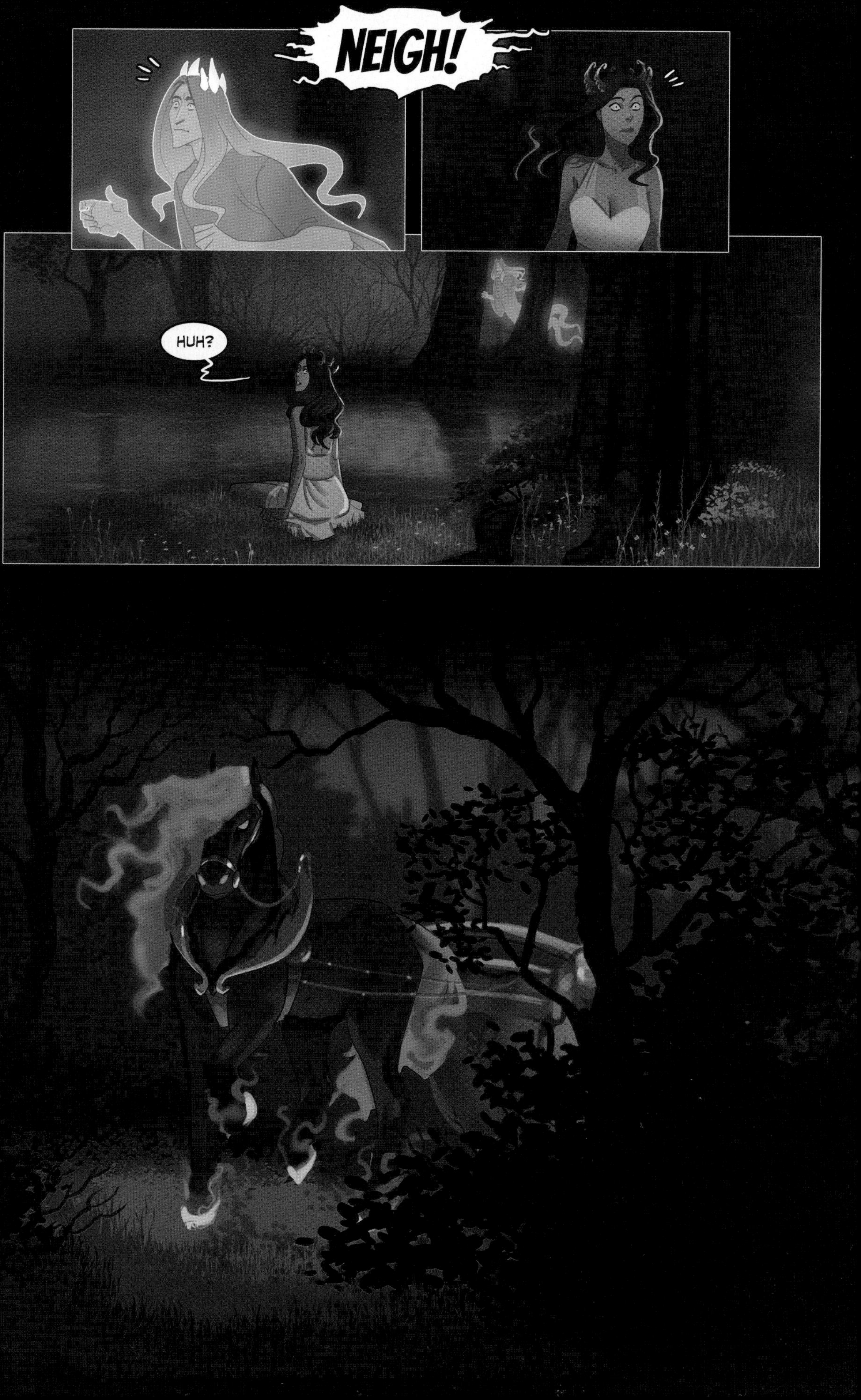
NEIGH!
HUH?

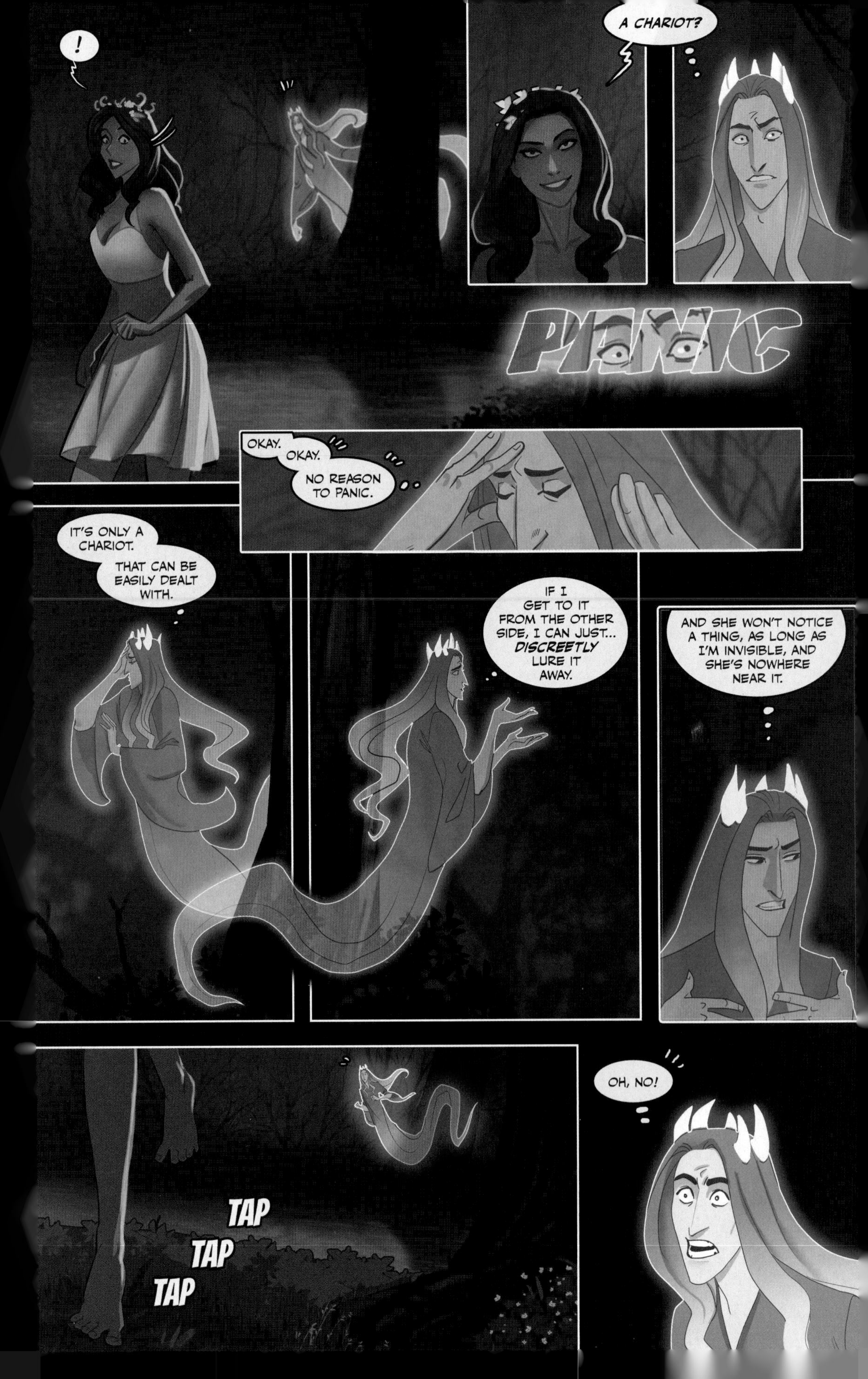

!
A CHARIOT?
PANIC
OKAY.
OKAY.
NO REASON TO PANIC.
IT'S ONLY A CHARIOT.
THAT CAN BE EASILY DEALT WITH.
IF I GET TO IT FROM THE OTHER SIDE, I CAN JUST... *DISCREETLY* LURE IT AWAY.
AND SHE WON'T NOTICE A THING, AS LONG AS I'M INVISIBLE, AND SHE'S NOWHERE NEAR IT.
OH, NO!
TAP
TAP
TAP

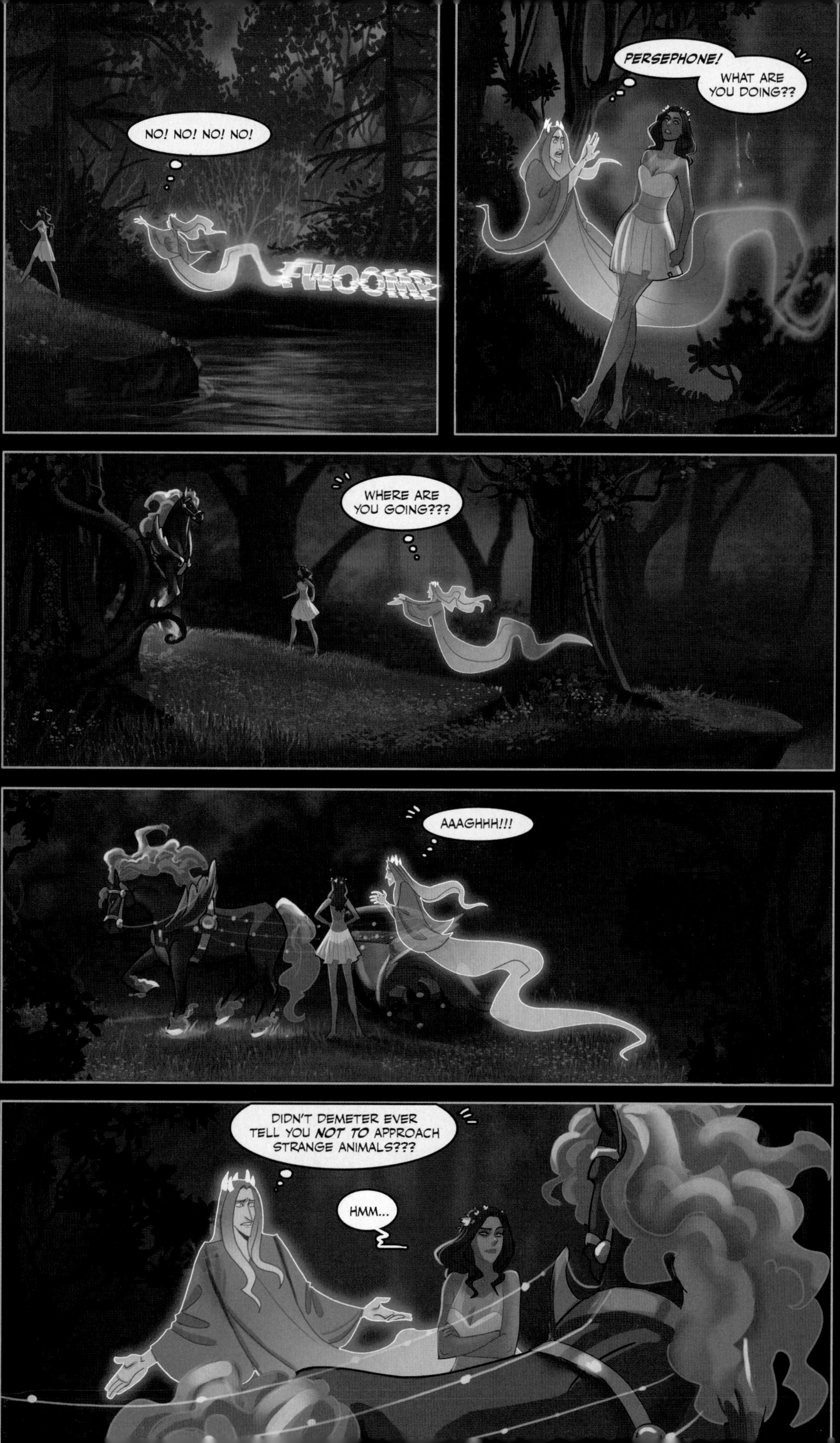
NO! NO! NO! NO!
FWOOMP
PERSEPHONE!
WHAT ARE YOU DOING??
WHERE ARE YOU GOING???
AAAGHHH!!!
DIDN'T DEMETER EVER TELL YOU NOT TO APPROACH STRANGE ANIMALS???
HMM...

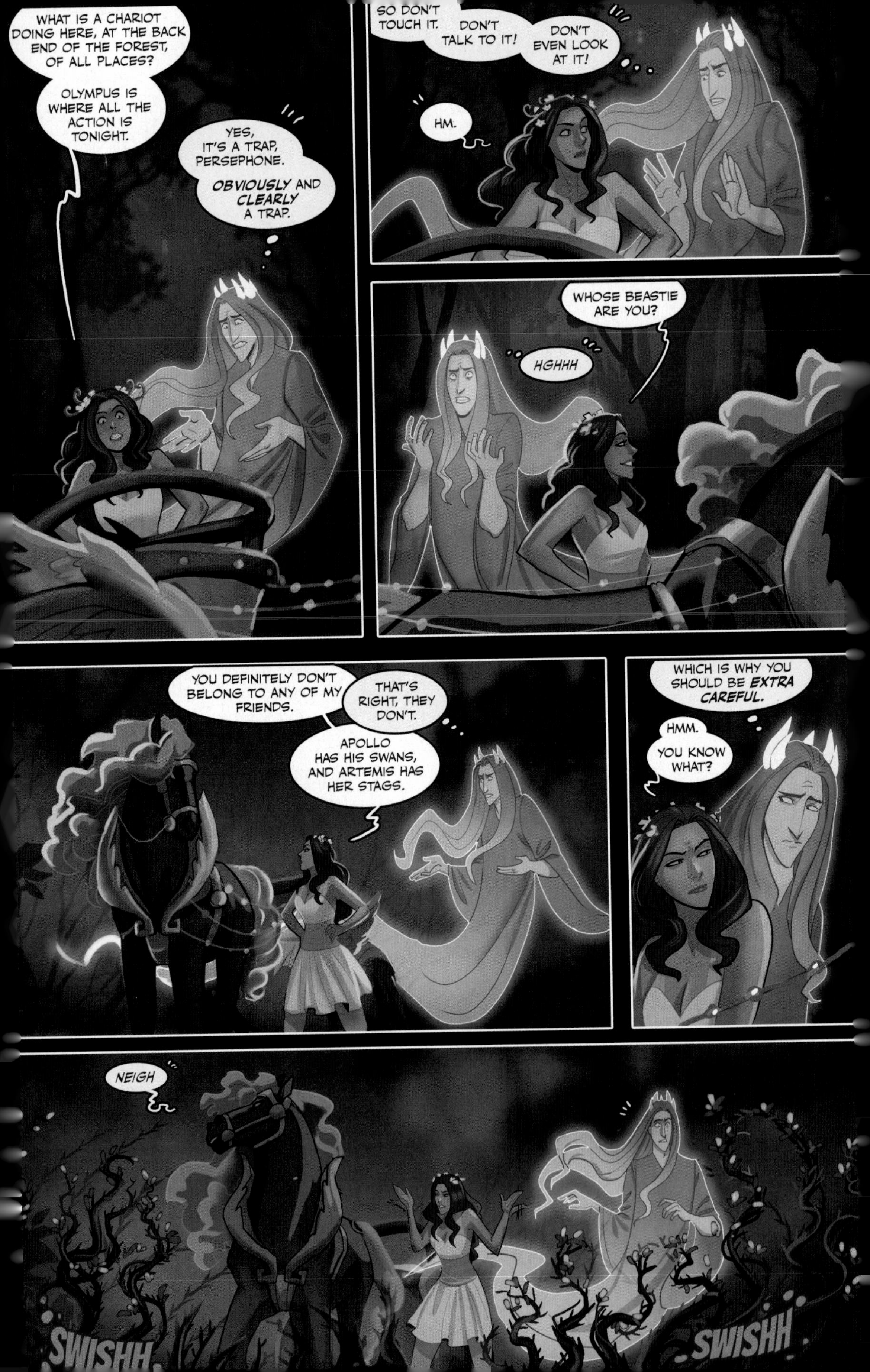
WHAT IS A CHARIOT DOING HERE, AT THE BACK END OF THE FOREST, OF ALL PLACES?
OLYMPUS IS WHERE ALL THE ACTION IS TONIGHT.
YES, IT'S A TRAP, PERSEPHONE.
OBVIOUSLY AND CLEARLY A TRAP.
SO DON'T TOUCH IT.
DON'T TALK TO IT!
DON'T EVEN LOOK AT IT!
HM.
WHOSE BEASTIE ARE YOU?
HGHHH
YOU DEFINITELY DON'T BELONG TO ANY OF MY FRIENDS.
THAT'S RIGHT, THEY DON'T.
APOLLO HAS HIS SWANS, AND ARTEMIS HAS HER STAGS.
WHICH IS WHY YOU SHOULD BE EXTRA CAREFUL.
HMM.
YOU KNOW WHAT?
NEIGH
SWISHH
SWISHH

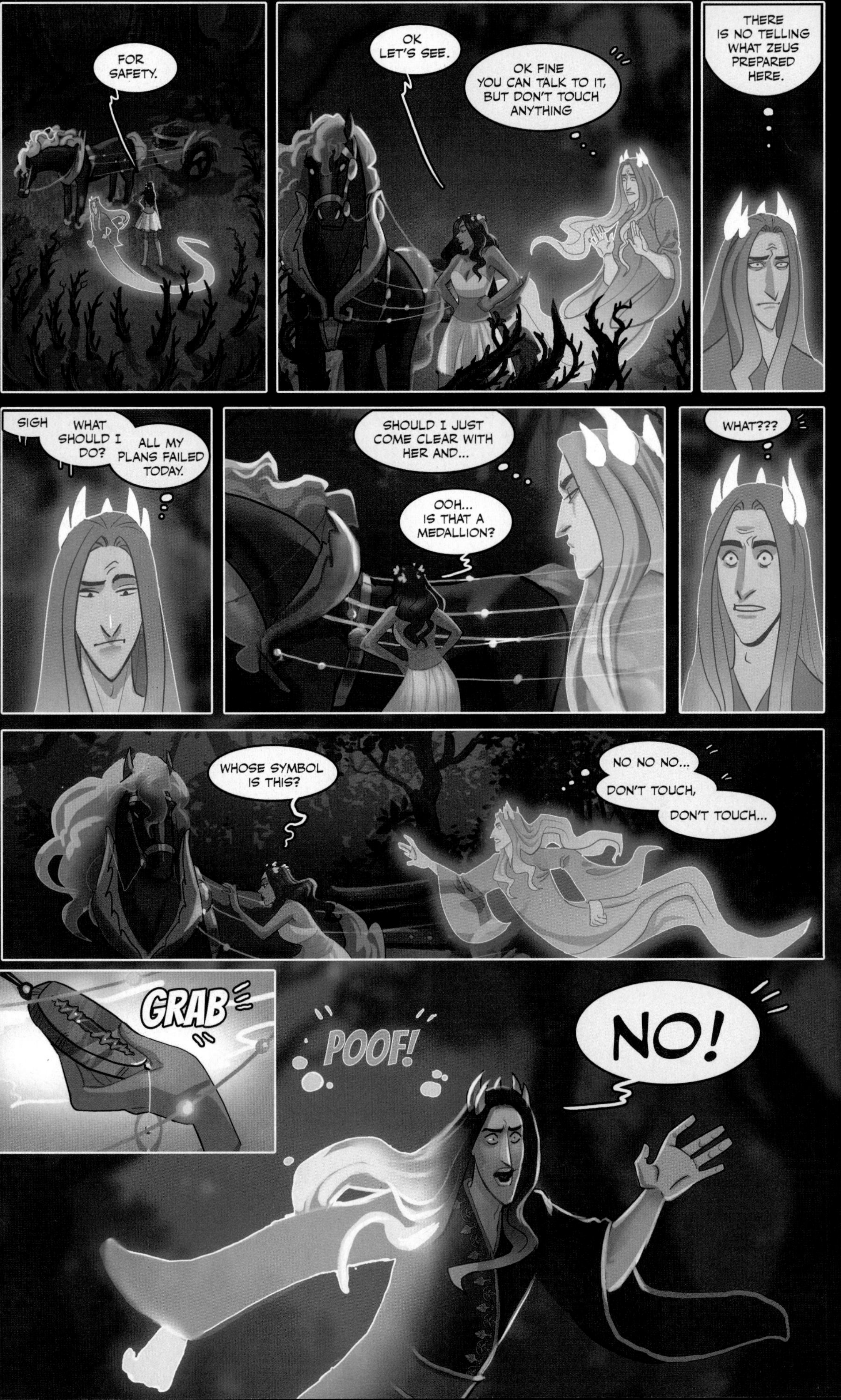

FOR SAFETY.
OK LET'S SEE.
OK FINE YOU CAN TALK TO IT, BUT DON'T TOUCH ANYTHING
THERE IS NO TELLING WHAT ZEUS PREPARED HERE.
SIGH
WHAT SHOULD I DO?
ALL MY PLANS FAILED TODAY.
SHOULD I JUST COME CLEAR WITH HER AND...
OOH... IS THAT A MEDALLION?
WHAT???
WHOSE SYMBOL IS THIS?
NO NO NO...
DON'T TOUCH,
DON'T TOUCH...
GRAB
POOF!
NO!

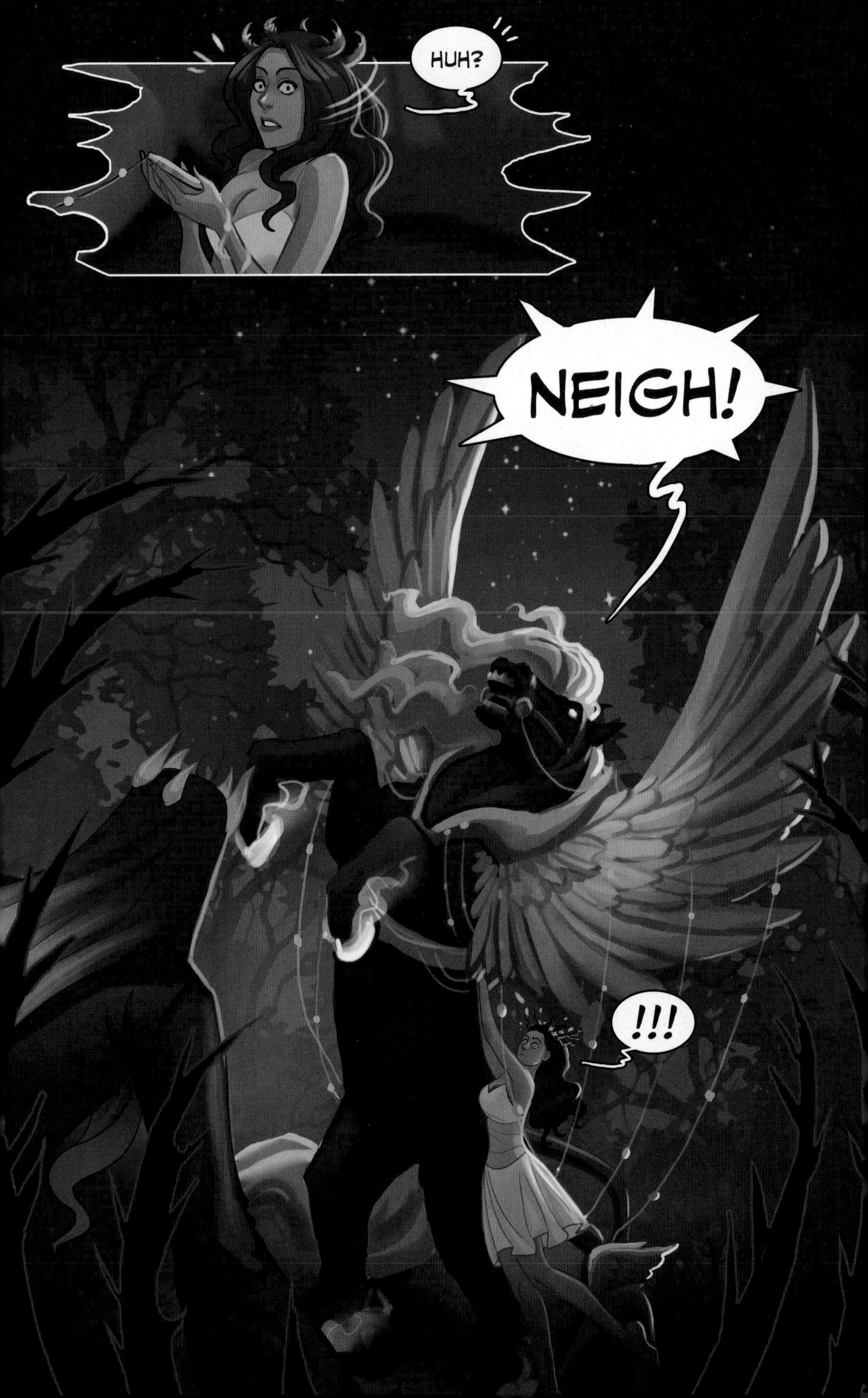
HUH?
NEIGH!
!!!

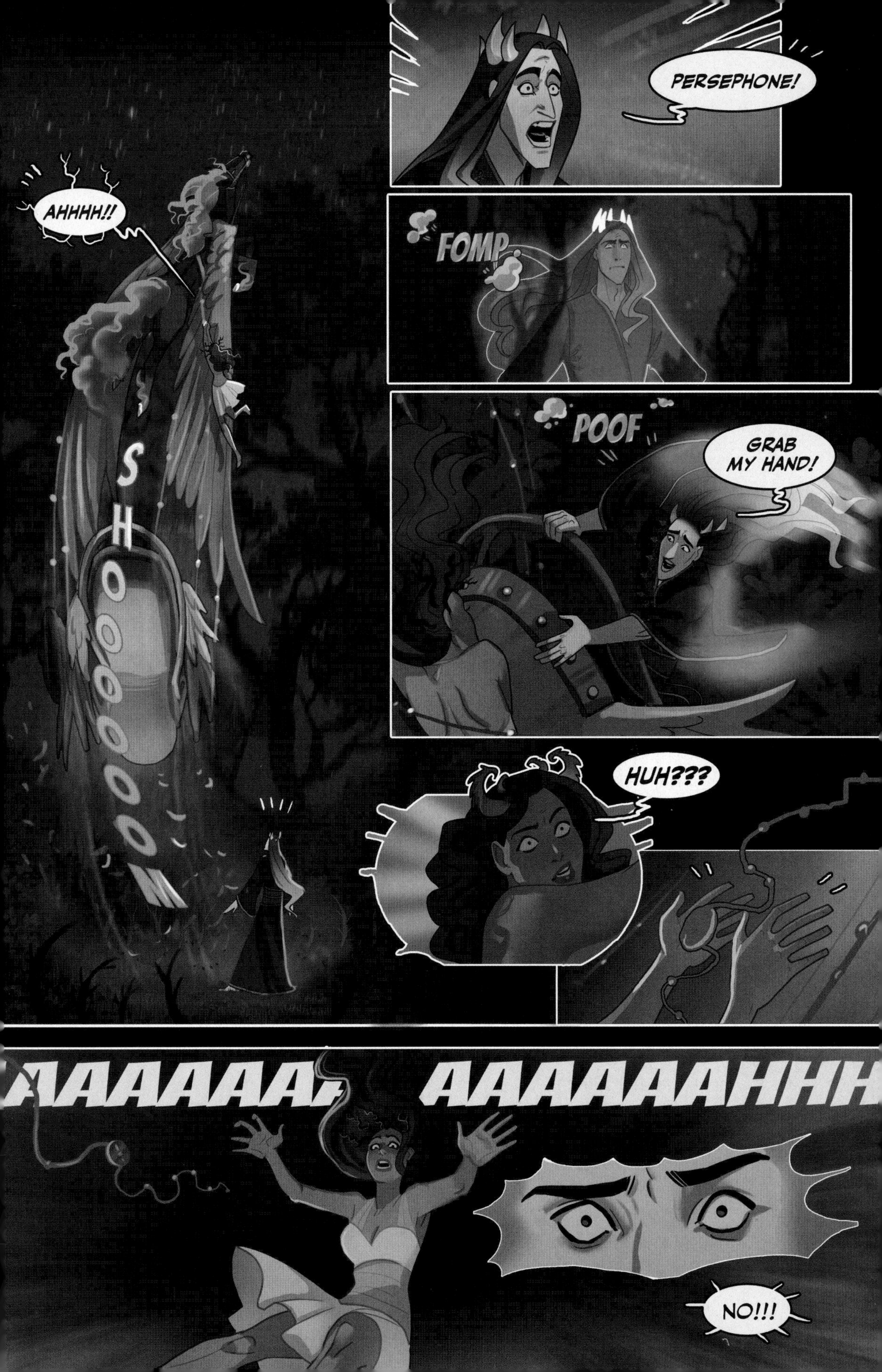
PERSEPHONE!
AHHHH!!
SHOOOOOOOO
FOMP
POOF
GRAB MY HAND!
HUH???
AAAAAA
AAAAAAAHHH
NO!!!

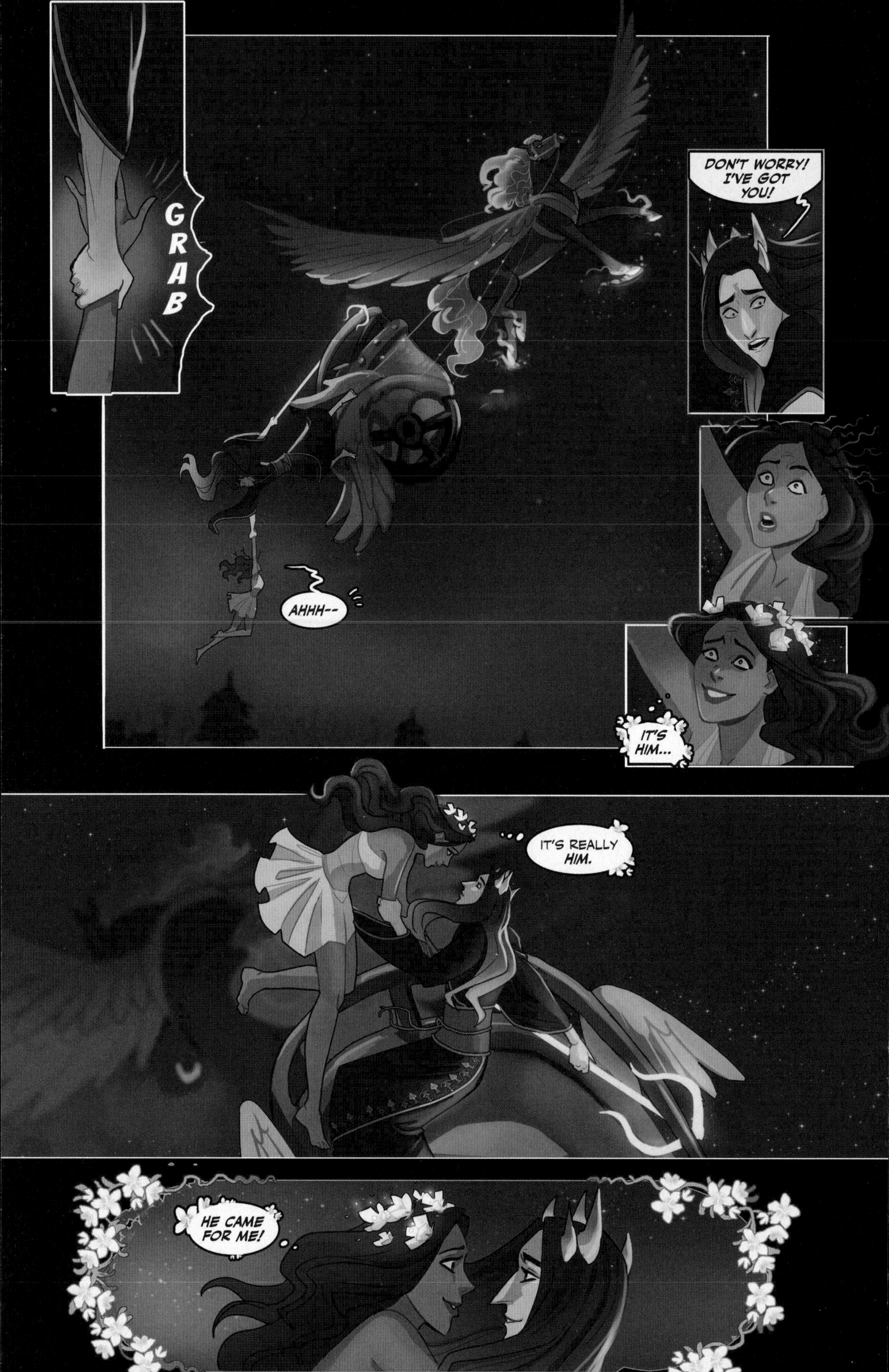
GRAB
DON'T WORRY! I'VE GOT YOU!
AHHH--
IT'S HIM...
IT'S REALLY HIM.
HE CAME FOR ME!

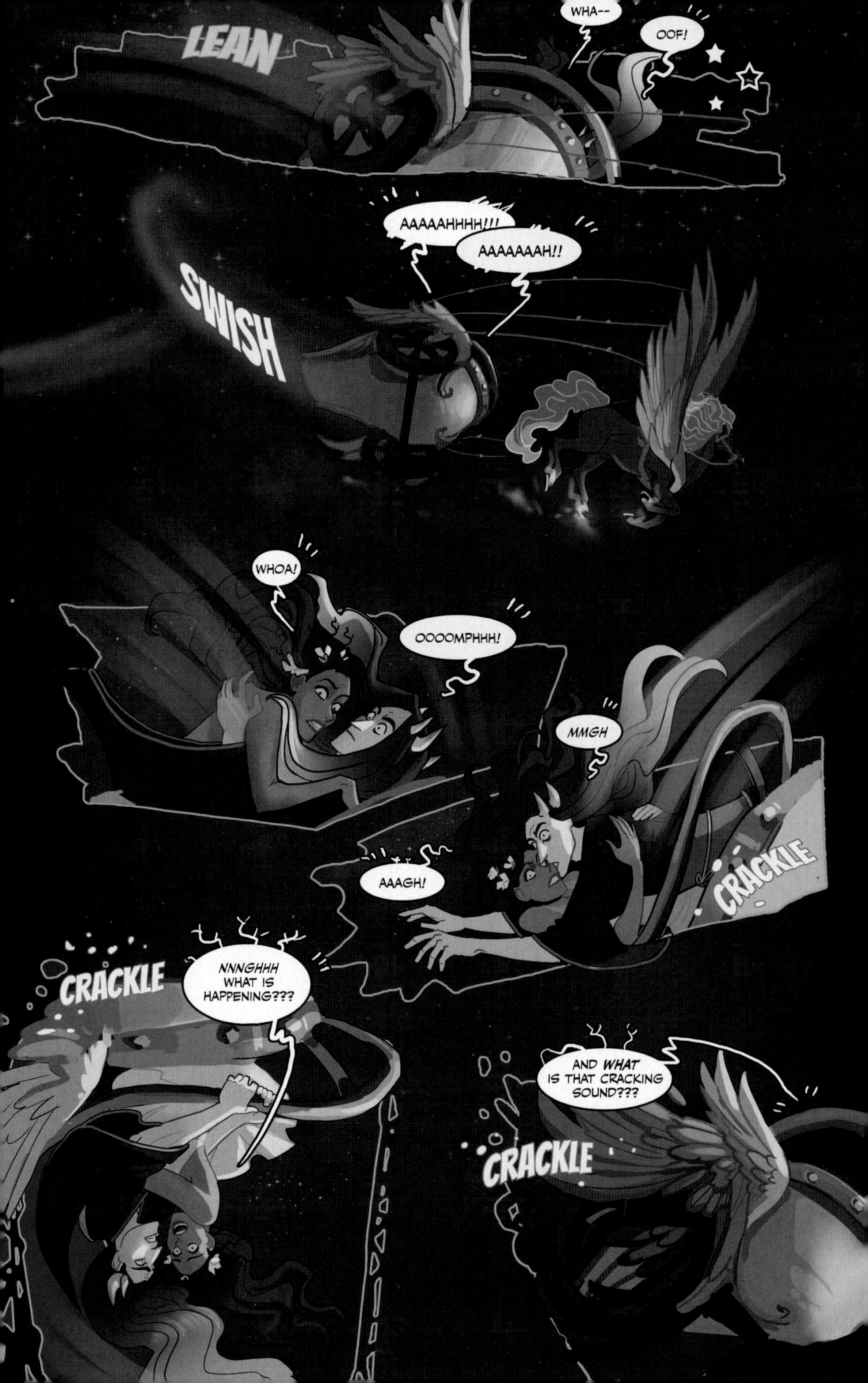
LEAN
WHA--
OOF!
SWISH
AAAAAHHHH!!!
AAAAAAAH!!
WHOA!
OOOOMPHHH!
MMGH
AAAGH!
CRACKLE
CRACKLE
NNNGHHH WHAT IS HAPPENING???
AND WHAT IS THAT CRACKING SOUND???
CRACKLE

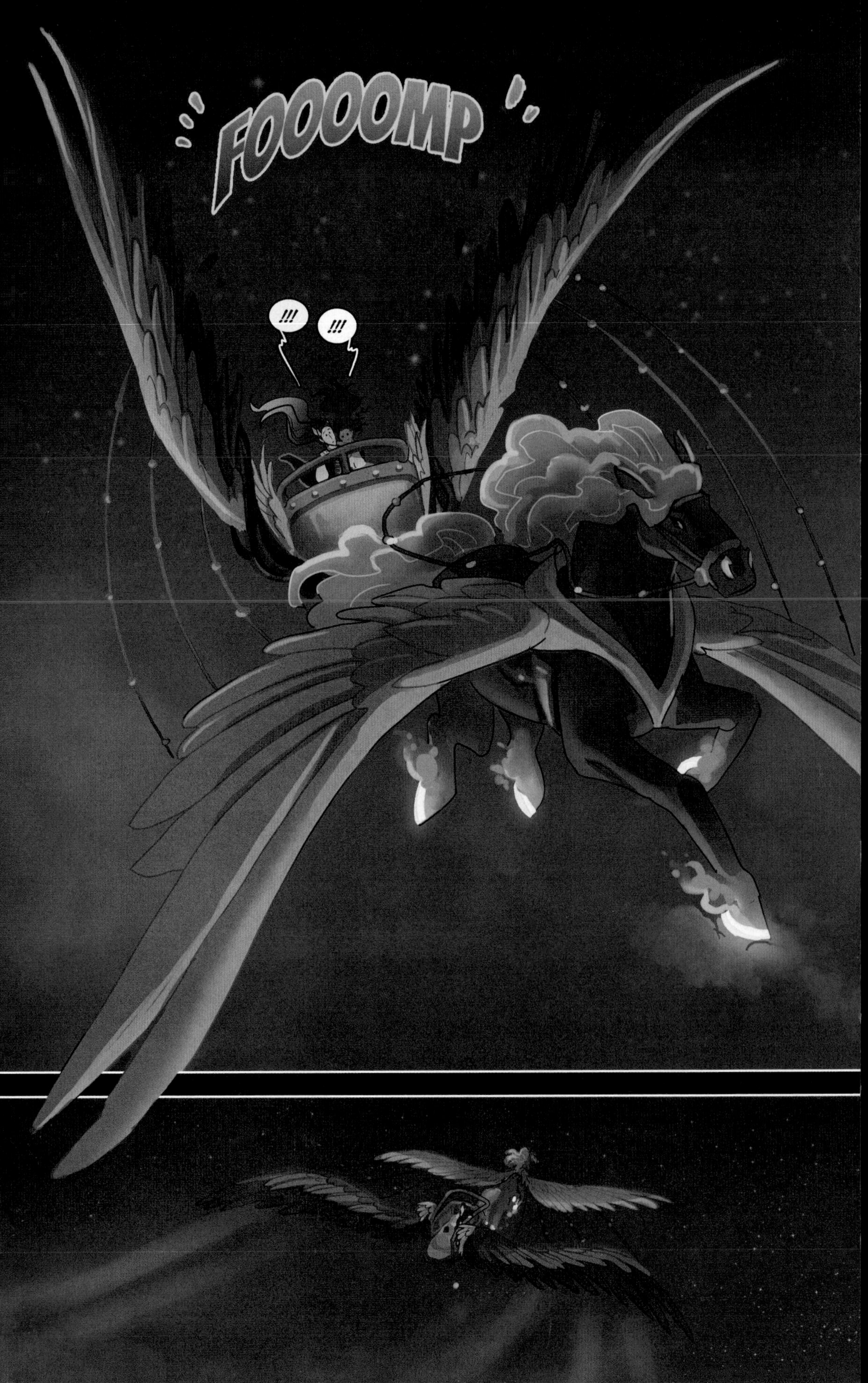
FOOOOMP
!!!
!!!

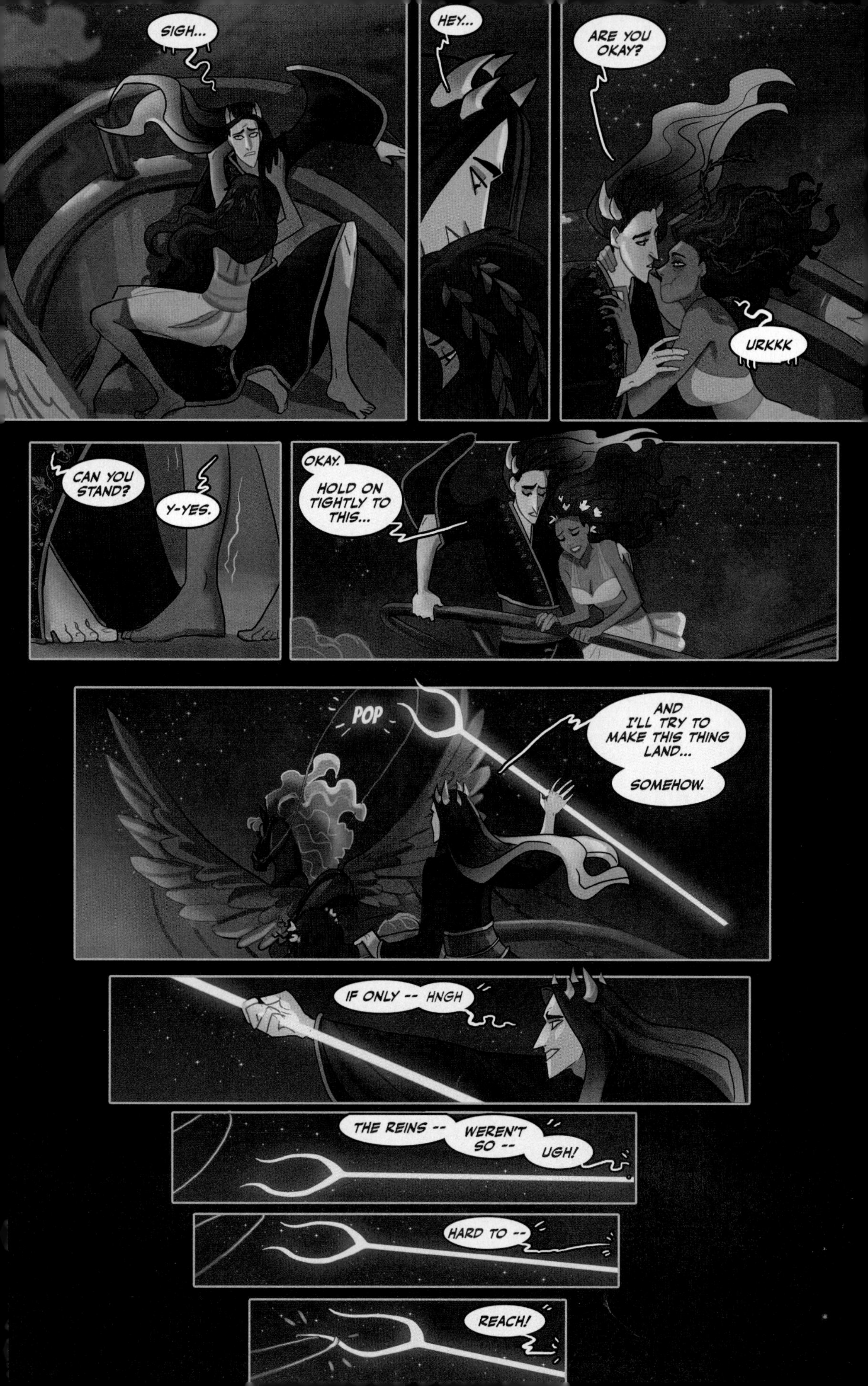
SIGH...
HEY...
ARE YOU OKAY?
URKKK
CAN YOU STAND?
Y-YES.
OKAY.
HOLD ON TIGHTLY TO THIS...
POP
AND I'LL TRY TO MAKE THIS THING LAND...
SOMEHOW.
IF ONLY -- HNGH
THE REINS --
WEREN'T SO --
UGH!
HARD TO --
REACH!

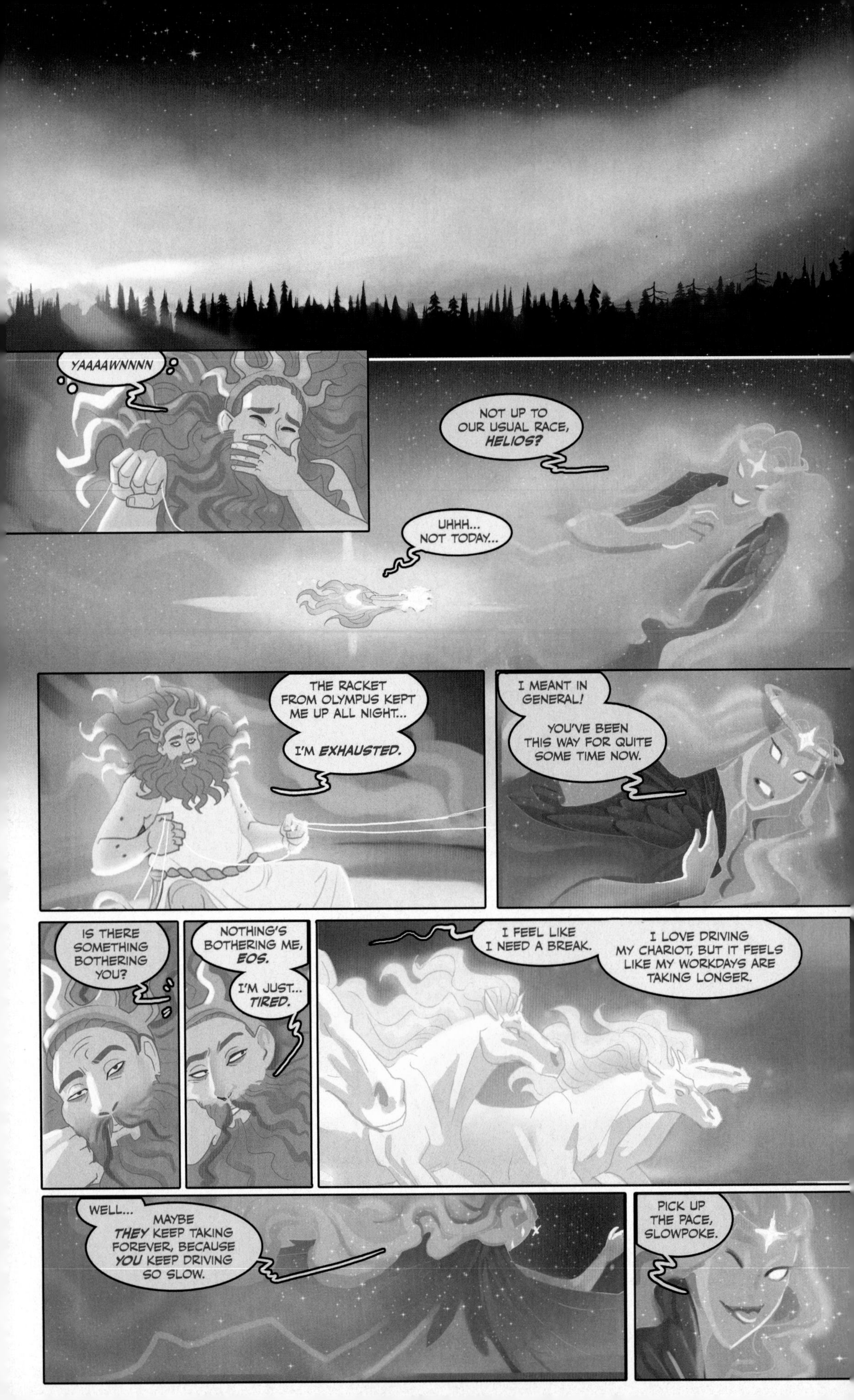
YAAAAWNNNN
NOT UP TO OUR USUAL RACE, HELIOS?
UHHH... NOT TODAY...
THE RACKET FROM OLYMPUS KEPT ME UP ALL NIGHT...
I'M EXHAUSTED.
I MEANT IN GENERAL!
YOU'VE BEEN THIS WAY FOR QUITE SOME TIME NOW.
IS THERE SOMETHING BOTHERING YOU?
NOTHING'S BOTHERING ME, EOS.
I'M JUST... TIRED.
I FEEL LIKE I NEED A BREAK.
I LOVE DRIVING MY CHARIOT, BUT IT FEELS LIKE MY WORKDAYS ARE TAKING LONGER.
WELL...
MAYBE THEY KEEP TAKING FOREVER, BECAUSE YOU KEEP DRIVING SO SLOW.
PICK UP THE PACE, SLOWPOKE.

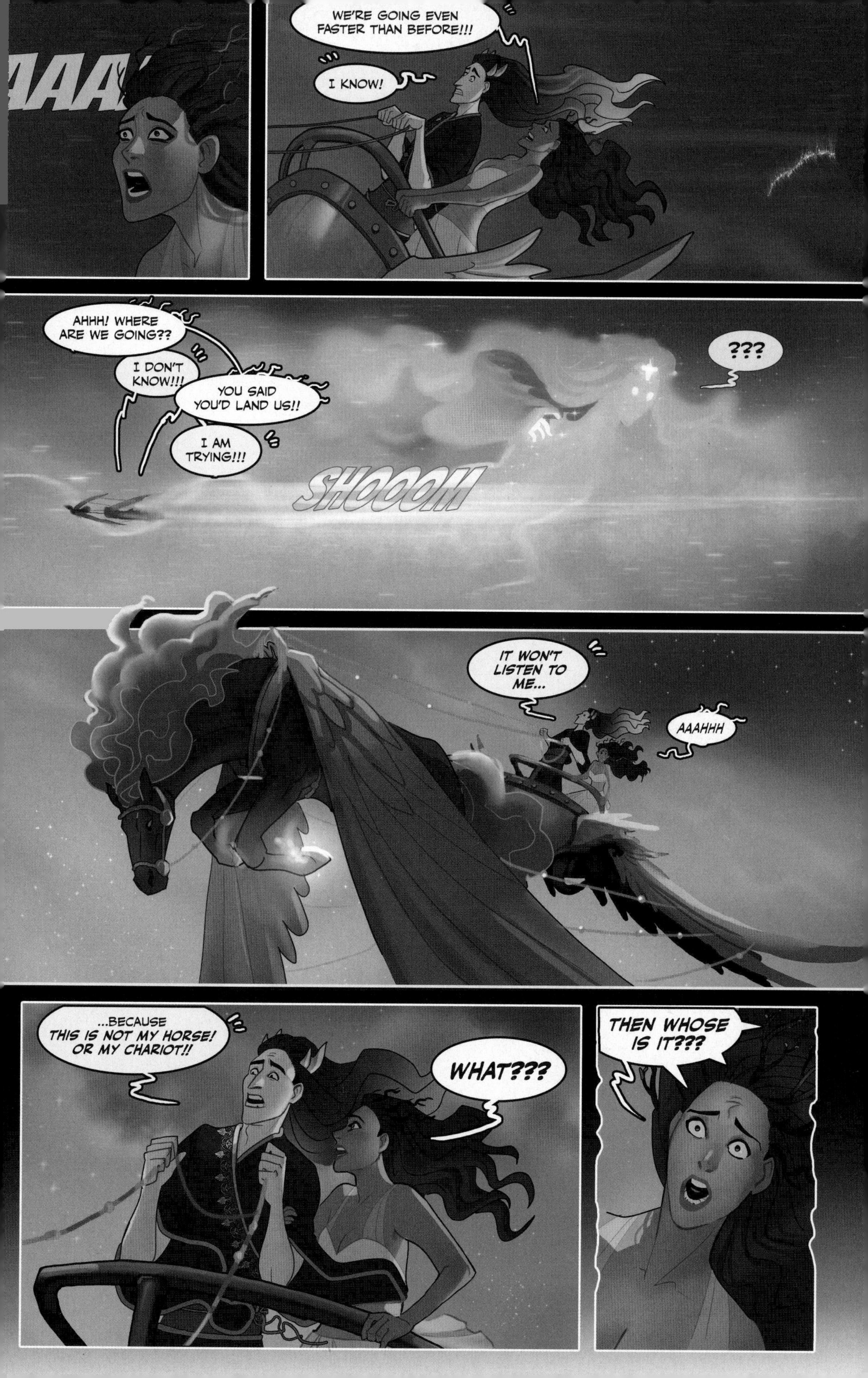
AAAA
WE'RE GOING EVEN FASTER THAN BEFORE!!!
I KNOW!
AHHH! WHERE ARE WE GOING??
I DON'T KNOW!!!
YOU SAID YOU'D LAND US!!
I AM TRYING!!!
???
SHOOOM
IT WON'T LISTEN TO ME...
AAAHHH
...BECAUSE THIS IS NOT MY HORSE! OR MY CHARIOT!!
WHAT???
THEN WHOSE IS IT???

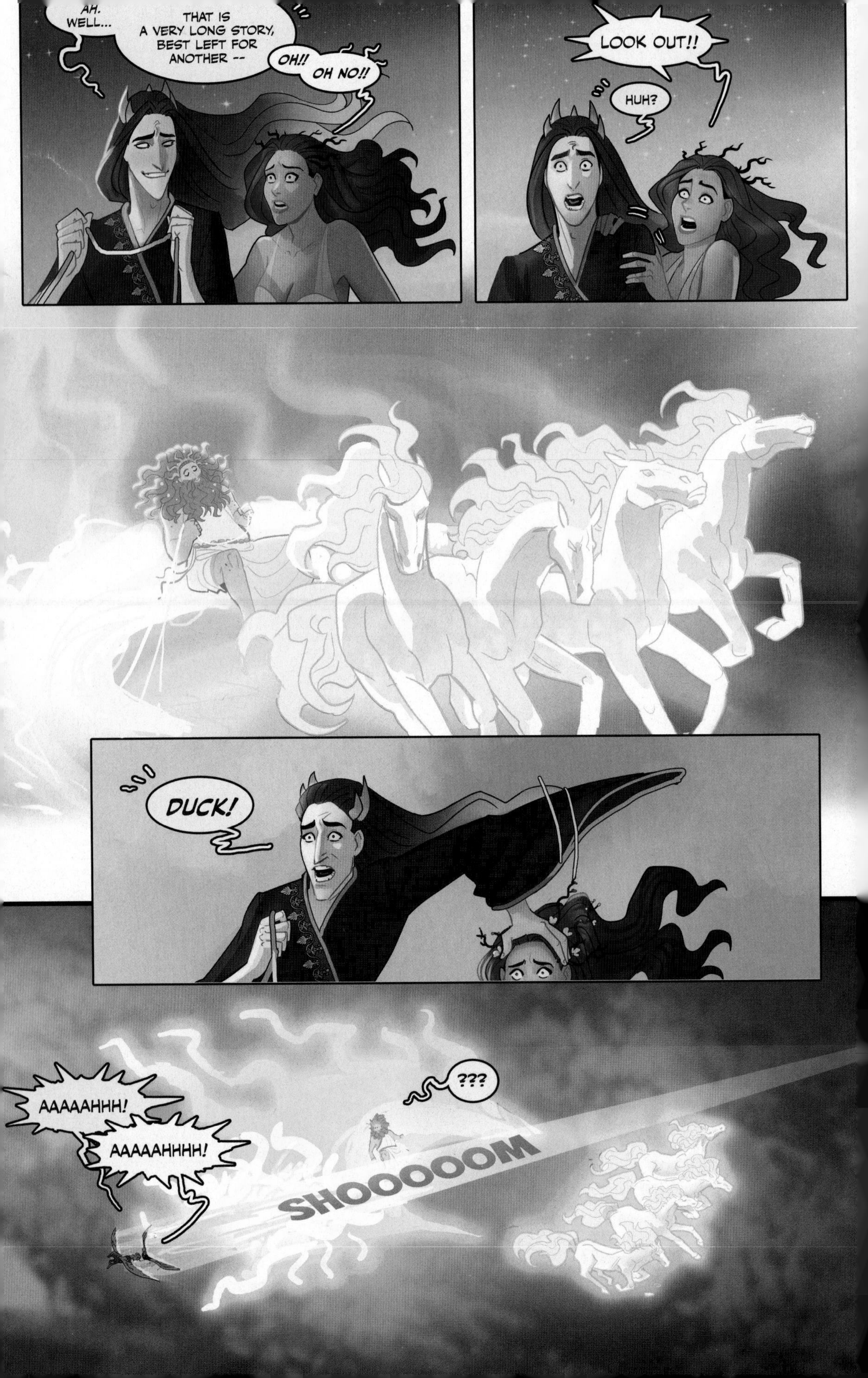
AH. WELL...
THAT IS A VERY LONG STORY, BEST LEFT FOR ANOTHER --
OH!!
OH NO!!
LOOK OUT!!
HUH?
DUCK!
???
AAAAAHHH!
AAAAAHHHH!
SHOOOOOOM

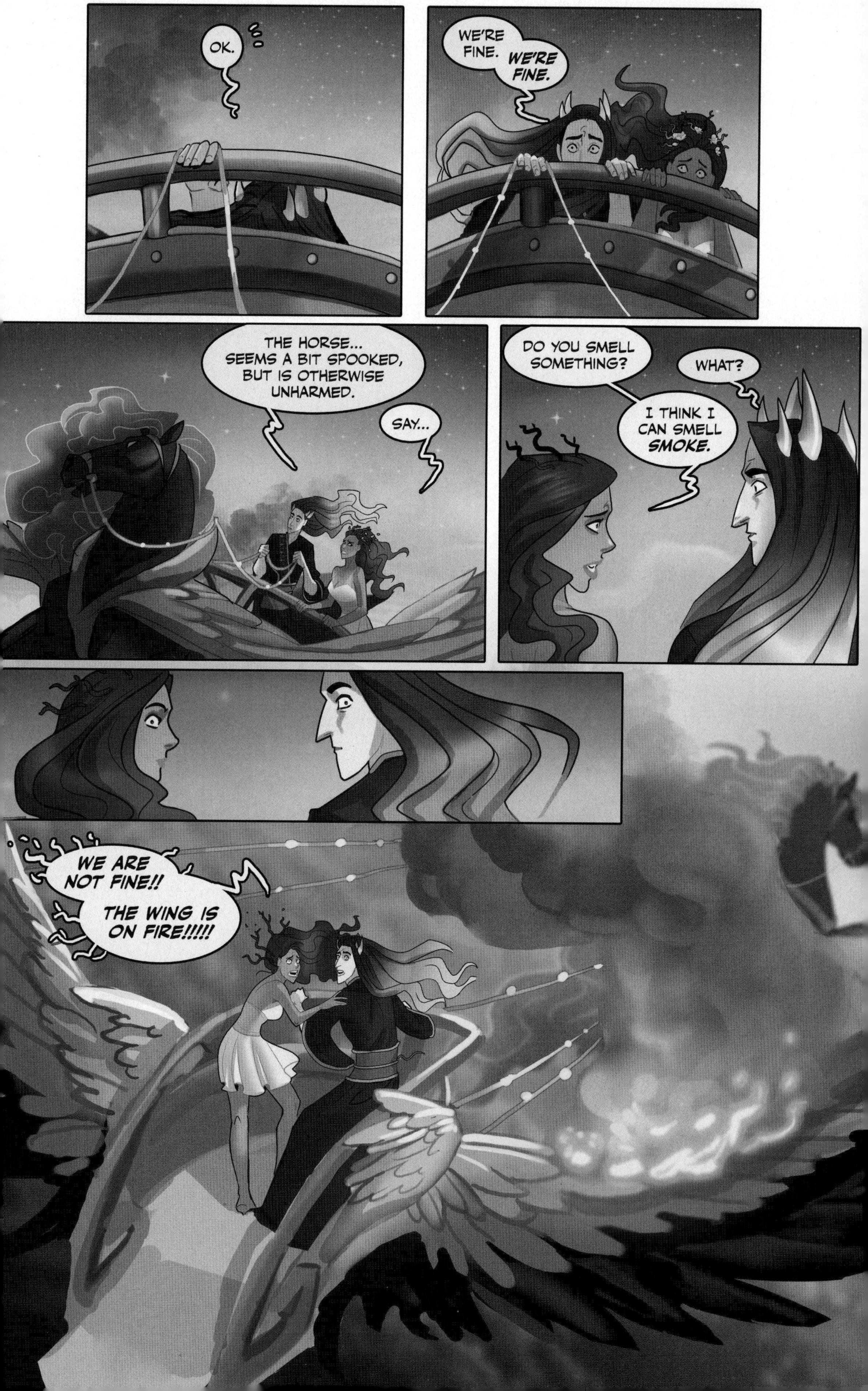
OK.
WE'RE FINE.
WE'RE FINE.
THE HORSE... SEEMS A BIT SPOOKED, BUT IS OTHERWISE UNHARMED.
SAY...
DO YOU SMELL SOMETHING?
WHAT?
I THINK I CAN SMELL SMOKE.
WE ARE NOT FINE!!
THE WING IS ON FIRE!!!!!

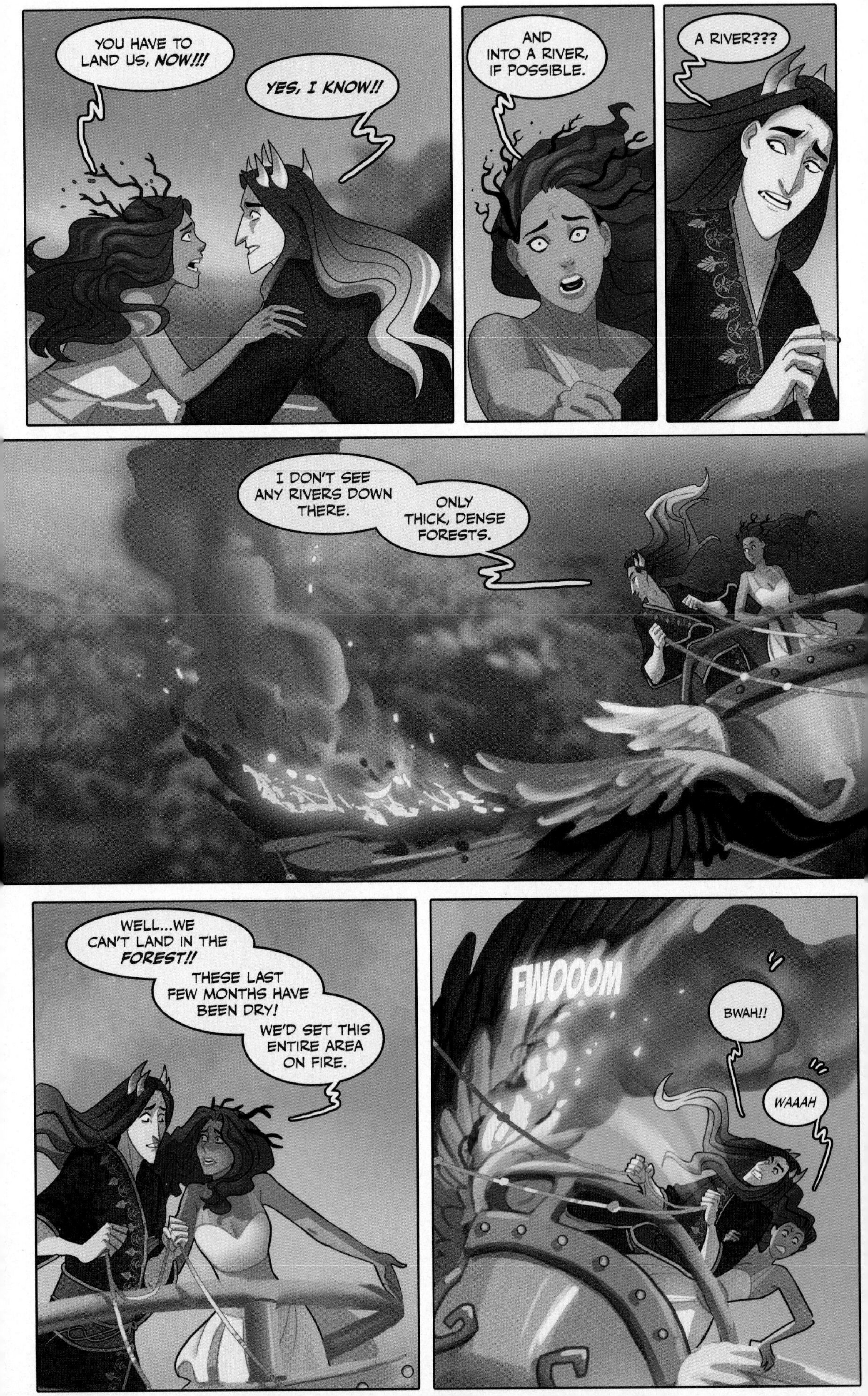
YOU HAVE TO LAND US, NOW!!!
YES, I KNOW!!
AND INTO A RIVER, IF POSSIBLE.
A RIVER???
I DON'T SEE ANY RIVERS DOWN THERE.
ONLY THICK, DENSE FORESTS.
WELL...WE CAN'T LAND IN THE FOREST!!
THESE LAST FEW MONTHS HAVE BEEN DRY!
WE'D SET THIS ENTIRE AREA ON FIRE.
FWOOOM
BWAH!!
WAAAH

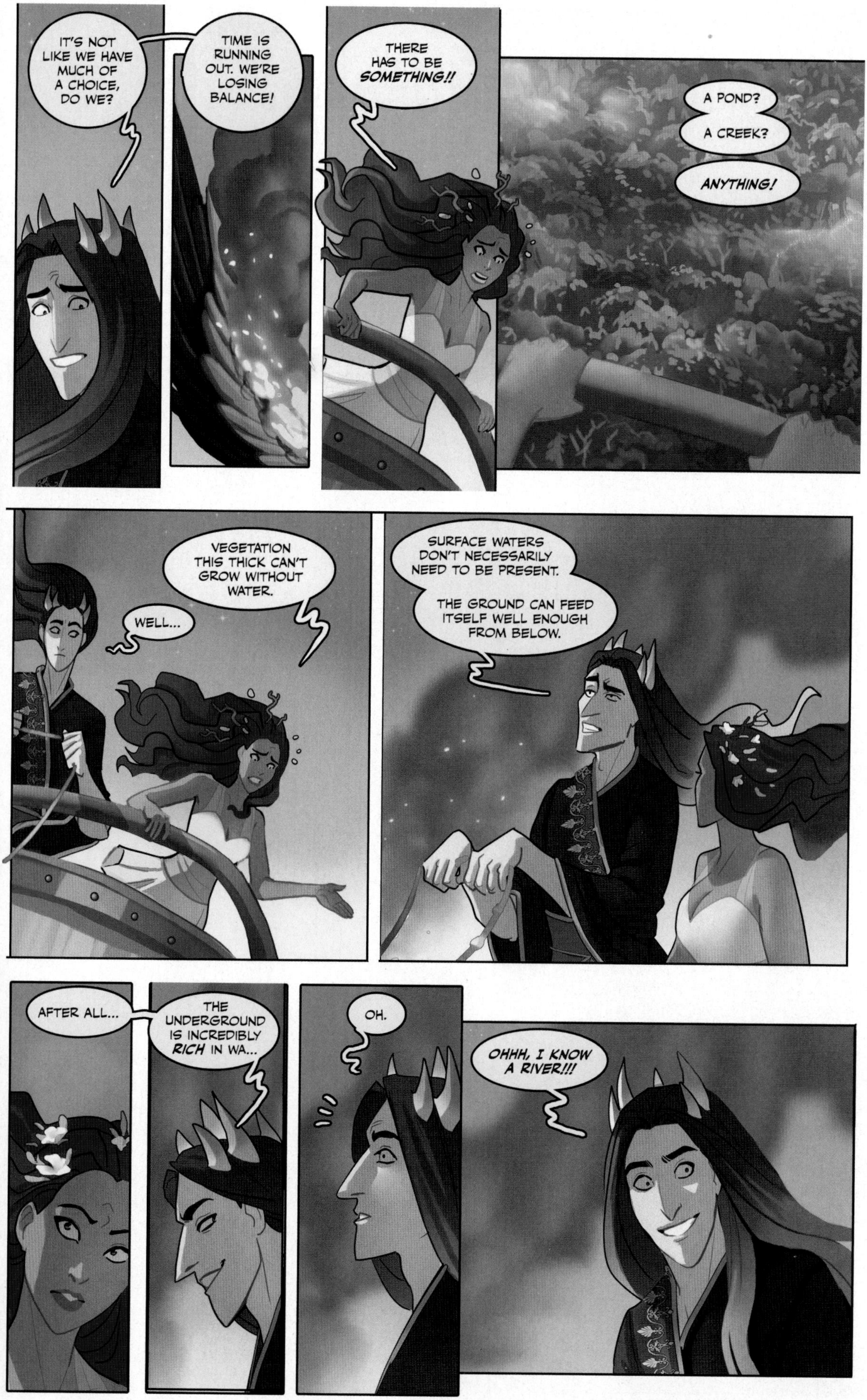
IT'S NOT LIKE WE HAVE MUCH OF A CHOICE, DO WE?
TIME IS RUNNING OUT. WE'RE LOSING BALANCE!
THERE HAS TO BE *SOMETHING!!*
A POND?
A CREEK?
ANYTHING!
VEGETATION THIS THICK CAN'T GROW WITHOUT WATER.
WELL...
SURFACE WATERS DON'T NECESSARILY NEED TO BE PRESENT.
THE GROUND CAN FEED ITSELF WELL ENOUGH FROM BELOW.
AFTER ALL...
THE UNDERGROUND IS INCREDIBLY *RICH* IN WA...
OH.
OHHH, I KNOW A RIVER!!!

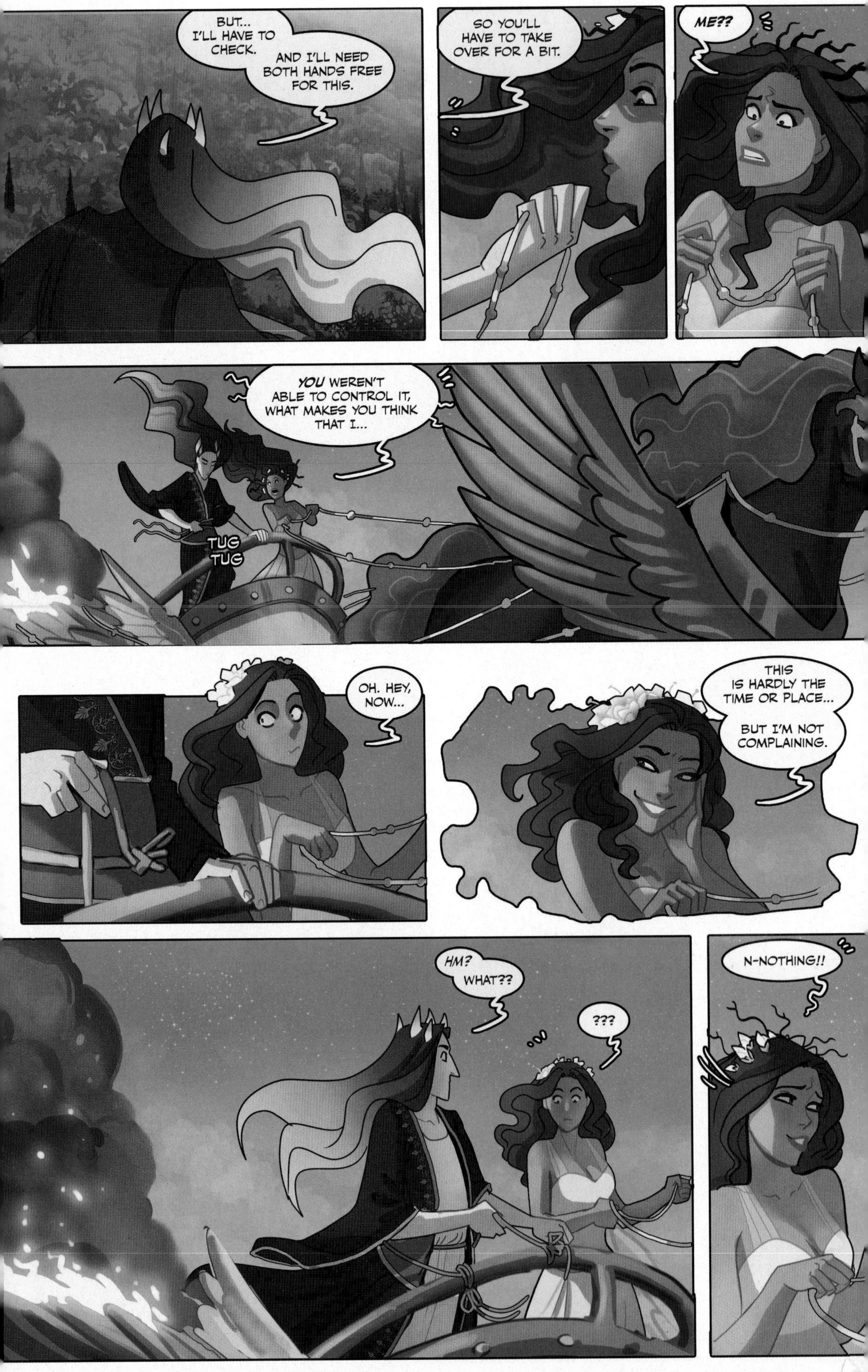
BUT... I'LL HAVE TO CHECK.
AND I'LL NEED BOTH HANDS FREE FOR THIS.
SO YOU'LL HAVE TO TAKE OVER FOR A BIT.
ME??
YOU WEREN'T ABLE TO CONTROL IT, WHAT MAKES YOU THINK THAT I...
TUG TUG
OH. HEY, NOW...
THIS IS HARDLY THE TIME OR PLACE...
BUT I'M NOT COMPLAINING.
HM? WHAT??
???
N-NOTHING!!

SO WHAT ARE YOU DO--

SHHHH

I'M DOWSING.*

SWISH

*LOOKING FOR UNDERGROUND WATER THROUGH DIVINATION

AND... UHHH

SWISH

...IT'S PULLING STRONGLY IN ALL DIRECTIONS.

SWISH

HM... I'LL NEED A MOMENT TO LOCATE IT PROPERLY.

PLEASE HURRY!!!

HNGH

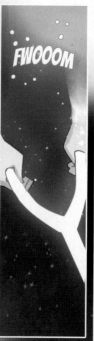

FWOOOM

OH!

YES!! THERE SHE IS!
HELLO, STYX, BELOVED GODDESS OF OATHS.
HELLO, HADES.
WILL YOU RECEIVE ME IN THE SAFETY OF YOUR WATERS?
YES. ALWAYS. WELCOME HOME.

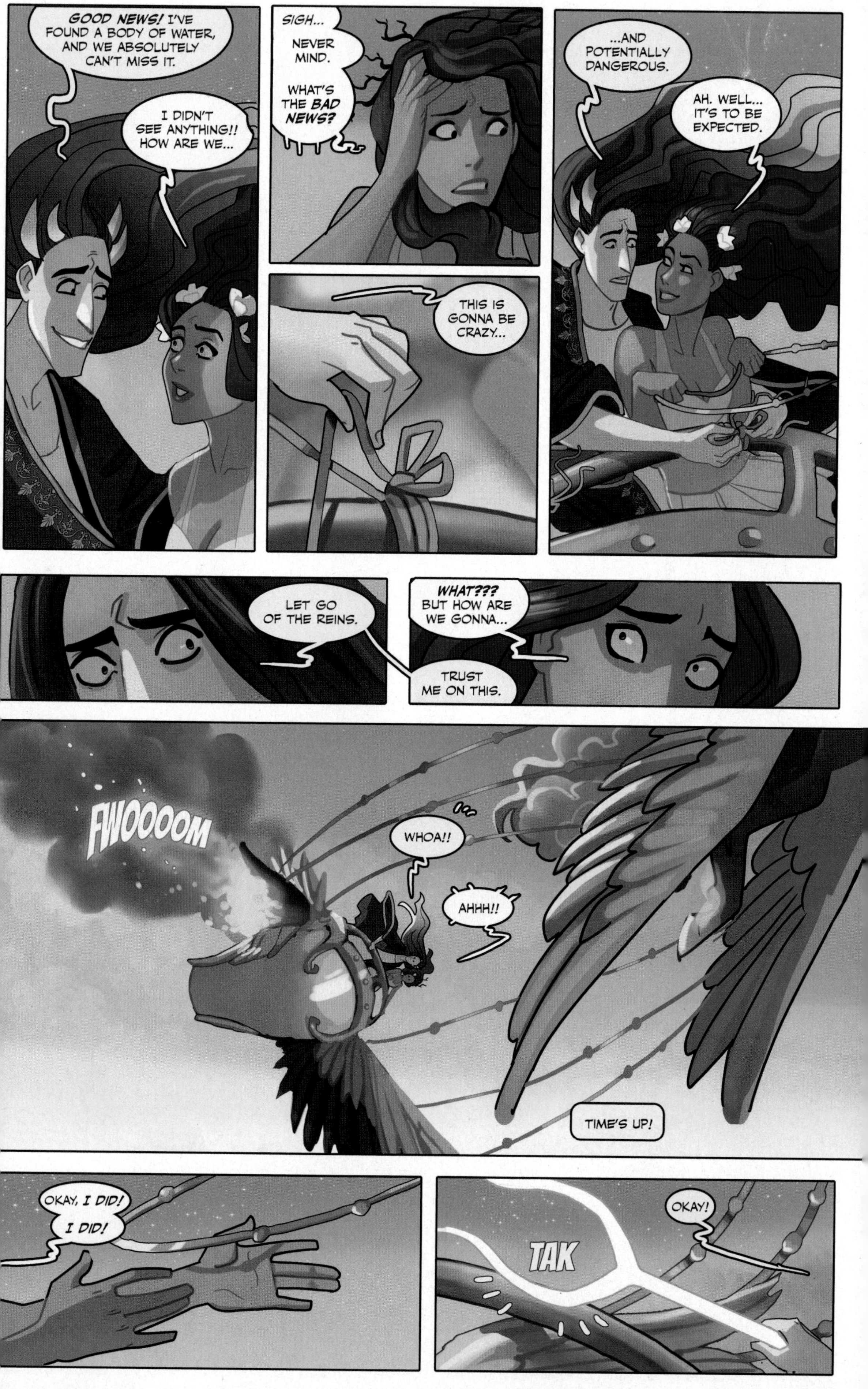
GOOD NEWS! I'VE FOUND A BODY OF WATER, AND WE ABSOLUTELY CAN'T MISS IT.
I DIDN'T SEE ANYTHING!! HOW ARE WE...
SIGH...
NEVER MIND.
WHAT'S THE BAD NEWS?
THIS IS GONNA BE CRAZY...
...AND POTENTIALLY DANGEROUS.
AH. WELL... IT'S TO BE EXPECTED.
LET GO OF THE REINS.
WHAT??? BUT HOW ARE WE GONNA...
TRUST ME ON THIS.
FWOOOOM
WHOA!!
AHHH!!
TIME'S UP!
OKAY, I DID!
I DID!
OKAY!
TAK

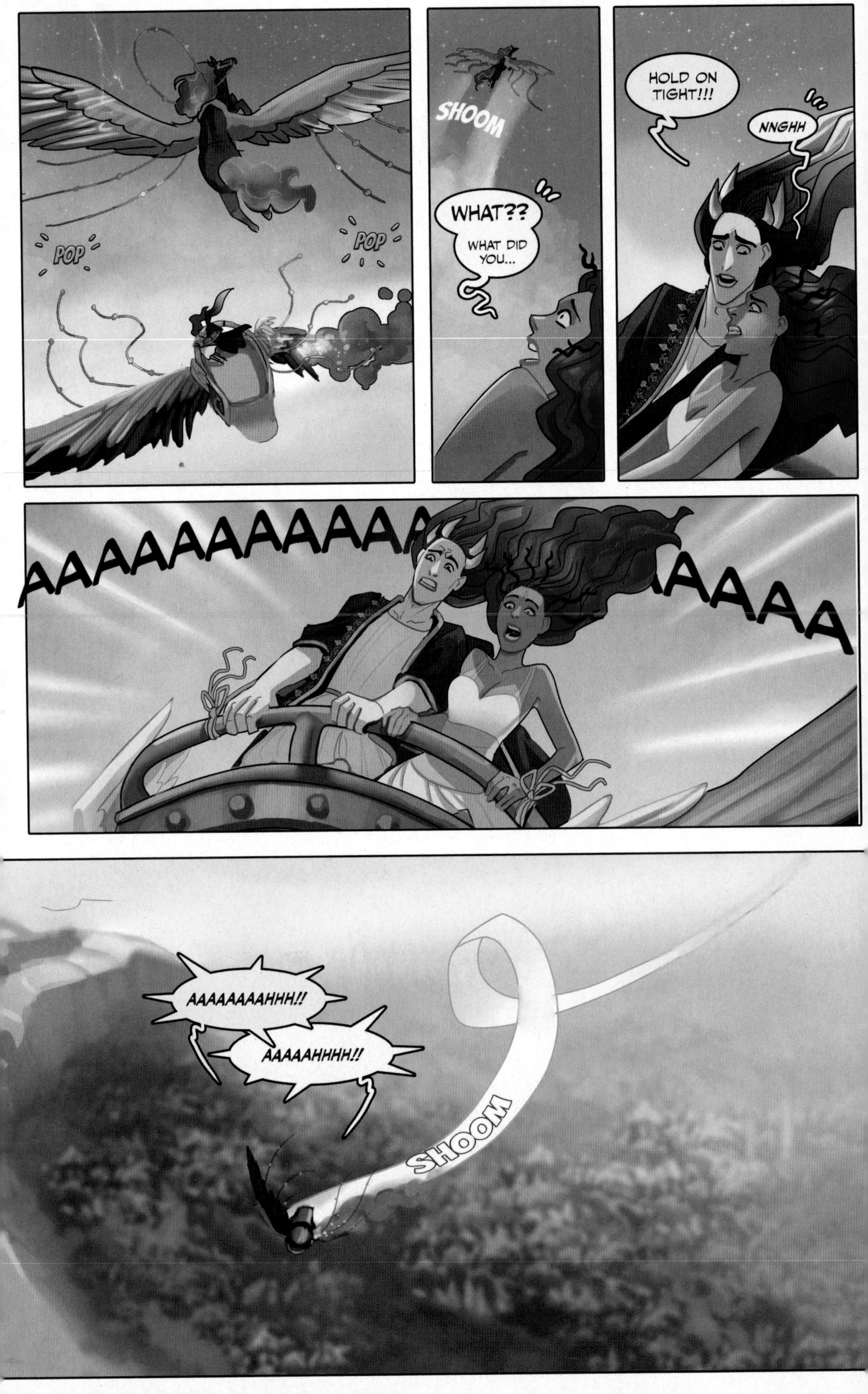
POP
POP
SHOOM
WHAT??
WHAT DID YOU...
HOLD ON TIGHT!!!
NNGHH
AAAAAAAAAAAAAAAAAAAAA
AAAAAAAAAHHH!!
AAAAAHHHH!!
SHOOM

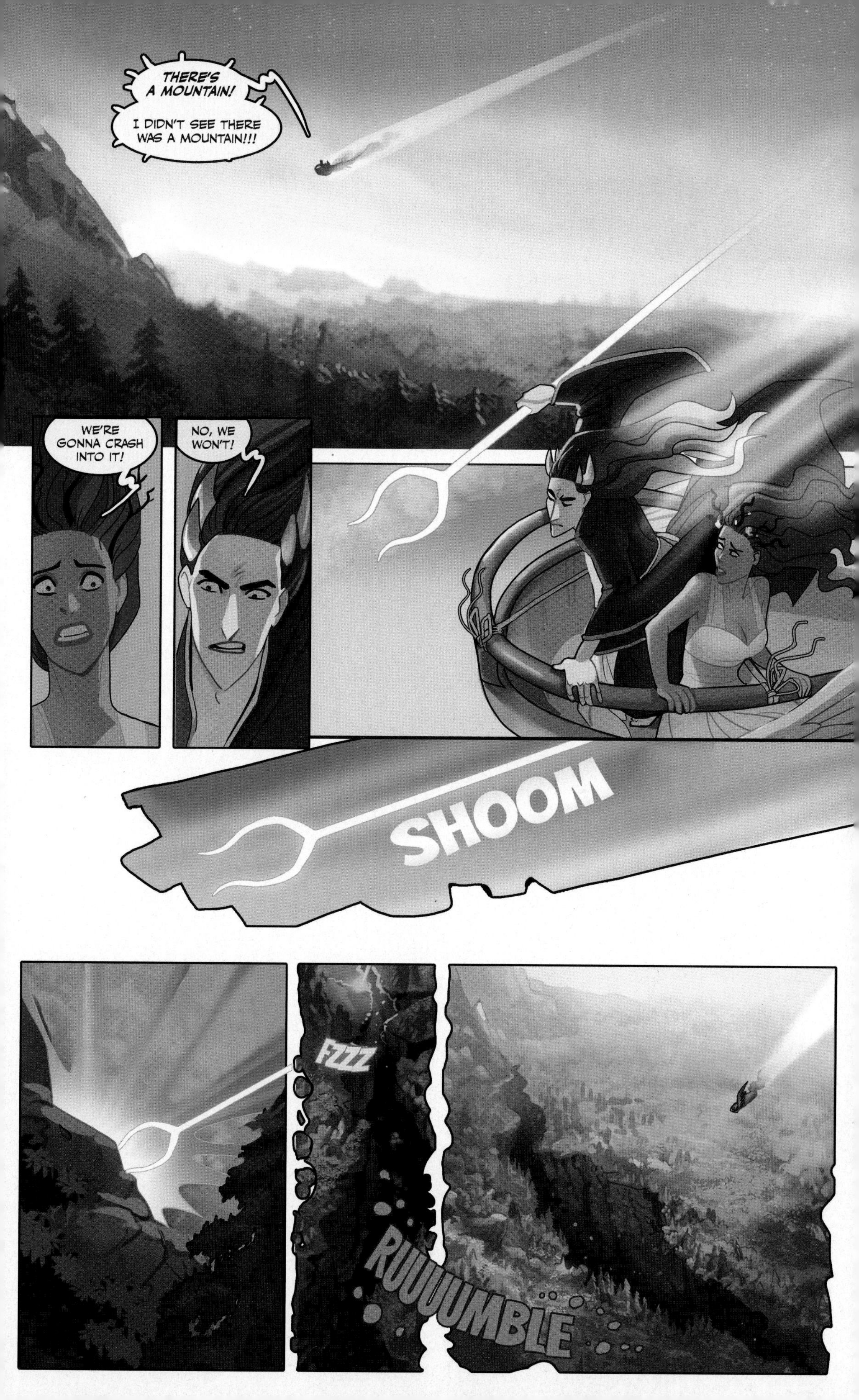
THERE'S A MOUNTAIN!
I DIDN'T SEE THERE WAS A MOUNTAIN!!!
WE'RE GONNA CRASH INTO IT!
NO, WE WON'T!
SHOOM
FZZZ
RUUUUMBLE

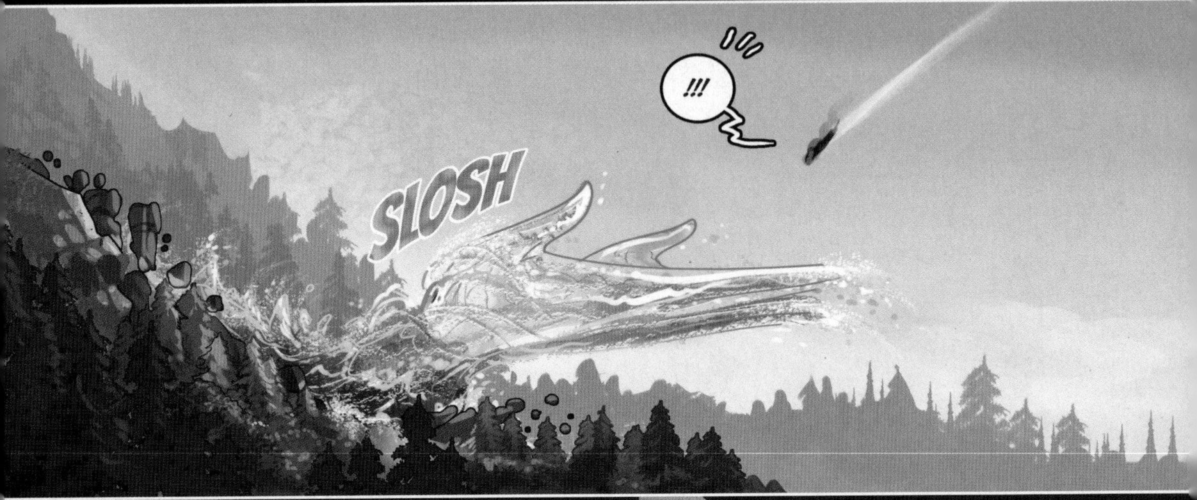
!!!
SLOSH

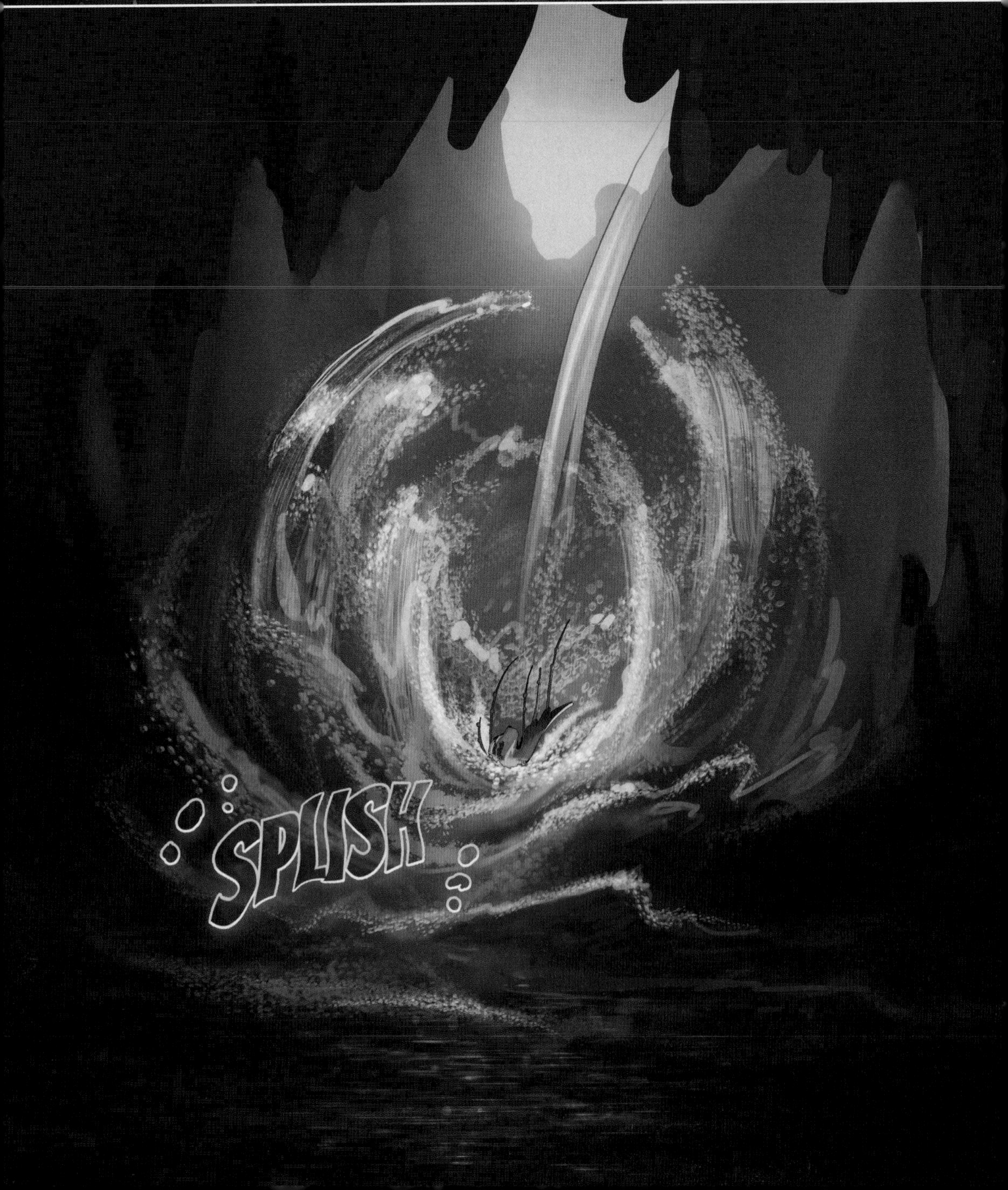
SPLISH

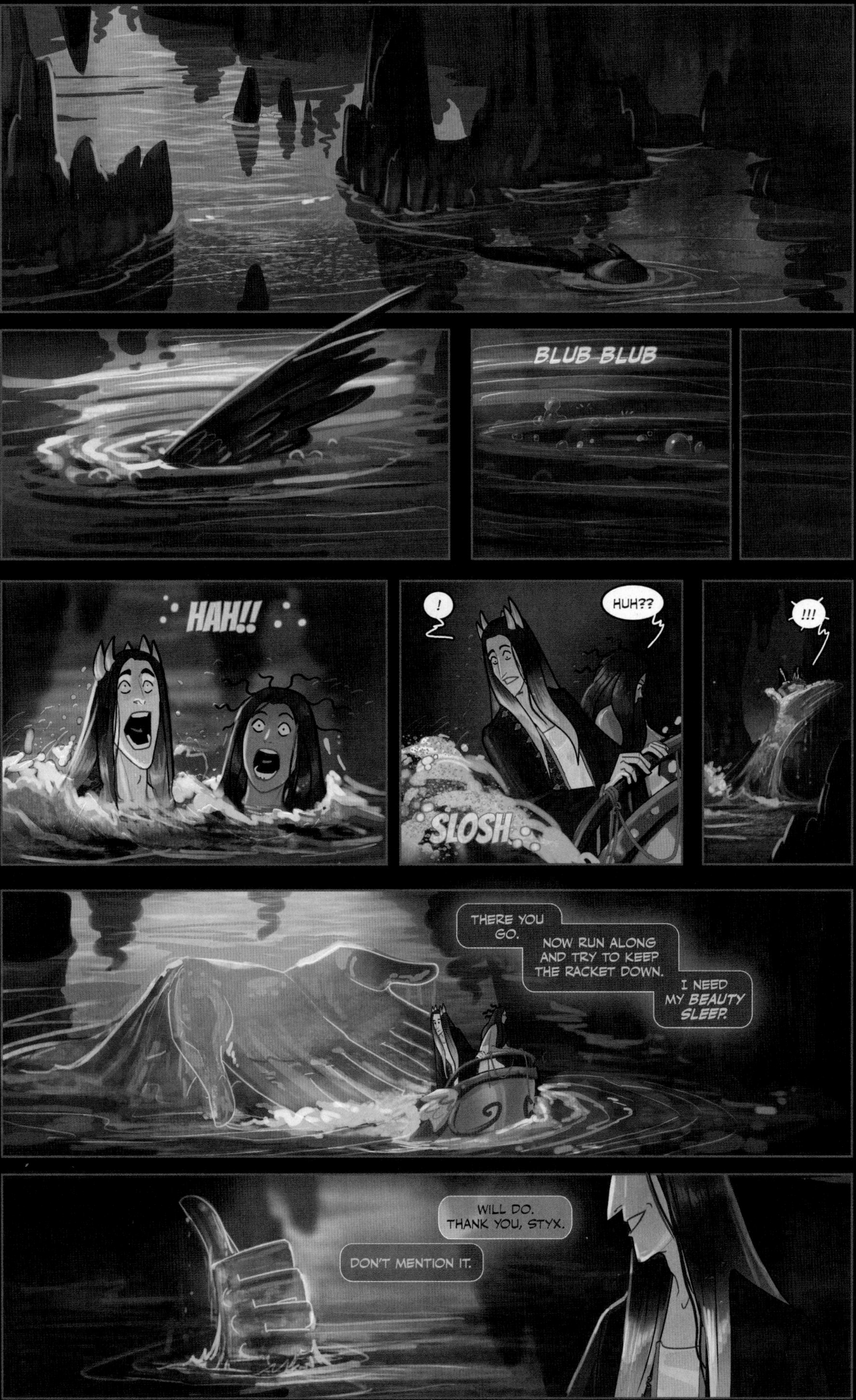
BLUB BLUB
HAH!!
!
HUH??
SLOSH
!!!
THERE YOU GO.
NOW RUN ALONG AND TRY TO KEEP THE RACKET DOWN.
I NEED MY BEAUTY SLEEP.
WILL DO. THANK YOU, STYX.
DON'T MENTION IT.

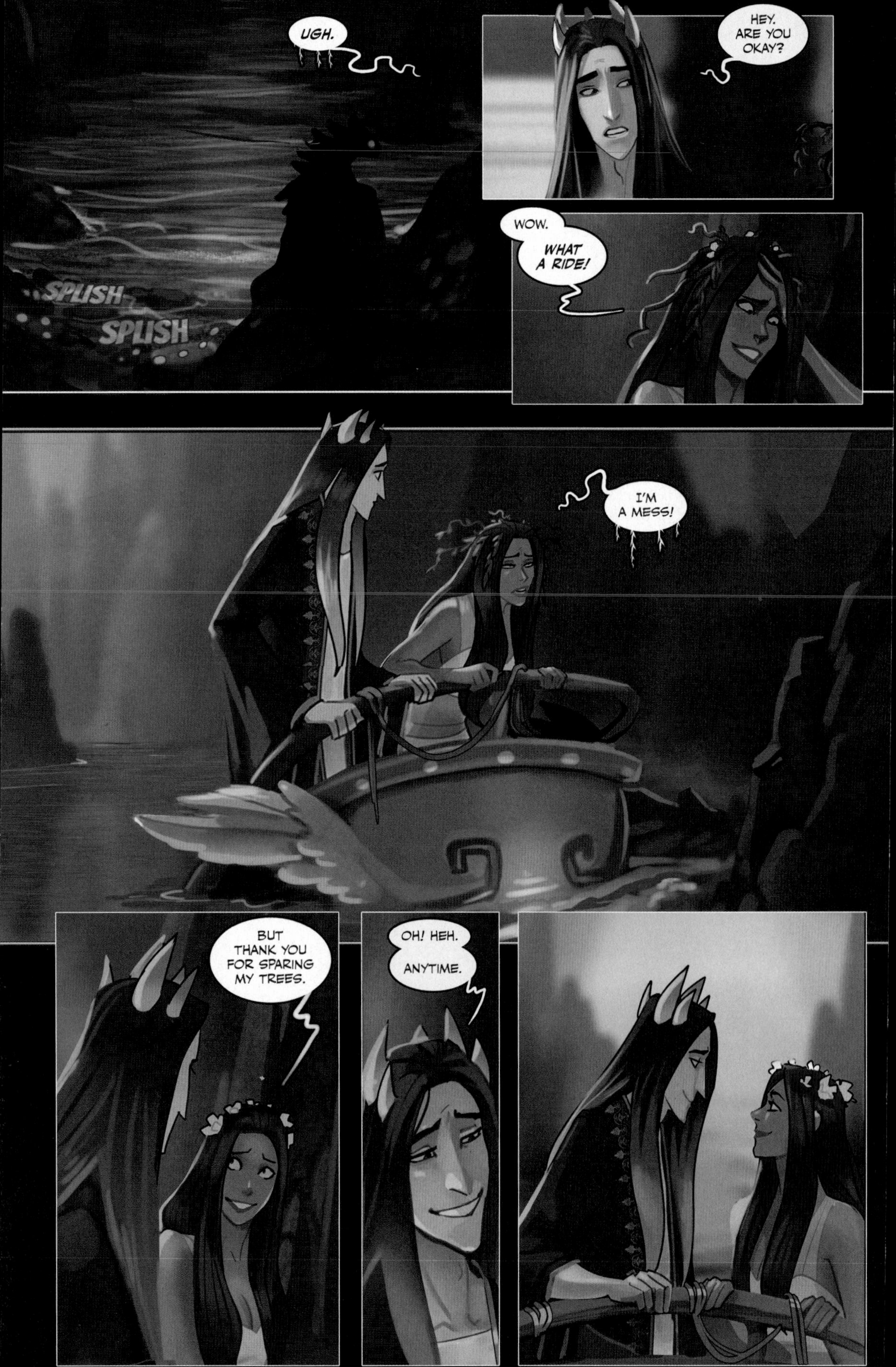
UGH.
SPLISH
SPLISH
HEY. ARE YOU OKAY?
WOW.
WHAT A RIDE!
I'M A MESS!
BUT THANK YOU FOR SPARING MY TREES.
OH! HEH.
ANYTIME.

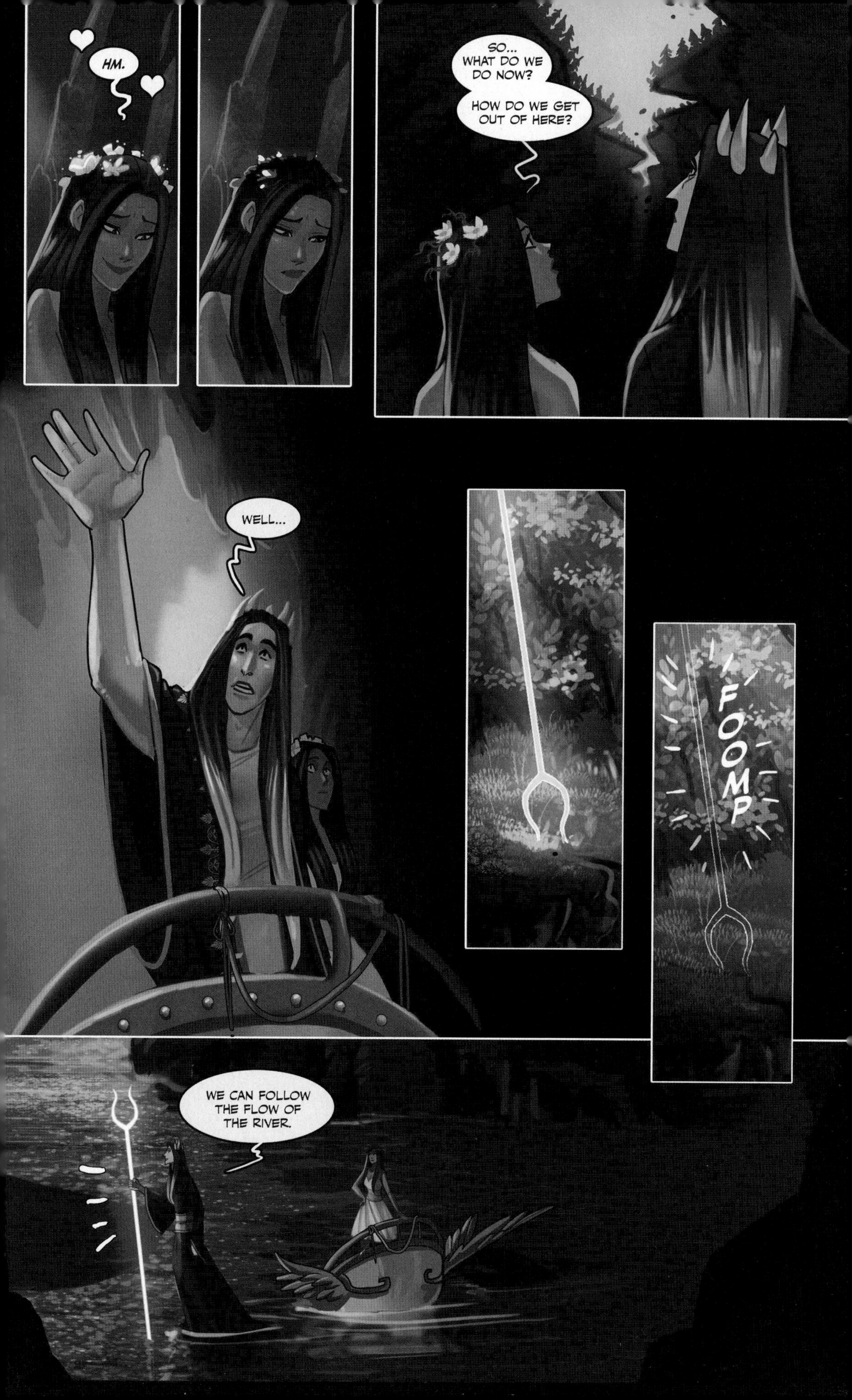
HM.
SO... WHAT DO WE DO NOW?
HOW DO WE GET OUT OF HERE?
WELL...
FOOMP
WE CAN FOLLOW THE FLOW OF THE RIVER.

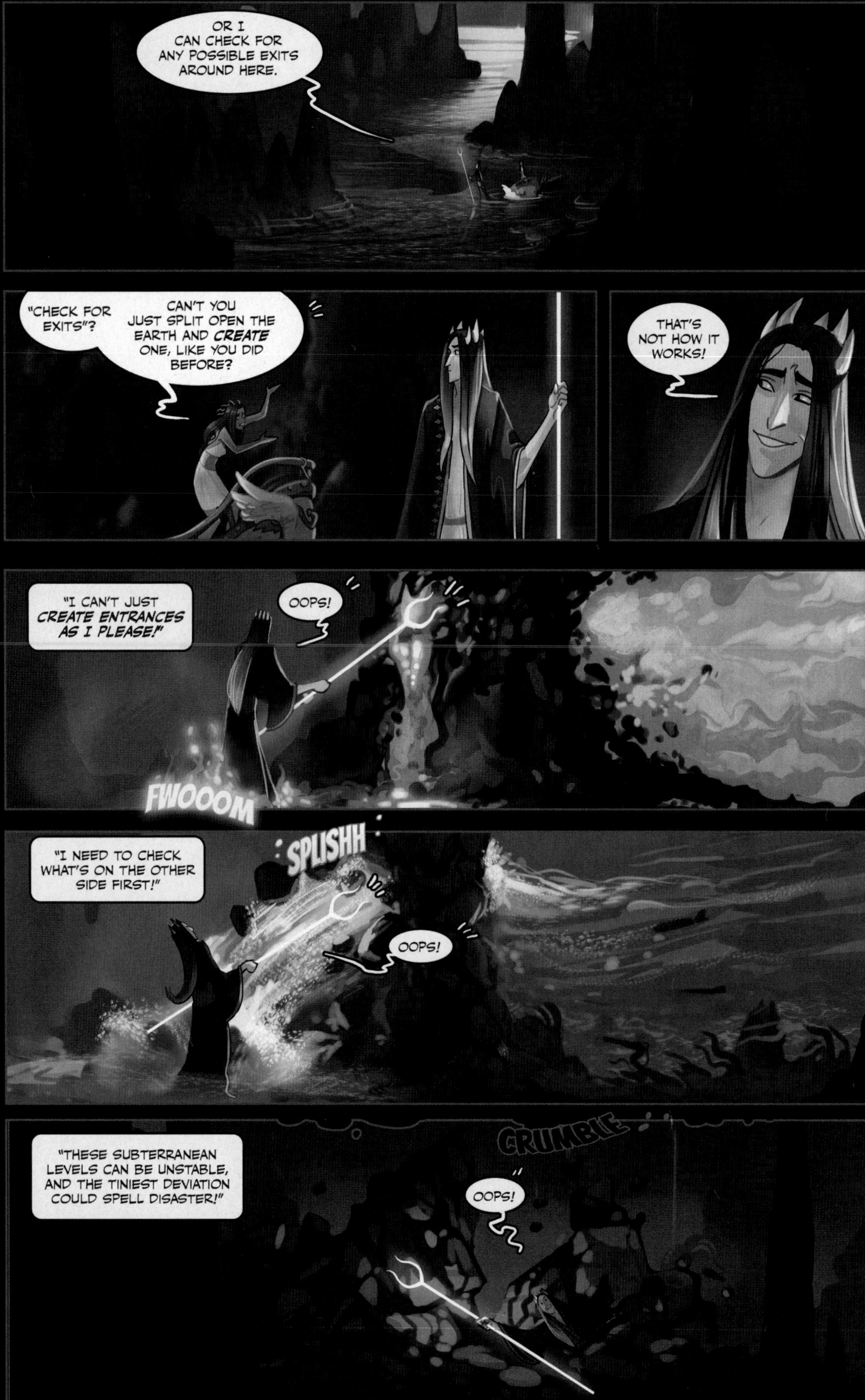
OR I CAN CHECK FOR ANY POSSIBLE EXITS AROUND HERE.
"CHECK FOR EXITS"?
CAN'T YOU JUST SPLIT OPEN THE EARTH AND *CREATE* ONE, LIKE YOU DID BEFORE?
THAT'S NOT HOW IT WORKS!
"I CAN'T JUST *CREATE ENTRANCES* AS I PLEASE!"
OOPS!
FWOOOM
"I NEED TO CHECK WHAT'S ON THE OTHER SIDE FIRST!"
SPLISHH
OOPS!
"THESE SUBTERRANEAN LEVELS CAN BE UNSTABLE, AND THE TINIEST DEVIATION COULD SPELL DISASTER!"
CRUMBLE
OOPS!

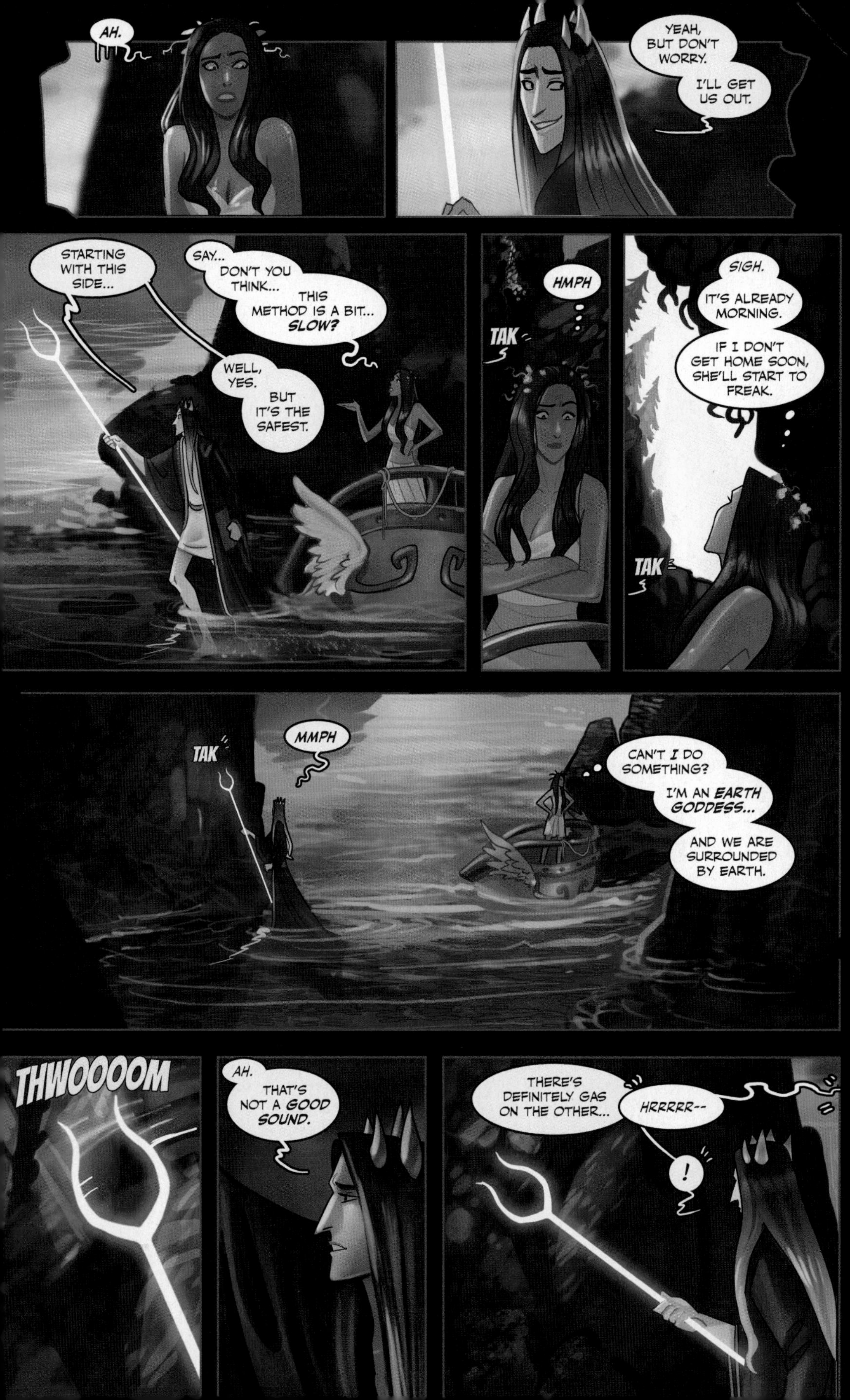
AH.
YEAH, BUT DON'T WORRY.
I'LL GET US OUT.
STARTING WITH THIS SIDE...
SAY... DON'T YOU THINK...
THIS METHOD IS A BIT... SLOW?
WELL, YES.
BUT IT'S THE SAFEST.
HMPH
TAK
SIGH.
IT'S ALREADY MORNING.
IF I DON'T GET HOME SOON, SHE'LL START TO FREAK.
TAK
TAK
MMPH
CAN'T I DO SOMETHING?
I'M AN EARTH GODDESS...
AND WE ARE SURROUNDED BY EARTH.
THWOOOOM
AH.
THAT'S NOT A GOOD SOUND.
THERE'S DEFINITELY GAS ON THE OTHER...
HRRRRR--
!

HRRRGHH
????
HRRRRGH!
BLOOP
BLOOP
HNGH
HRRGHHH!
...WHAT ARE YOU DOING?
GNNNGGHH!
GAH!
I CAN'T DO IT!
WHAT?
WHY CAN'T I DO IT???
DO WHAT?

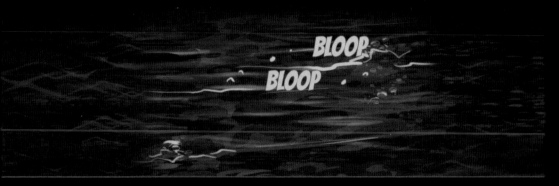

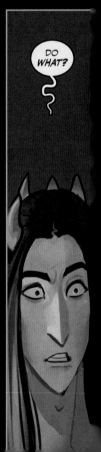

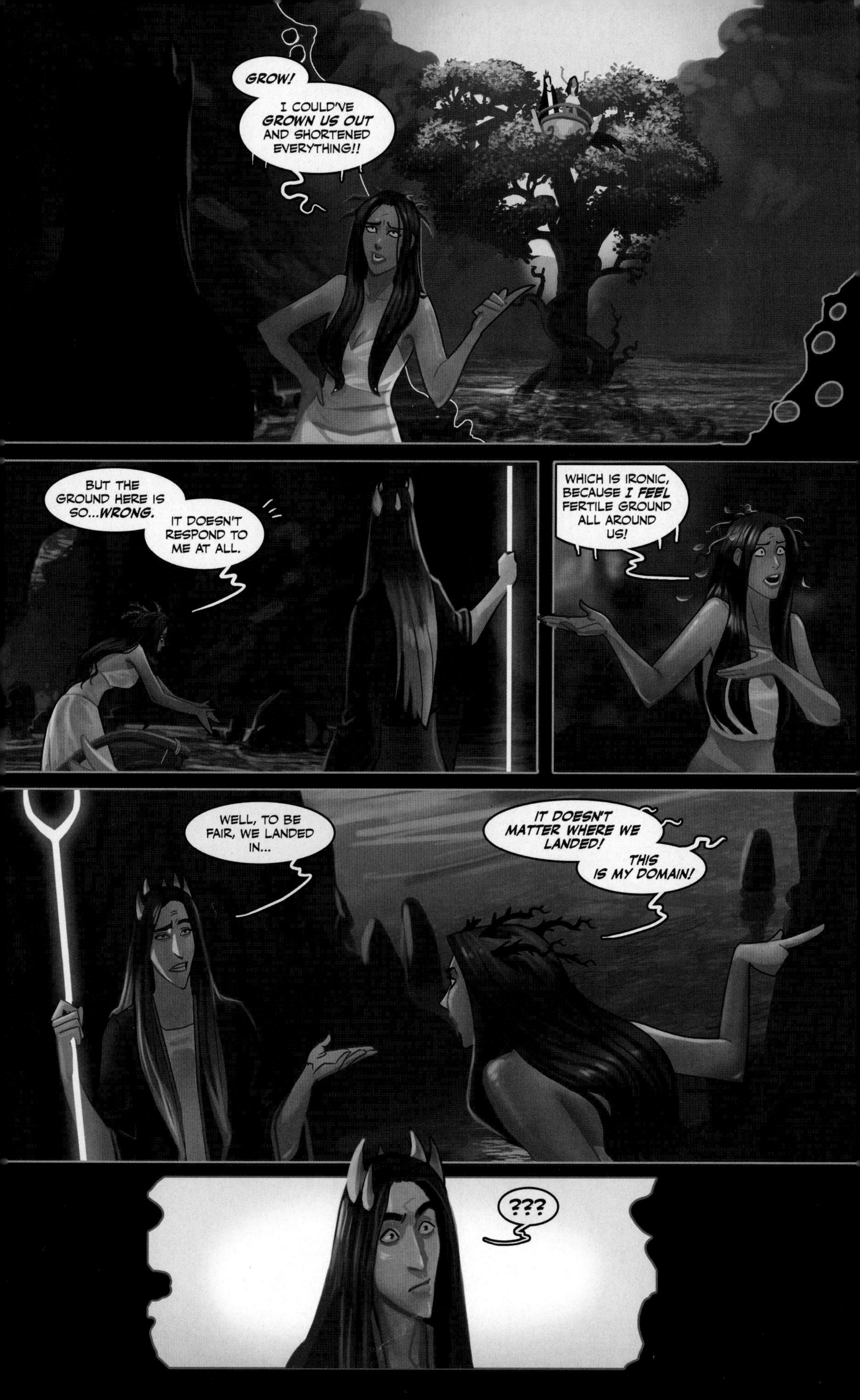
GROW!
I COULD'VE GROWN US OUT AND SHORTENED EVERYTHING!!
BUT THE GROUND HERE IS SO...WRONG.
IT DOESN'T RESPOND TO ME AT ALL.
WHICH IS IRONIC, BECAUSE I FEEL FERTILE GROUND ALL AROUND US!
WELL, TO BE FAIR, WE LANDED IN...
IT DOESN'T MATTER WHERE WE LANDED!
THIS IS MY DOMAIN!
???

THE EARTH IS MY DOMAIN. IT'S *SUPPOSED* TO LISTEN TO ME.

I DON'T UNDERSTAND!

DOESN'T IT KNOW *WHO I AM?*

I'M NOT SOME *MINOR GODDESS!*

I'M *PERSEPHONE!*

SIGH. *LOOK.*

I'M SORRY. I KNOW YOU'RE TRYING TO HELP... BUT I DON'T HAVE THE TIME OR THE PATIENCE TO CHECK EVERY LAST ROCK AND CRANNY.

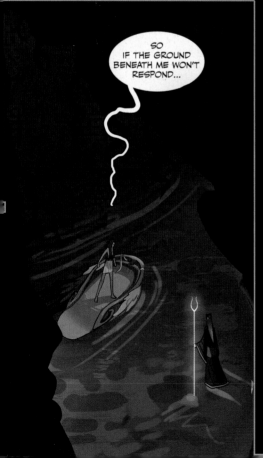

SO IF THE GROUND BENEATH ME WON'T RESPOND...

...THEN I WILL *MAKE THE ROOTS* CRADLE US FROM ABOVE.

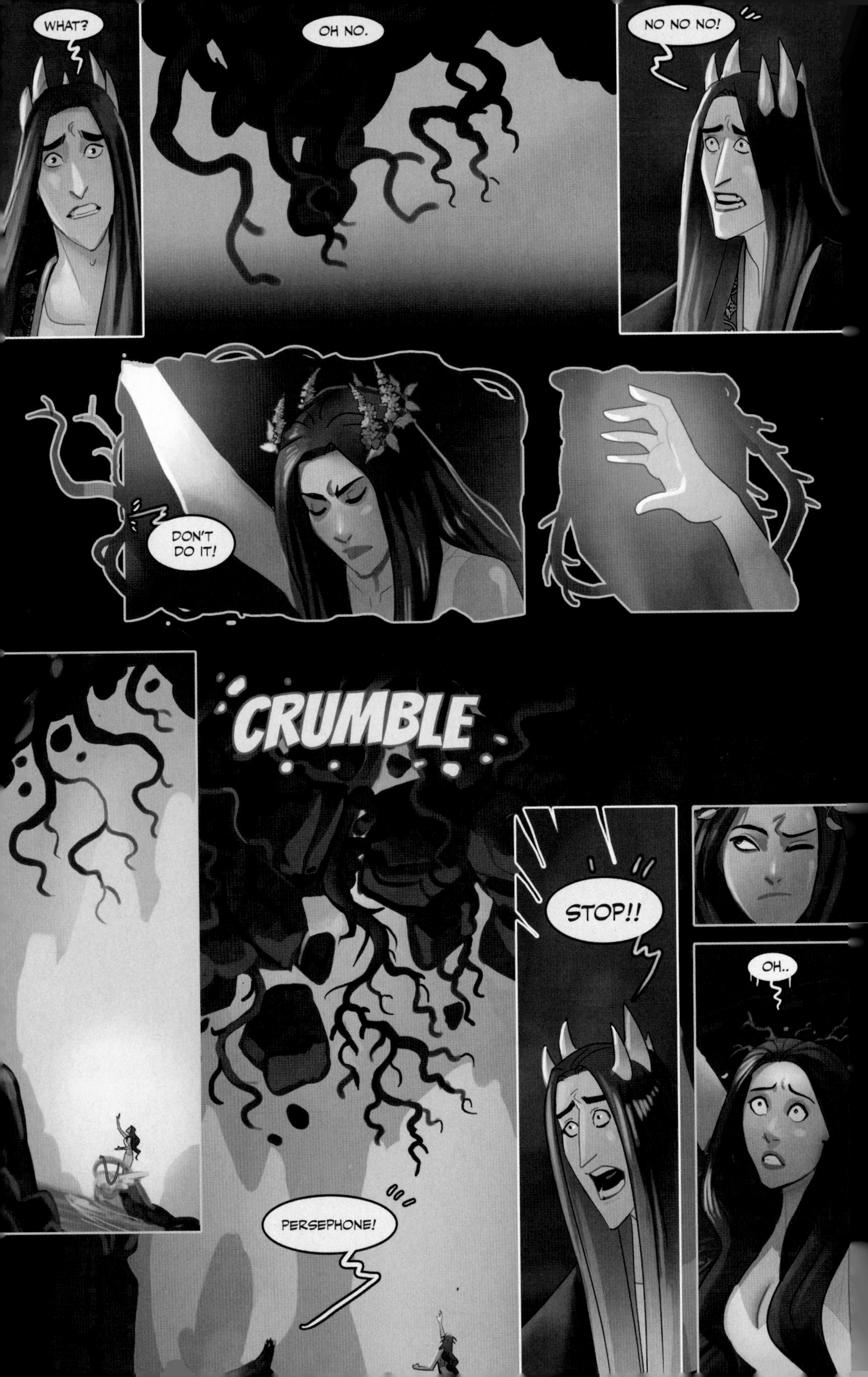

WHAT?
OH NO.
NO NO NO!
DON'T DO IT!
CRUMBLE
STOP!!
OH..
PERSEPHONE!

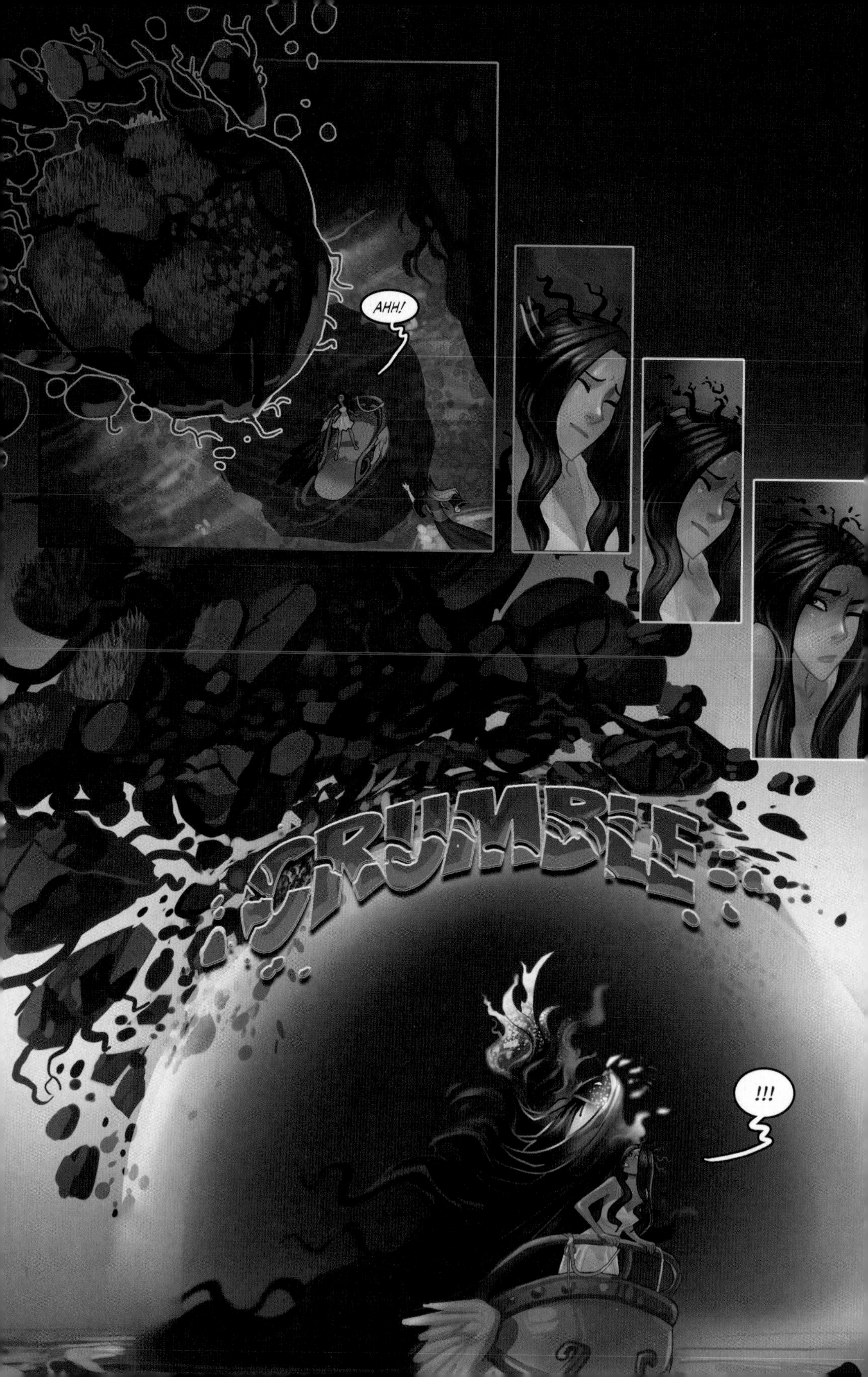
AHH!
CRUMBLE
!!!

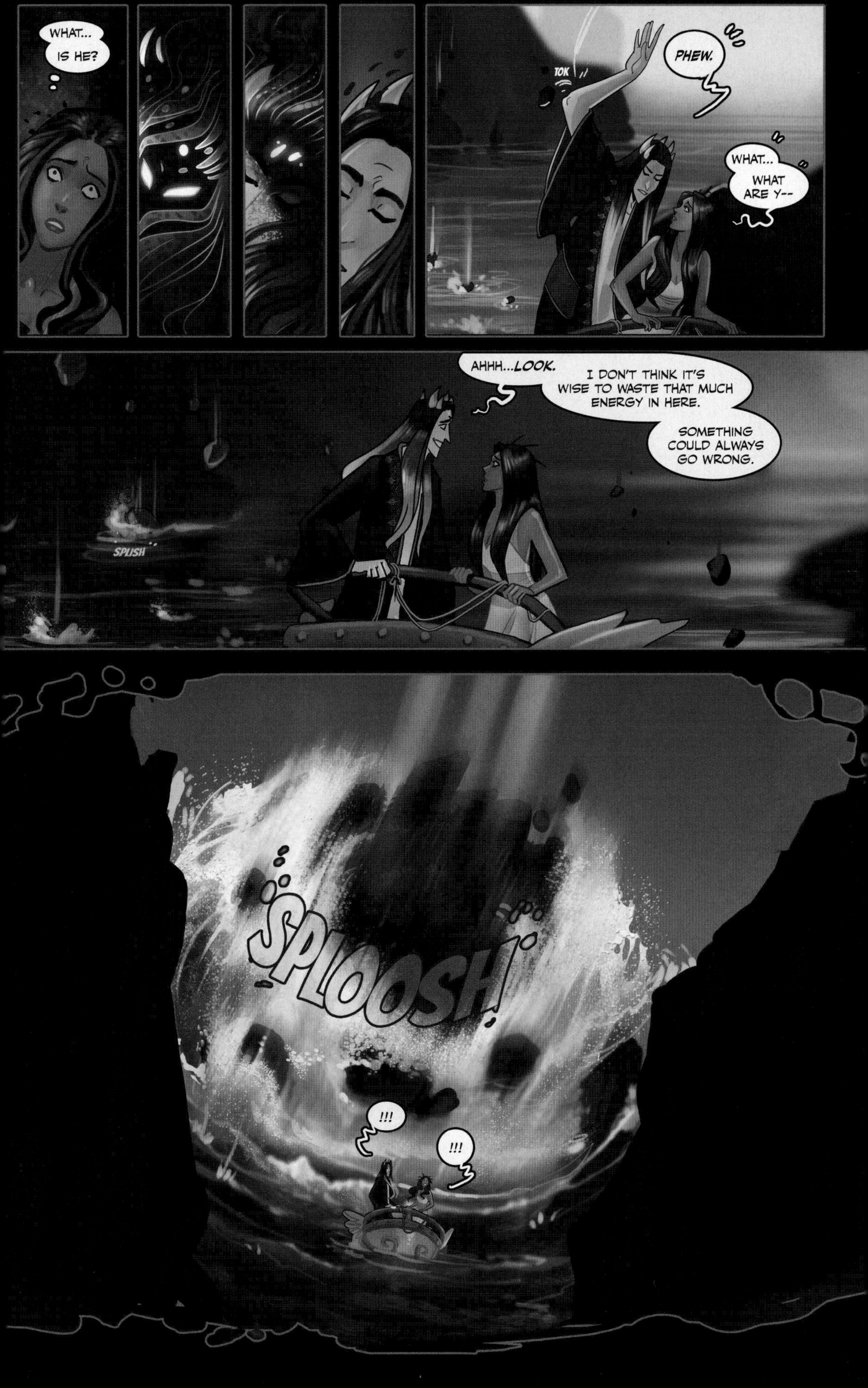
WHAT... IS HE?
TOK
PHEW.
WHAT... WHAT ARE Y--
AHHH...LOOK.
I DON'T THINK IT'S WISE TO WASTE THAT MUCH ENERGY IN HERE.
SOMETHING COULD ALWAYS GO WRONG.
SPLISH
SPLOOSH!
!!!
!!!

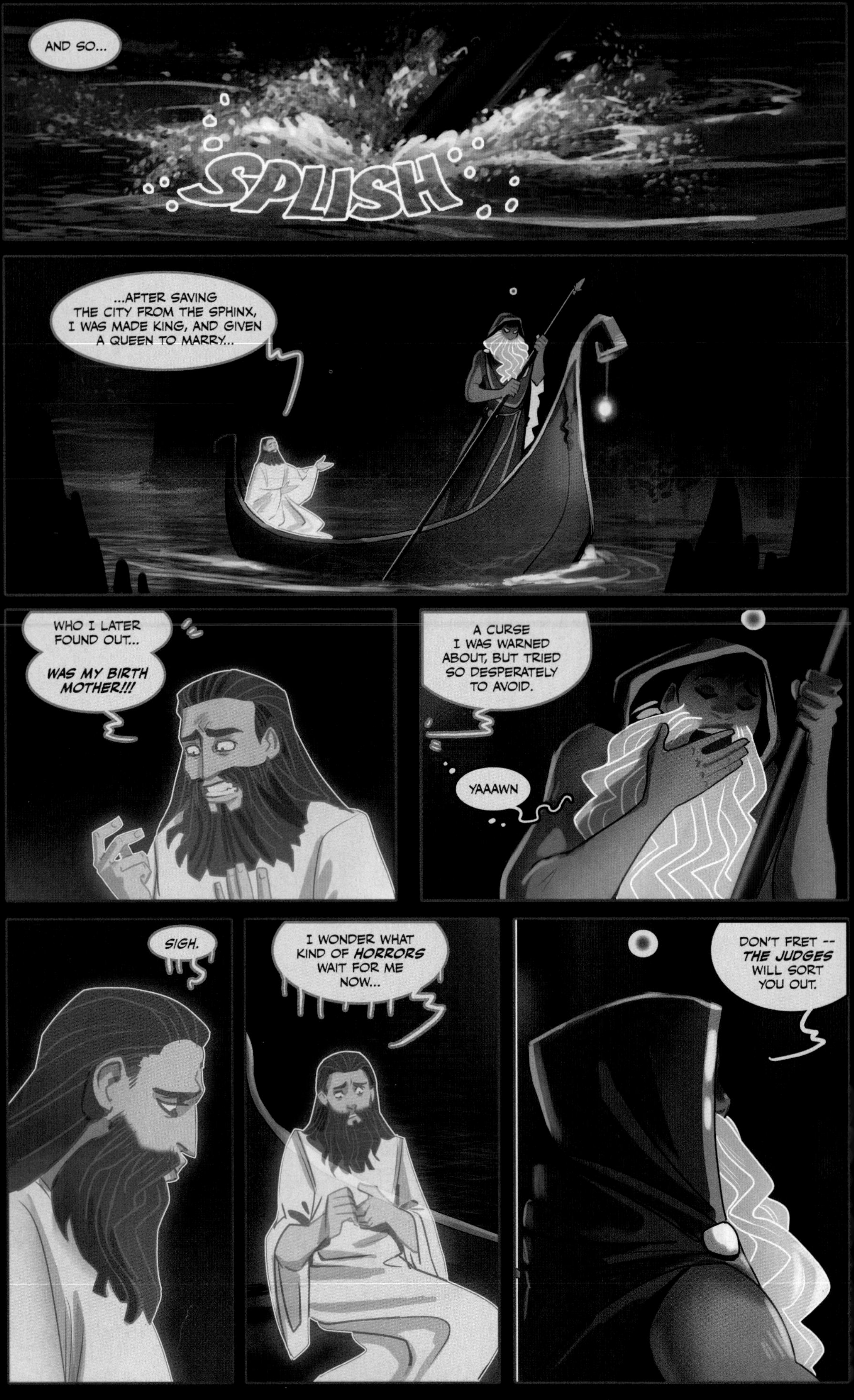
AND SO...
SPLISH
...AFTER SAVING THE CITY FROM THE SPHINX, I WAS MADE KING, AND GIVEN A QUEEN TO MARRY...
WHO I LATER FOUND OUT...
WAS MY BIRTH MOTHER!!!
A CURSE I WAS WARNED ABOUT, BUT TRIED SO DESPERATELY TO AVOID.
YAAAWN
SIGH.
I WONDER WHAT KIND OF HORRORS WAIT FOR ME NOW...
DON'T FRET -- THE JUDGES WILL SORT YOU OUT.

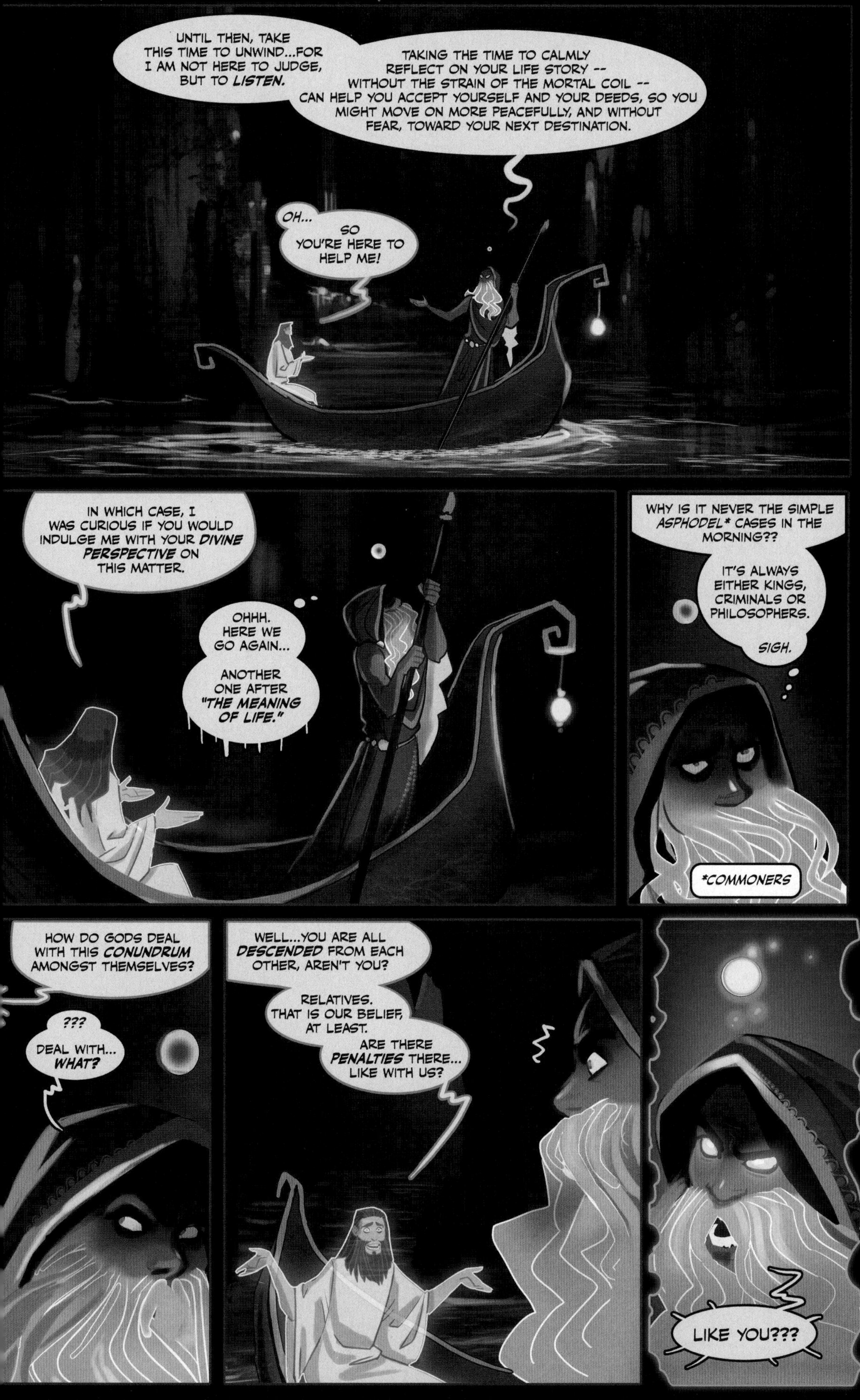
UNTIL THEN, TAKE THIS TIME TO UNWIND...FOR I AM NOT HERE TO JUDGE, BUT TO *LISTEN.*
TAKING THE TIME TO CALMLY REFLECT ON YOUR LIFE STORY -- WITHOUT THE STRAIN OF THE MORTAL COIL -- CAN HELP YOU ACCEPT YOURSELF AND YOUR DEEDS, SO YOU MIGHT MOVE ON MORE PEACEFULLY, AND WITHOUT FEAR, TOWARD YOUR NEXT DESTINATION.
OH...
SO YOU'RE HERE TO HELP ME!
IN WHICH CASE, I WAS CURIOUS IF YOU WOULD INDULGE ME WITH YOUR *DIVINE PERSPECTIVE* ON THIS MATTER.
OHHH. HERE WE GO AGAIN...
ANOTHER ONE AFTER *"THE MEANING OF LIFE."*
WHY IS IT NEVER THE SIMPLE *ASPHODEL** CASES IN THE MORNING??
IT'S ALWAYS EITHER KINGS, CRIMINALS OR PHILOSOPHERS.
SIGH.
*COMMONERS
HOW DO GODS DEAL WITH THIS *CONUNDRUM* AMONGST THEMSELVES?
???
DEAL WITH... *WHAT?*
WELL...YOU ARE ALL *DESCENDED* FROM EACH OTHER, AREN'T YOU?
RELATIVES. THAT IS OUR BELIEF, AT LEAST.
ARE THERE *PENALTIES* THERE... LIKE WITH US?
LIKE YOU???

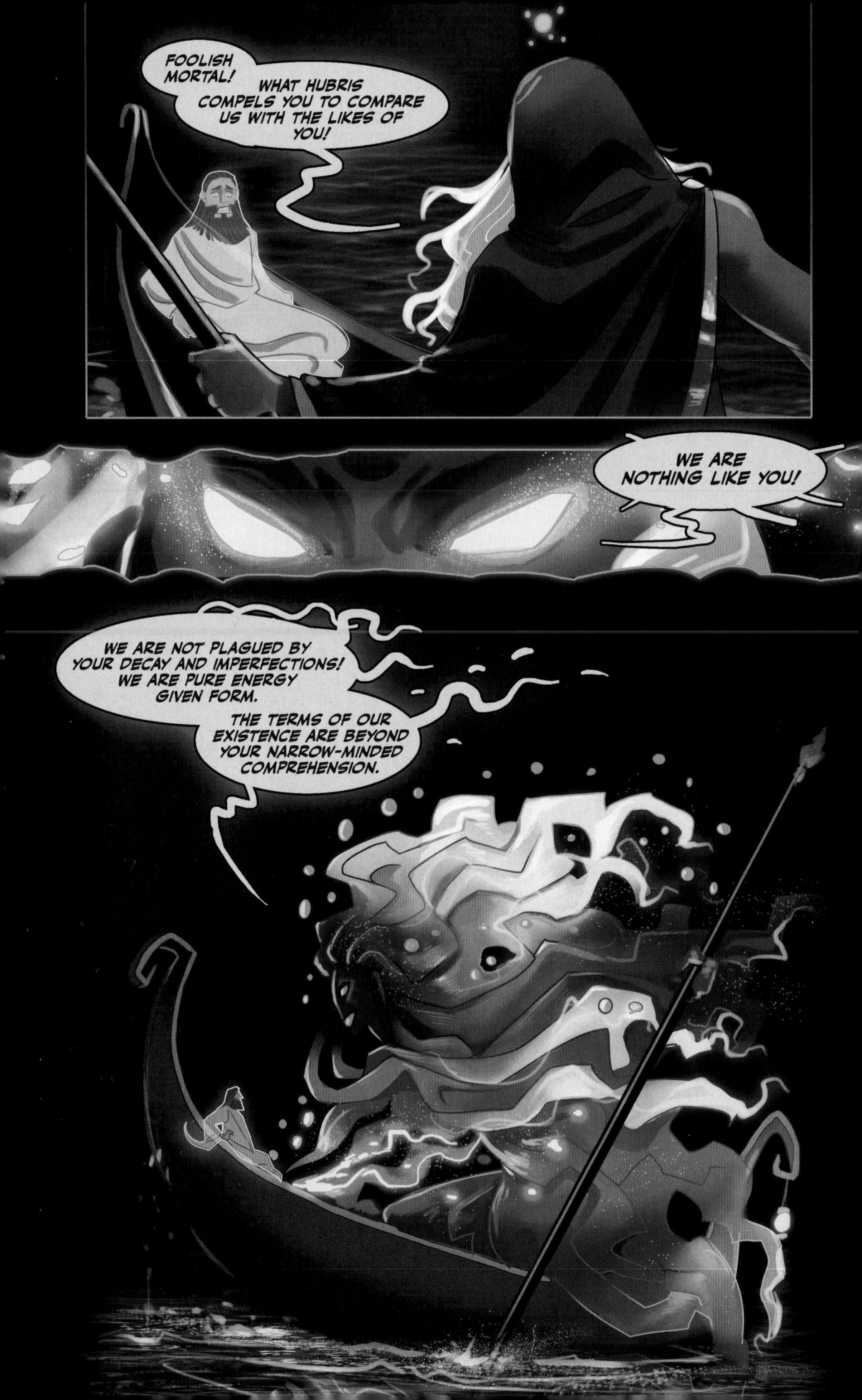
FOOLISH MORTAL!
WHAT HUBRIS COMPELS YOU TO COMPARE US WITH THE LIKES OF YOU!
WE ARE NOTHING LIKE YOU!
WE ARE NOT PLAGUED BY YOUR DECAY AND IMPERFECTIONS! WE ARE PURE ENERGY GIVEN FORM.
THE TERMS OF OUR EXISTENCE ARE BEYOND YOUR NARROW-MINDED COMPREHENSION.

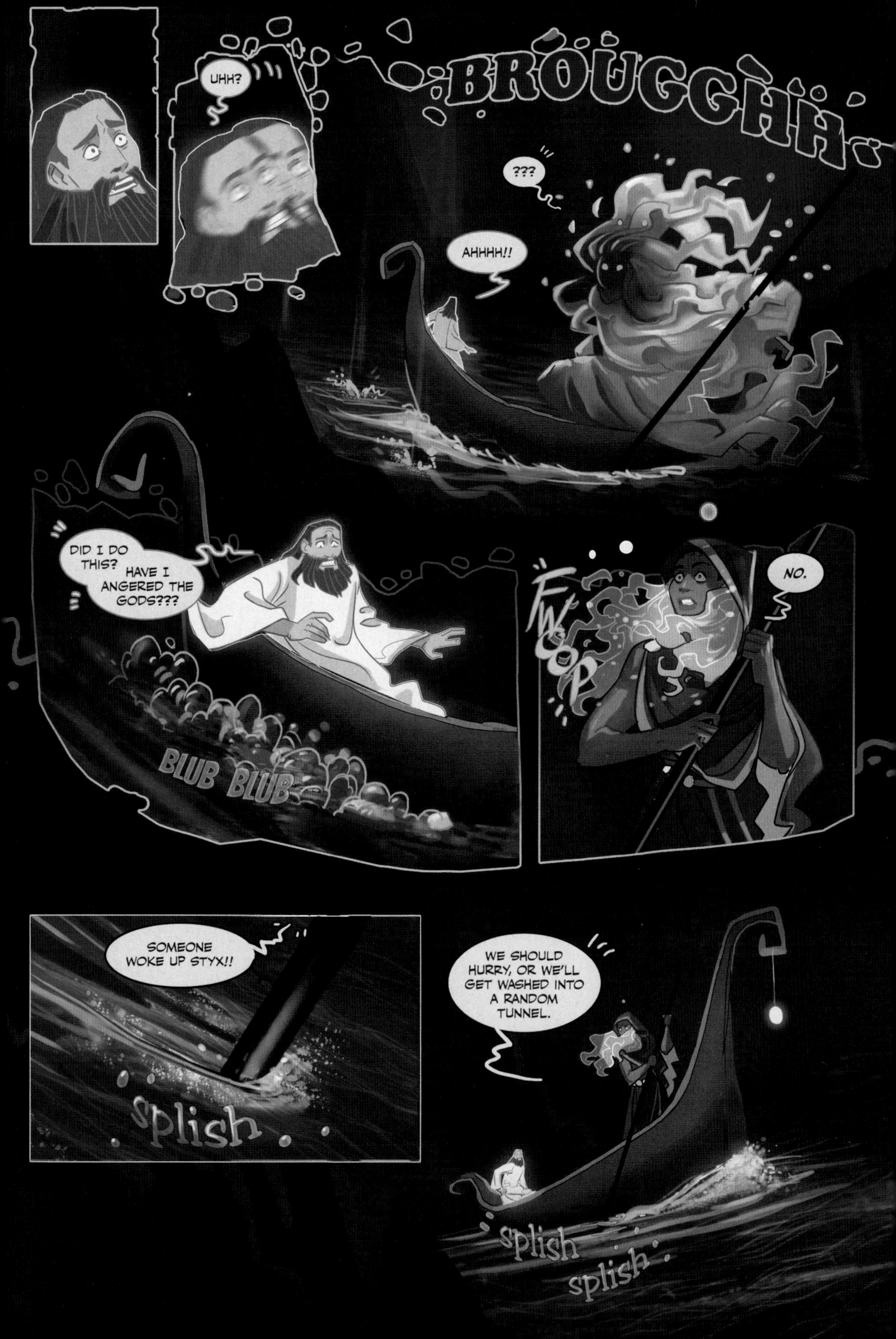
UHH?
BROUGGHH
???
AHHHH!!
DID I DO THIS? HAVE I ANGERED THE GODS???
BLUB BLUB
FWOOP
NO.
SOMEONE WOKE UP STYX!!
splish
WE SHOULD HURRY, OR WE'LL GET WASHED INTO A RANDOM TUNNEL.
splish
splish

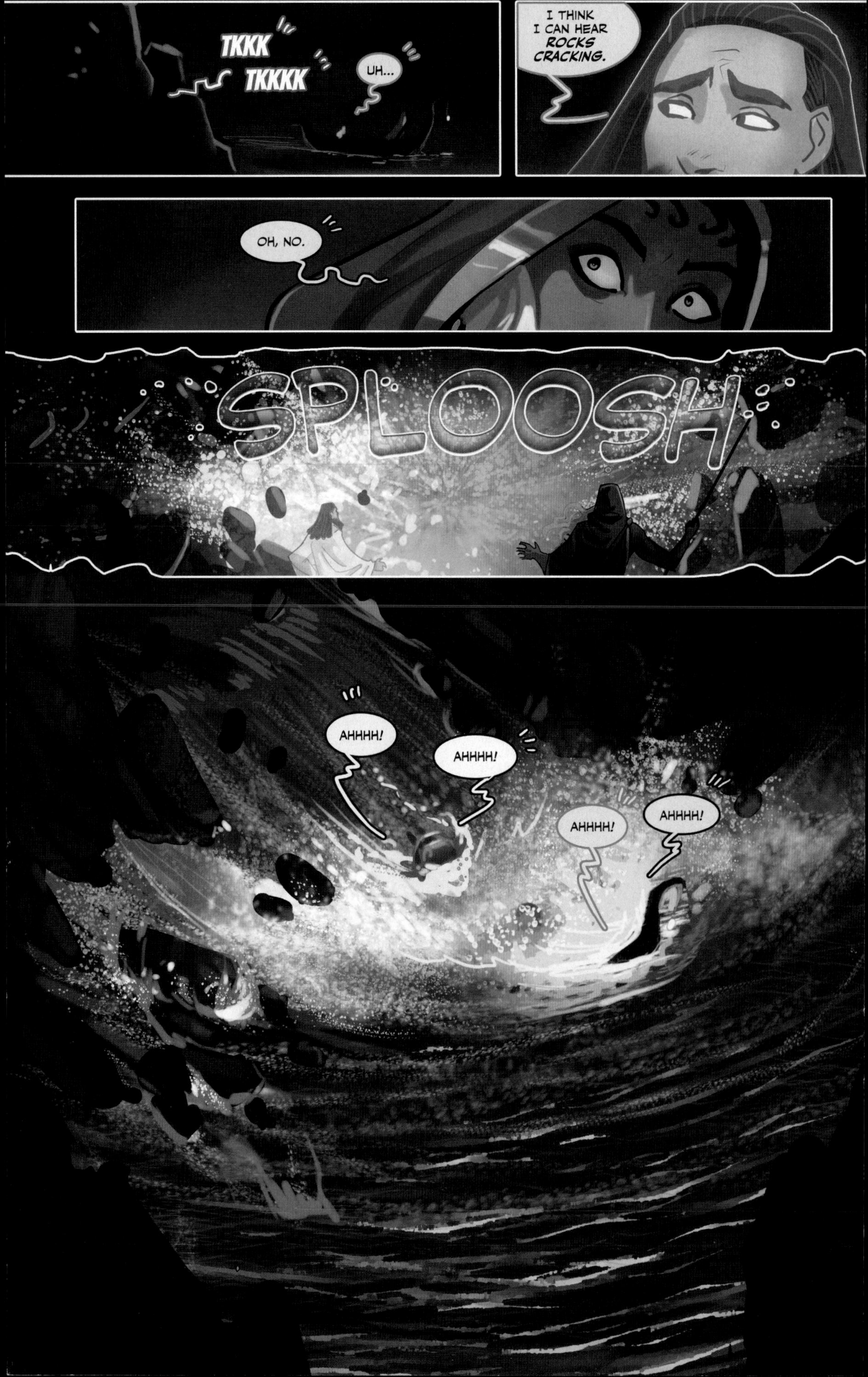
TKKK
TKKKK
UH...
I THINK I CAN HEAR ROCKS CRACKING.
OH, NO.
SPLOOSH
AHHHH!
AHHHH!
AHHHH!
AHHHH!

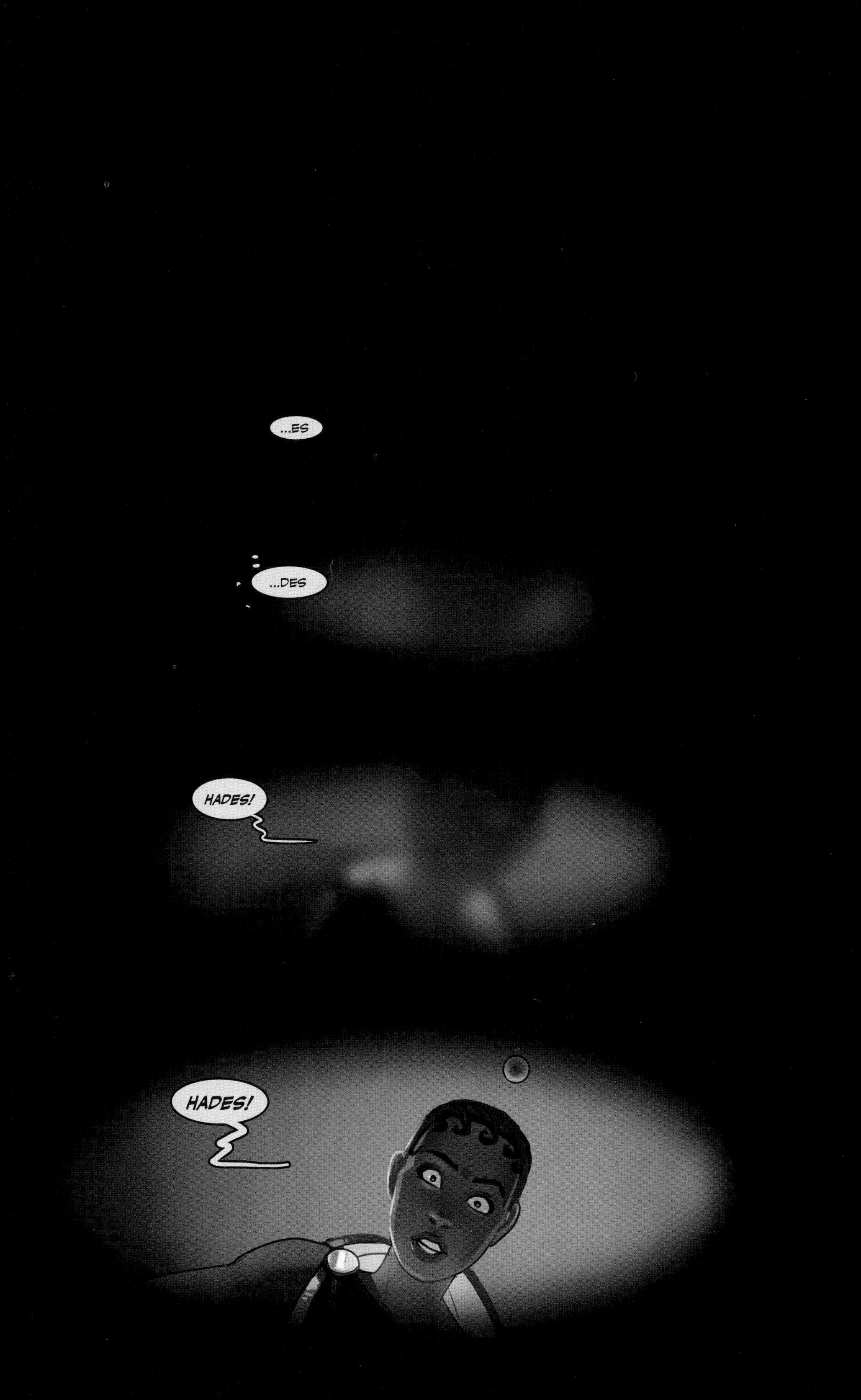
...ES
...DES
HADES!
HADES!

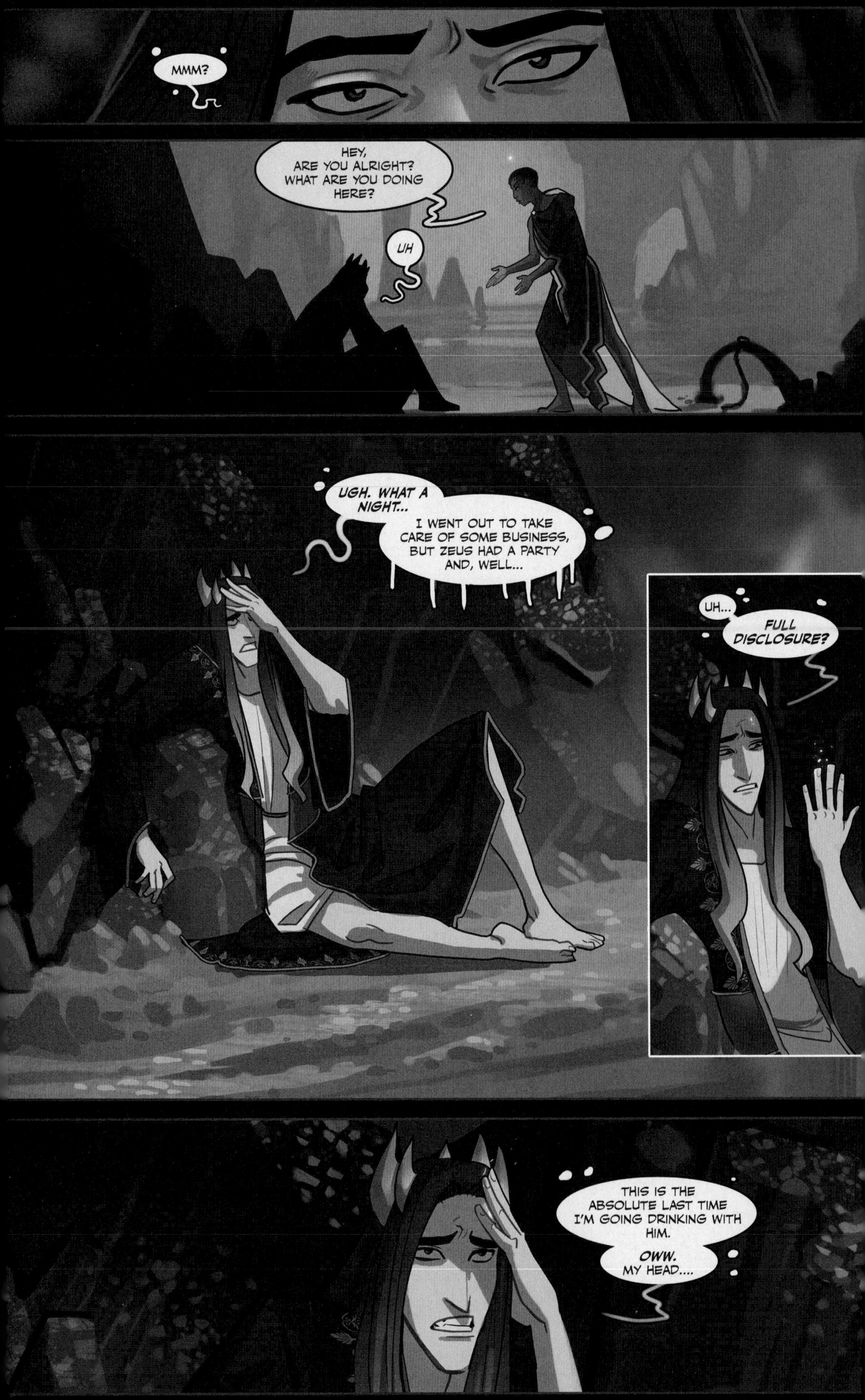
MMM?
HEY, ARE YOU ALRIGHT? WHAT ARE YOU DOING HERE?
UH
UGH. WHAT A NIGHT...
I WENT OUT TO TAKE CARE OF SOME BUSINESS, BUT ZEUS HAD A PARTY AND, WELL...
UH...
FULL DISCLOSURE?
THIS IS THE ABSOLUTE LAST TIME I'M GOING DRINKING WITH HIM.
OWW. MY HEAD....

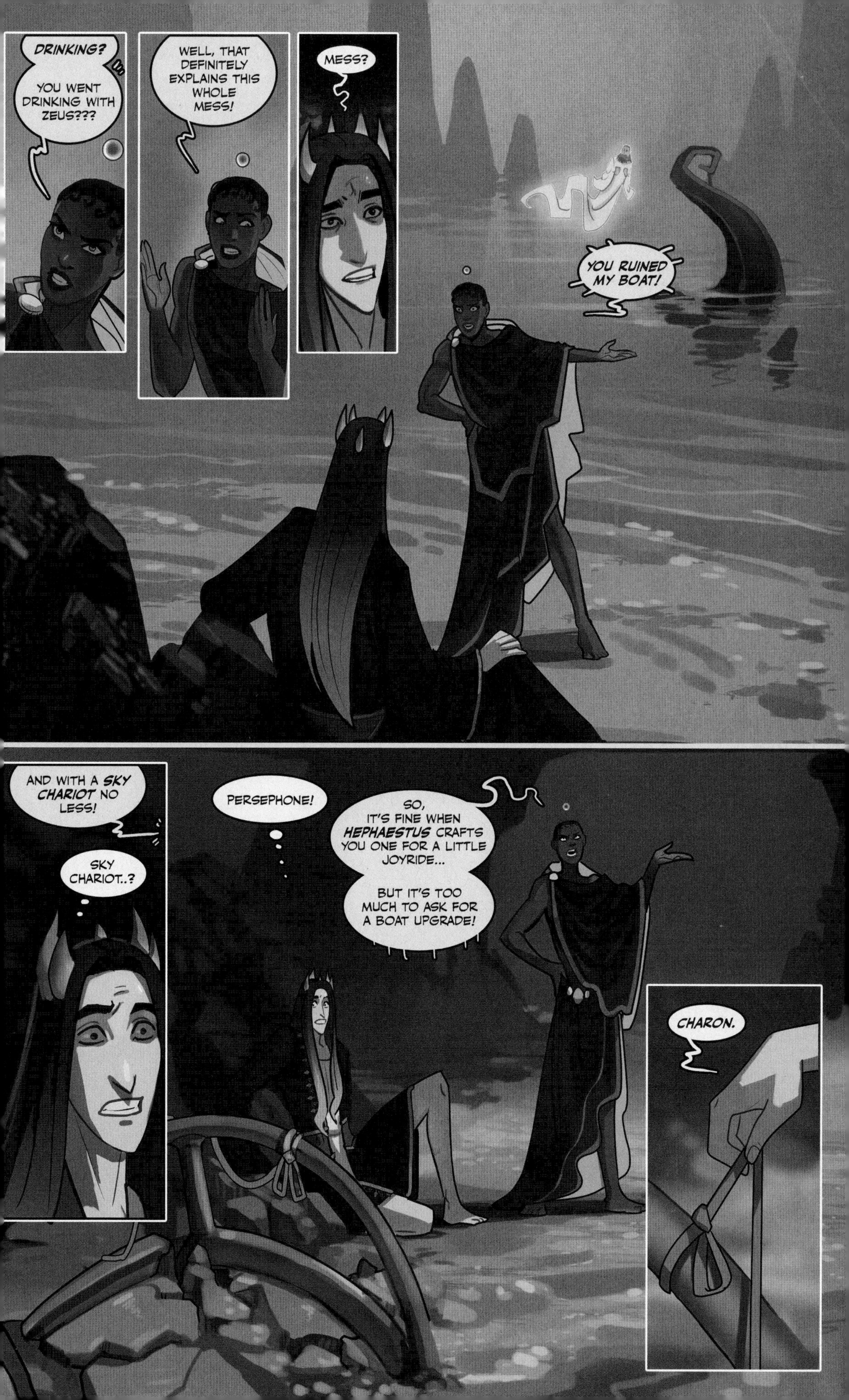
DRINKING?
YOU WENT DRINKING WITH ZEUS???
WELL, THAT DEFINITELY EXPLAINS THIS WHOLE MESS!
MESS?
YOU RUINED MY BOAT!
AND WITH A SKY CHARIOT NO LESS!
SKY CHARIOT..?
PERSEPHONE!
SO, IT'S FINE WHEN HEPHAESTUS CRAFTS YOU ONE FOR A LITTLE JOYRIDE...
BUT IT'S TOO MUCH TO ASK FOR A BOAT UPGRADE!
CHARON.

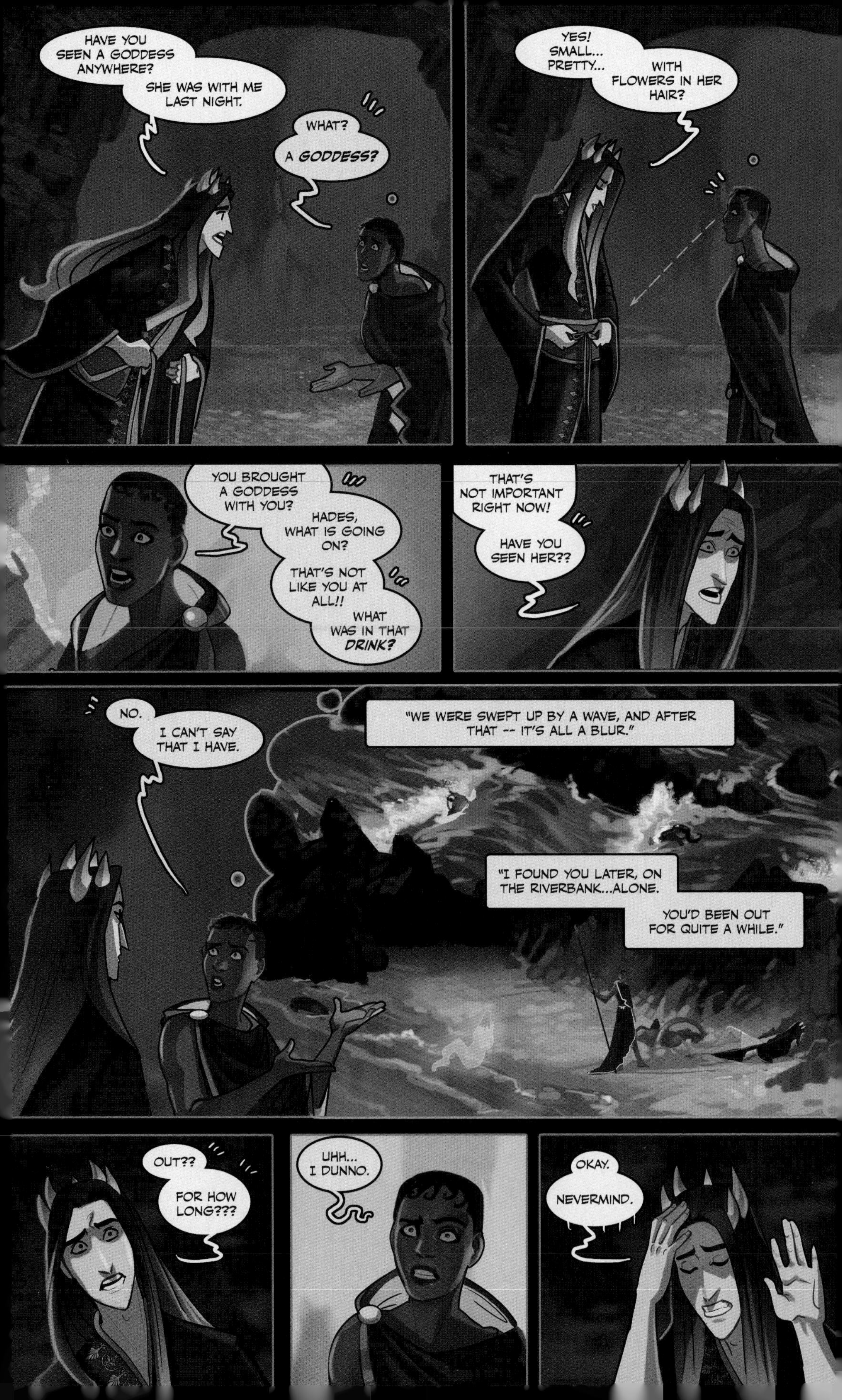
HAVE YOU SEEN A GODDESS ANYWHERE?
SHE WAS WITH ME LAST NIGHT.
WHAT?
A *GODDESS?*
YES! SMALL... PRETTY...
WITH FLOWERS IN HER HAIR?
YOU BROUGHT A GODDESS WITH YOU?
HADES, WHAT IS GOING ON?
THAT'S NOT LIKE YOU AT ALL!!
WHAT WAS IN THAT *DRINK?*
THAT'S NOT IMPORTANT RIGHT NOW!
HAVE YOU SEEN HER??
NO.
I CAN'T SAY THAT I HAVE.
"WE WERE SWEPT UP BY A WAVE, AND AFTER THAT -- IT'S ALL A BLUR."
"I FOUND YOU LATER, ON THE RIVERBANK...ALONE.
YOU'D BEEN OUT FOR QUITE A WHILE."
OUT??
FOR HOW LONG???
UHH... I DUNNO.
OKAY.
NEVERMIND.

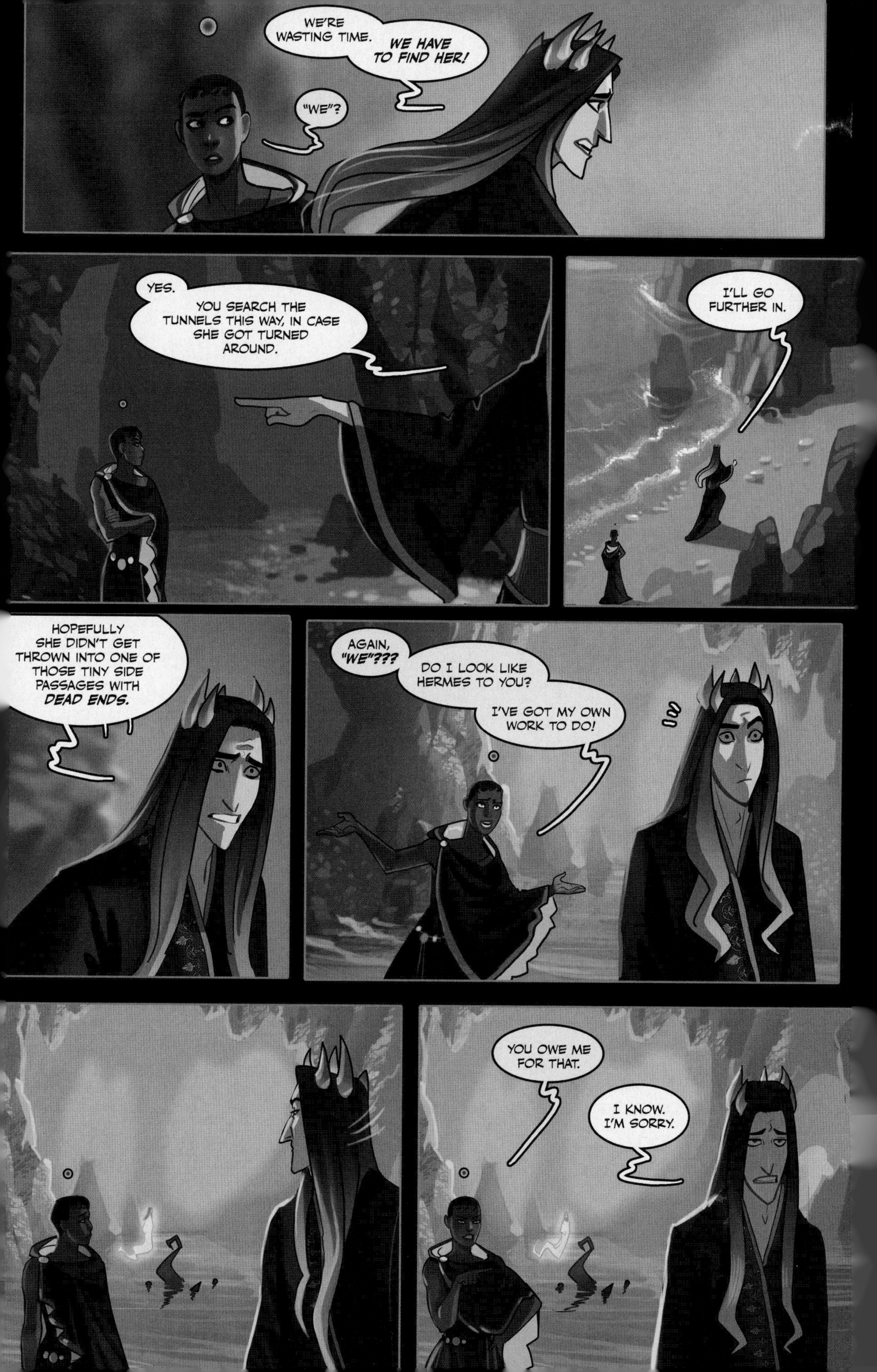
WE'RE WASTING TIME. *WE HAVE TO FIND HER!*
"WE"?
YES.
YOU SEARCH THE TUNNELS THIS WAY, IN CASE SHE GOT TURNED AROUND.
I'LL GO FURTHER IN.
HOPEFULLY SHE DIDN'T GET THROWN INTO ONE OF THOSE TINY SIDE PASSAGES WITH *DEAD ENDS.*
AGAIN, *"WE"???*
DO I LOOK LIKE HERMES TO YOU?
I'VE GOT MY OWN WORK TO DO!
YOU OWE ME FOR THAT.
I KNOW. I'M SORRY.

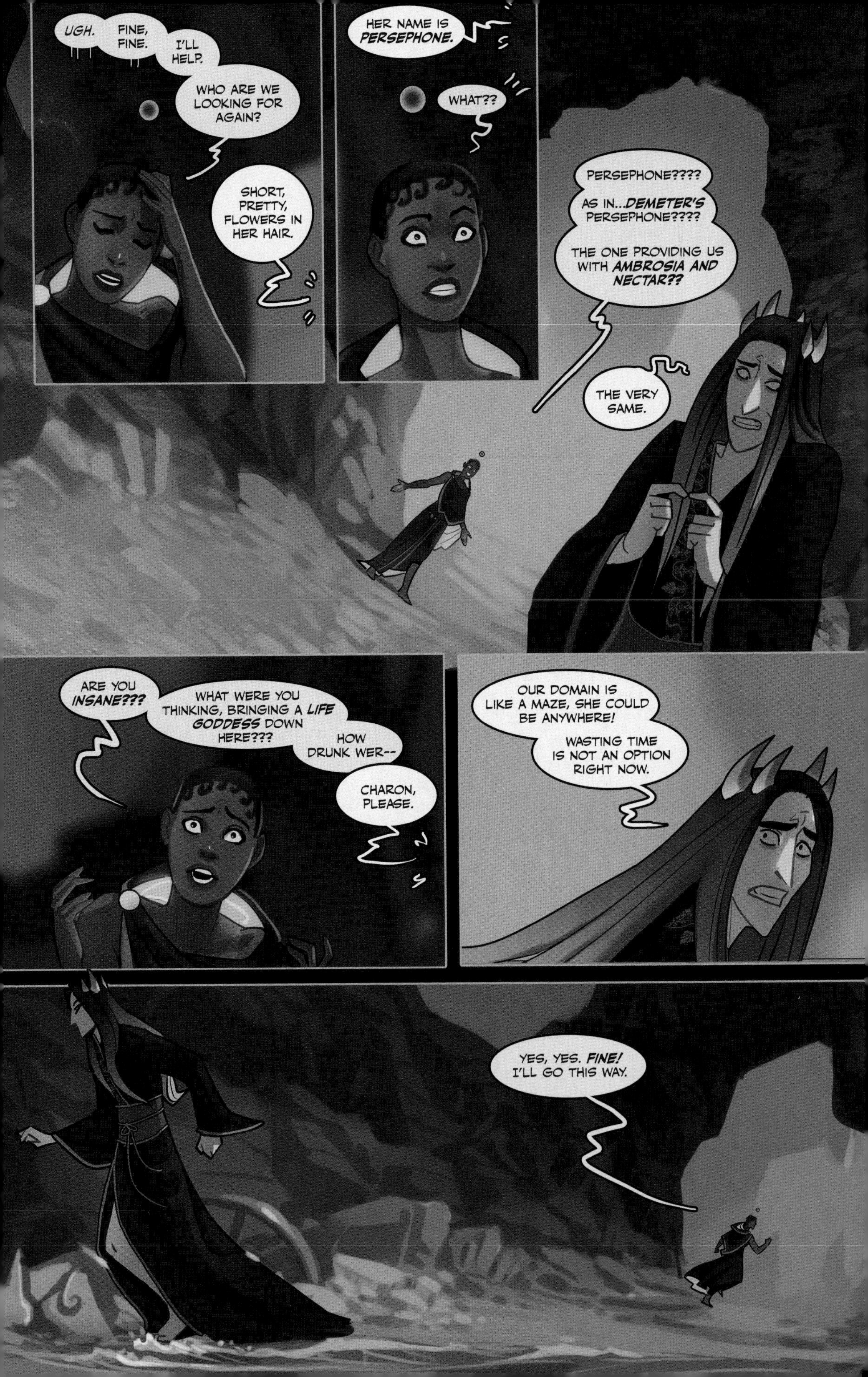
UGH.
FINE, FINE.
I'LL HELP.
WHO ARE WE LOOKING FOR AGAIN?
SHORT, PRETTY, FLOWERS IN HER HAIR.
HER NAME IS *PERSEPHONE.*
WHAT??
PERSEPHONE????
AS IN...*DEMETER'S* PERSEPHONE????
THE ONE PROVIDING US WITH *AMBROSIA AND NECTAR??*
THE VERY SAME.
ARE YOU *INSANE???*
WHAT WERE YOU THINKING, BRINGING A *LIFE GODDESS* DOWN HERE???
HOW DRUNK WER--
CHARON, PLEASE.
OUR DOMAIN IS LIKE A MAZE, SHE COULD BE ANYWHERE!
WASTING TIME IS NOT AN OPTION RIGHT NOW.
YES, YES. *FINE!* I'LL GO THIS WAY.

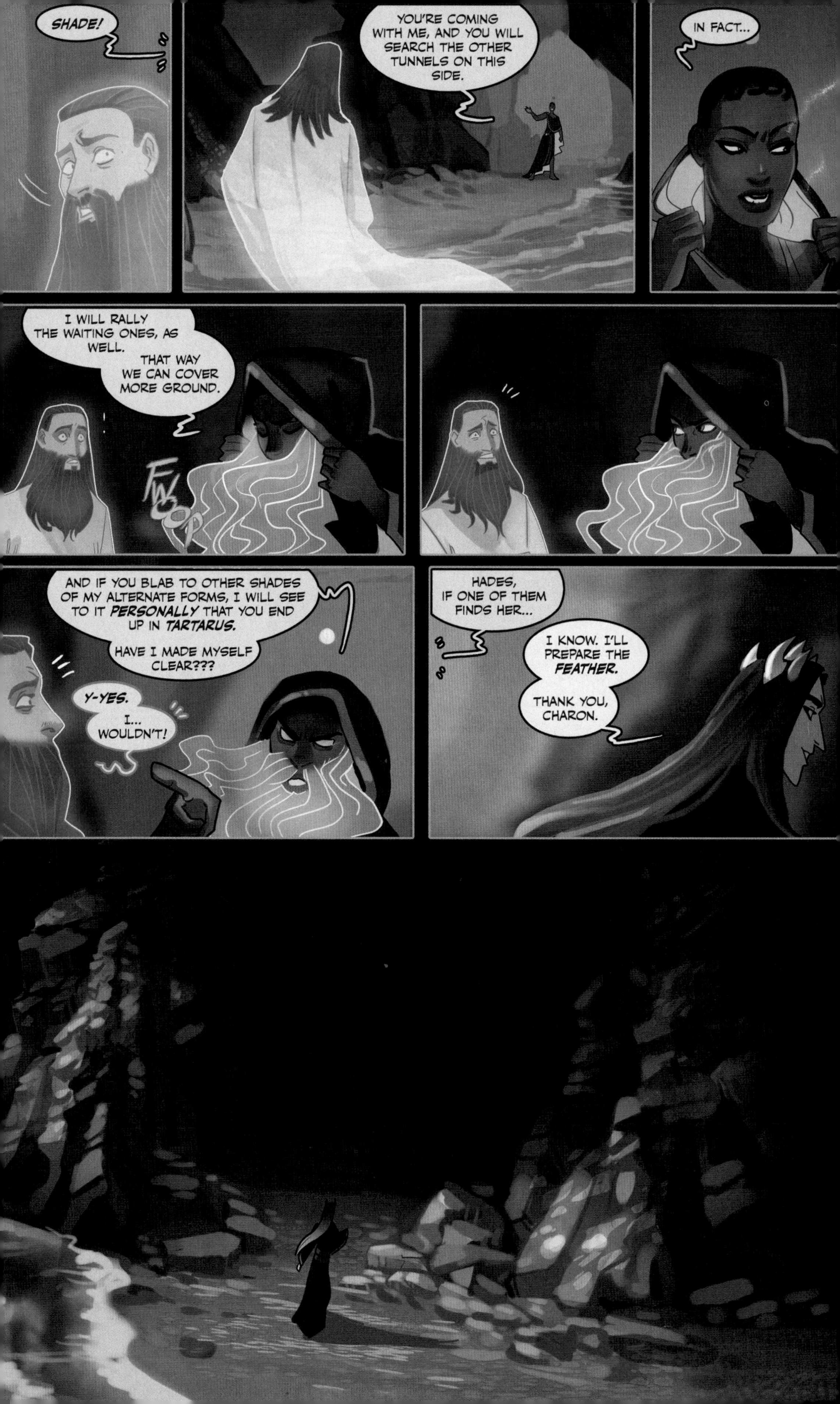
SHADE!
YOU'RE COMING WITH ME, AND YOU WILL SEARCH THE OTHER TUNNELS ON THIS SIDE.
IN FACT...
I WILL RALLY THE WAITING ONES, AS WELL.
THAT WAY WE CAN COVER MORE GROUND.
FWOOP
AND IF YOU BLAB TO OTHER SHADES OF MY ALTERNATE FORMS, I WILL SEE TO IT PERSONALLY THAT YOU END UP IN TARTARUS.
HAVE I MADE MYSELF CLEAR???
Y-YES.
I... WOULDN'T!
HADES, IF ONE OF THEM FINDS HER...
I KNOW. I'LL PREPARE THE FEATHER.
THANK YOU, CHARON.

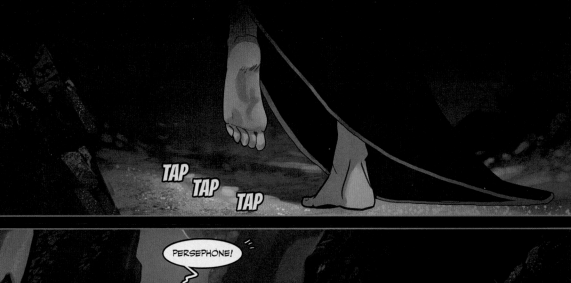

TAP TAP TAP

PERSEPHONE!

PERSEPHONE!!

UGH... SO DARK.

POP

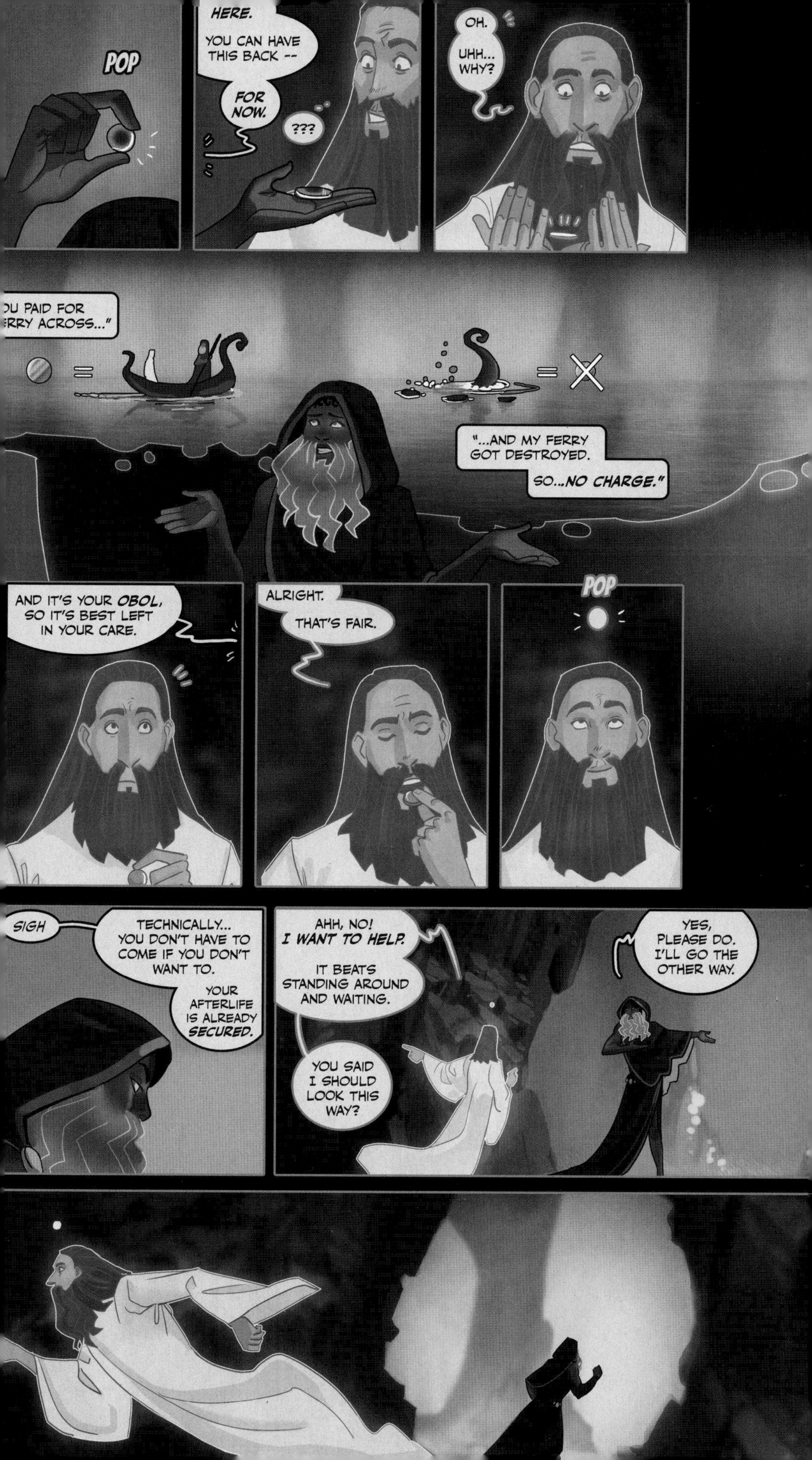
POP
HERE.
YOU CAN HAVE THIS BACK --
FOR NOW.
???
OH.
UHH... WHY?
OU PAID FOR
ERRY ACROSS..."
"...AND MY FERRY GOT DESTROYED.
SO...NO CHARGE."
AND IT'S YOUR OBOL, SO IT'S BEST LEFT IN YOUR CARE.
ALRIGHT.
THAT'S FAIR.
POP
SIGH
TECHNICALLY... YOU DON'T HAVE TO COME IF YOU DON'T WANT TO.
YOUR AFTERLIFE IS ALREADY SECURED.
AHH, NO! I WANT TO HELP.
IT BEATS STANDING AROUND AND WAITING.
YOU SAID I SHOULD LOOK THIS WAY?
YES, PLEASE DO. I'LL GO THE OTHER WAY.

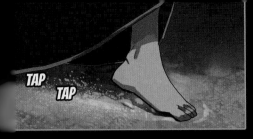

TAP
TAP

PERSEPHONE!

NOT HERE

NOT HERE

AHH!!

TAP   TAP

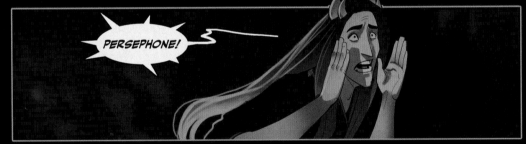

PERSEPHONE!

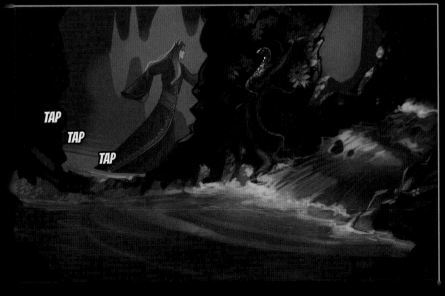

TAP

TAP

TAP

WHERE DID
THE RIVER TAKE
HER...

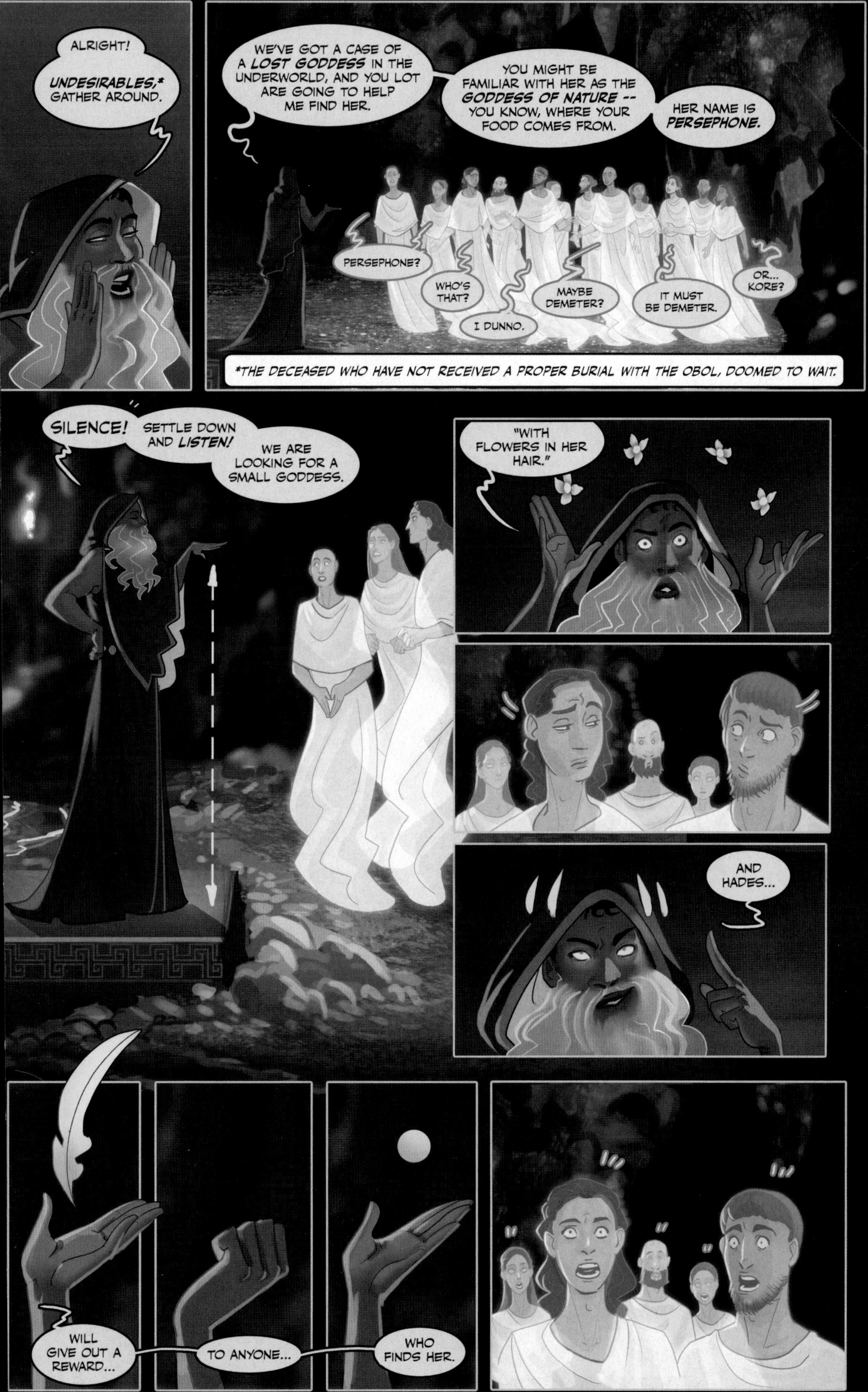

ALRIGHT!
UNDESIRABLES,* GATHER AROUND.
WE'VE GOT A CASE OF A LOST GODDESS IN THE UNDERWORLD, AND YOU LOT ARE GOING TO HELP ME FIND HER.
YOU MIGHT BE FAMILIAR WITH HER AS THE GODDESS OF NATURE -- YOU KNOW, WHERE YOUR FOOD COMES FROM.
HER NAME IS PERSEPHONE.
PERSEPHONE?
WHO'S THAT?
I DUNNO.
MAYBE DEMETER?
IT MUST BE DEMETER.
OR... KORE?
*THE DECEASED WHO HAVE NOT RECEIVED A PROPER BURIAL WITH THE OBOL, DOOMED TO WAIT.
SILENCE!
SETTLE DOWN AND LISTEN!
WE ARE LOOKING FOR A SMALL GODDESS.
"WITH FLOWERS IN HER HAIR."
AND HADES...
WILL GIVE OUT A REWARD...
TO ANYONE...
WHO FINDS HER.

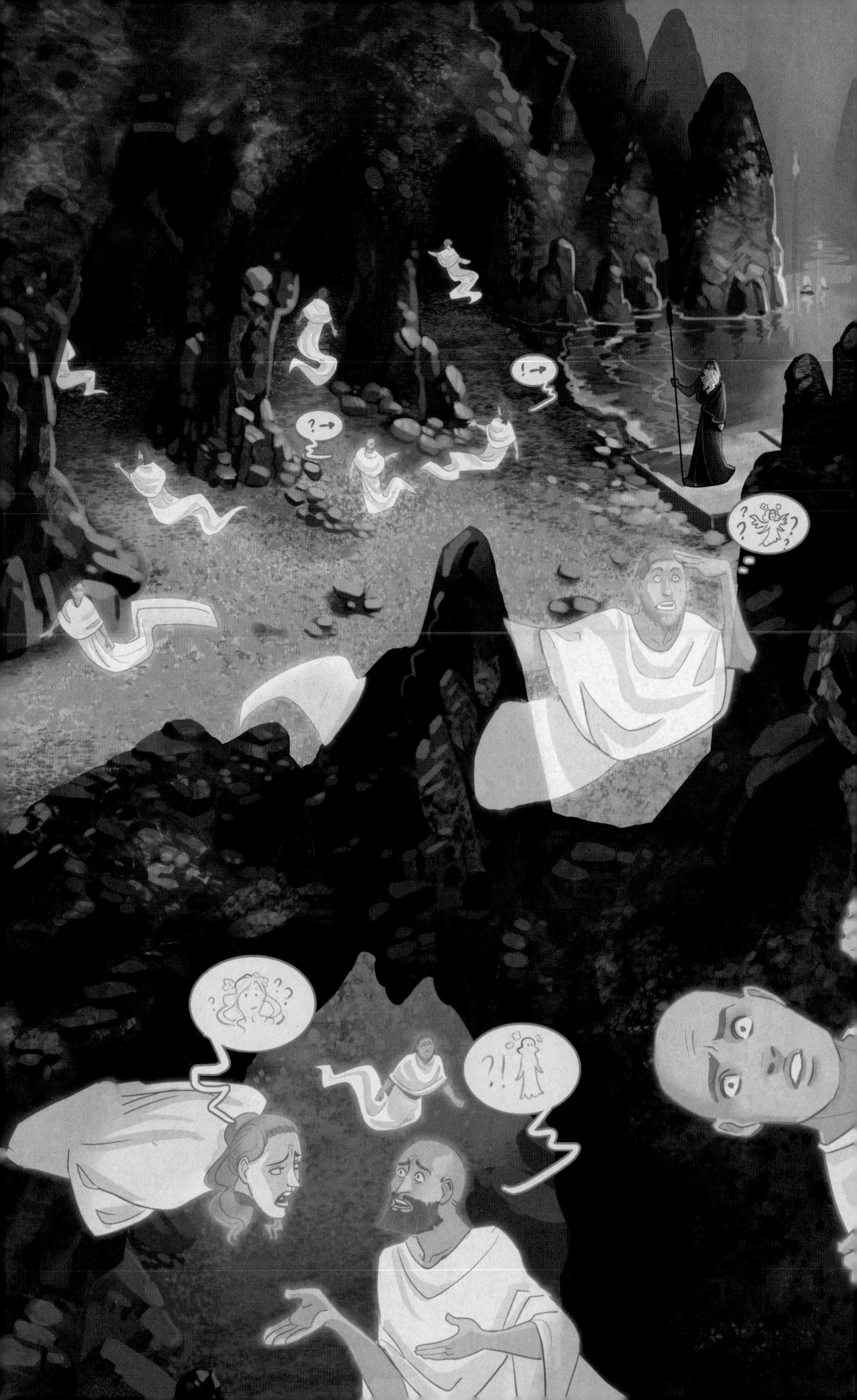

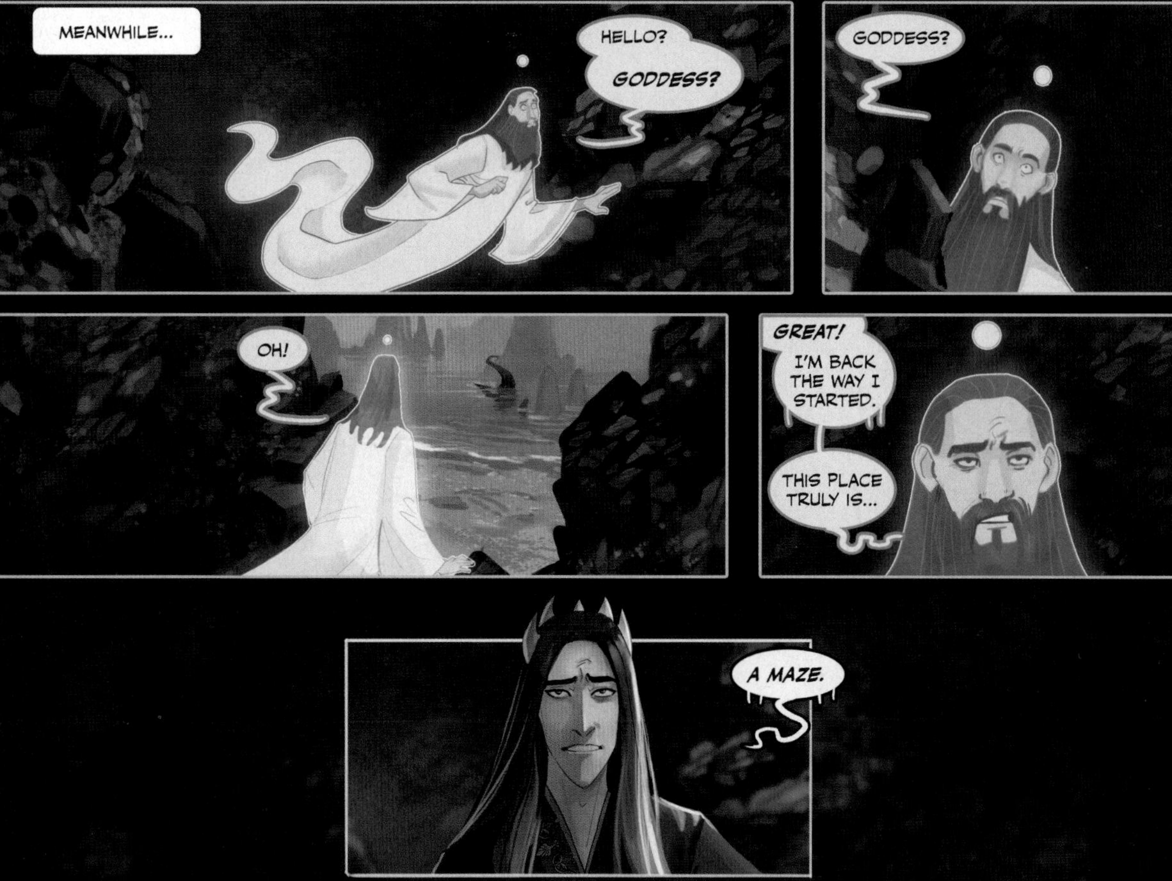
MEANWHILE...
HELLO?
GODDESS?
GODDESS?
OH!
GREAT!
I'M BACK THE WAY I STARTED.
THIS PLACE TRULY IS...
A MAZE.

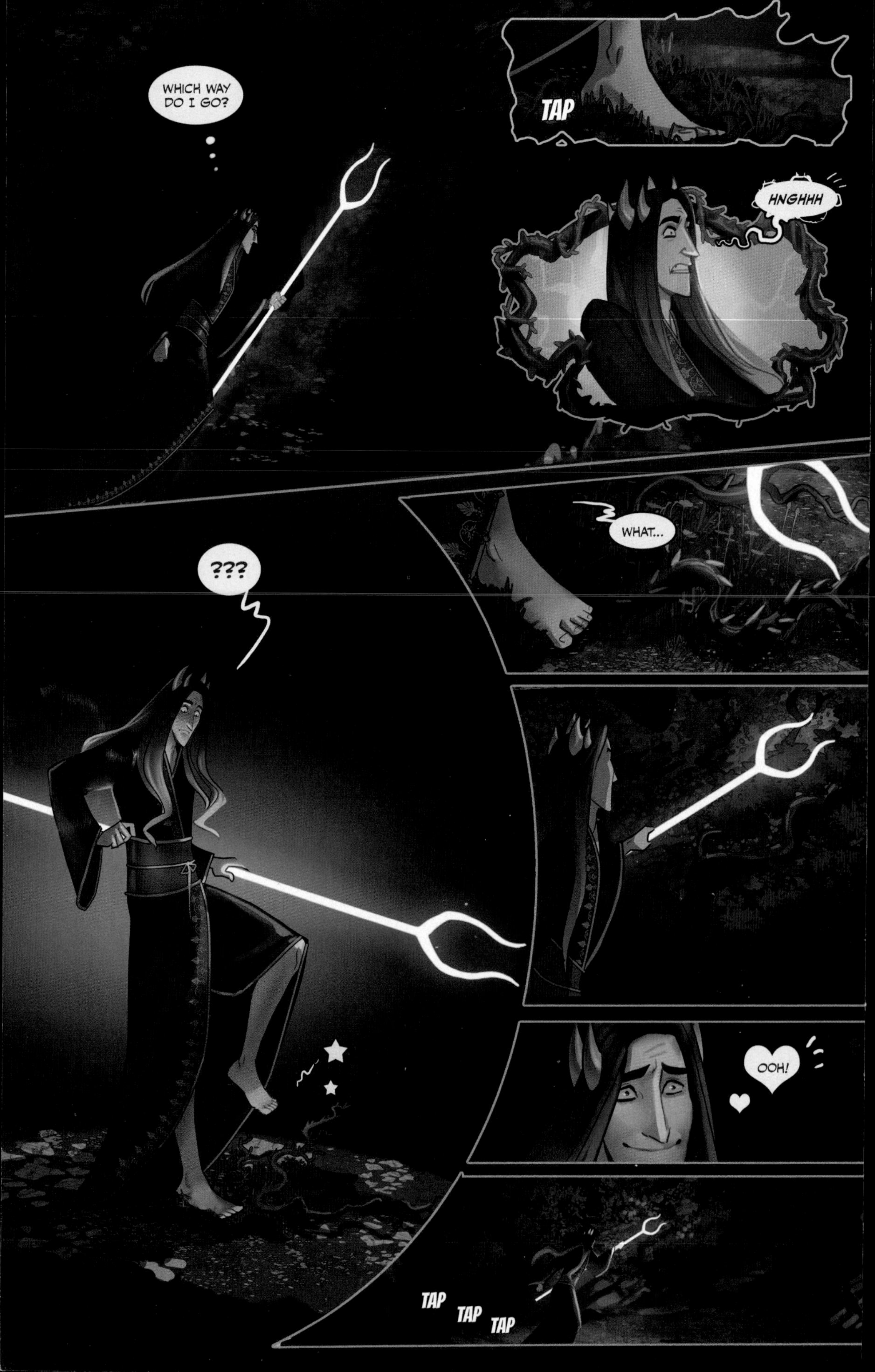

WHICH WAY DO I GO?
TAP
HNGHHH
WHAT...
???
OOH!
TAP
TAP
TAP

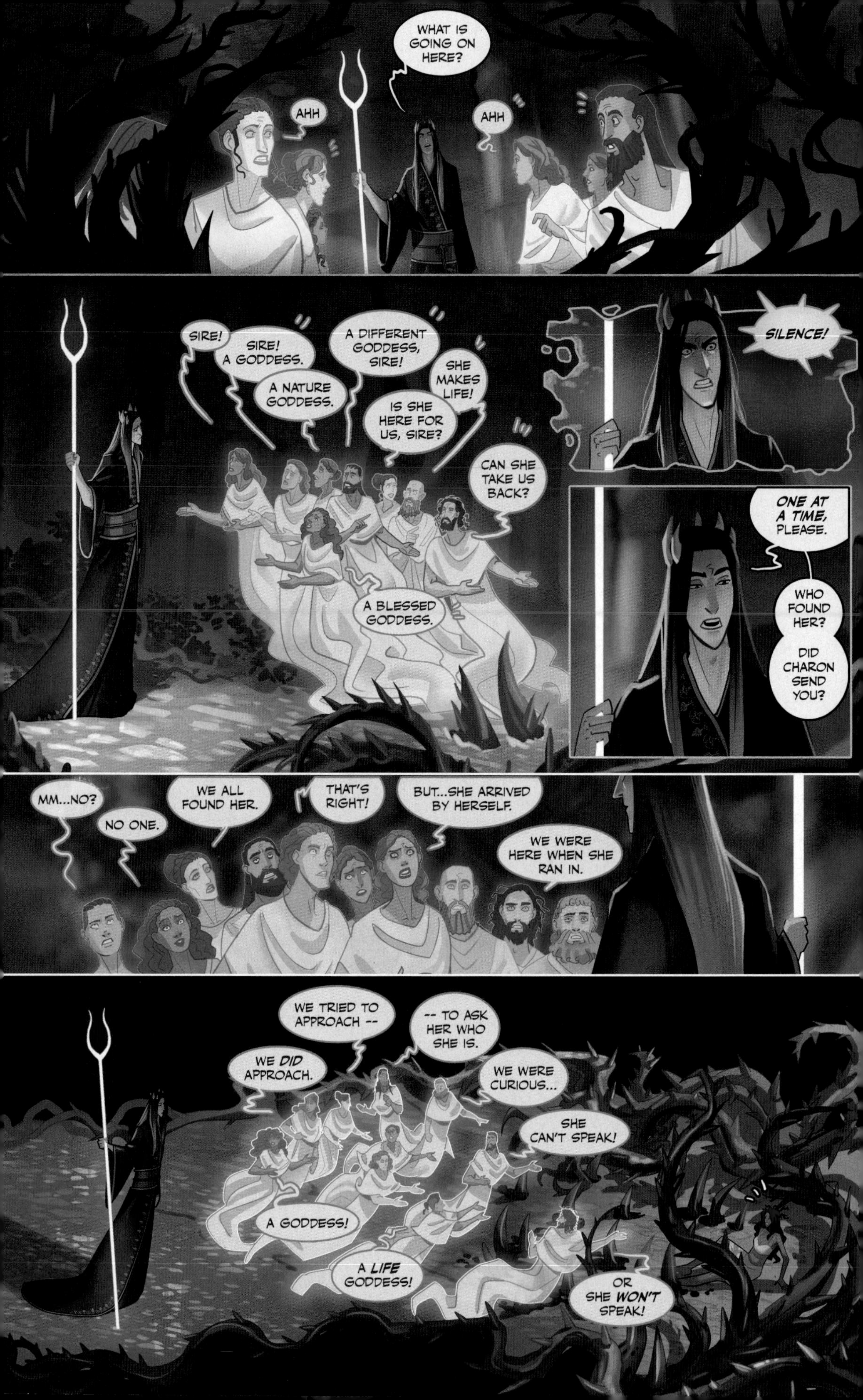
WHAT IS GOING ON HERE?
AHH
AHH
SIRE!
SIRE! A GODDESS.
A NATURE GODDESS.
A DIFFERENT GODDESS, SIRE!
SHE MAKES LIFE!
IS SHE HERE FOR US, SIRE?
CAN SHE TAKE US BACK?
A BLESSED GODDESS.
SILENCE!
ONE AT A TIME, PLEASE.
WHO FOUND HER?
DID CHARON SEND YOU?
MM...NO?
NO ONE.
WE ALL FOUND HER.
THAT'S RIGHT!
BUT...SHE ARRIVED BY HERSELF.
WE WERE HERE WHEN SHE RAN IN.
WE TRIED TO APPROACH --
-- TO ASK HER WHO SHE IS.
WE DID APPROACH.
WE WERE CURIOUS...
SHE CAN'T SPEAK!
A GODDESS!
A LIFE GODDESS!
OR SHE WON'T SPEAK!

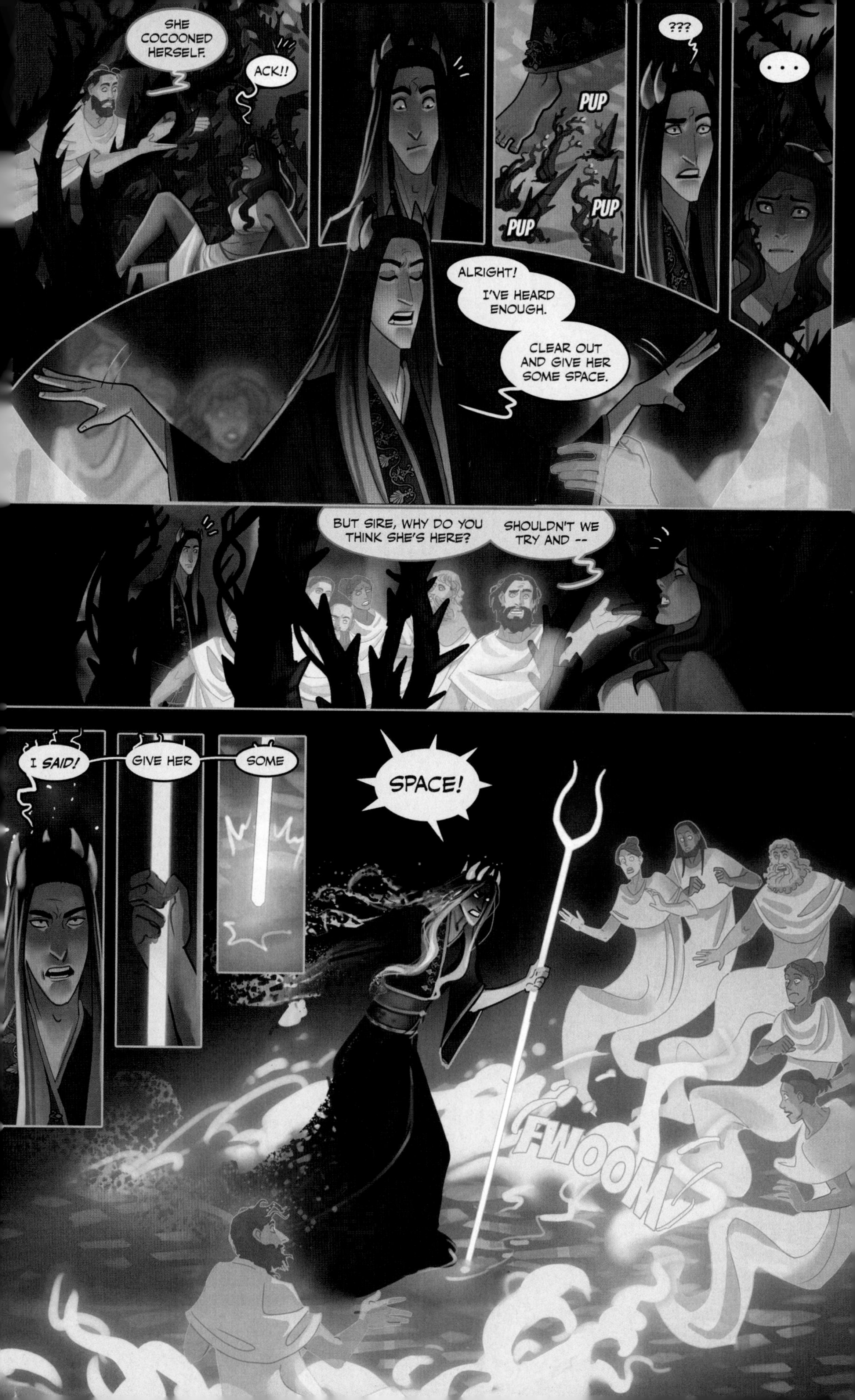
SHE COCOONED HERSELF.
ACK!!
PUP
PUP
PUP
???
...
ALRIGHT!
I'VE HEARD ENOUGH.
CLEAR OUT AND GIVE HER SOME SPACE.
BUT SIRE, WHY DO YOU THINK SHE'S HERE?
SHOULDN'T WE TRY AND --
I SAID!
GIVE HER
SOME
SPACE!
FWOOM

WE CAN DISCUSS THIS *FURTHER* IN MY OFFICE.

HERE.

POOF!

YOU ALL GET A *DOT*, SO I CAN REMEMBER YOU.

TIP

I PROMISED CHARON THAT I WOULD REWARD ONE OF YOU FOR FINDING HER, SO MAKE SURE TO DECIDE AMONGST YOURSELVES WHO IT WILL BE.

NOW RUN ALONG, WHILE I TAKE CARE OF THIS.

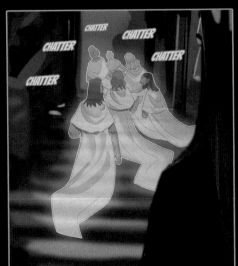

CHATTER
CHATTER
CHATTER
CHATTER
CHATTER

SIGH...

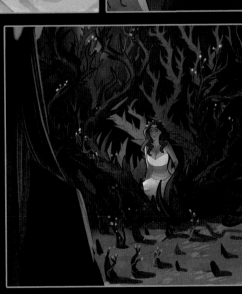

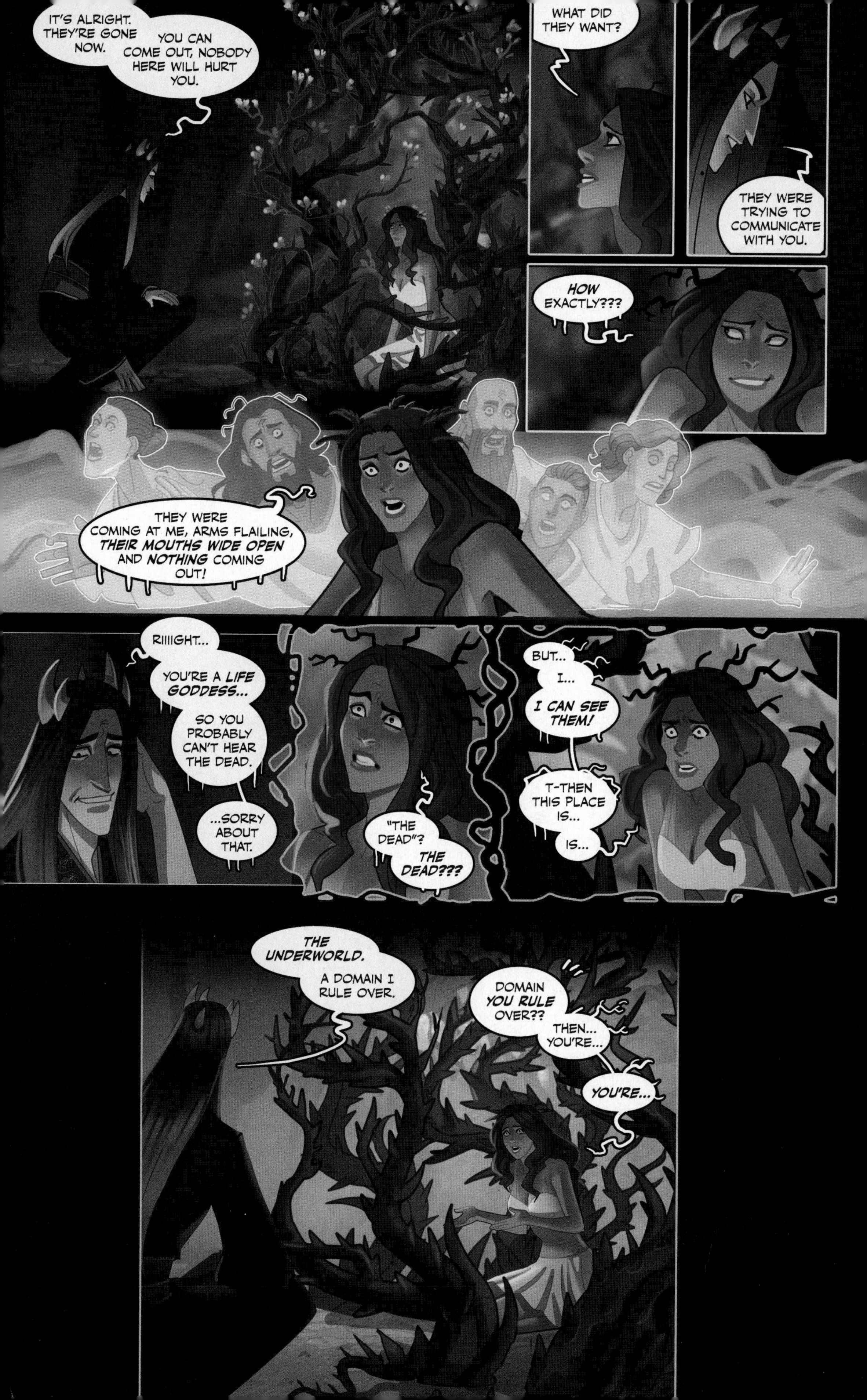
IT'S ALRIGHT. THEY'RE GONE NOW.
YOU CAN COME OUT, NOBODY HERE WILL HURT YOU.
WHAT DID THEY WANT?
THEY WERE TRYING TO COMMUNICATE WITH YOU.
HOW EXACTLY???
THEY WERE COMING AT ME, ARMS FLAILING, *THEIR MOUTHS WIDE OPEN* AND *NOTHING* COMING OUT!
RIIIIGHT...
YOU'RE A *LIFE GODDESS...*
SO YOU PROBABLY CAN'T HEAR THE DEAD.
...SORRY ABOUT THAT.
"THE DEAD"?
THE DEAD???
BUT...
I...
I CAN SEE THEM!
T-THEN THIS PLACE IS...
IS...
THE UNDERWORLD.
A DOMAIN I RULE OVER.
DOMAIN *YOU RULE* OVER??
THEN... YOU'RE...
YOU'RE...

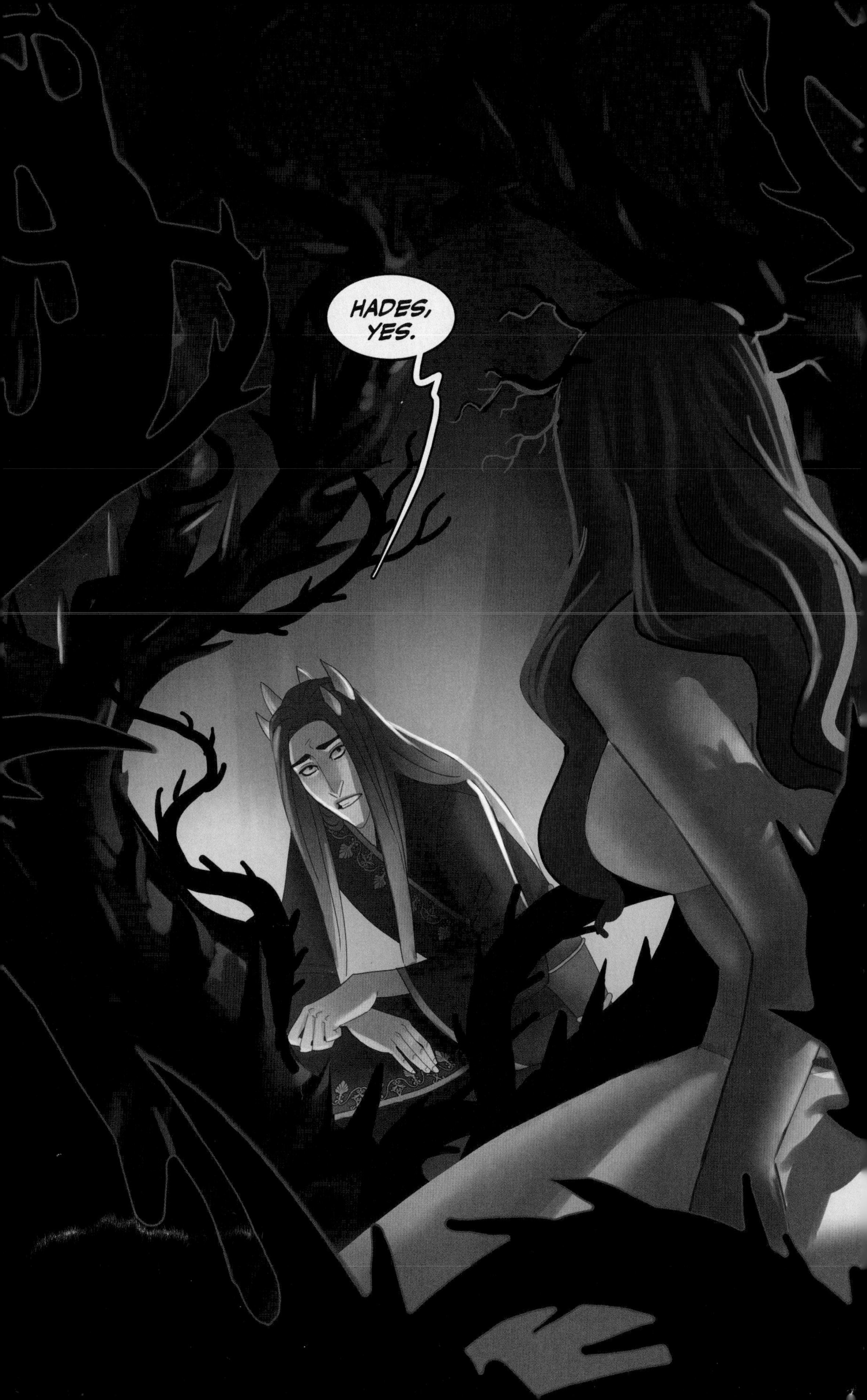
HADES, YES.

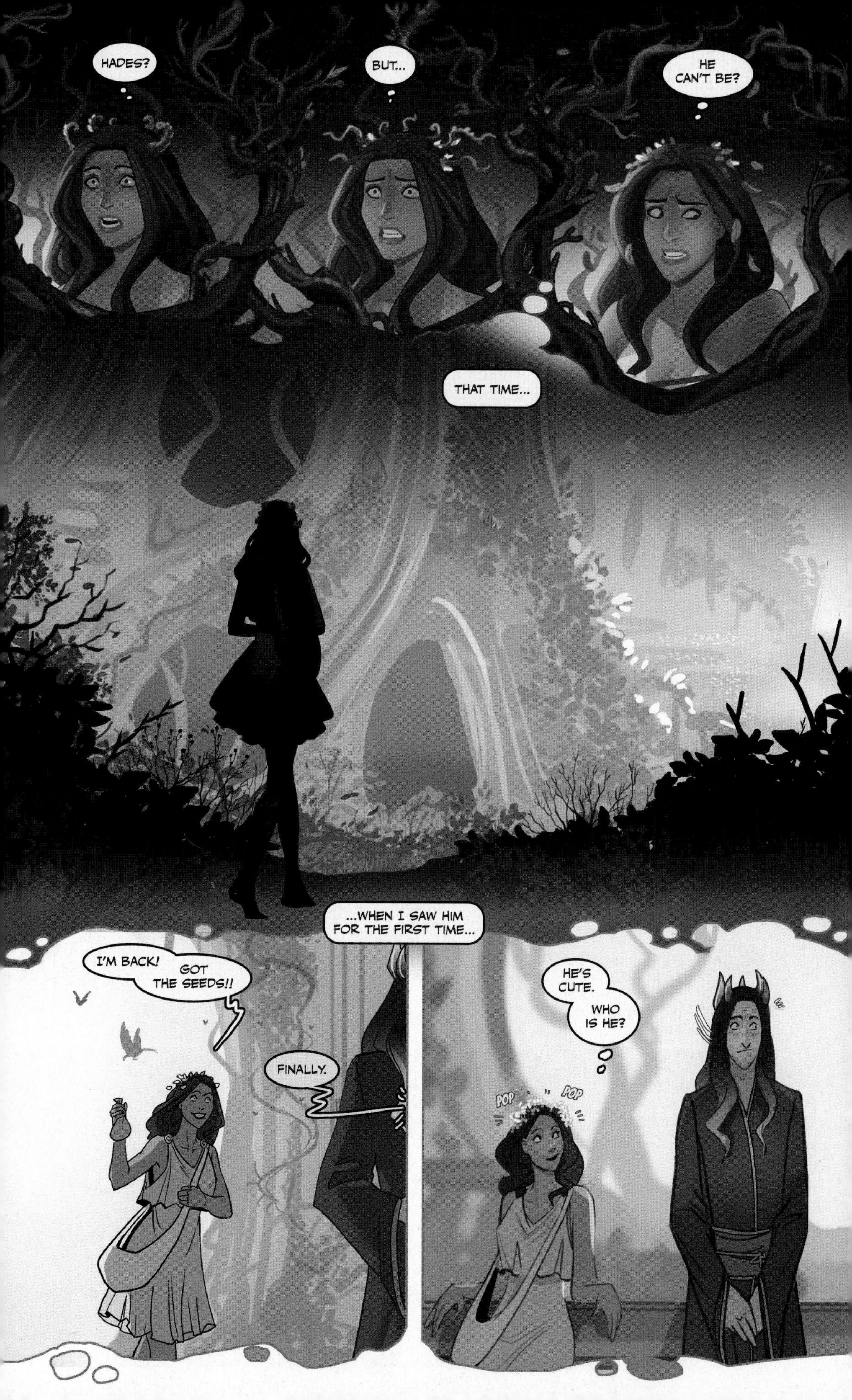
HADES?
BUT...
HE CAN'T BE?
THAT TIME...
...WHEN I SAW HIM FOR THE FIRST TIME...
I'M BACK! GOT THE SEEDS!!
FINALLY.
HE'S CUTE. WHO IS HE?
POP
POP

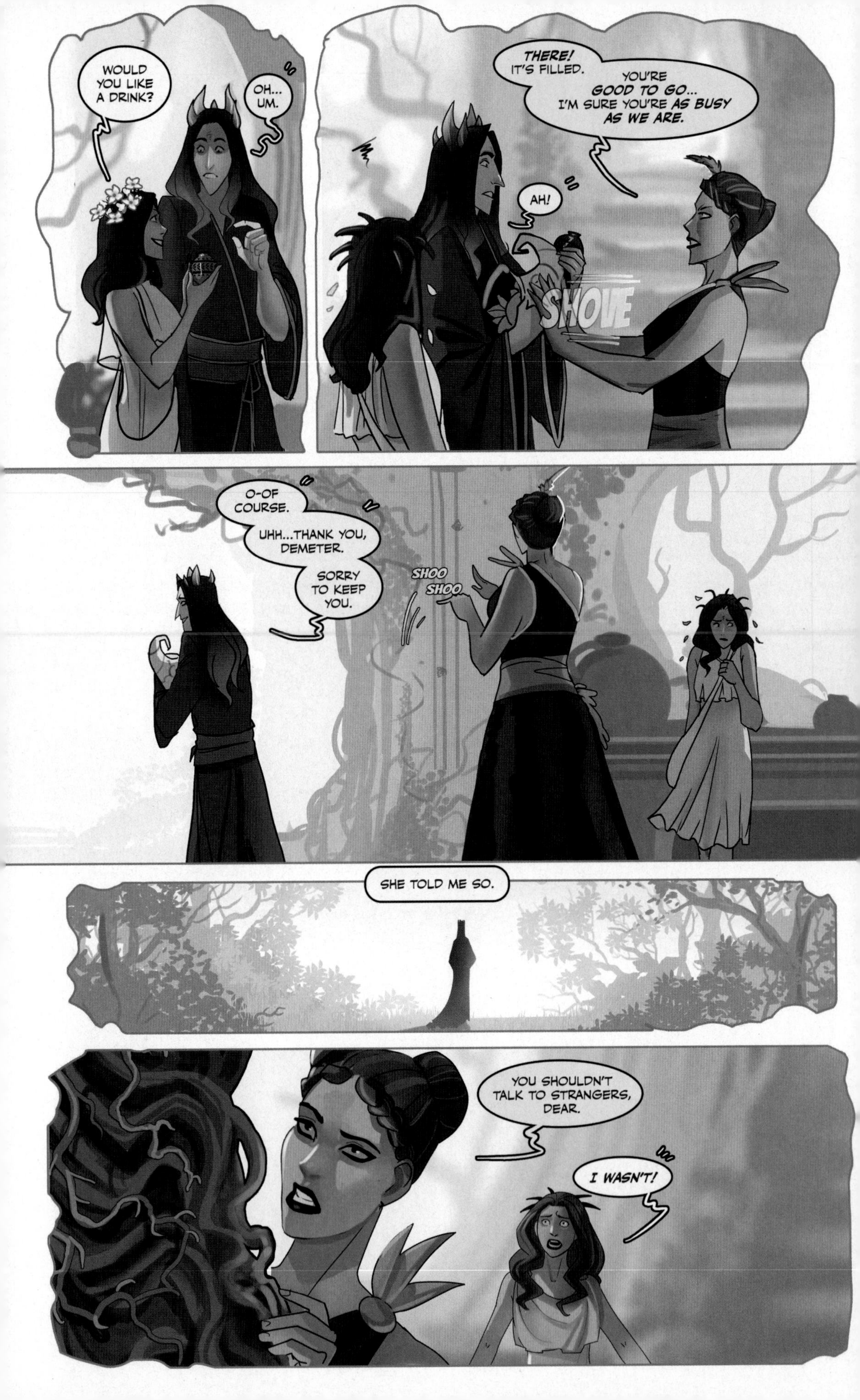
WOULD YOU LIKE A DRINK?
OH... UM.
THERE! IT'S FILLED.
YOU'RE GOOD TO GO... I'M SURE YOU'RE AS BUSY AS WE ARE.
AH!
SHOVE
O-OF COURSE.
UHH...THANK YOU, DEMETER.
SORRY TO KEEP YOU.
SHOO SHOO
SHE TOLD ME SO.
YOU SHOULDN'T TALK TO STRANGERS, DEAR.
I WASN'T!

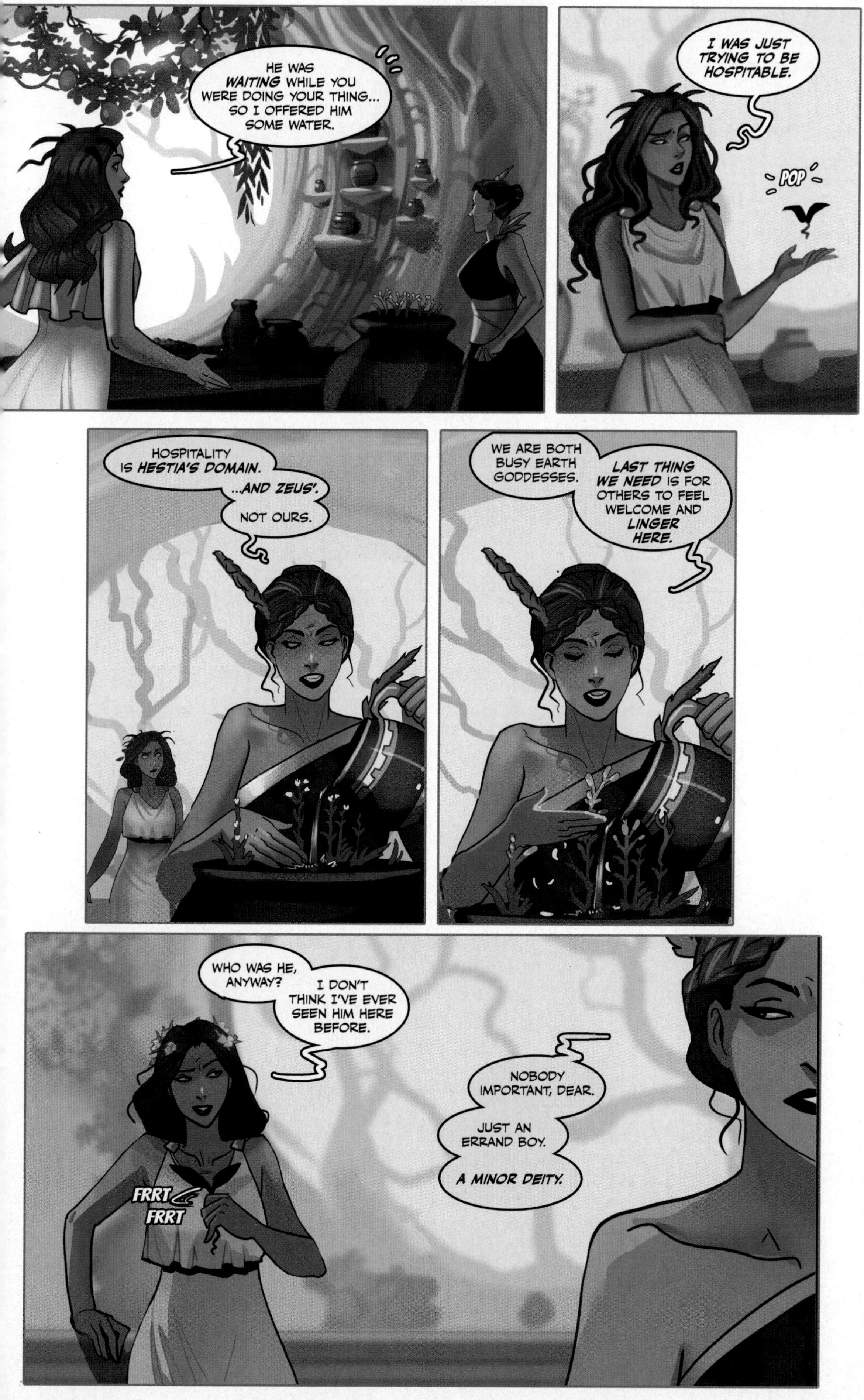
HE WAS WAITING WHILE YOU WERE DOING YOUR THING... SO I OFFERED HIM SOME WATER.
I WAS JUST TRYING TO BE HOSPITABLE.
POP
HOSPITALITY IS HESTIA'S DOMAIN.
...AND ZEUS'.
NOT OURS.
WE ARE BOTH BUSY EARTH GODDESSES.
LAST THING WE NEED IS FOR OTHERS TO FEEL WELCOME AND LINGER HERE.
WHO WAS HE, ANYWAY?
I DON'T THINK I'VE EVER SEEN HIM HERE BEFORE.
NOBODY IMPORTANT, DEAR.
JUST AN ERRAND BOY.
A MINOR DEITY.
FRRT
FRRT

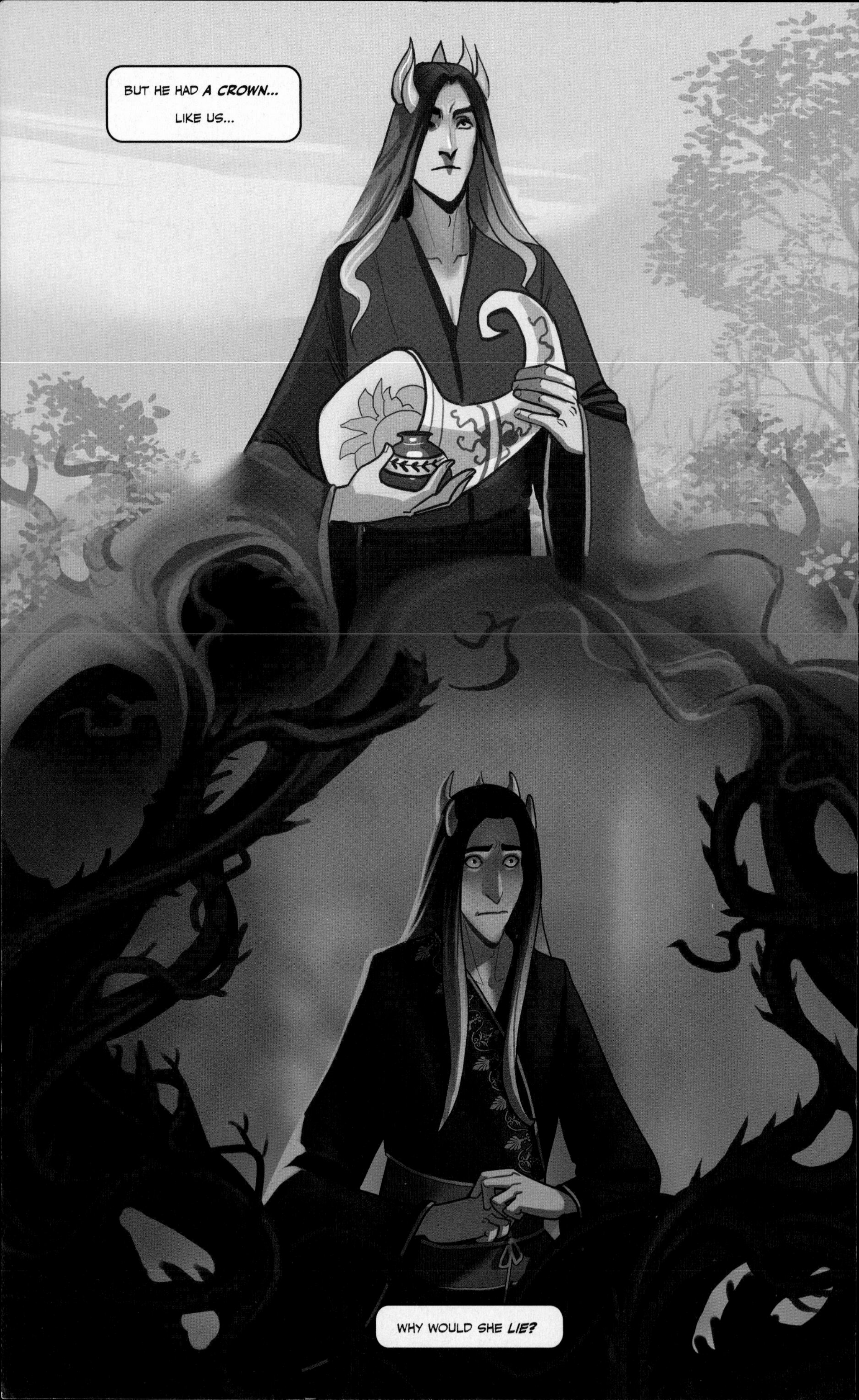
BUT HE HAD A CROWN...
LIKE US...
WHY WOULD SHE LIE?

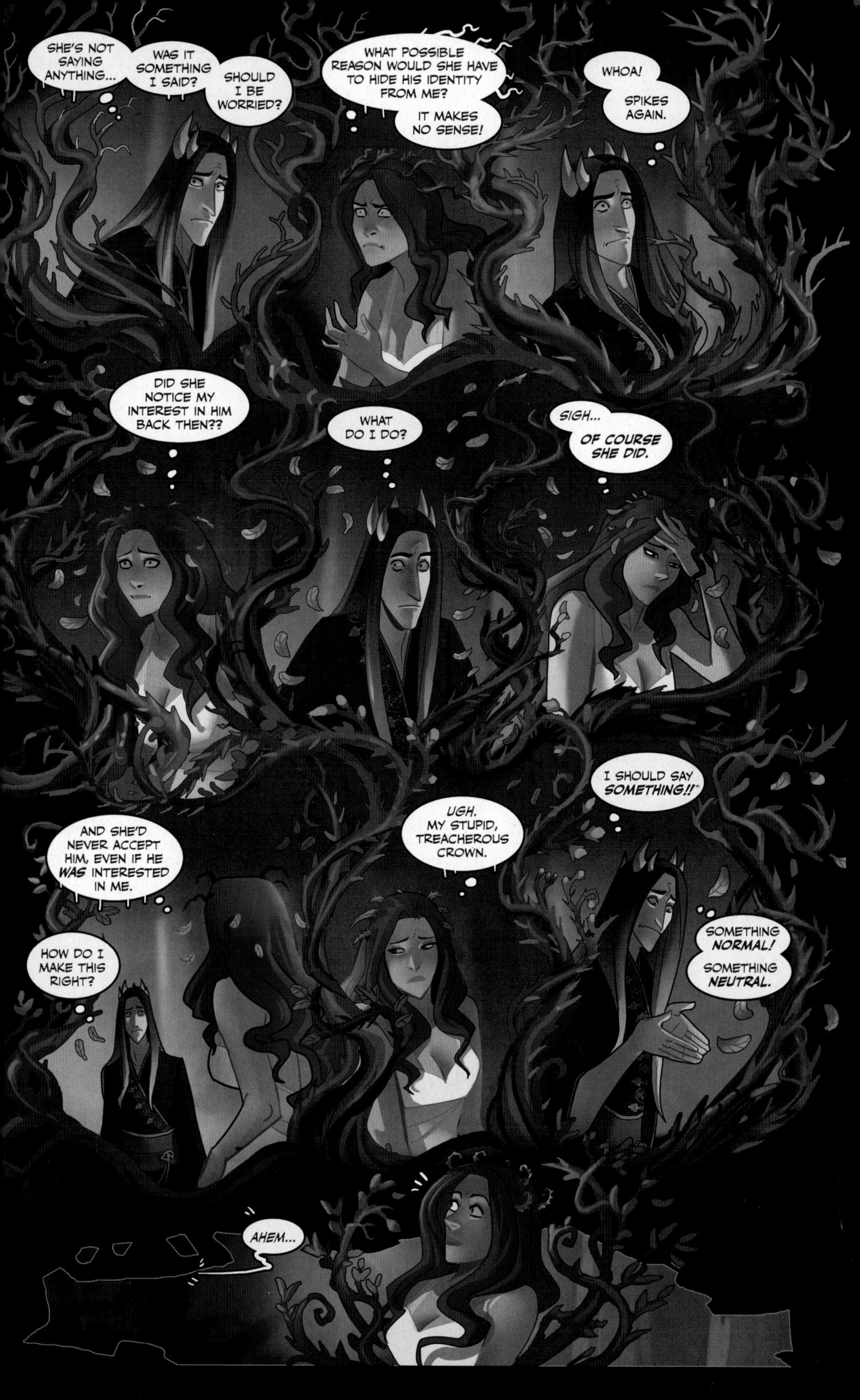
SHE'S NOT SAYING ANYTHING...
WAS IT SOMETHING I SAID?
SHOULD I BE WORRIED?
WHAT POSSIBLE REASON WOULD SHE HAVE TO HIDE HIS IDENTITY FROM ME?
IT MAKES NO SENSE!
WHOA!
SPIKES AGAIN.
DID SHE NOTICE MY INTEREST IN HIM BACK THEN??
WHAT DO I DO?
SIGH...
OF COURSE SHE DID.
AND SHE'D NEVER ACCEPT HIM, EVEN IF HE WAS INTERESTED IN ME.
UGH. MY STUPID, TREACHEROUS CROWN.
I SHOULD SAY SOMETHING!!
HOW DO I MAKE THIS RIGHT?
SOMETHING NORMAL!
SOMETHING NEUTRAL.
AHEM...

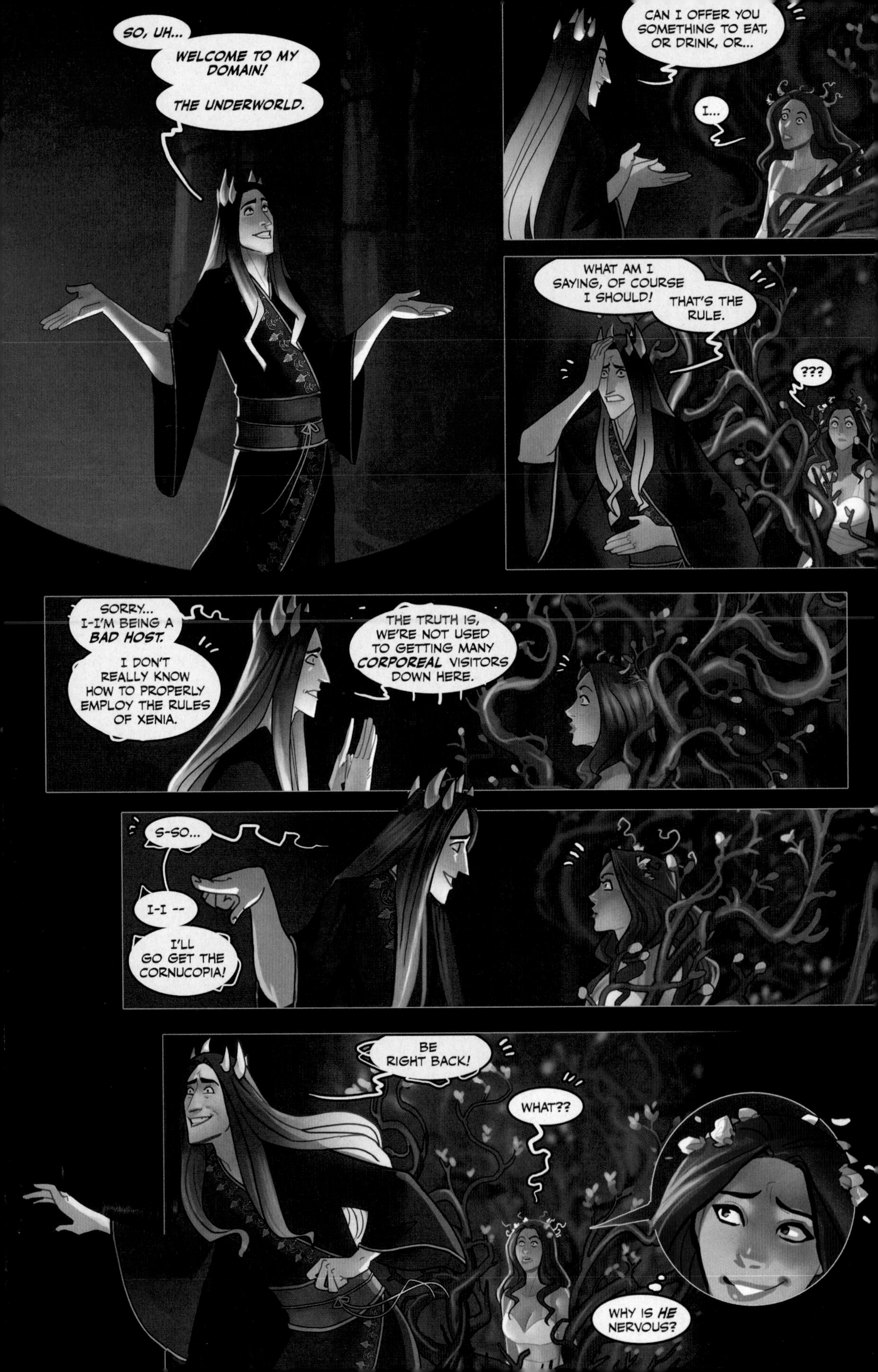
SO, UH...
WELCOME TO MY DOMAIN!
THE UNDERWORLD.
CAN I OFFER YOU SOMETHING TO EAT, OR DRINK, OR...
I...
WHAT AM I SAYING, OF COURSE I SHOULD!
THAT'S THE RULE.
???
SORRY... I-I'M BEING A BAD HOST.
I DON'T REALLY KNOW HOW TO PROPERLY EMPLOY THE RULES OF XENIA.
THE TRUTH IS, WE'RE NOT USED TO GETTING MANY CORPOREAL VISITORS DOWN HERE.
S-SO...
I-I --
I'LL GO GET THE CORNUCOPIA!
BE RIGHT BACK!
WHAT??
WHY IS HE NERVOUS?

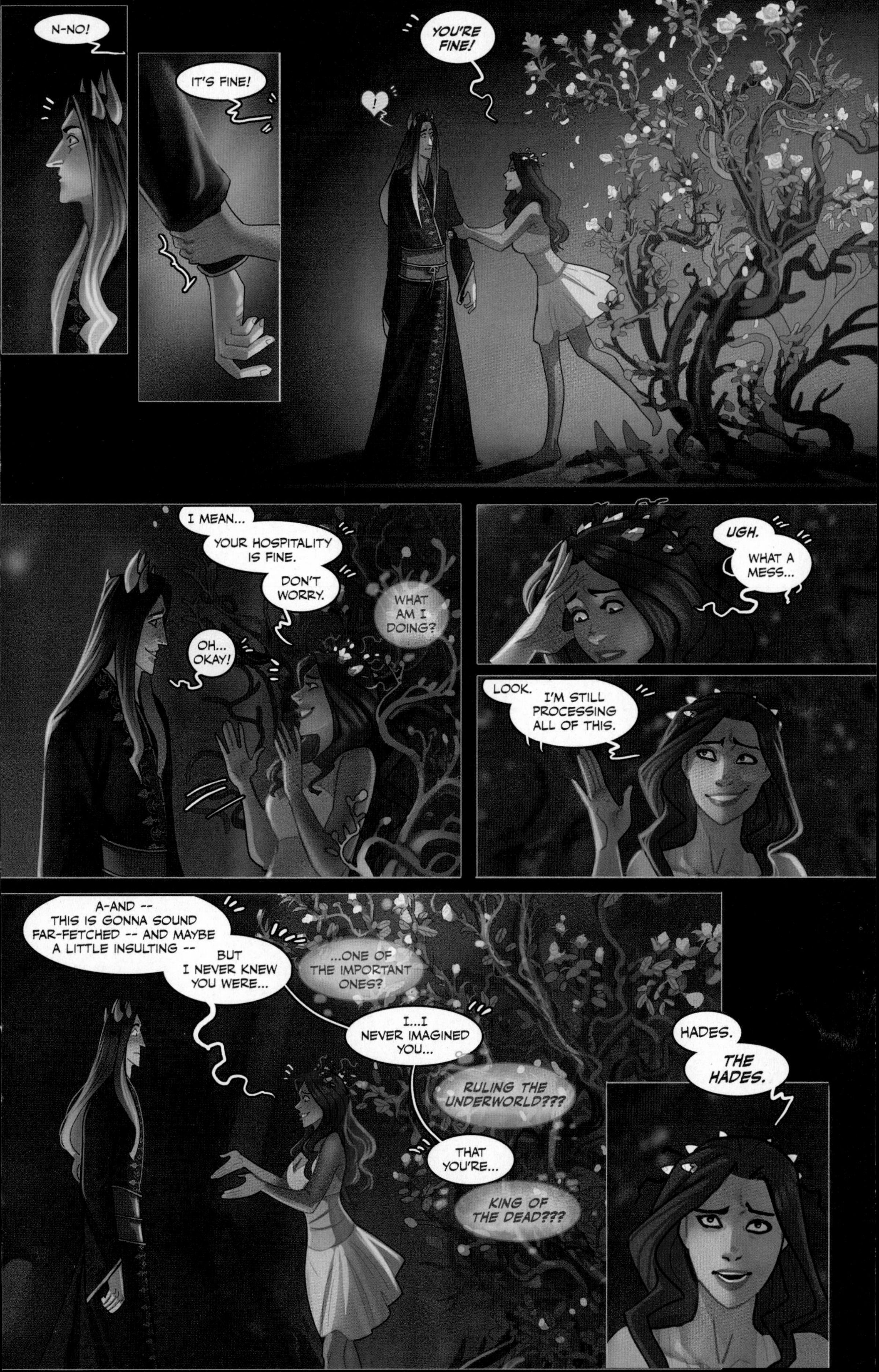
N-NO!
IT'S FINE!
YOU'RE FINE!
I MEAN...
YOUR HOSPITALITY IS FINE.
DON'T WORRY.
WHAT AM I DOING?
OH... OKAY!
UGH.
WHAT A MESS...
LOOK.
I'M STILL PROCESSING ALL OF THIS.
A-AND -- THIS IS GONNA SOUND FAR-FETCHED -- AND MAYBE A LITTLE INSULTING --
BUT I NEVER KNEW YOU WERE...
...ONE OF THE IMPORTANT ONES?
I...I NEVER IMAGINED YOU...
RULING THE UNDERWORLD???
THAT YOU'RE...
KING OF THE DEAD???
HADES.
THE HADES.

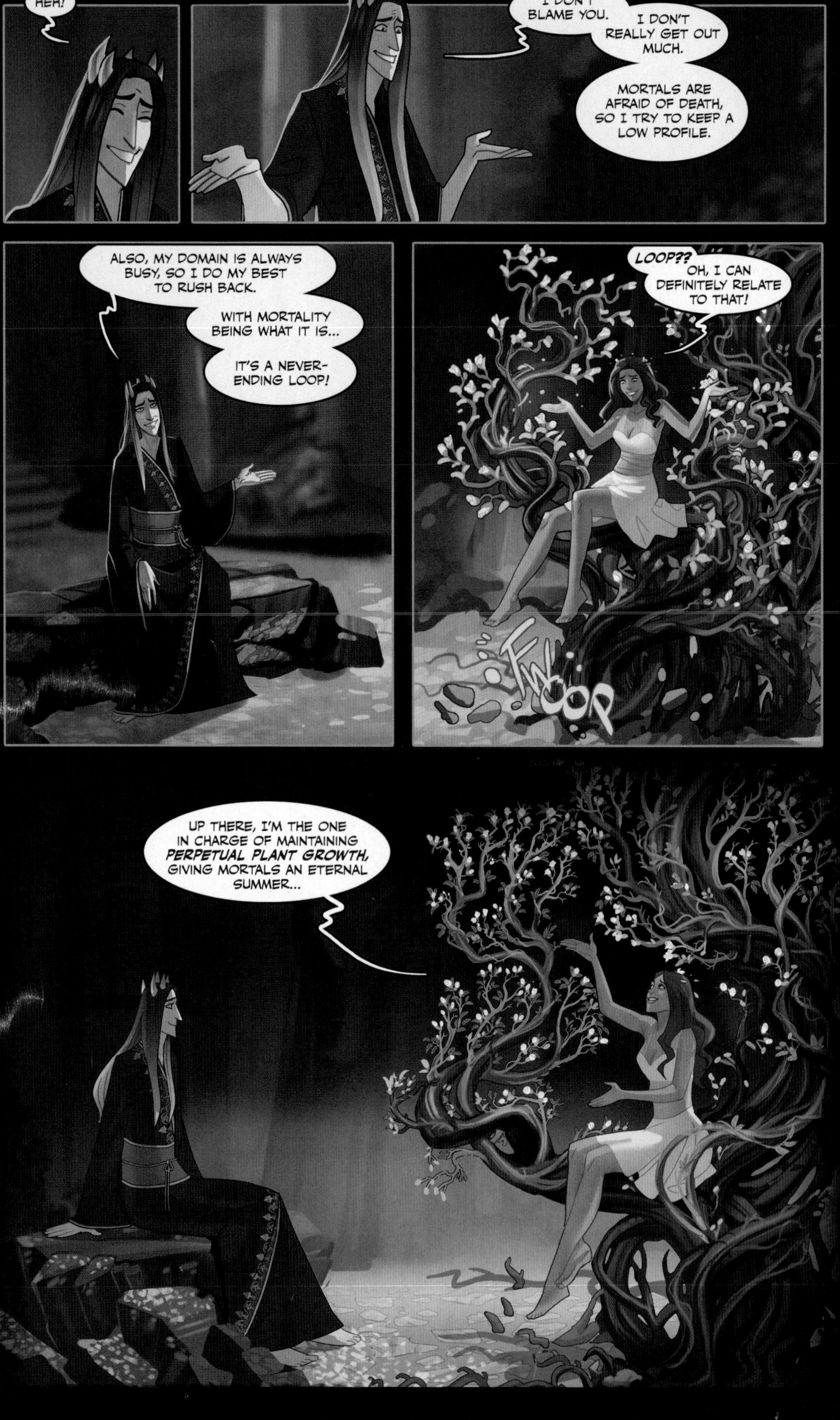
HEH!
I DON'T BLAME YOU.
I DON'T REALLY GET OUT MUCH.
MORTALS ARE AFRAID OF DEATH, SO I TRY TO KEEP A LOW PROFILE.
ALSO, MY DOMAIN IS ALWAYS BUSY, SO I DO MY BEST TO RUSH BACK.
WITH MORTALITY BEING WHAT IT IS...
IT'S A NEVER-ENDING LOOP!
LOOP?? OH, I CAN DEFINITELY RELATE TO THAT!
FWOOP
UP THERE, I'M THE ONE IN CHARGE OF MAINTAINING PERPETUAL PLANT GROWTH, GIVING MORTALS AN ETERNAL SUMMER...

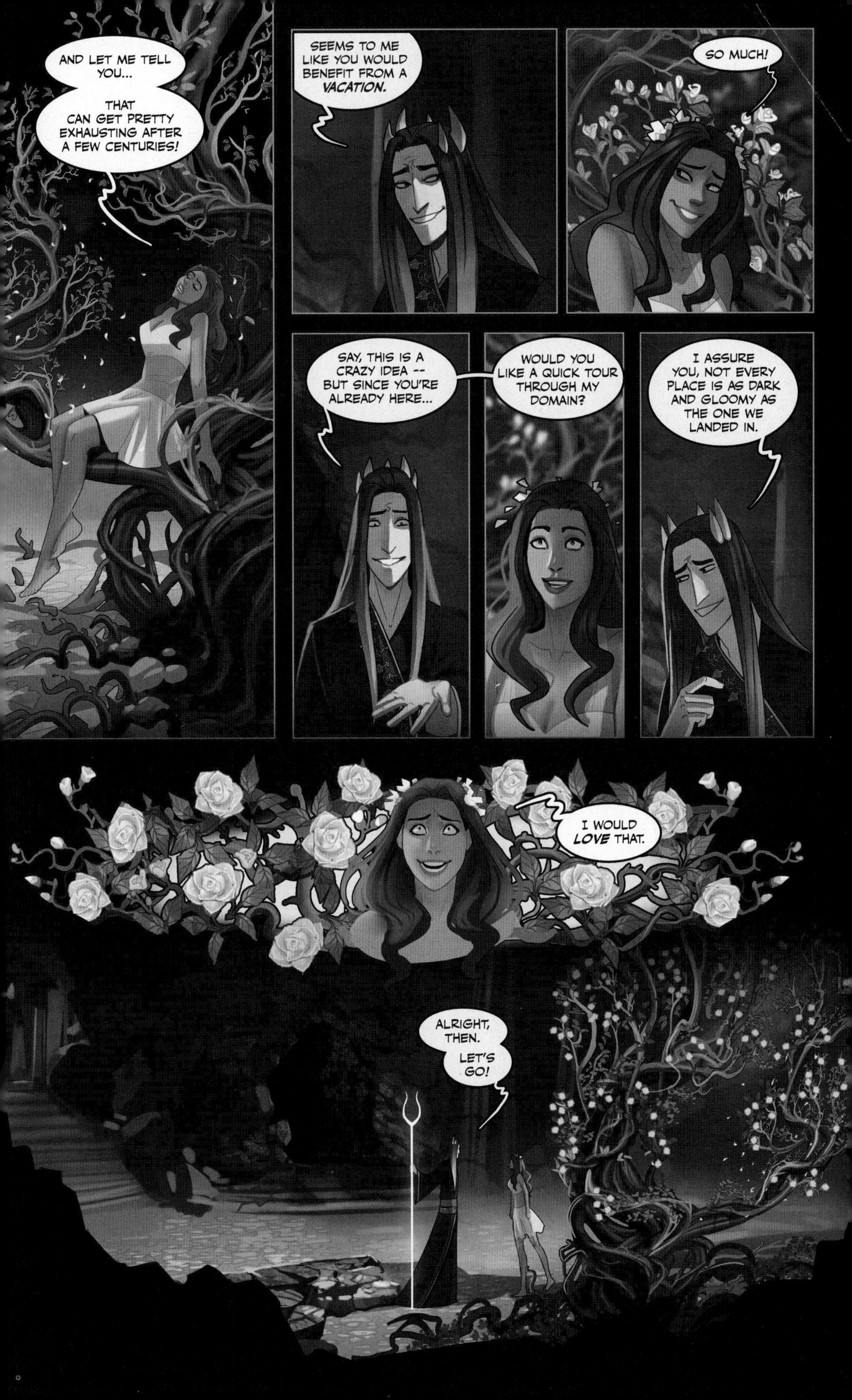
AND LET ME TELL YOU...
THAT CAN GET PRETTY EXHAUSTING AFTER A FEW CENTURIES!
SEEMS TO ME LIKE YOU WOULD BENEFIT FROM A *VACATION.*
SO MUCH!
SAY, THIS IS A CRAZY IDEA -- BUT SINCE YOU'RE ALREADY HERE...
WOULD YOU LIKE A QUICK TOUR THROUGH MY DOMAIN?
I ASSURE YOU, NOT EVERY PLACE IS AS DARK AND GLOOMY AS THE ONE WE LANDED IN.
I WOULD *LOVE* THAT.
ALRIGHT, THEN.
LET'S GO!

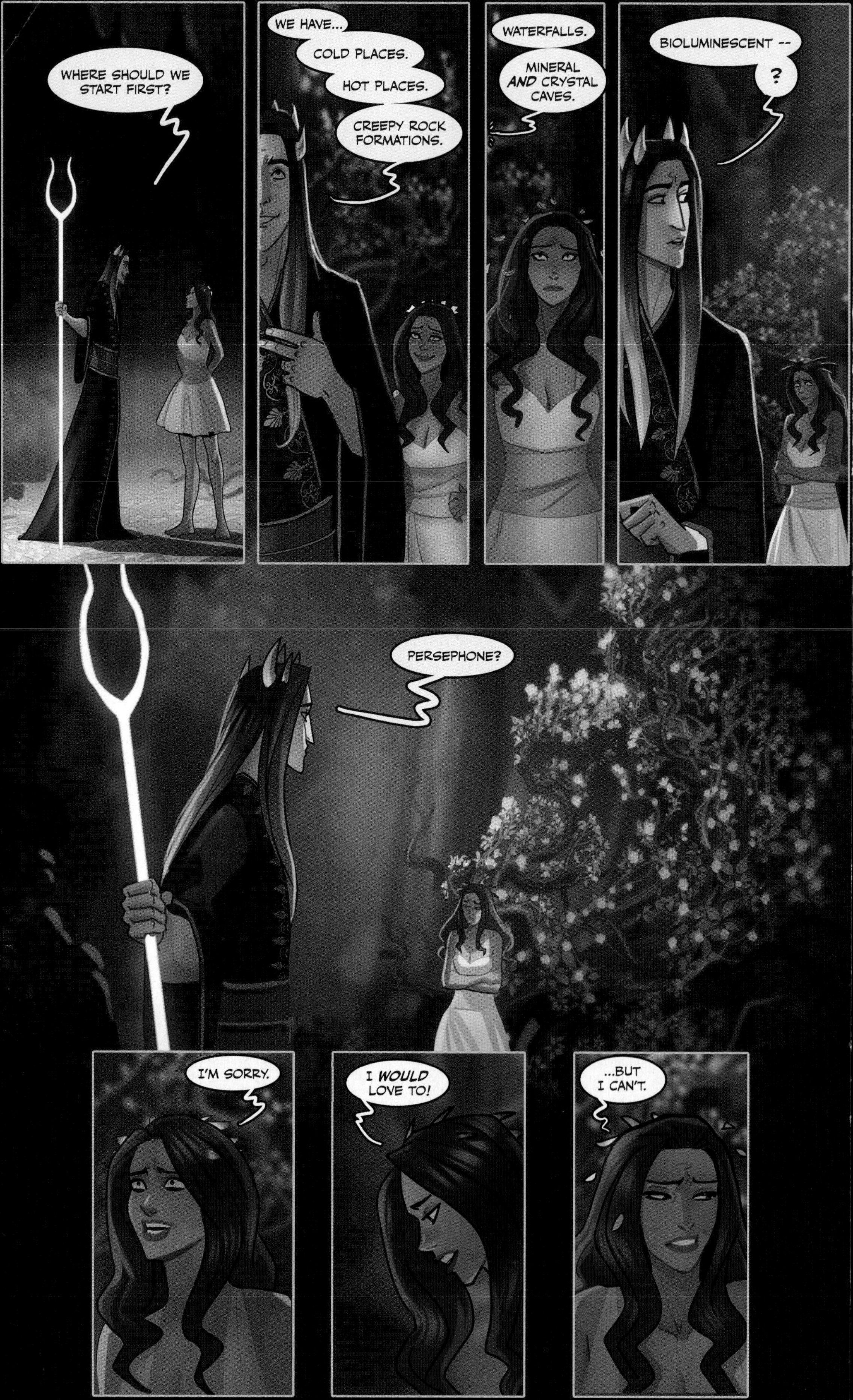
WHERE SHOULD WE START FIRST?
WE HAVE...
COLD PLACES.
HOT PLACES.
CREEPY ROCK FORMATIONS.
WATERFALLS.
MINERAL *AND* CRYSTAL CAVES.
BIOLUMINESCENT --
?
PERSEPHONE?
I'M SORRY.
I *WOULD* LOVE TO!
...BUT I CAN'T.

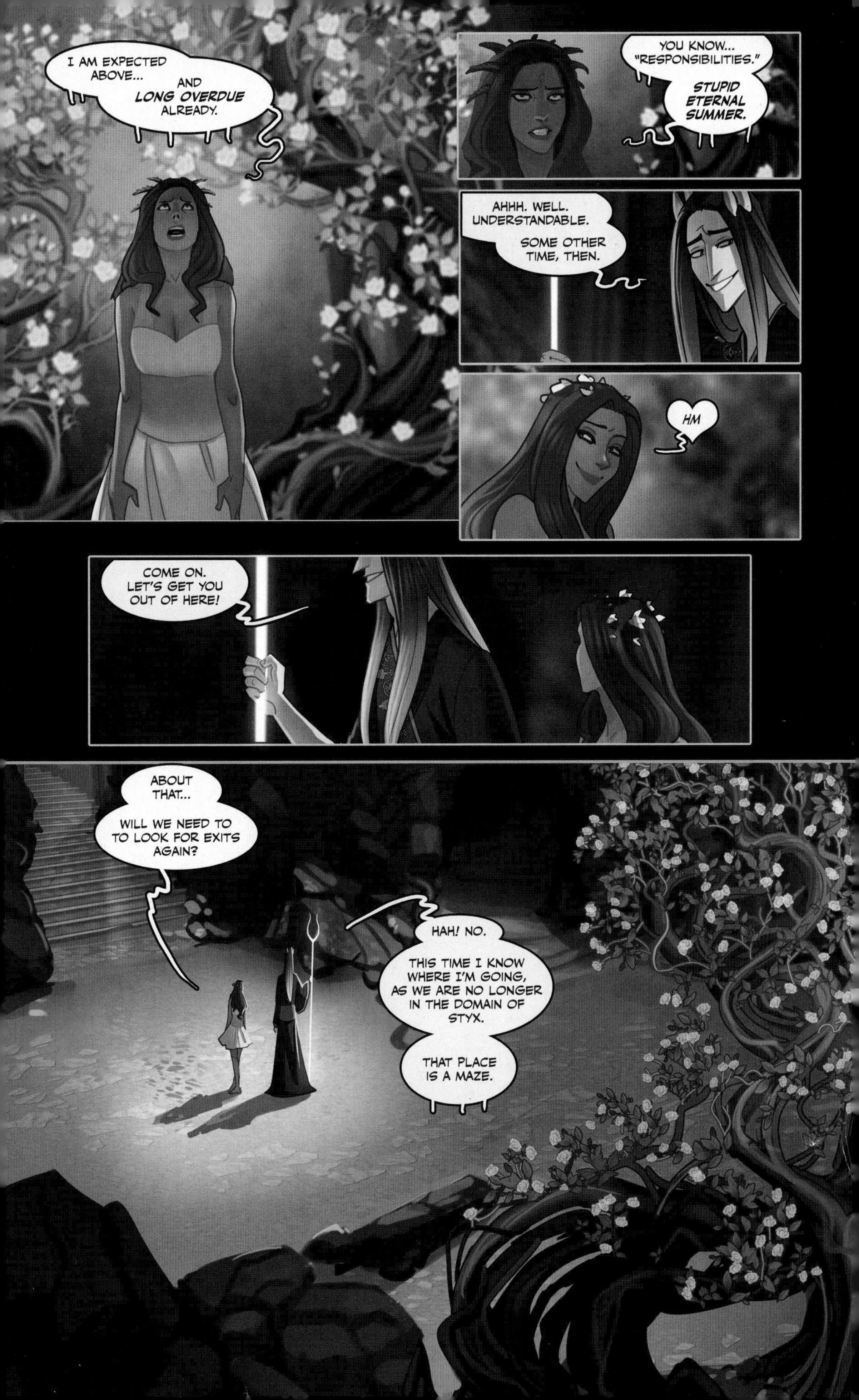

I AM EXPECTED ABOVE... AND LONG OVERDUE ALREADY.
YOU KNOW... "RESPONSIBILITIES."
STUPID ETERNAL SUMMER.
AHHH. WELL. UNDERSTANDABLE.
SOME OTHER TIME, THEN.
HM
COME ON. LET'S GET YOU OUT OF HERE!
ABOUT THAT...
WILL WE NEED TO TO LOOK FOR EXITS AGAIN?
HAH! NO.
THIS TIME I KNOW WHERE I'M GOING, AS WE ARE NO LONGER IN THE DOMAIN OF STYX.
THAT PLACE IS A MAZE.

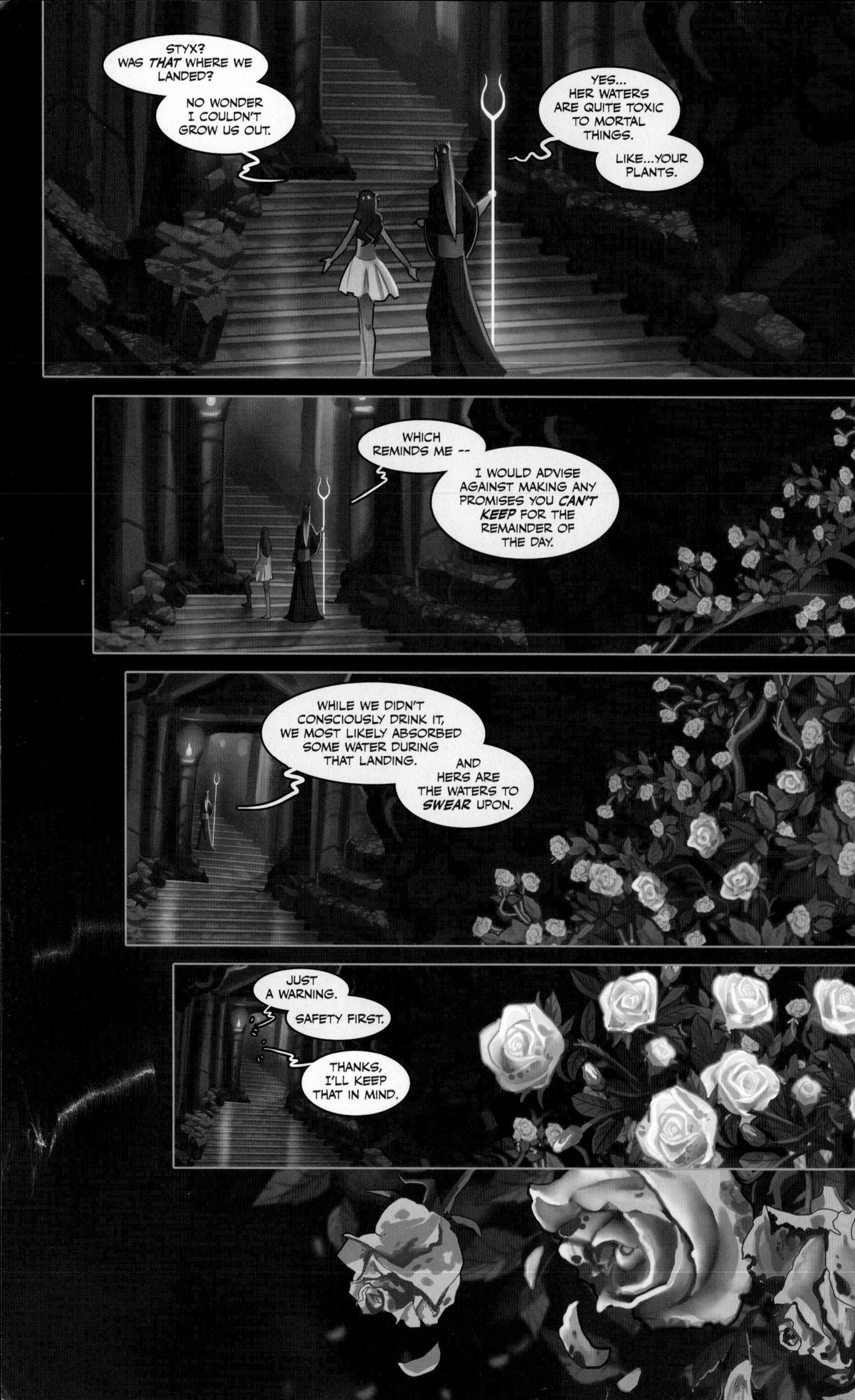

STYX? WAS *THAT* WHERE WE LANDED?
NO WONDER I COULDN'T GROW US OUT.
YES... HER WATERS ARE QUITE TOXIC TO MORTAL THINGS.
LIKE...YOUR PLANTS.
WHICH REMINDS ME --
I WOULD ADVISE AGAINST MAKING ANY PROMISES YOU *CAN'T KEEP* FOR THE REMAINDER OF THE DAY.
WHILE WE DIDN'T CONSCIOUSLY DRINK IT, WE MOST LIKELY ABSORBED SOME WATER DURING THAT LANDING.
AND HERS ARE THE WATERS TO *SWEAR* UPON.
JUST A WARNING.
SAFETY FIRST.
THANKS, I'LL KEEP THAT IN MIND.

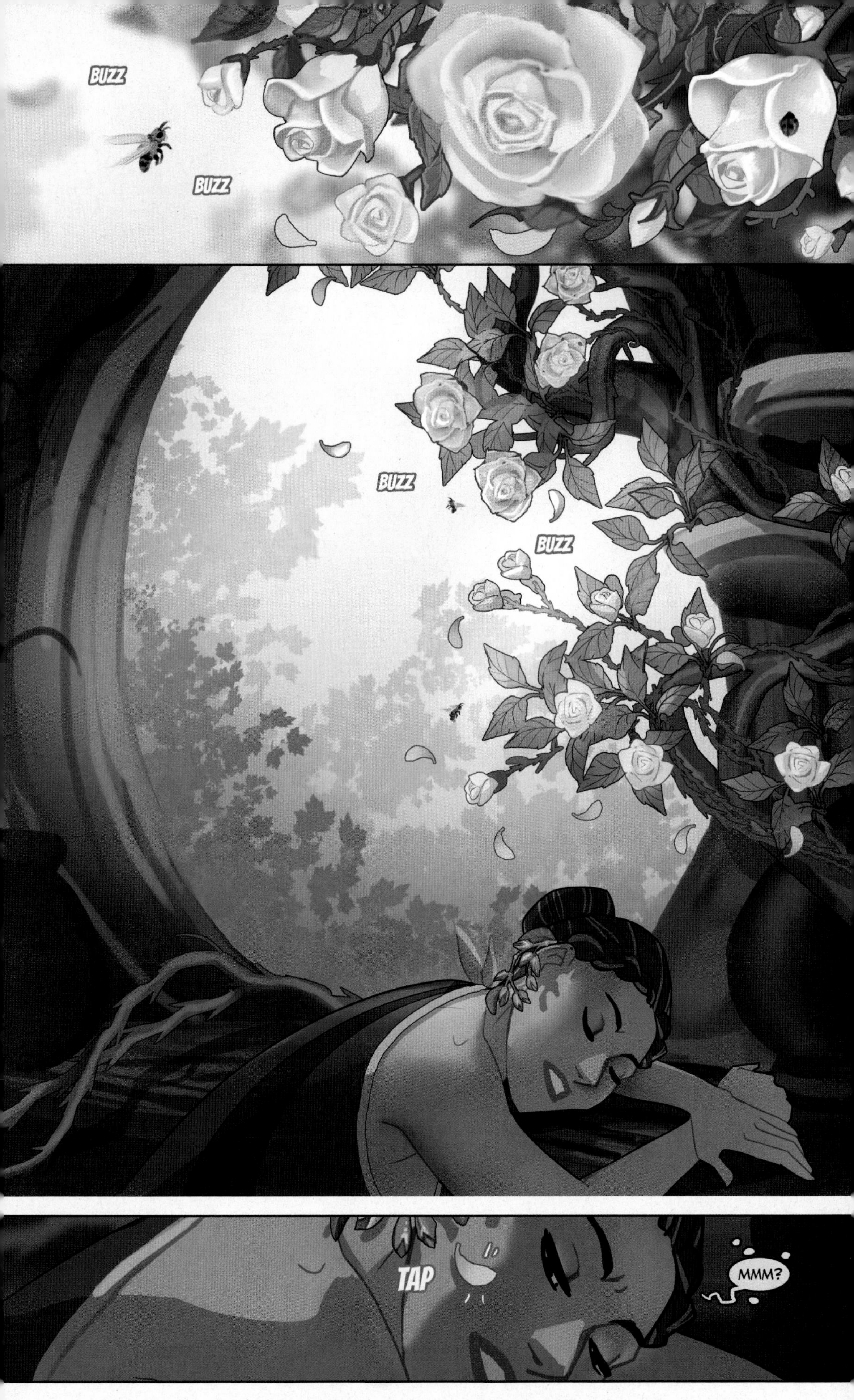

BUZZ
BUZZ
BUZZ
BUZZ
TAP
MMM?

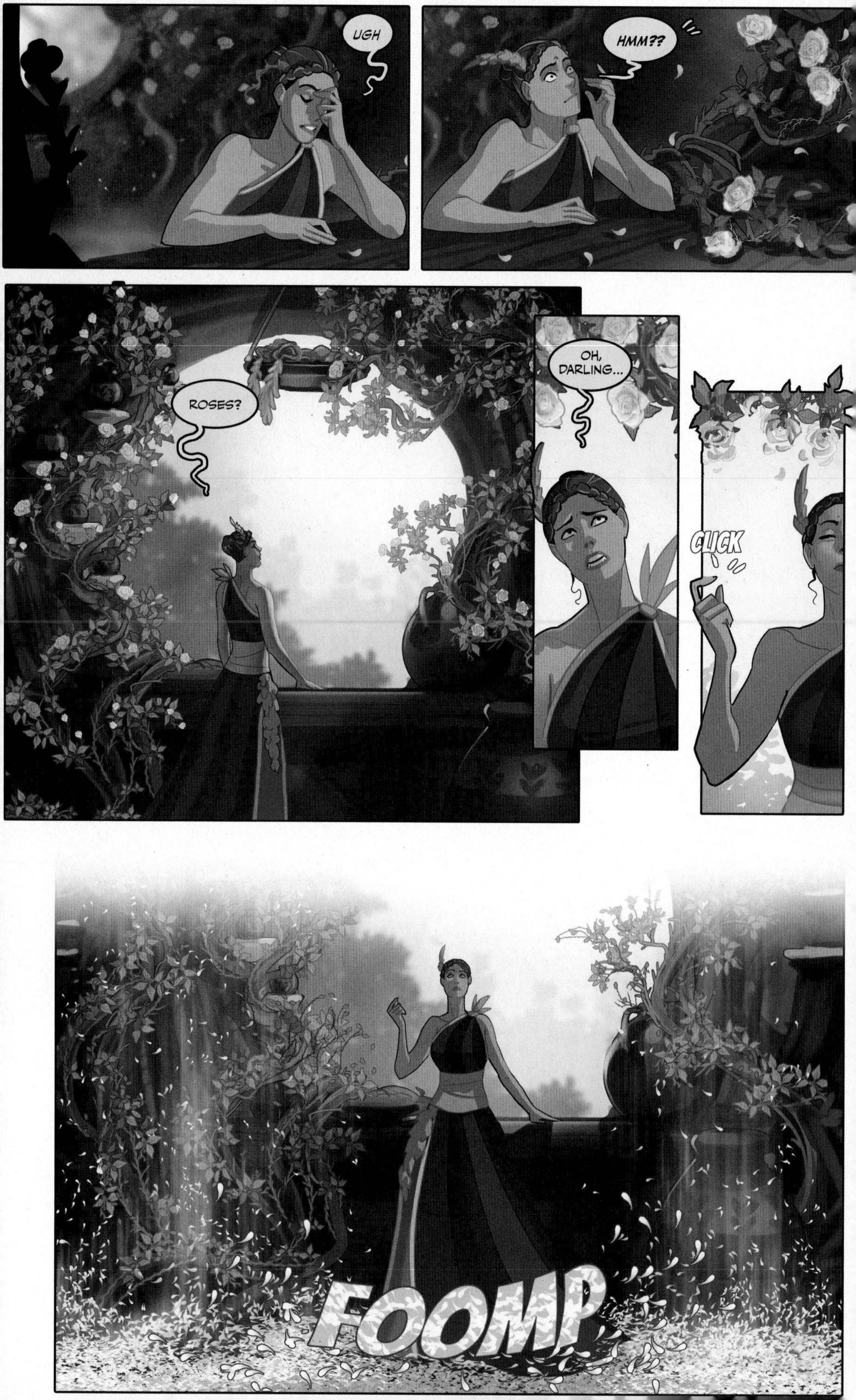
UGH
HMM??
ROSES?
OH, DARLING...
CLICK
FOOMP

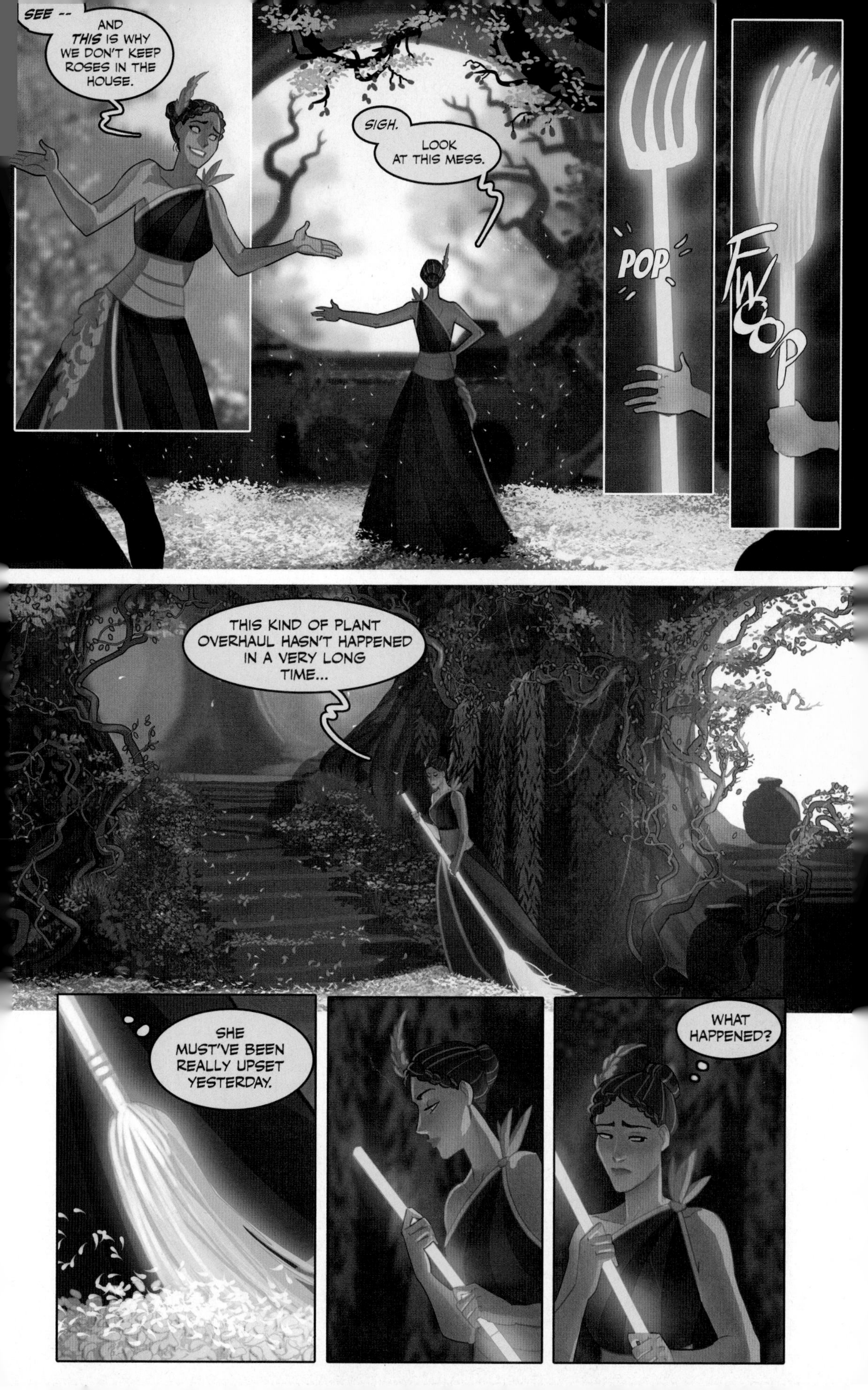
SEE --
AND THIS IS WHY WE DON'T KEEP ROSES IN THE HOUSE.
SIGH.
LOOK AT THIS MESS.
POP
FWOOP
THIS KIND OF PLANT OVERHAUL HASN'T HAPPENED IN A VERY LONG TIME...
SHE MUST'VE BEEN REALLY UPSET YESTERDAY.
WHAT HAPPENED?

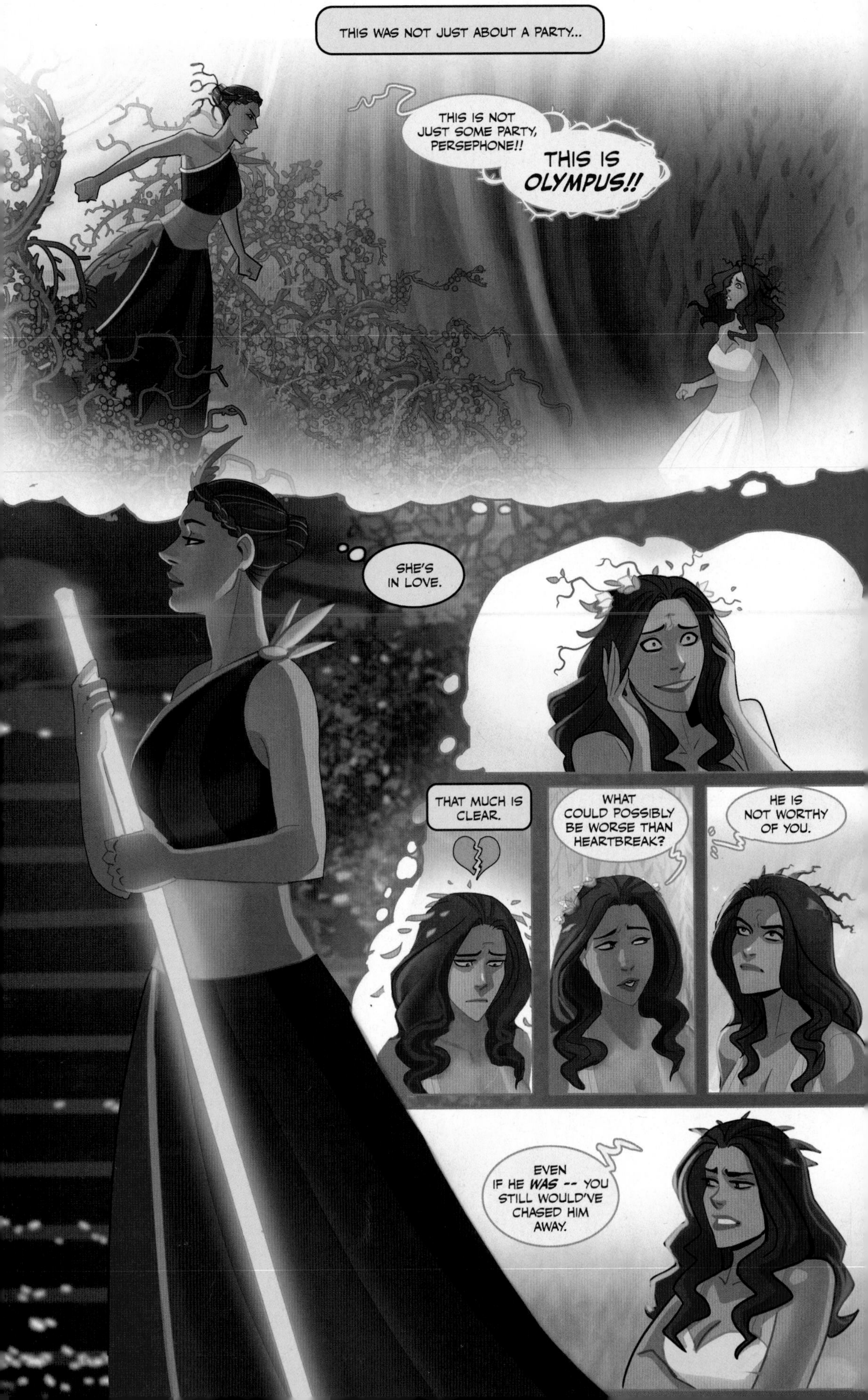
THIS WAS NOT JUST ABOUT A PARTY...
THIS IS NOT JUST SOME PARTY, PERSEPHONE!!
THIS IS OLYMPUS!!
SHE'S IN LOVE.
THAT MUCH IS CLEAR.
WHAT COULD POSSIBLY BE WORSE THAN HEARTBREAK?
HE IS NOT WORTHY OF YOU.
EVEN IF HE WAS -- YOU STILL WOULD'VE CHASED HIM AWAY.

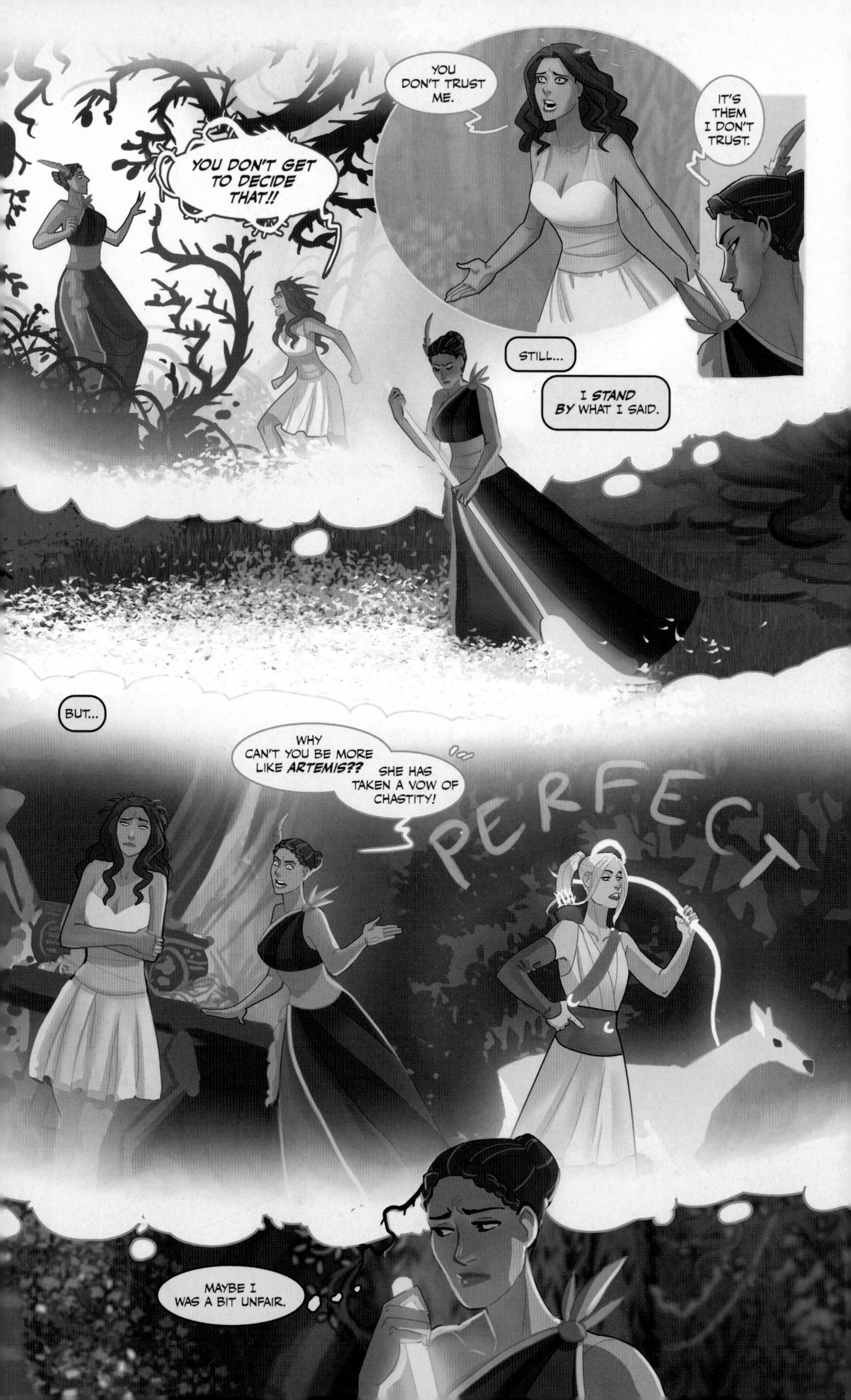
YOU DON'T GET TO DECIDE THAT!!
YOU DON'T TRUST ME.
IT'S THEM I DON'T TRUST.
STILL...
I STAND BY WHAT I SAID.
BUT...
WHY CAN'T YOU BE MORE LIKE ARTEMIS??
SHE HAS TAKEN A VOW OF CHASTITY!
PERFECT
MAYBE I WAS A BIT UNFAIR.

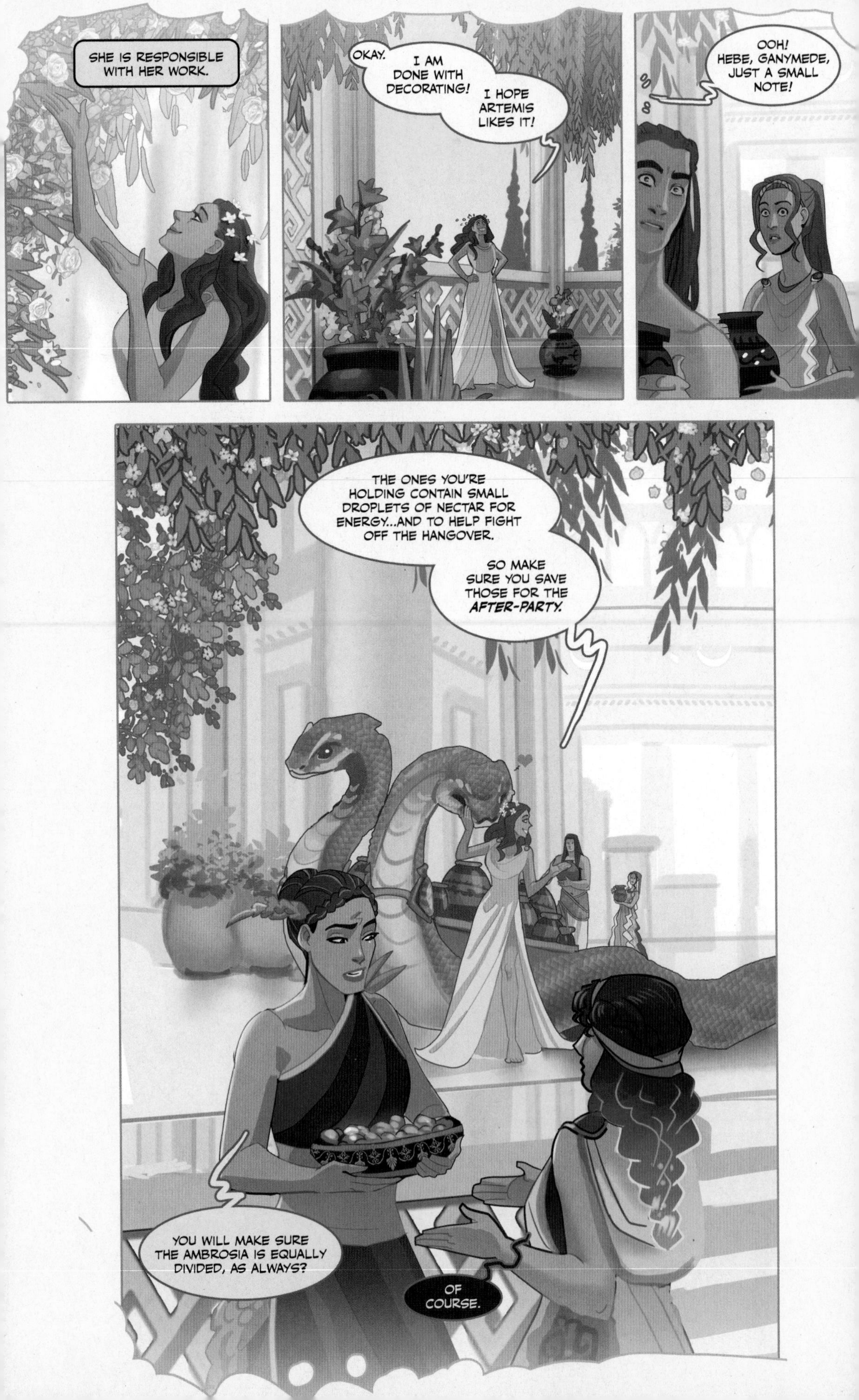
SHE IS RESPONSIBLE WITH HER WORK.
OKAY.
I AM DONE WITH DECORATING!
I HOPE ARTEMIS LIKES IT!
OOH! HEBE, GANYMEDE, JUST A SMALL NOTE!
THE ONES YOU'RE HOLDING CONTAIN SMALL DROPLETS OF NECTAR FOR ENERGY...AND TO HELP FIGHT OFF THE HANGOVER.
SO MAKE SURE YOU SAVE THOSE FOR THE *AFTER-PARTY.*
YOU WILL MAKE SURE THE AMBROSIA IS EQUALLY DIVIDED, AS ALWAYS?
OF COURSE.

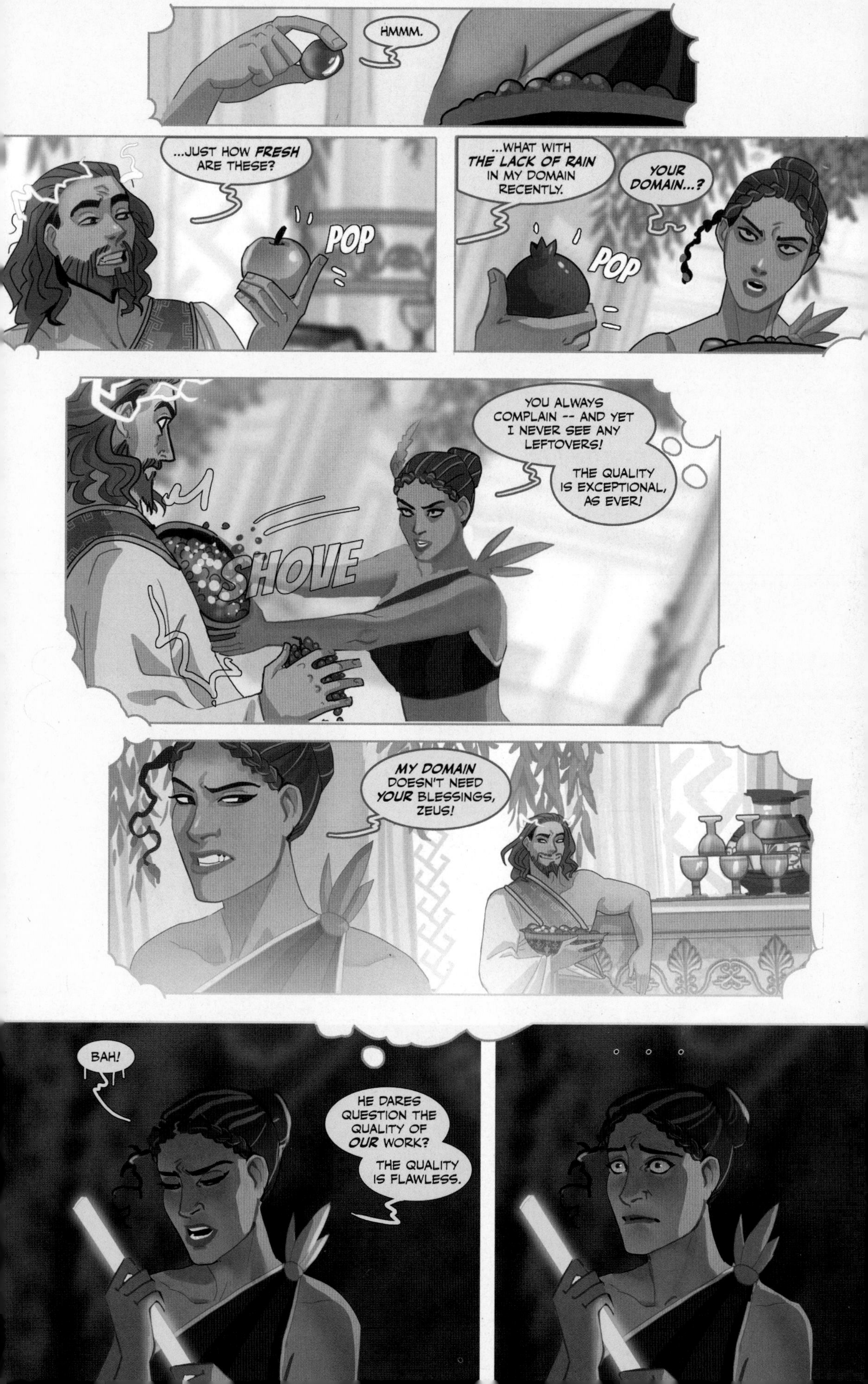
HMMM.
...JUST HOW FRESH ARE THESE?
POP
...WHAT WITH THE LACK OF RAIN IN MY DOMAIN RECENTLY.
YOUR DOMAIN...?
POP
YOU ALWAYS COMPLAIN -- AND YET I NEVER SEE ANY LEFTOVERS!
THE QUALITY IS EXCEPTIONAL, AS EVER!
SHOVE
MY DOMAIN DOESN'T NEED YOUR BLESSINGS, ZEUS!
BAH!
HE DARES QUESTION THE QUALITY OF OUR WORK?
THE QUALITY IS FLAWLESS.

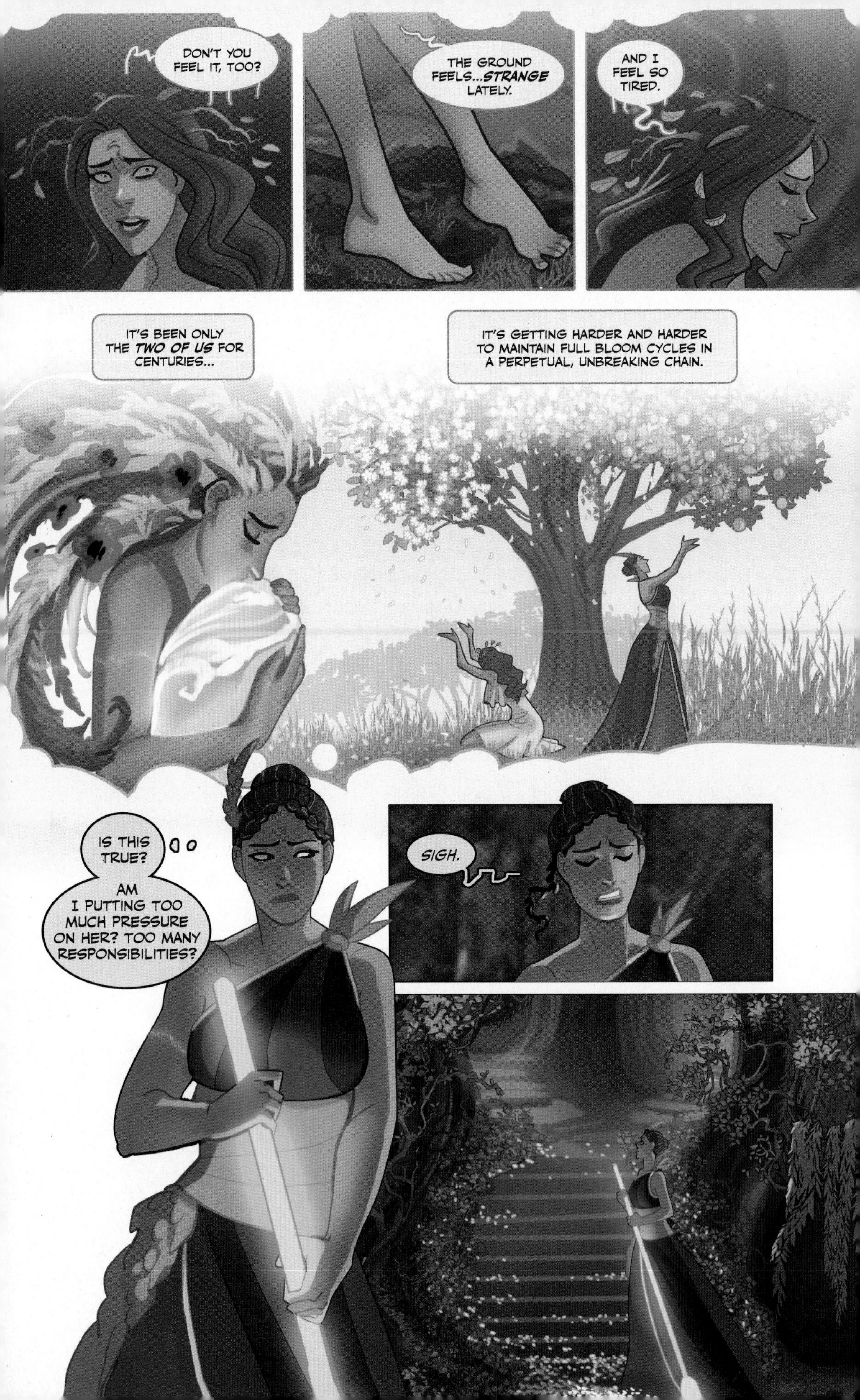
DON'T YOU FEEL IT, TOO?
THE GROUND FEELS...STRANGE LATELY.
AND I FEEL SO TIRED.
IT'S BEEN ONLY THE TWO OF US FOR CENTURIES...
IT'S GETTING HARDER AND HARDER TO MAINTAIN FULL BLOOM CYCLES IN A PERPETUAL, UNBREAKING CHAIN.
IS THIS TRUE?
AM I PUTTING TOO MUCH PRESSURE ON HER? TOO MANY RESPONSIBILITIES?
SIGH.

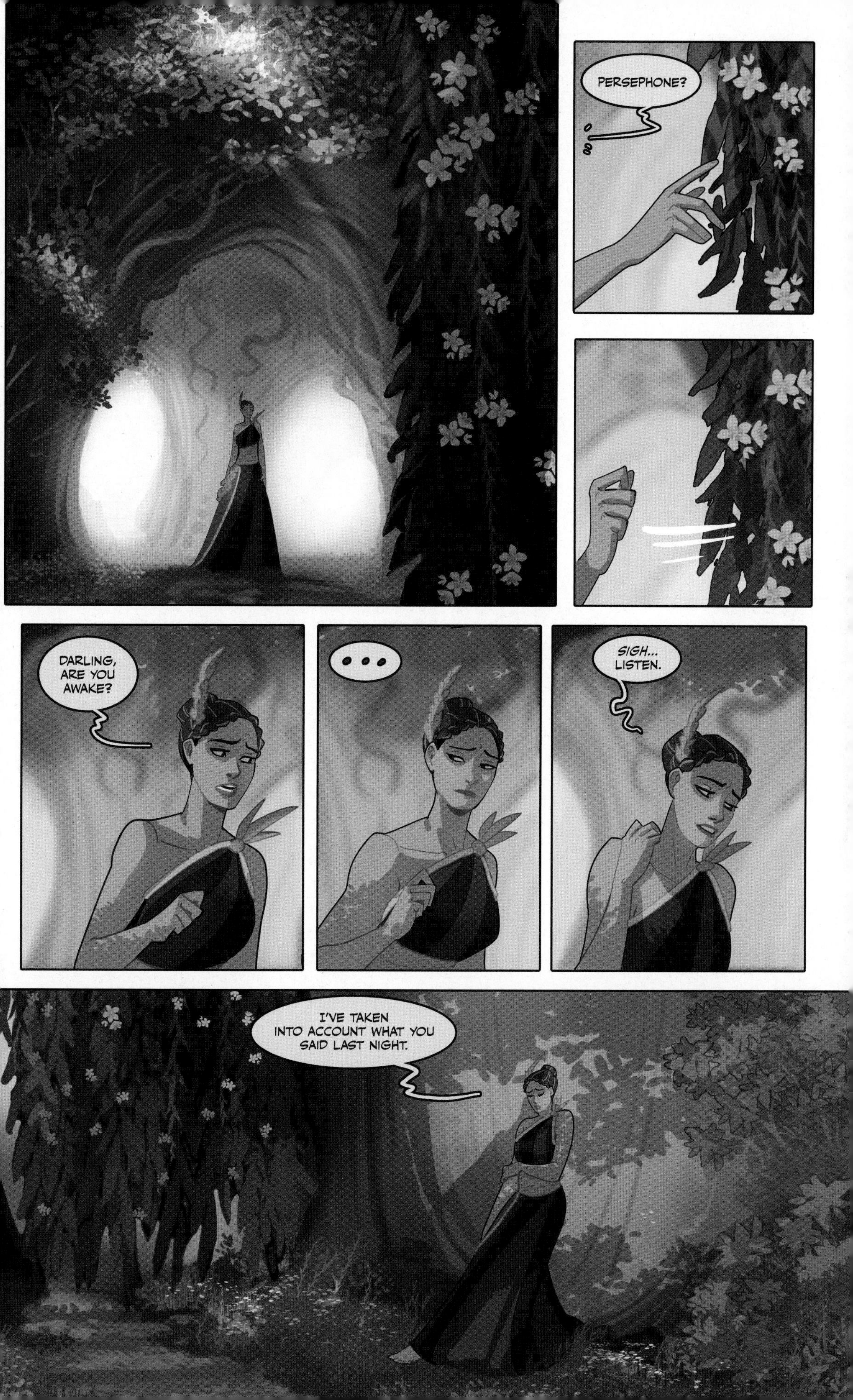
PERSEPHONE?
DARLING, ARE YOU AWAKE?
...
SIGH... LISTEN.
I'VE TAKEN INTO ACCOUNT WHAT YOU SAID LAST NIGHT.

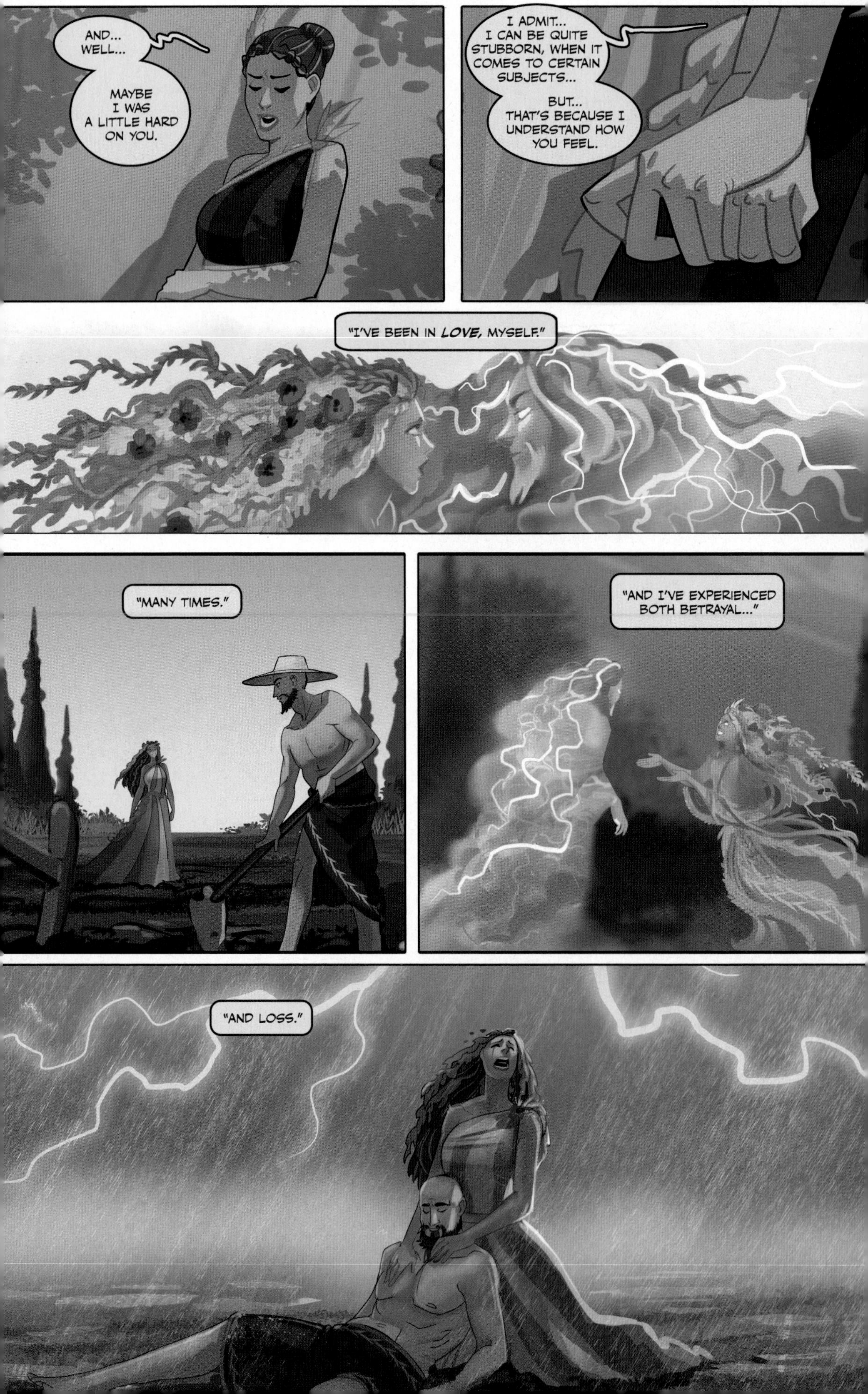
AND... WELL...
MAYBE I WAS A LITTLE HARD ON YOU.
I ADMIT... I CAN BE QUITE STUBBORN, WHEN IT COMES TO CERTAIN SUBJECTS...
BUT... THAT'S BECAUSE I UNDERSTAND HOW YOU FEEL.
"I'VE BEEN IN *LOVE,* MYSELF."
"MANY TIMES."
"AND I'VE EXPERIENCED BOTH BETRAYAL..."
"AND LOSS."

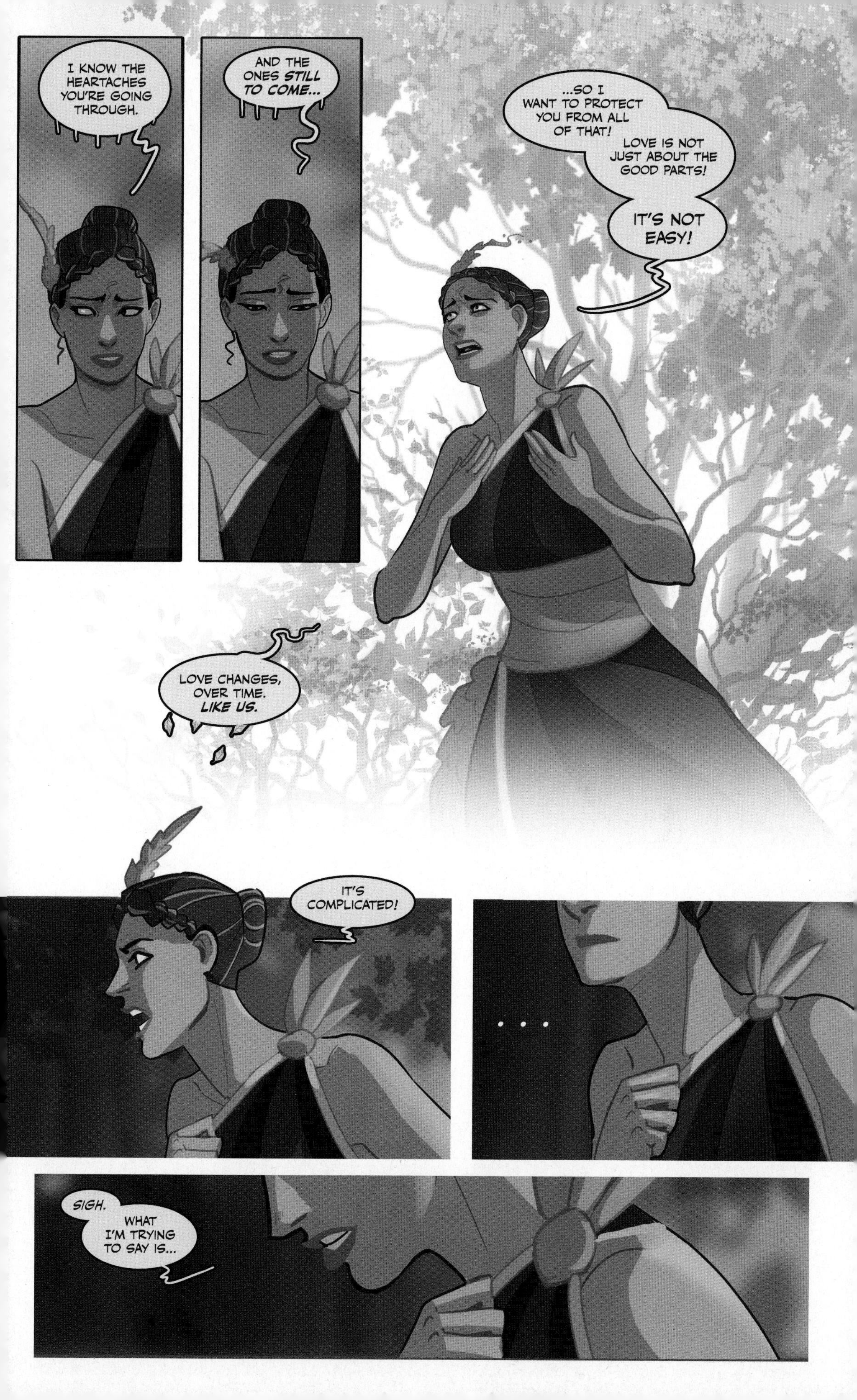
I KNOW THE HEARTACHES YOU'RE GOING THROUGH.
AND THE ONES STILL TO COME...
...SO I WANT TO PROTECT YOU FROM ALL OF THAT!
LOVE IS NOT JUST ABOUT THE GOOD PARTS!
IT'S NOT EASY!
LOVE CHANGES, OVER TIME. LIKE US.
IT'S COMPLICATED!
. . .
SIGH.
WHAT I'M TRYING TO SAY IS...

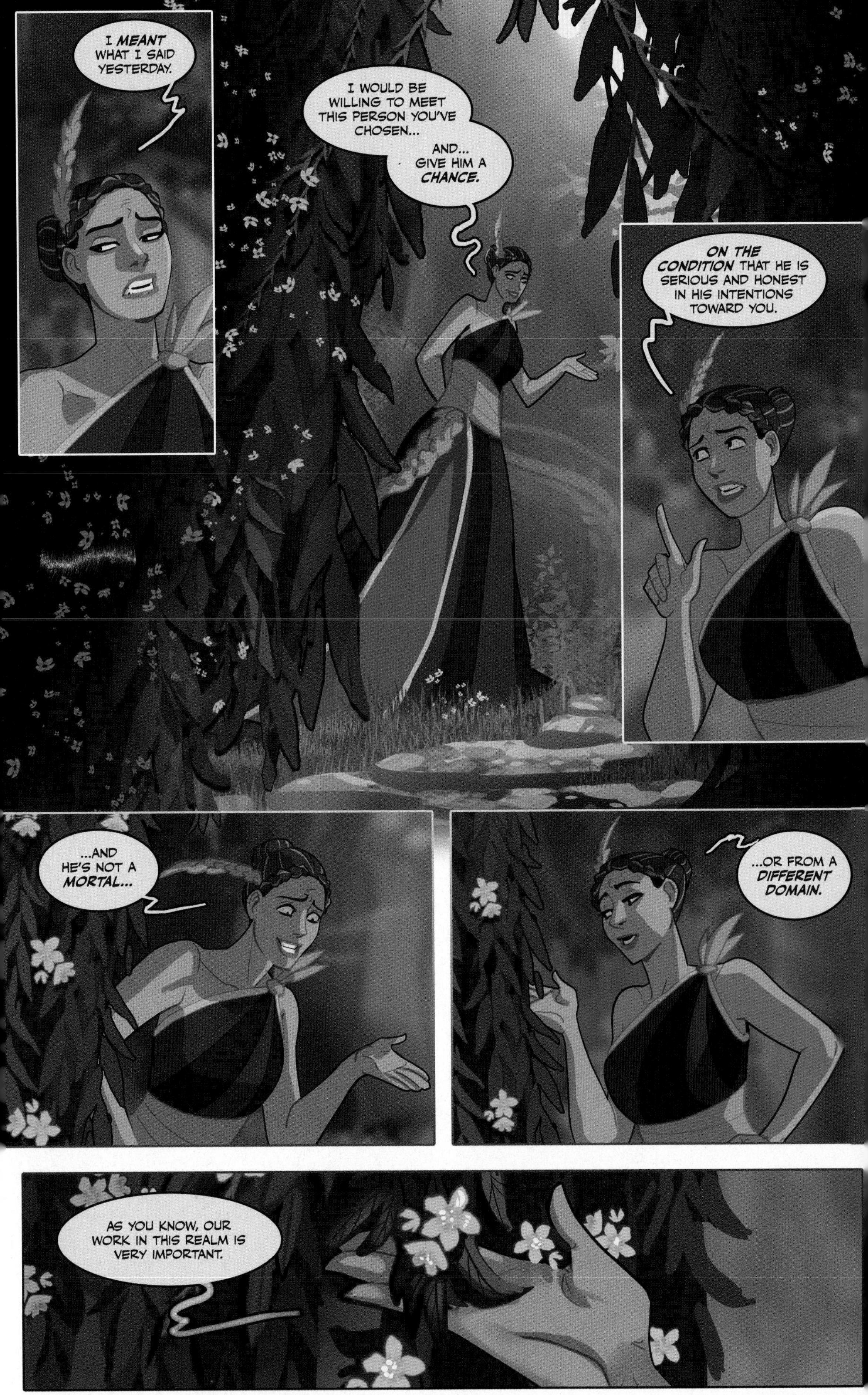
I MEANT WHAT I SAID YESTERDAY.
I WOULD BE WILLING TO MEET THIS PERSON YOU'VE CHOSEN...
AND... GIVE HIM A CHANCE.
ON THE CONDITION THAT HE IS SERIOUS AND HONEST IN HIS INTENTIONS TOWARD YOU.
...AND HE'S NOT A MORTAL...
...OR FROM A DIFFERENT DOMAIN.
AS YOU KNOW, OUR WORK IN THIS REALM IS VERY IMPORTANT.

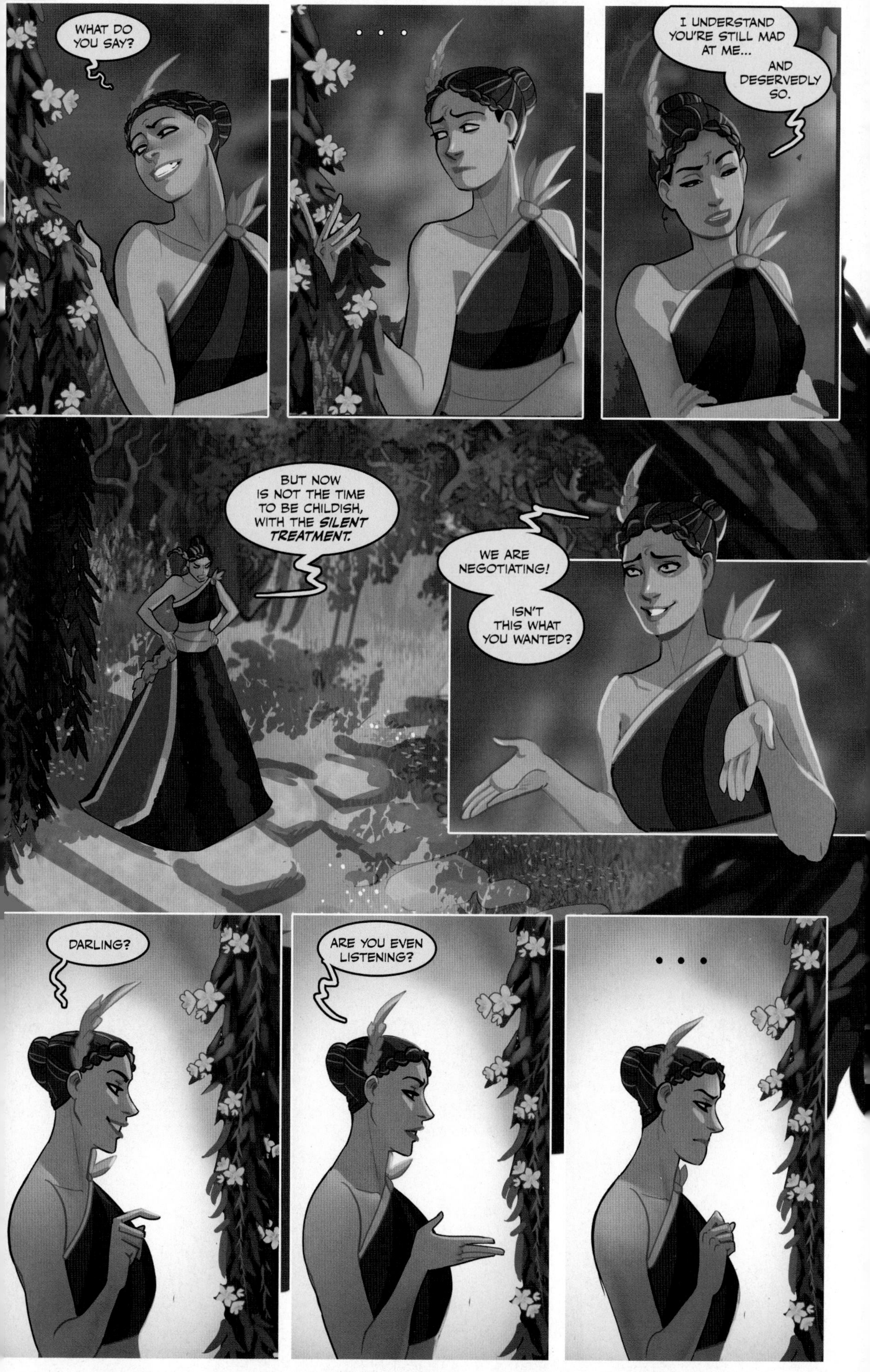
WHAT DO YOU SAY?
. . .
I UNDERSTAND YOU'RE STILL MAD AT ME...
AND DESERVEDLY SO.
BUT NOW IS NOT THE TIME TO BE CHILDISH, WITH THE *SILENT TREATMENT.*
WE ARE NEGOTIATING!
ISN'T THIS WHAT YOU WANTED?
DARLING?
ARE YOU EVEN LISTENING?
. . .

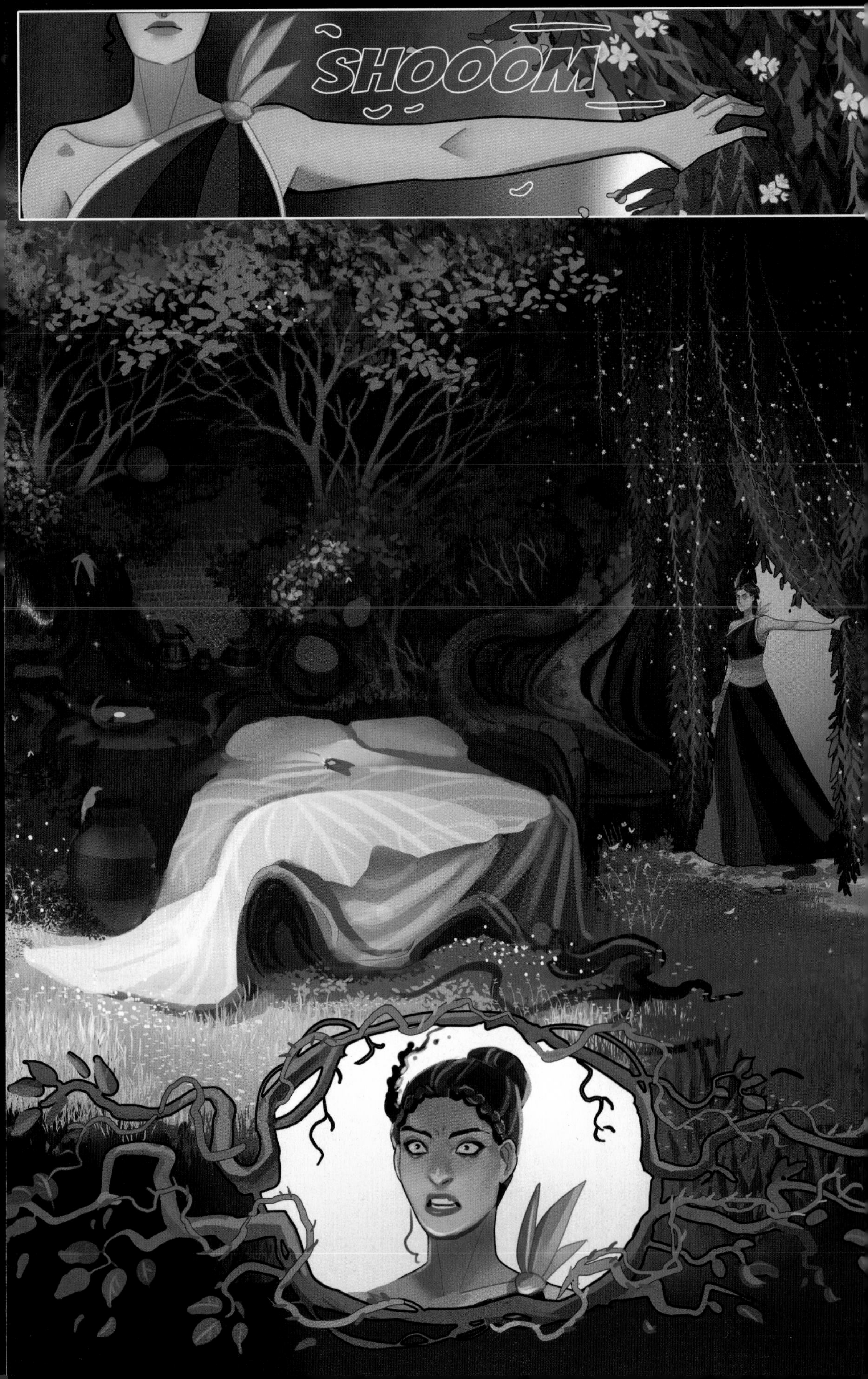
SHOOOM

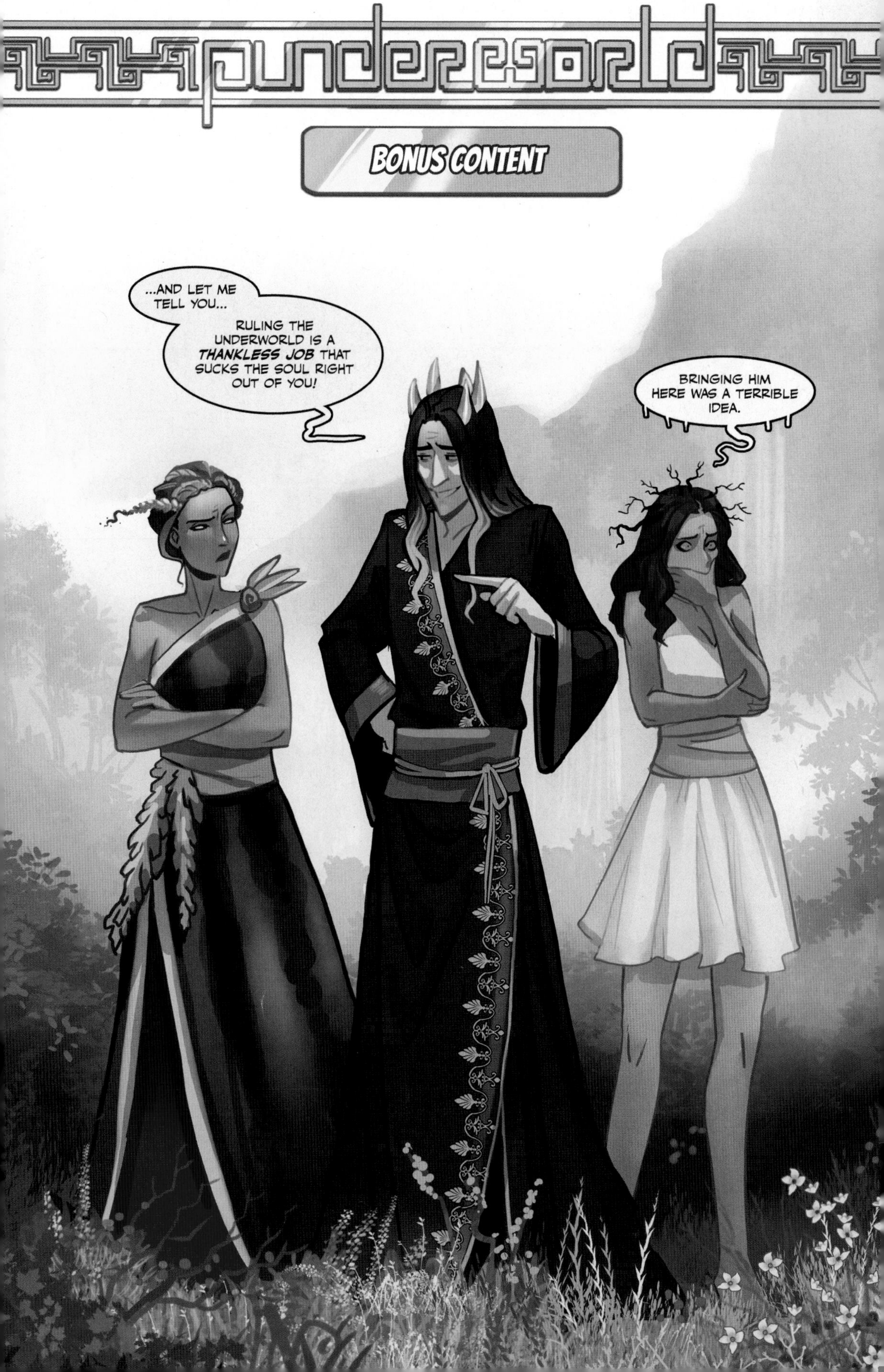
UNDERWORLD
BONUS CONTENT
...AND LET ME TELL YOU...
RULING THE UNDERWORLD IS A THANKLESS JOB THAT SUCKS THE SOUL RIGHT OUT OF YOU!
BRINGING HIM HERE WAS A TERRIBLE IDEA.

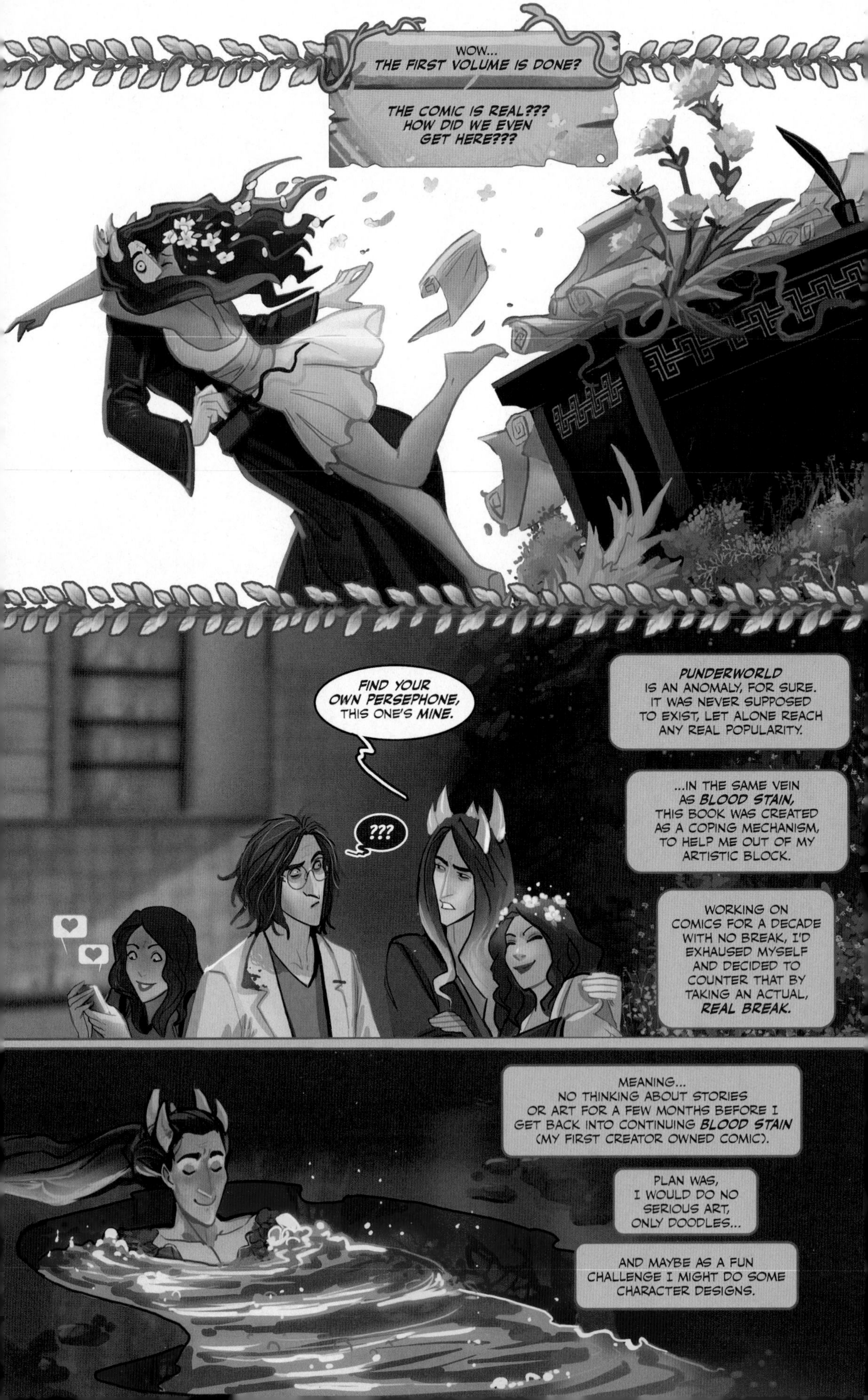
WOW...
THE FIRST VOLUME IS DONE?
THE COMIC IS REAL??? HOW DID WE EVEN GET HERE???
PUNDERWORLD IS AN ANOMALY, FOR SURE. IT WAS NEVER SUPPOSED TO EXIST, LET ALONE REACH ANY REAL POPULARITY.
FIND YOUR OWN PERSEPHONE, THIS ONE'S MINE.
???
...IN THE SAME VEIN AS BLOOD STAIN, THIS BOOK WAS CREATED AS A COPING MECHANISM, TO HELP ME OUT OF MY ARTISTIC BLOCK.
WORKING ON COMICS FOR A DECADE WITH NO BREAK, I'D EXHAUSED MYSELF AND DECIDED TO COUNTER THAT BY TAKING AN ACTUAL, REAL BREAK.
MEANING... NO THINKING ABOUT STORIES OR ART FOR A FEW MONTHS BEFORE I GET BACK INTO CONTINUING BLOOD STAIN (MY FIRST CREATOR OWNED COMIC).
PLAN WAS, I WOULD DO NO SERIOUS ART, ONLY DOODLES...
AND MAYBE AS A FUN CHALLENGE I MIGHT DO SOME CHARACTER DESIGNS.

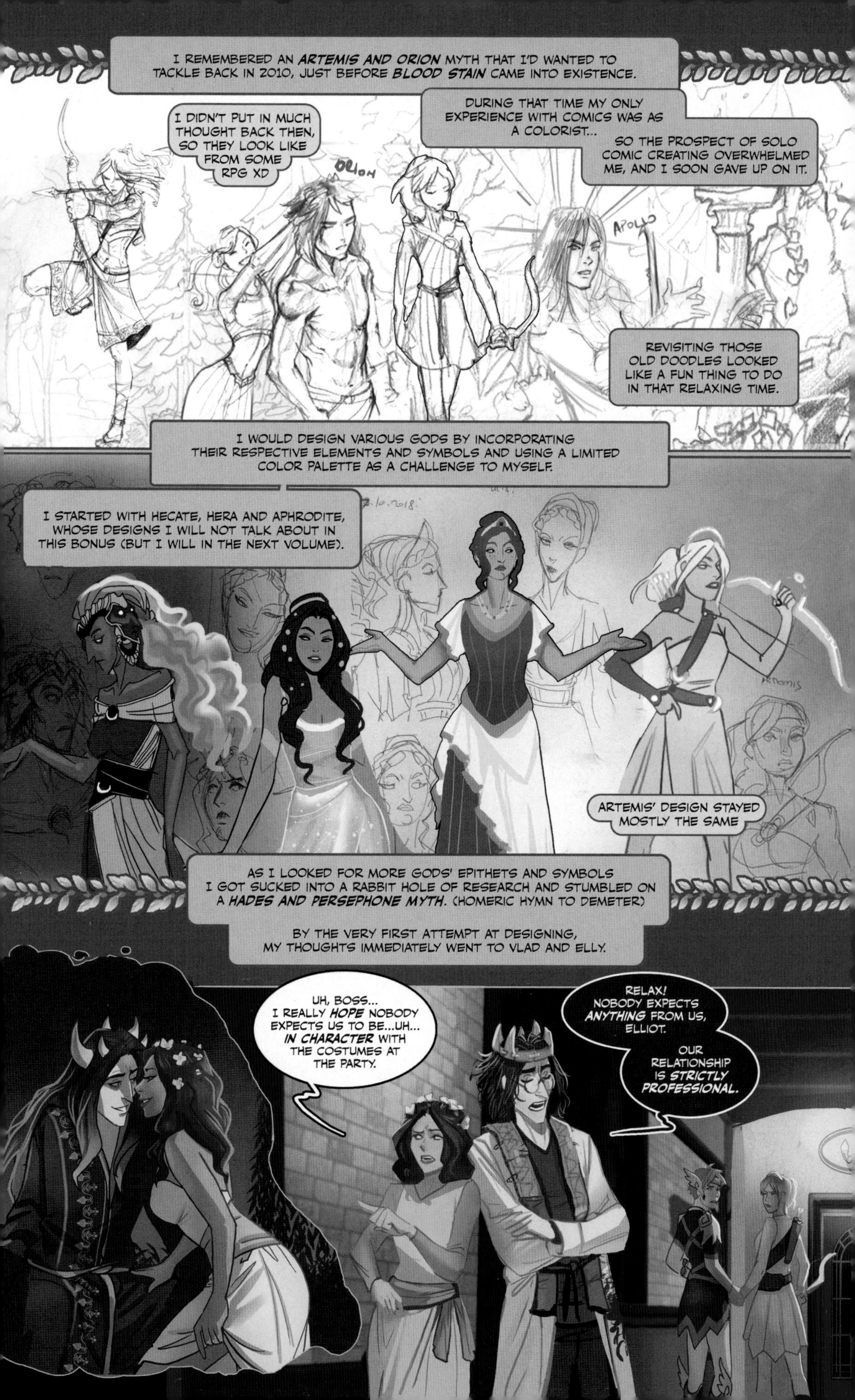
I REMEMBERED AN *ARTEMIS AND ORION* MYTH THAT I'D WANTED TO TACKLE BACK IN 2010, JUST BEFORE *BLOOD STAIN* CAME INTO EXISTENCE.
I DIDN'T PUT IN MUCH THOUGHT BACK THEN, SO THEY LOOK LIKE FROM SOME RPG XD
DURING THAT TIME MY ONLY EXPERIENCE WITH COMICS WAS AS A COLORIST...
SO THE PROSPECT OF SOLO COMIC CREATING OVERWHELMED ME, AND I SOON GAVE UP ON IT.
ORION
APOLLO
REVISITING THOSE OLD DOODLES LOOKED LIKE A FUN THING TO DO IN THAT RELAXING TIME.
I WOULD DESIGN VARIOUS GODS BY INCORPORATING THEIR RESPECTIVE ELEMENTS AND SYMBOLS AND USING A LIMITED COLOR PALETTE AS A CHALLENGE TO MYSELF.
I STARTED WITH HECATE, HERA AND APHRODITE, WHOSE DESIGNS I WILL NOT TALK ABOUT IN THIS BONUS (BUT I WILL IN THE NEXT VOLUME).
ARTEMIS' DESIGN STAYED MOSTLY THE SAME
AS I LOOKED FOR MORE GODS' EPITHETS AND SYMBOLS I GOT SUCKED INTO A RABBIT HOLE OF RESEARCH AND STUMBLED ON A *HADES AND PERSEPHONE MYTH*. (HOMERIC HYMN TO DEMETER)
BY THE VERY FIRST ATTEMPT AT DESIGNING, MY THOUGHTS IMMEDIATELY WENT TO VLAD AND ELLY.
UH, BOSS... I REALLY *HOPE* NOBODY EXPECTS US TO BE...UH... *IN CHARACTER* WITH THE COSTUMES AT THE PARTY.
RELAX! NOBODY EXPECTS *ANYTHING* FROM US, ELLIOT.
OUR RELATIONSHIP IS *STRICTLY PROFESSIONAL.*

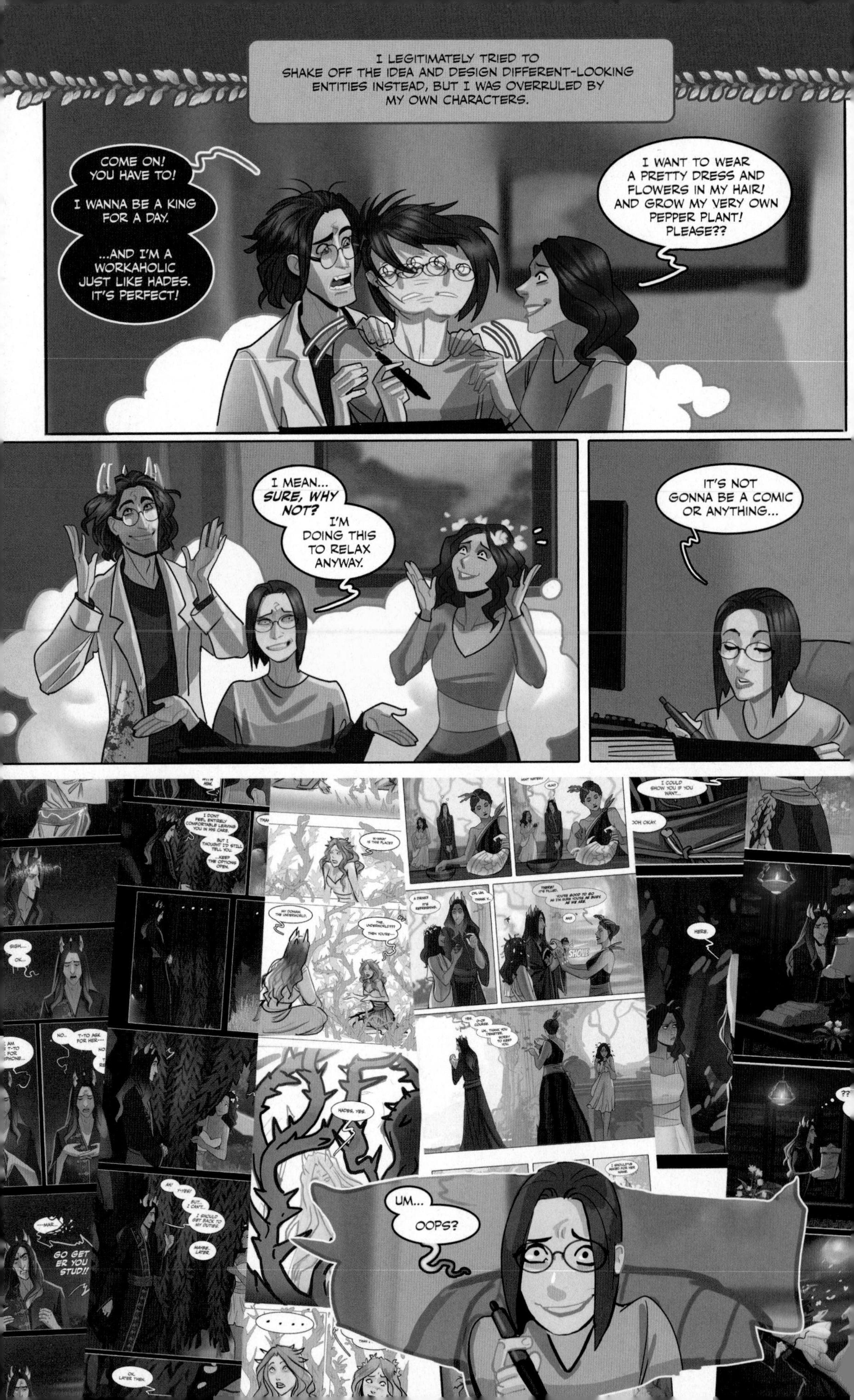
I LEGITIMATELY TRIED TO SHAKE OFF THE IDEA AND DESIGN DIFFERENT-LOOKING ENTITIES INSTEAD, BUT I WAS OVERRULED BY MY OWN CHARACTERS.
COME ON! YOU HAVE TO!
I WANNA BE A KING FOR A DAY.
...AND I'M A WORKAHOLIC JUST LIKE HADES. IT'S PERFECT!
I WANT TO WEAR A PRETTY DRESS AND FLOWERS IN MY HAIR! AND GROW MY VERY OWN PEPPER PLANT! PLEASE??
I MEAN... SURE, WHY NOT?
I'M DOING THIS TO RELAX ANYWAY.
IT'S NOT GONNA BE A COMIC OR ANYTHING...
UM...
OOPS?

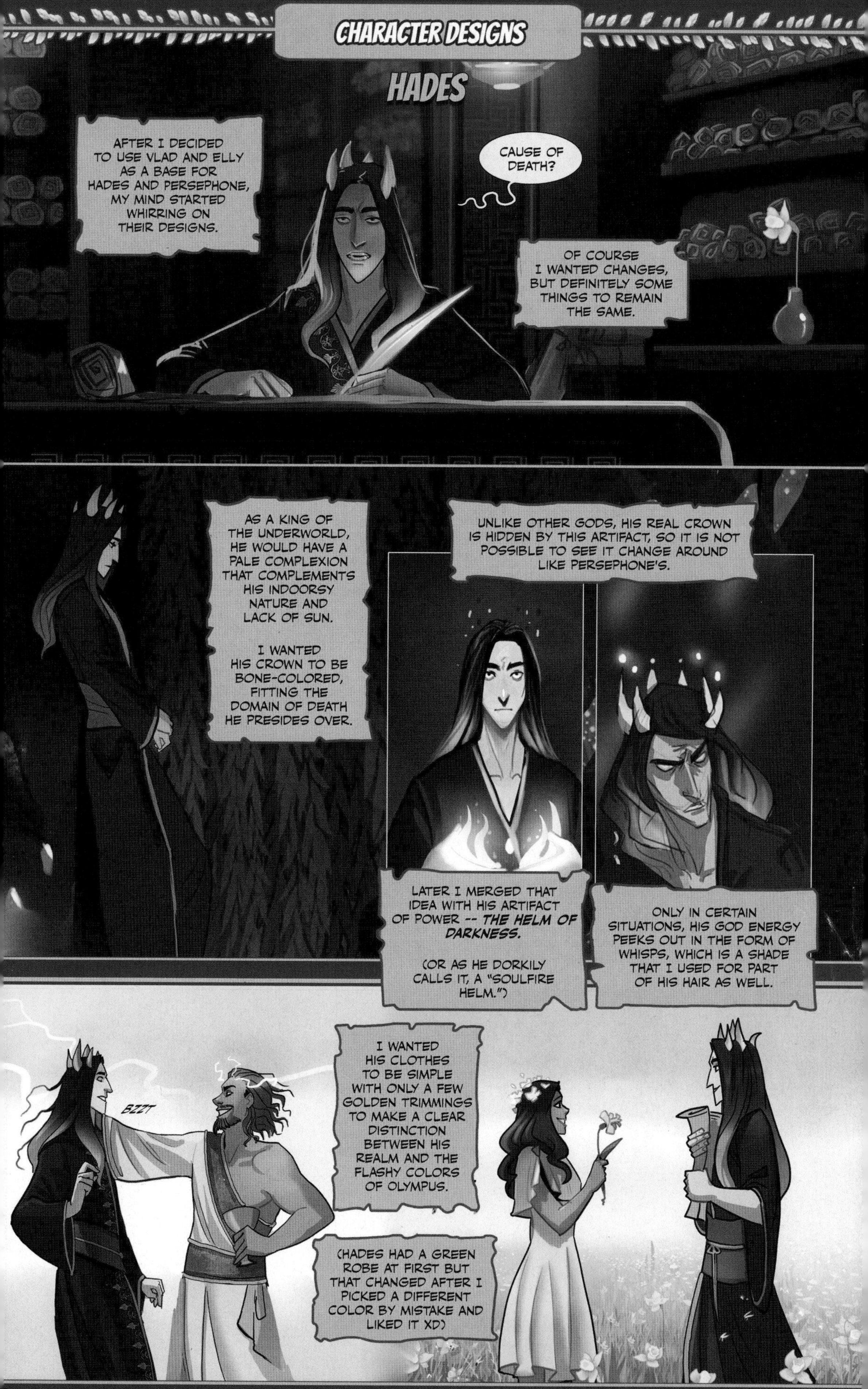
CHARACTER DESIGNS
HADES
AFTER I DECIDED TO USE VLAD AND ELLY AS A BASE FOR HADES AND PERSEPHONE, MY MIND STARTED WHIRRING ON THEIR DESIGNS.
CAUSE OF DEATH?
OF COURSE I WANTED CHANGES, BUT DEFINITELY SOME THINGS TO REMAIN THE SAME.
AS A KING OF THE UNDERWORLD, HE WOULD HAVE A PALE COMPLEXION THAT COMPLEMENTS HIS INDOORSY NATURE AND LACK OF SUN.
I WANTED HIS CROWN TO BE BONE-COLORED, FITTING THE DOMAIN OF DEATH HE PRESIDES OVER.
UNLIKE OTHER GODS, HIS REAL CROWN IS HIDDEN BY THIS ARTIFACT, SO IT IS NOT POSSIBLE TO SEE IT CHANGE AROUND LIKE PERSEPHONE'S.
LATER I MERGED THAT IDEA WITH HIS ARTIFACT OF POWER -- THE HELM OF DARKNESS.
(OR AS HE DORKILY CALLS IT, A "SOULFIRE HELM.")
ONLY IN CERTAIN SITUATIONS, HIS GOD ENERGY PEEKS OUT IN THE FORM OF WHISPS, WHICH IS A SHADE THAT I USED FOR PART OF HIS HAIR AS WELL.
BZZT
I WANTED HIS CLOTHES TO BE SIMPLE WITH ONLY A FEW GOLDEN TRIMMINGS TO MAKE A CLEAR DISTINCTION BETWEEN HIS REALM AND THE FLASHY COLORS OF OLYMPUS.
(HADES HAD A GREEN ROBE AT FIRST BUT THAT CHANGED AFTER I PICKED A DIFFERENT COLOR BY MISTAKE AND LIKED IT XD)

PERSEPHONE

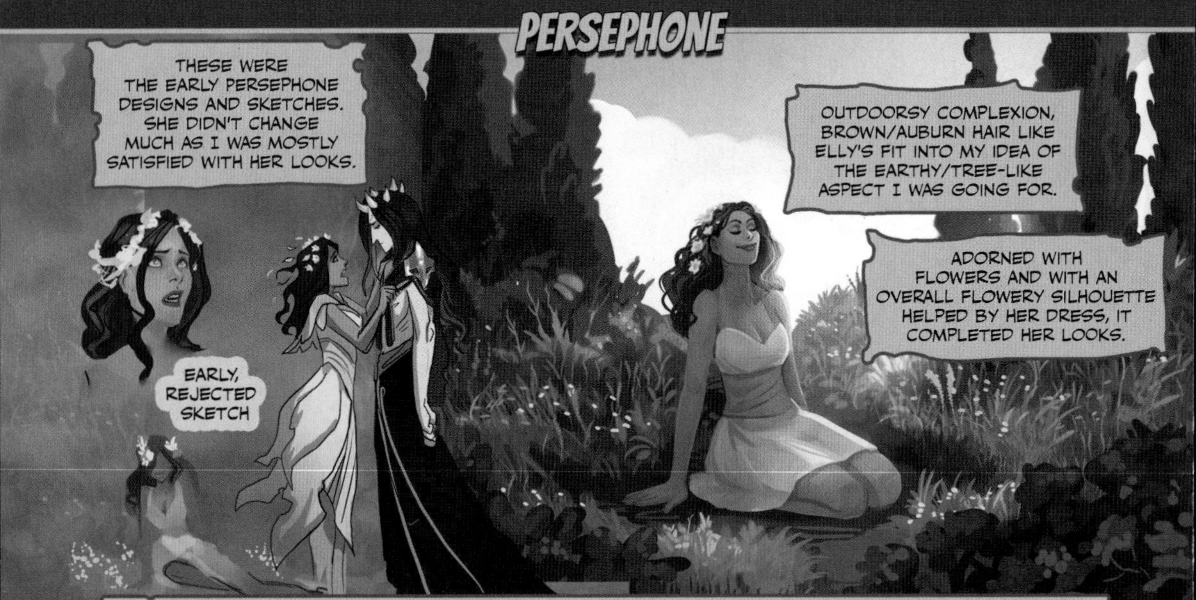
THESE WERE THE EARLY PERSEPHONE DESIGNS AND SKETCHES. SHE DIDN'T CHANGE MUCH AS I WAS MOSTLY SATISFIED WITH HER LOOKS.
EARLY, REJECTED SKETCH
OUTDOORSY COMPLEXION, BROWN/AUBURN HAIR LIKE ELLY'S FIT INTO MY IDEA OF THE EARTHY/TREE-LIKE ASPECT I WAS GOING FOR.
ADORNED WITH FLOWERS AND WITH AN OVERALL FLOWERY SILHOUETTE HELPED BY HER DRESS, IT COMPLETED HER LOOKS.

THEIR STORY INTRIGUED ME, BECAUSE IT GAVE ME A LOT OF ROOM TO EXPLORE THEIR DYNAMICS. SO I KEPT DOODLING THEIR INTERACTIONS.

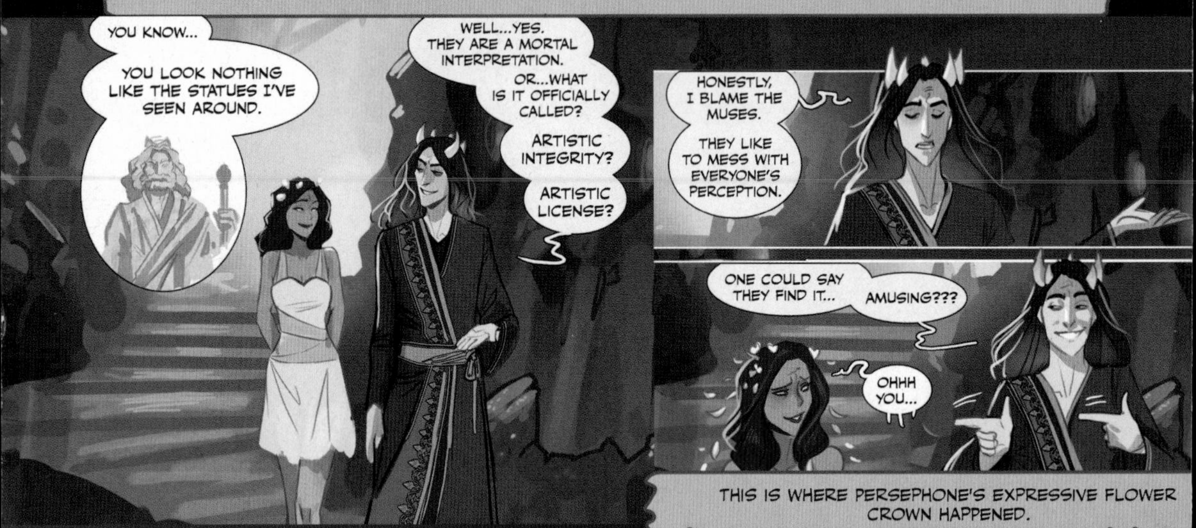
YOU KNOW...
YOU LOOK NOTHING LIKE THE STATUES I'VE SEEN AROUND.
WELL...YES. THEY ARE A MORTAL INTERPRETATION.
OR...WHAT IS IT OFFICIALLY CALLED?
ARTISTIC INTEGRITY?
ARTISTIC LICENSE?
HONESTLY, I BLAME THE MUSES.
THEY LIKE TO MESS WITH EVERYONE'S PERCEPTION.
ONE COULD SAY THEY FIND IT...
AMUSING???
OHHH YOU...
THIS IS WHERE PERSEPHONE'S EXPRESSIVE FLOWER CROWN HAPPENED.

BECAUSE OF MY INHERENT LAZINESS TO DRAW THE SAME THING MULTIPLE TIMES, DURING MY THUMBNAIL PHASE I INSTINCTIVELY DREW DIFFERENT PLANTS FOR EACH EXPRESSIVE FACE.

THOSE SOMEWHAT CORRESPONDED TO CAT EARS' WAY OF EMOTING, SO I KEPT IT BECAUSE IT SEEMED LIKE A FUN IDEA TO PLAY WITH :)

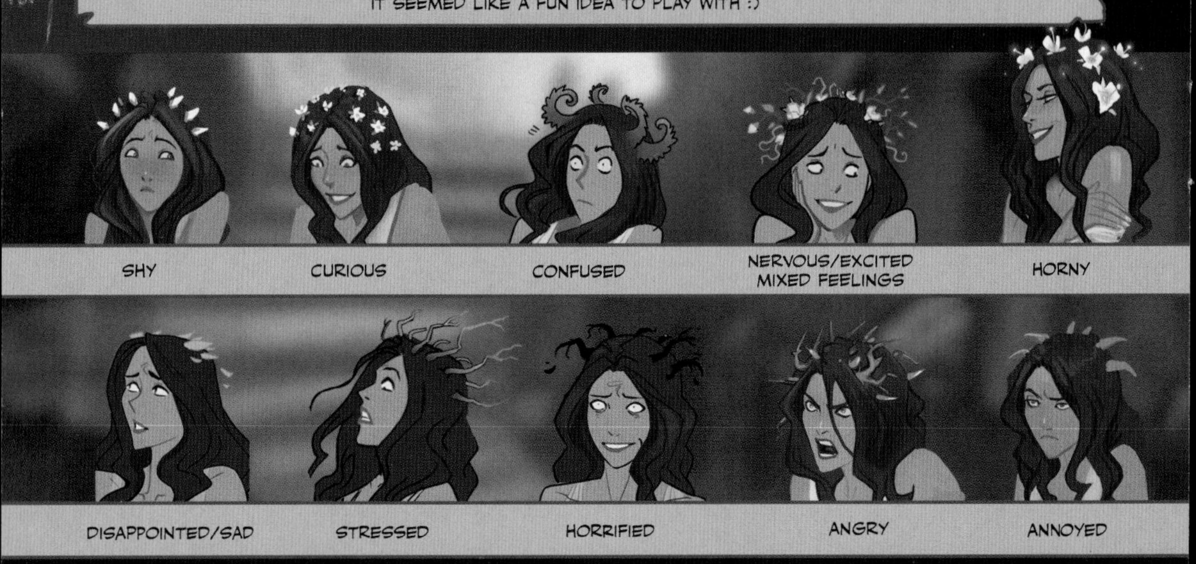
SHY
CURIOUS
CONFUSED
NERVOUS/EXCITED MIXED FEELINGS
HORNY
DISAPPOINTED/SAD
STRESSED
HORRIFIED
ANGRY
ANNOYED

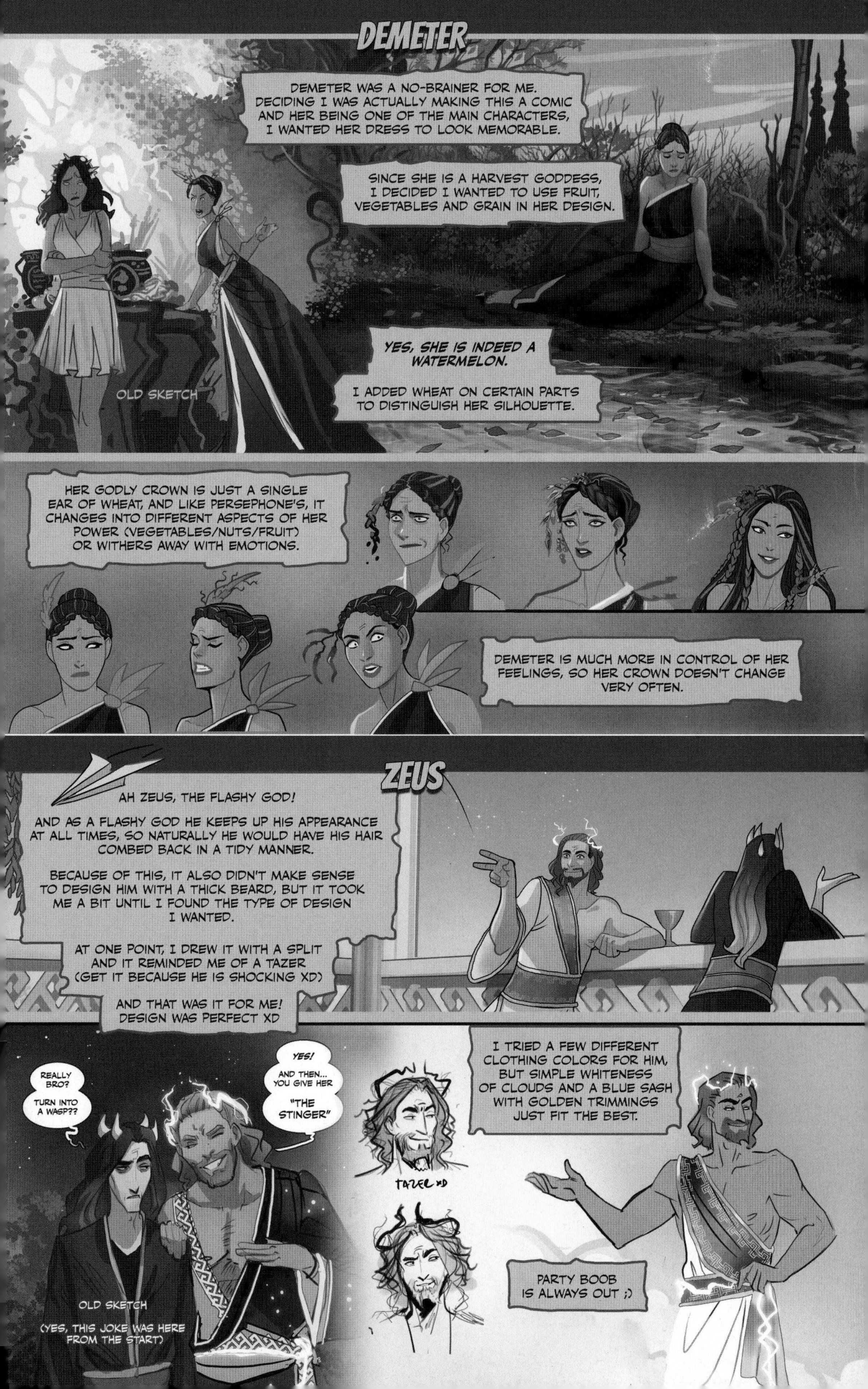
DEMETER
DEMETER WAS A NO-BRAINER FOR ME. DECIDING I WAS ACTUALLY MAKING THIS A COMIC AND HER BEING ONE OF THE MAIN CHARACTERS, I WANTED HER DRESS TO LOOK MEMORABLE.
SINCE SHE IS A HARVEST GODDESS, I DECIDED I WANTED TO USE FRUIT, VEGETABLES AND GRAIN IN HER DESIGN.
OLD SKETCH
YES, SHE IS INDEED A WATERMELON.
I ADDED WHEAT ON CERTAIN PARTS TO DISTINGUISH HER SILHOUETTE.
HER GODLY CROWN IS JUST A SINGLE EAR OF WHEAT, AND LIKE PERSEPHONE'S, IT CHANGES INTO DIFFERENT ASPECTS OF HER POWER (VEGETABLES/NUTS/FRUIT) OR WITHERS AWAY WITH EMOTIONS.
DEMETER IS MUCH MORE IN CONTROL OF HER FEELINGS, SO HER CROWN DOESN'T CHANGE VERY OFTEN.
ZEUS
AH ZEUS, THE FLASHY GOD!
AND AS A FLASHY GOD HE KEEPS UP HIS APPEARANCE AT ALL TIMES, SO NATURALLY HE WOULD HAVE HIS HAIR COMBED BACK IN A TIDY MANNER.
BECAUSE OF THIS, IT ALSO DIDN'T MAKE SENSE TO DESIGN HIM WITH A THICK BEARD, BUT IT TOOK ME A BIT UNTIL I FOUND THE TYPE OF DESIGN I WANTED.
AT ONE POINT, I DREW IT WITH A SPLIT AND IT REMINDED ME OF A TAZER (GET IT BECAUSE HE IS SHOCKING XD)
AND THAT WAS IT FOR ME! DESIGN WAS PERFECT XD
REALLY BRO? TURN INTO A WASP??
YES! AND THEN... YOU GIVE HER "THE STINGER"
OLD SKETCH
(YES, THIS JOKE WAS HERE FROM THE START)
I TRIED A FEW DIFFERENT CLOTHING COLORS FOR HIM, BUT SIMPLE WHITENESS OF CLOUDS AND A BLUE SASH WITH GOLDEN TRIMMINGS JUST FIT THE BEST.
TAZER XD
PARTY BOOB IS ALWAYS OUT ;)

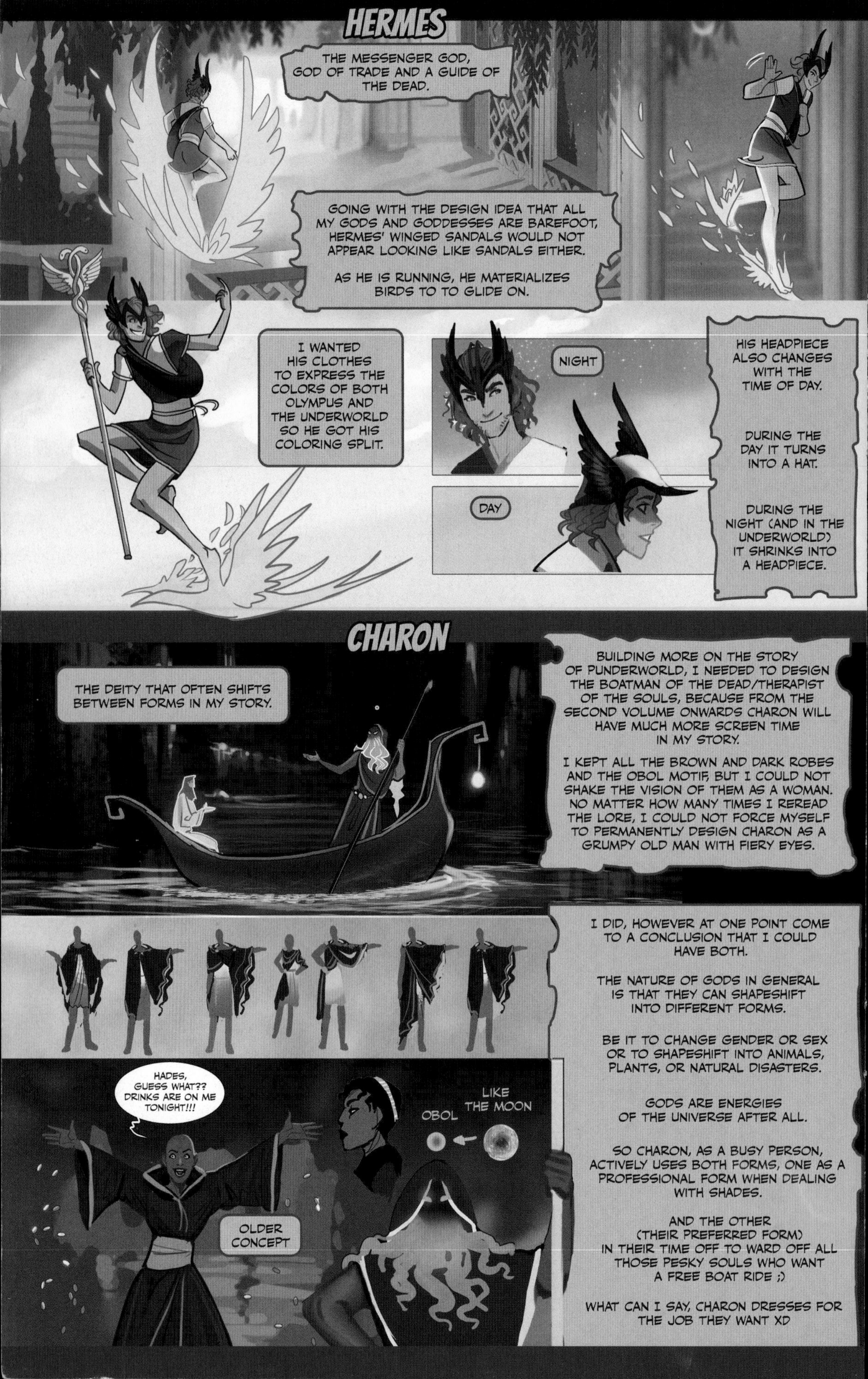
HERMES
THE MESSENGER GOD, GOD OF TRADE AND A GUIDE OF THE DEAD.
GOING WITH THE DESIGN IDEA THAT ALL MY GODS AND GODDESSES ARE BAREFOOT, HERMES' WINGED SANDALS WOULD NOT APPEAR LOOKING LIKE SANDALS EITHER.
AS HE IS RUNNING, HE MATERIALIZES BIRDS TO TO GLIDE ON.
I WANTED HIS CLOTHES TO EXPRESS THE COLORS OF BOTH OLYMPUS AND THE UNDERWORLD SO HE GOT HIS COLORING SPLIT.
NIGHT
DAY
HIS HEADPIECE ALSO CHANGES WITH THE TIME OF DAY.
DURING THE DAY IT TURNS INTO A HAT.
DURING THE NIGHT (AND IN THE UNDERWORLD) IT SHRINKS INTO A HEADPIECE.
CHARON
THE DEITY THAT OFTEN SHIFTS BETWEEN FORMS IN MY STORY.
BUILDING MORE ON THE STORY OF PUNDERWORLD, I NEEDED TO DESIGN THE BOATMAN OF THE DEAD/THERAPIST OF THE SOULS, BECAUSE FROM THE SECOND VOLUME ONWARDS CHARON WILL HAVE MUCH MORE SCREEN TIME IN MY STORY.
I KEPT ALL THE BROWN AND DARK ROBES AND THE OBOL MOTIF, BUT I COULD NOT SHAKE THE VISION OF THEM AS A WOMAN. NO MATTER HOW MANY TIMES I REREAD THE LORE, I COULD NOT FORCE MYSELF TO PERMANENTLY DESIGN CHARON AS A GRUMPY OLD MAN WITH FIERY EYES.
I DID, HOWEVER AT ONE POINT COME TO A CONCLUSION THAT I COULD HAVE BOTH.
THE NATURE OF GODS IN GENERAL IS THAT THEY CAN SHAPESHIFT INTO DIFFERENT FORMS.
BE IT TO CHANGE GENDER OR SEX OR TO SHAPESHIFT INTO ANIMALS, PLANTS, OR NATURAL DISASTERS.
GODS ARE ENERGIES OF THE UNIVERSE AFTER ALL.
SO CHARON, AS A BUSY PERSON, ACTIVELY USES BOTH FORMS, ONE AS A PROFESSIONAL FORM WHEN DEALING WITH SHADES.
AND THE OTHER (THEIR PREFERRED FORM) IN THEIR TIME OFF TO WARD OFF ALL THOSE PESKY SOULS WHO WANT A FREE BOAT RIDE ;)
WHAT CAN I SAY, CHARON DRESSES FOR THE JOB THEY WANT XD
HADES, GUESS WHAT?? DRINKS ARE ON ME TONIGHT!!!
LIKE THE MOON
OBOL
OLDER CONCEPT

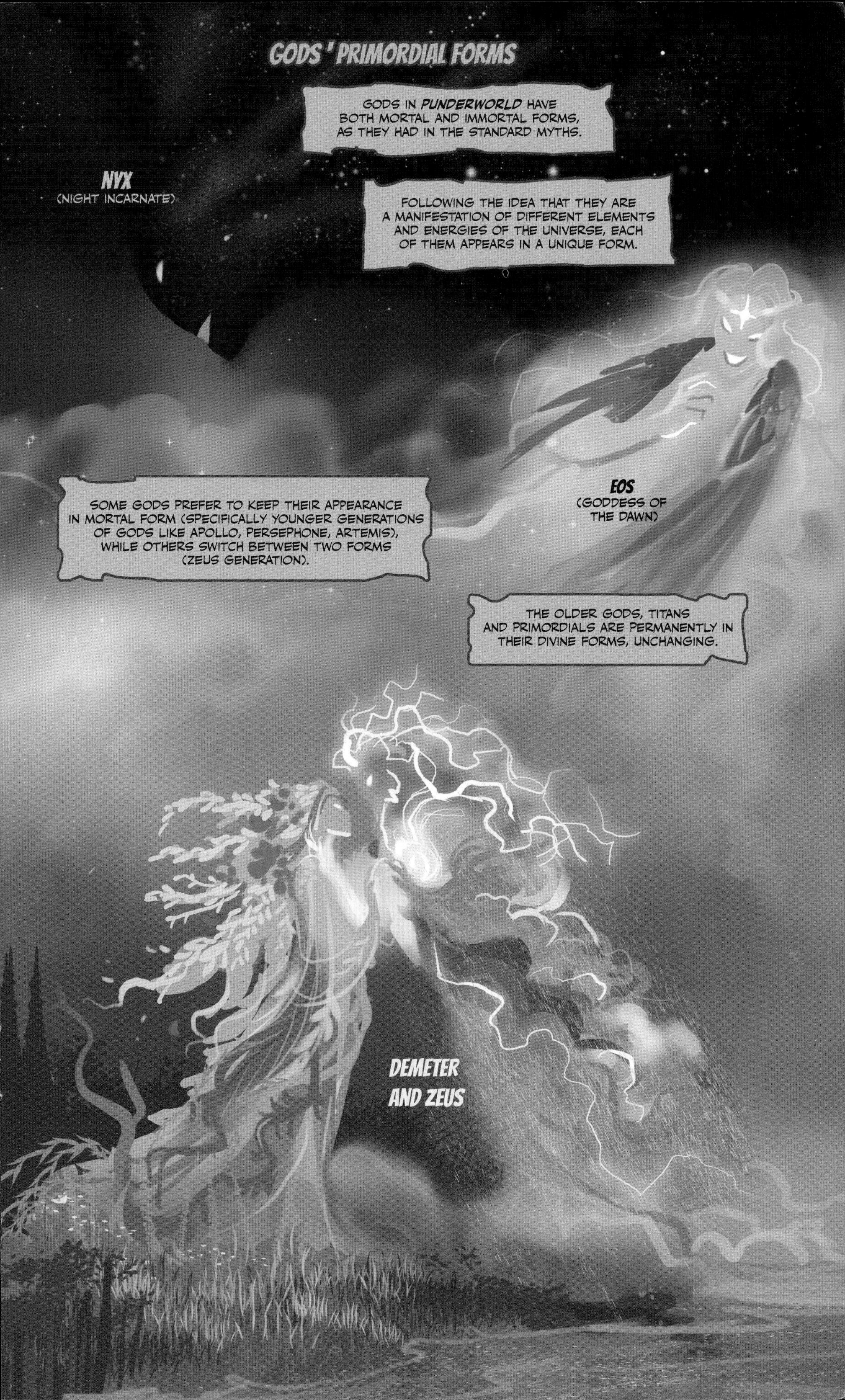
GODS' PRIMORDIAL FORMS
GODS IN PUNDERWORLD HAVE BOTH MORTAL AND IMMORTAL FORMS, AS THEY HAD IN THE STANDARD MYTHS.
NYX
(NIGHT INCARNATE)
FOLLOWING THE IDEA THAT THEY ARE A MANIFESTATION OF DIFFERENT ELEMENTS AND ENERGIES OF THE UNIVERSE, EACH OF THEM APPEARS IN A UNIQUE FORM.
SOME GODS PREFER TO KEEP THEIR APPEARANCE IN MORTAL FORM (SPECIFICALLY YOUNGER GENERATIONS OF GODS LIKE APOLLO, PERSEPHONE, ARTEMIS), WHILE OTHERS SWITCH BETWEEN TWO FORMS (ZEUS GENERATION).
EOS
(GODDESS OF THE DAWN)
THE OLDER GODS, TITANS AND PRIMORDIALS ARE PERMANENTLY IN THEIR DIVINE FORMS, UNCHANGING.
DEMETER AND ZEUS

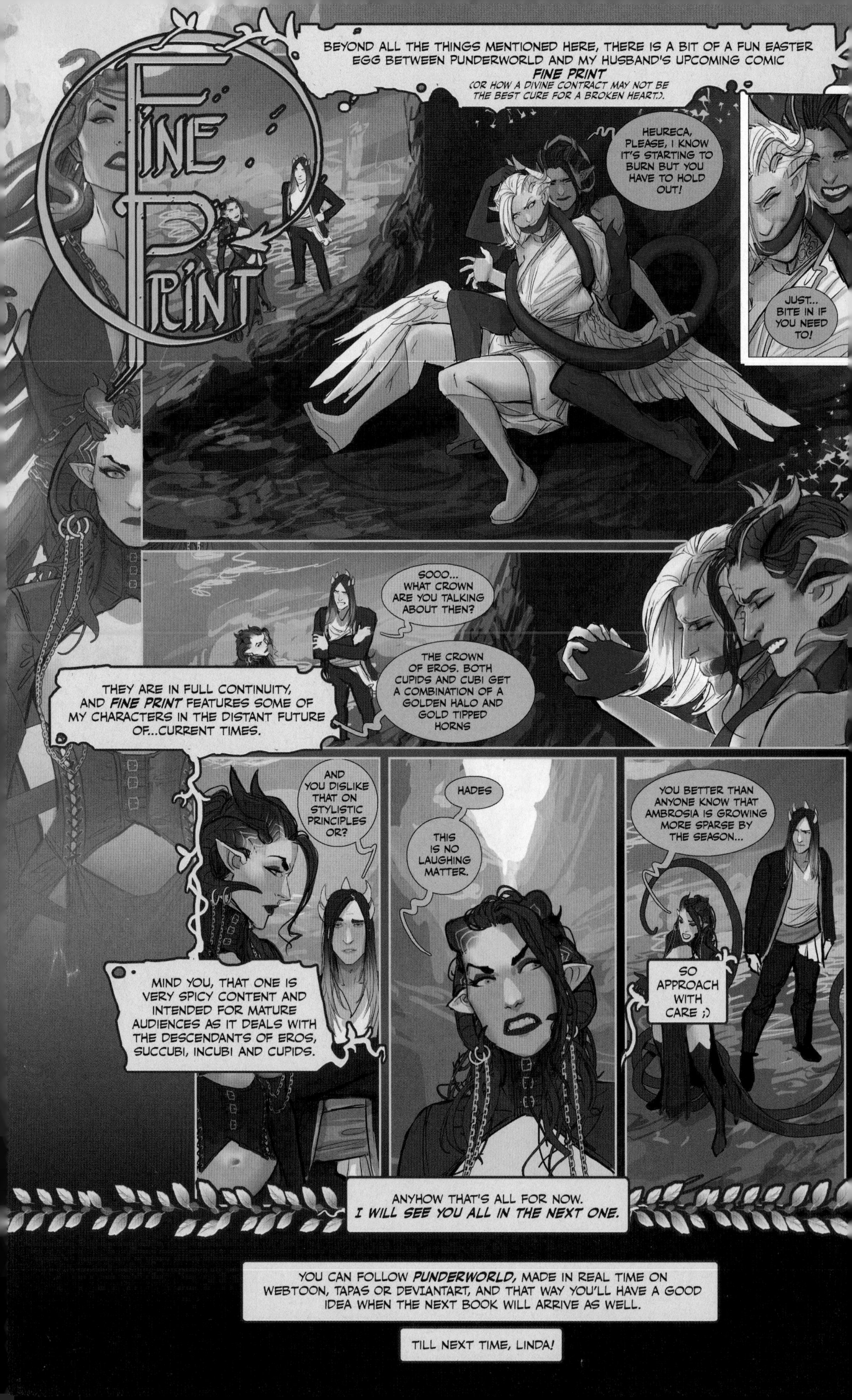
BEYOND ALL THE THINGS MENTIONED HERE, THERE IS A BIT OF A FUN EASTER EGG BETWEEN PUNDERWORLD AND MY HUSBAND'S UPCOMING COMIC
FINE PRINT
(OR HOW A DIVINE CONTRACT MAY NOT BE THE BEST CURE FOR A BROKEN HEART.).
FINE PRINT
HEURECA, PLEASE, I KNOW IT'S STARTING TO BURN BUT YOU HAVE TO HOLD OUT!
JUST... BITE IN IF YOU NEED TO!
SOOO... WHAT CROWN ARE YOU TALKING ABOUT THEN?
THE CROWN OF EROS. BOTH CUPIDS AND CUBI GET A COMBINATION OF A GOLDEN HALO AND GOLD TIPPED HORNS
THEY ARE IN FULL CONTINUITY, AND FINE PRINT FEATURES SOME OF MY CHARACTERS IN THE DISTANT FUTURE OF...CURRENT TIMES.
AND YOU DISLIKE THAT ON STYLISTIC PRINCIPLES OR?
MIND YOU, THAT ONE IS VERY SPICY CONTENT AND INTENDED FOR MATURE AUDIENCES AS IT DEALS WITH THE DESCENDANTS OF EROS, SUCCUBI, INCUBI AND CUPIDS.
HADES
THIS IS NO LAUGHING MATTER.
YOU BETTER THAN ANYONE KNOW THAT AMBROSIA IS GROWING MORE SPARSE BY THE SEASON...
SO APPROACH WITH CARE ;)
ANYHOW THAT'S ALL FOR NOW.
I WILL SEE YOU ALL IN THE NEXT ONE.
YOU CAN FOLLOW PUNDERWORLD, MADE IN REAL TIME ON WEBTOON, TAPAS OR DEVIANTART, AND THAT WAY YOU'LL HAVE A GOOD IDEA WHEN THE NEXT BOOK WILL ARRIVE AS WELL.
TILL NEXT TIME, LINDA!

The Top Cow essentials checklist:

Aphrodite IX: Rebirth, Volume 1
(ISBN: 978-1-60706-828-0)

Blood Stain, Volume 1
(ISBN: 978-1-63215-544-3)

Bonehead, Volume 1
(ISBN: 978-1-5343-0664-6)

Cyber Force: Awakening, Volume 1
(ISBN: 978-1-5343-0980-7)

The Clock, Volume 1
(ISBN: 978-1-5343-1611-9)

The Darkness: Origins, Volume 1
(ISBN: 978-1-60706-097-0)

Death Vigil, Volume 1
(ISBN: 978-1-63215-278-7)

Dissonance, Volume 1
(ISBN: 978-1-5343-0742-1)

Eclipse, Volume 1
(ISBN: 978-1-5343-0038-5)

Eden's Fall, Volume 1
(ISBN: 978-1-5343-0065-1)

The Freeze, OGN
(ISBN: 978-1-5343-1211-1)

God Complex, Volume 1
(ISBN: 978-1-5343-0657-8)

Infinite Dark, Volume 1
(ISBN: 978-1-5343-1056-8)

Paradox Girl, Volume 1
(ISBN: 978-1-5343-1220-3)

Port of Earth, Volume 1
(ISBN: 978-1-5343-0646-2)

Postal, Volume 1
(ISBN: 978-1-63215-342-5)

Stairway Anthology
(ISBN: 978-1-5343-1702-4)

Sugar, Volume 1
(ISBN: 978-1-5343-1641-7)

Sunstone, Volume 1
(ISBN: 978-1-63215-212-1)

Swing, Volume 1
(ISBN: 978-1-5343-0516-8)

Symmetry, Volume 1
(ISBN: 978-1-63215-699-0)

The Tithe, Volume 1
(ISBN: 978-1-63215-324-1)

Think Tank, Volume 1
(ISBN: 978-1-60706-660-6)

Vindication, OGN
(ISBN: 978-1-5343-1237-1)

Warframe, Volume 1
(ISBN: 978-1-5343-0512-0)

Witchblade 2017, Volume 1
(ISBN: 978-1-5343-0685-1)

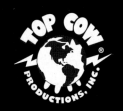

For more ISBN and ordering information on our latest collections go to:
www.topcow.com
Ask your retailer about our catalogue of collected editions, digests, and hard covers or check the listings at:
Barnes and Noble, Amazon.com,
and other fine retailers.

To find your nearest comic shop go to:
www.comicshoplocator.com